Dear Reader,

While I love a good edge-of-your-seat, action-packed
thriller as much as the next person, I've long believed
the most compelling stories are those found in everyday
life—the day-to-day challenges of raising kids and dealing
with family relationships; the way life forces us to grow in
ways we never expected to; the breath-stealing awe of
finding new love. To this end, I tend to write about people
the average reader might know, or even be, characters
no less exceptional simply because they do eight loads
of laundry a week or worry about a learning disabled child
or sometimes wonder how they're going to make it to the
next payday. These are people who find joy in the scent
of a roasting turkey, the feel of a child in their arms, the
satisfaction of knowing that beat-up old minivan in the
driveway is theirs. And these are people no less worthy
of finding true love simply because they're "ordinary."

This book, my first single title for Silhouette, is no
exception. Since the story is set in my adopted hometown
of Albuquerque, New Mexico, these people see what I
see every day, shop where I shop, deal with many of the
same issues I—and most of you—face every day. Yet for
five months, as they revealed their fears and hopes and
deepest desires to me, their quiet drama kept me on the
edge of my seat. I pray they do the same for you.

Karen Templeton

Karen Templeton

Playing for Keeps

Silhouette Books

Published by Silhouette Books
America's Publisher of Contemporary Romance

SILHOUETTE BOOKS

PLAYING FOR KEEPS

ISBN 0-373-21834-6

To everyone who hangs out in the AOL Books Community
Writing Series Romance folder—
thanks for seven years (and counting)
of cheers and commiseration. (Not to mention answers
to any off-the-wall question I can think up!)
I love you guys.

And to Trish, Holly, Susan and Alice,
for reassuring me the story made sense.

And to Gail—
I'm holding you to that promise
to edit my next three hundred books!

Chapter 1

If Joanna Swann had learned nothing else in her thirty-two years, it was that bad news rarely came à la carte. If one thing went wrong, it was only a matter of time before the other shoe would drop. This phone call, however, had to make at least the thirty-fourth shoe to drop within the past few weeks, which was sorely taxing her good humor.

For a single bright, glistening moment, the temptation to leave her three children to fend for themselves and to take to her bed was nearly overwhelming. However she scraped together her last ounce of reserve and said, ''Mr. Shaw—'' she tried to place her relatively new neighbor, but all she was getting was a beer belly and a cowboy hat large enough to shelter a family of six ''—how is that even possible? Chester doesn't even come up to Glady's knees. Let alone her—''

''I saw 'em with my own eyes! Right out here in my own goddamn backyard! Your goddamn dog got up on the top step of my goddamn back porch and got my bitch pregnant! We were just about to have her bred, too, and we were counting on that income! You have any idea how much a Great Dane puppy with papers brings?''

Her neck muscles cramped from cradling the cordless between her jaw and her shoulder as she tossed Bob the Builder fruit snacks into the boys' lunch boxes. Joanna glared at the furbag lying with his head on his paws, bushy white eyebrows twitching. Damn dog had been nothing but trouble from the moment her ex-husband had brought him home for the kids' Christmas present, year before last. Without consulting her first, natch. And if the kids hadn't been so attached to the mangy beast, he would've long since been history. His manners were atrocious, his libido embarrassingly healthy, and there hadn't been a fence or wall invented he couldn't dig out of. But Chester was pure-bred, so Bobby had said it didn't make sense to get him fixed until they'd put him out to stud a few times, at least. Apparently, Chester had decided to take the initiative on his own.

Heaven help them, this was going be one butt-ugly batch of puppies.

''No, Mr. Shaw,'' Joanna said, eyeing the clock and frowning—Bobby was late picking up the kids for school. Again. ''I have no idea how much—''

''Six hundred bucks a pop, that's how much! And Gladys always has at least ten pups! That means I'm out six thousand dollars, lady. So what're you gonna do about it?''

''Me?'' she squeaked, the sleep-deprivation fog lifting just enough for her to realize where this conversation was going. Glowering, she dumped out an inch of murky water from the bowl she'd left on the counter last night to catch the drip from the leaky roof. ''You expect me to compensate you for an…an…accident?''

''Damn straight I expect you to compensate me! Wasn't my dog that got out, it was yours! Your fault—you have to pay up. We can go to petty court if you like, but that'd only add court costs to what you already owe me. So I'll be sending you a bill soon as Gladys delivers.''

Wham! went the receiver in her ear just as the father of her three children picked that inauspicious moment to drag his sorry hide through her back door.

"Next time you bring me an unneutered dog, Bobby Alvarez, make sure he knows how to use a condom!'' And long as the gun was loaded, might as well get off another round. "And where the *hell* have you been? *Kids!*'' she bellowed in the general direction of their rooms. "Your father's here!''

"Whoa, babe, back up.'' Bobby dug a blue-and-red-striped tie from the pocket of his top-of-the-line JCPenney sportsjacket, threading it through his shirt collar. "What's this about the dog and condoms?''

Joanna pointed to Chester, whose eyebrows twitched some more.

"That…thing knocked up the neighbor's Great Dane.''

Bobby stopped knotting his tie to grin at the dog. "Chester! My man!'' He bent at the knees, extending one hand. "Give me five!'' The dog hesitated, then belly-crawled to Bobby, eyeing Joanna warily as he shook hands with the only person in the room who currently didn't wish to see him stuffed. Bobby did the praising thing, then sidled over to the coffeemaker. "This fresh?''

Fumbling to hook an earring one-handed into her left lobe, Joanna gulped down the cold remnants of her first cup of coffee, refusing to let the crooked, charming, you-wouldn't-really-smack-somebody-this-cute-wouldja? look in those hot-fudge eyes get to her.

"Touch that coffee and die. And since you find *your* dog's sexual escapades so amusing, then I guess it's okay to send the bill to you.''

"Bill?''

"Yeah, bill. As in, for the loss of what would have been a purebred litter. For which the mother-to-be's daddy is suing me. Us. Which is just what I need on top of the roof leaking. Again. And why the hell are you late?''

"How can you be mad at me for so many things in one breath?''

"A time-saving strategy fine-honed after nine years of marriage. Well?''

"Hey, I'm really sorry, babe. But Tori—''

"And don't even try to blame this on your girlfriend—''

"Fiancée.''

Joanna reeled for a second or two as shoe number thirty-five bounced off her head. "Since when?''

Something almost like apology flickered in his eyes. "Last night. I mean, this probably isn't the best time to spring this on you—''

"No, no…'' Joanna inserted the second earring. "Now, later, whenever. Congratulations. I guess. Although that's neither here nor there,'' she added, scrambling to get back up on her high horse. "The whole point of my asking you to take the kids to school today was so I could get to my appointment on time…dammit, what are they *doing?*'' Joanna tromped across the kitchen's tiled floor, her curly hair boinging around her face and annoying the life out of her. "Dulcy! Matt! Ryder! *Now!*''

"Jo,'' Bobby said behind her. "It's been more than three years since we split up. Time at least one of us moved on.''

Joanna whirled around at the precise moment the dog decided to shuffle back across the kitchen floor. Right in front of her. She clutched the edge of the counter, sloshing coffee all over her left boob. Cursing, she grabbed a napkin and started rubbing at the spot, even though some small, tired part of her brain knew coffee and peach cotton did not mix. She glared at Bobby as her breast jiggled from the onslaught. "One word about wanting to help and you're dead meat,'' she said, then added, "As for your *moving on*…as I recall, you did that before the ink was dry on the divorce papers.''

"You're still pissed about the dog, aren't you?"

"The dog, the roof, your being late…take your pick. Oh, and Ryder's teacher called. She wants us to come in for a conference."

To give Bobby credit, concern flashed across his features. "I thought he was doing better this year."

"Yeah, well, so did I. But apparently not. So believe me, your getting married again doesn't even make the short list. But honestly, Bobby…" Joanna gave up on the rubbing and looked at her ex. "Can Tori even *vote* yet?"

"She's twenty-one, for God's sake. Besides, in some ways she's older than I am—"

Which, Joanna thought uncharitably, wasn't all that much of a stretch.

"—and she's pregnant."

At this rate Joanna could open a damn shoe store. "Well," she said after a moment, "at least no one's holding Chester accountable for *that* puppy."

"That's why I'm late," Bobby said, ignoring her. "Tori was so sick this morning, she didn't want me to leave."

Oh, no. Uh-uh. Not that she didn't genuinely feel badly for Bobby's girlfriend, who clearly had no idea what she was getting herself into. But no way was Joanna about to let sympathy sully the righteous indignation she'd spent the past half hour polishing to a high gloss.

"You are totally out of your mind," she said.

The corners of Bobby's mouth pulled down. "Why do you say that? You know how much I love kids."

"Yeah. I also know you barely make enough to support the ones you already have. Not to mention this problem you have with picking them up on time."

"I told you—"

"I don't just mean this morning. I mean…oh, never mind," Joanna said as her daughter and twin sons finally came trooping into the kitchen, huge grins erupting on their faces when they saw their father. All three began chattering at once, even though they talked to their father every single night and spent every weekend with him. Joanna watched the interaction with an aching heart, thinking, as she had many, many times since the divorce, what a shame it was that the man was so pitifully clueless in every other aspect of his life but this.

He really did love his kids. Of that, she'd never had a single doubt. For that, she'd be eternally grateful. But their marriage had been built on the sands of impulse and boredom and infatuation; its collapse had been inevitable from their wedding day. That he seemed about to embark on the journey with someone new...

None of your business, Joanna. Let go.

So she kissed each of her dark-haired babies goodbye, slipping in an extra word of encouragement for Ryder who, thank goodness, wasn't complaining about his stomach hurting this morning. The kids filed out the back door, Joanna barely noticing the sheet of paper on the counter in time to call Bobby back. He eyed it as if it was a snake coiled for attack. And rightfully so.

"What's that?"

"Plumber's bill. I already paid it, so you owe me half."

His eyes twitched to hers. "I told you I'd fix that leak—"

"That was two weeks ago, Bobby. What was I supposed to do? Go without the second toilet until you 'got around' to fixing it?"

"It's just things are kinda tight right now, y'know?"

"Oh, forget it!" Joanna snatched the bill out of his hand. "I don't know why I bother trying to get you to do anything—"

"Dammit, Jo—there you go with the drama queen act again." He stuck out his hand. "Give me the bill. I'll take care of it as soon as I can."

"And what about the roof? And taking care of Chester's

little indiscretion? And Mrs. Kellogg wants me to set up that appointment ASAP—''

"Jeez, Jo—why can't we deal with one thing at a time?''

"Because life doesn't *hand* me one thing at a time!''

He let out a heavy sigh, then gestured toward the bill again. "Give me the damn bill,'' he said quietly. "I'll call you later about the other stuff. I swear.''

She passed it back to him, even though she knew he'd put it somewhere and never look at it again.

"Da-ad!''

"I'm there, sweetheart,'' he shouted to his daughter. He turned back to Jo, that damn smile spreading across olive-skinned features a little less sharply defined than they had been in his twenties despite the field of one-inch black spikes jutting from his scalp. Figured he'd manage to get younger-looking as time passed, while Jo was rapidly approaching hagdom. "You know, babe, you really gotta trust me a little more.''

"I'm going to pretend I didn't hear that. And I don't mean the calling me 'babe' part, although that's not exactly winning you points, either.''

He shrugged off her comment, the gesture of a man determined to never let the turkeys—or anybody else—get him down. Then his eyes tangled with hers. "You know I wanted to have more kids. With you, I mean.''

This, she didn't need. "Wasn't in the cards, Bobby.''

"No. I guess not.'' Then off he went, leaving Joanna to wonder if it was too early to start drinking. Oh, right. She didn't drink. An unfortunate oversight on her part.

After a millisecond's pang of empathy for Tori, she flew down the hall to her bedroom, stripping off the coffee-stained jersey dress as worries pelted her like sleet. Not that, in theory, Bobby's news was a worry. Joanna hadn't had a claim on his affections in years. He was free to marry whomever he liked and to have as many kids as he liked. But she knew Bobby and his *Trust me, babe…it'll work out, you'll see.* If he couldn't handle his responsibilities to her and the kids when they were all still living under one roof, how the hell did he think he was going to add a new wife and child to the mix?

The man couldn't take anything seriously if his life depended on it. Which ironically was exactly what had appealed to the twenty-year-old Joanna, exhausted from trying to live up to her parents' expectations. She, however, had come to grips with reality. Bobby Alvarez's view of "reality" began and ended with *Survivor.* Hence the divorce.

Hey. It was better than murder.

Now sporting a denim dress she prayed wouldn't turn her into Melba toast when the cool early October morning gave way to the blistering hot October afternoon, she rammed a pair of silver combs into the chaos that was her hair and sailed back down the hall, ignoring the cyclonized kitchen as she zipped through into the converted garage that served as her workshop. She now had less than forty-five minutes to load up the van and get across town to the hotsy-totsy gallery that had agreed to take a couple of her handmade Santa Clauses.

Not that she was thrilled about leaving them on consignment, something she hadn't done since the early days when she'd been doing well to sell one or two at a craft show here and there. But the High Desert Gallery carried some of the most prestigious names in the Southwest art world. Placing her work there was a coup of no small proportion, well worth the commission she'd pay the gallery for any special orders that resulted. Her mother thought she was insane, looking to take on even more work when she could barely keep up with the orders she had. Yeah, well, Joanna thought, slinging her saddlebag up onto her left shoulder as she carefully lifted the sturdy shopping bag packed with a pair of Father Christmasses off her worktable, she'd given up sanity about the same time she'd stopped wearing panty hose.

She and the bulging bag forged through the small sea of cats who called her rambling Albuquerque North Valley adobe home. Some minutes later she was tearing across Paseo del Norte in the Blue Bomb when her cell phone rang.

Ever since some yahoo yakking on his cell had nearly creamed her after running a red light, Joanna had been none too keen about talking on the phone while driving. But— damn—a glance at the readout revealed her mother's number.

"Hi, sweetheart," Glynnie Swann's voice chirped in her ear when she answered. "Why don't you swing by and pick me up on your way to the gallery? There's the most adorable new toy store right by there—Patty Kohler was telling me about it the other day—and since Barbara's oldest just had another baby, I thought this would save me a trip."

Why wasn't her mother at work? Why couldn't she go get Aunt Barb's oldest's baby a present by herself?

"I'm really running late, Mom—"

"I'll be right in front, so you won't even have to get out," Glynnie said, and hung up.

And what had Joanna done in some previous life to merit her present torment?

The word *railroading* had been invented expressly for her mother, Joanna thought on a weary sigh as she headed into the chamisa and sagebrush-infested Sandia foothills and toward her parents' new house, hidden so deep among the twisting, turning roads that Joanna managed to get lost every time she drove up here. The wind coming through her open window was making the curls tickle her face; she jabbed at the automatic button, only to realize that, once again, she'd missed a key turnoff.

Even as she realized that, for something that wasn't supposed to be bothering her, she was sure thinking about

Bobby's news an awful lot. But why? It wasn't as if she was jealous. And she certainly wasn't envious.

Her mouth twisted. Okay, so maybe that part wasn't exactly true, even if she of all people understood all too well the pitfalls of marriage. Such as waking up one morning and looking at the naked man snoring beside you and wondering, Who the hell *is* this person and what is he doing in my bed? And, hey, just because two people shared living space, body fluids and three kids, where had she gotten off thinking that that also meant they shared the responsibility for the living space and the three kids who were the direct result of sharing body fluids?

Still, it hadn't been all bad. The sex had been nice. And not infrequent, she thought on a despondent sigh. And there'd been laughter, at least in the beginning when she still believed she could count on Bobby to do what he'd said he'd do. She did miss that. And the sound of a man's voice booming out to the kids when he came home from work—even if ''work'' had been a hand-out job from her father. She missed family dinners and Christmas mornings with everybody in their pajamas and secret winks over small heads and clandestine gropes when nobody was looking.

What she didn't miss were the fights or the blank looks in Bobby's eyes when she'd light into him about something and he'd look at her as though she were speaking Klingon. What she didn't miss was who living with him had started to turn her into. Stewing in resentment was not her idea of a fun time. The thing was, she'd been more than prepared to give her fifty percent. Sixty, if push came to shove. But marrying Bobby had been like buying a jumbo bag of potato chips only to open the bag and discover it was half air. Even the make-up sex grew stale after a while. Phone calls from creditors really wreaked havoc on the afterglow, boy.

She'd felt cheated, is what. Although…well, to be truthful, not so much by Bobby as by her naive expectations. The nine years had definitely been a learning experience, that was for damn sure. But she also felt…what? Jolted awake? Something. Sort of a well-gee-there-he-goes-off-to-have-a-new-life-and-where-does-that-leave-me? kind of feeling.

Actually she knew where that left her. In a house with a leaky roof, ancient plumbing, a half-empty bed and three children with various and assorted issues probably stemming from the divorce and/or the shared custody backings and forthings. Oh, and two credit cards on the verge of meltdown. Although she supposed things could be worse: at least she had a roof, leaking though it might be, and everyone was healthy and…

And…

Well, hell. That was it?

Another frown bit into her forehead as she pulled into her mother's driveway. Eschewing the ten-second fashion trendiness known to fell many a lesser woman, Glynnie hot-footed it out to the van in a snazzy linen suit, silk blouse and a pair of classic slingbacks that sure as shooting hadn't come from Payless. Behind her mother loomed a two-story, rose-stuccoed monstrosity still glittering in its newness. Lots of arbitrary levels and grand arched windows and things. "Indigenous" landscaping. No grass, no trees, just lots of dirt, rocks and scruffy-looking bushes. Not exactly homey. But definitely impressive, in a Southwest bourgeois kind of way.

Joanna saw her mother's half-pitying, half-repulsed expression long before the woman reached the ten-year-old minivan. Sort of the way you might look at a homeless person.

"You know what, honey?" Glynnie said when she reached the car. "Why don't we take the Lexus? It's got a full tank."

"So does this."

"But, Jo—"

"Hey. You invite yourself along, you ride in the van. I don't have time to switch stuff over."

"But, honey—"

"Mom? Get in. You can always duck if you see anyone you know."

Glynnie did, her fashionably pale mouth set in a glistening line.

"And, if it makes you feel better," Jo said as she backed out of the drive, "I'll park far enough away from the gallery that nobody'll see it. 'Kay?"

"And aren't we being Miss Sensitive this morning?"

"I'm not the one who just looked at my car like it was dog poop."

"I just don't understand why you won't let your father find you something a little less…used-looking."

"Why, when this one already smells like the children?"

"I noticed," Glynnie said, then lifted a manicured, be-ringed left hand to her hair, which, much to Glynnie's perpetual chagrin, shot the control-freak image all to hell. Hundreds of itty-bitty corkscrew curls shuddered around her mother's face, curls that had triumphed over every straightening and relaxing process known to cosmetology. At one time—like last week—her mother's hair had been redder than Joanna's. Today, however, it was kind of a strawberry-blond.

"Nice color," Jo said.

"You really like it?"

"Yes, Mom, I really like it."

"Well, that's a relief," Glynnie said on a sigh. "Sylvia thought the natural color was getting too harsh for my face."

Joanna swallowed a smile, then said, "So how come you're not off slaying dragons this morning?"

"Because, my dear, your brilliant mother brought a particularly nasty one to its heels yesterday."

"You're kidding? Hawthorne versus Northstar? You won?"

"My ego really appreciates your confidence in my abilities."

"Sorry. But from what I've heard, the case was anything but a slam dunk."

Out of the corner of her eye, Joanna caught her mother's smug grin. "It wasn't. Which made victory all the sweeter." The grin widened. "Your father helped me celebrate."

"With champagne and dinner?"

"That, too." `

Joanna's already gloomy mood got gloomier. Her mother noticed.

"Okay. What's wrong?"

"Wrong? Nothing. Exactly."

Her mother waited. Joanna sighed. There wasn't a person alive who could withstand her mother's let-them-crumble-on-their-own tactic.

"Okay, Bobby came to take the kids to school this morning."

"No wonder you're grouchy."

"I am not grouchy. At least, not just because he came over," she muttered in response to her mother's raised brows. "Tori's pregnant. So they're getting married. Bobby and Tori."

"Sounds like a dance team from Lawrence Welk," her mother said, then added, "What *is* the child thinking?"

Joanna had to smile. Tori had been temping at her father's Lexus dealership—as a means of putting herself through college—when Bobby met her. By all accounts, she was bright, focused and mature for her age. How on earth she'd fallen prey to Bobby's charms was anybody's guess. But then...

"Ohmigod...Tori's practically the same age I was."

Beside her, curls bobbed. "Wondered how long it was

going to take for that to click in.'' She sensed her mother's eyes on her face. "How are you holding up?"

"Fine. I think. But not because I have any feelings left for Bobby,'' she hastily added.

After a moment her mother said, staring out the window, "You remember that blue Ellen Tracy suit I had, the one I gave away about five years ago?"

"Vaguely. Why?"

"I got rid of it because it no longer fit, for one thing. And I was bored with it, for another.'' She turned to Joanna. "But damn if I wasn't pissed when I saw some woman wearing it a few months later."

Joanna chuckled. "I get your point. But that's not it."

"Then what?"

And without warning, Joanna's mouth fell open and half of what she'd been thinking that morning flew out. Including, amazingly enough, a lot of the stuff about missing sex.

"Hell,'' her mother said, "If it was me, I'd be in the loony bin by now."

"I could have gone all morning without knowing that."

"And for somebody so determined to 'do her own thing' or whatever they call it these days, you're the biggest prude I know."

"That's not true!"

"Is, too. Honey, Bobby's moved on. He's started another family, scary as that thought is. The feelings you're having are perfectly normal. You need to get out there, go find a man, get—"

"—a life, I know, I know."

"That's not what I was going to say."

Joanna grimaced. "You're saying I should throw myself back into the dating pool?"

"Ding, ding, ding! And a point to the beautiful woman on my left."

"Beautiful, my ass."

"Well, that's probably pretty nice, too, but I haven't seen that since you were ten."

Joanna ignored her. "Right. One slightly worn, slightly droopy, recycled singleton seeks the company—"

Her mother grunted.

"—of a breathing male with a reasonable understanding of personal hygiene, most of his own teeth and at least a moderate grasp on reality."

"See, that's your problem. You're too picky."

In spite of herself, Joanna laughed as they pulled into the parking lot in front of the gallery. "I suppose the part about having most of his teeth was pushing it."

"Better they need dentures than Viagra."

Thinking, *Hmm*, Joanna parked the car and got out, retrieving the Santas from the back. When she straightened, blowing her hair out of her face, she noticed her mother frowning at her dress.

"What?"

"Somebody needs to go shopping. Bad."

"Hey. This is New Mexico," Joanna said. "Denim is always in style."

Glynnie came as close as she ever did to rolling her eyes.

Dale McConnaughy happened to look out the store window right as the two women got out of the dusty, suburban-blue minivan and just in time to see an explosion of red curls catch fire in the morning sun. The women disappeared inside the art gallery next door, however, before he had a chance to get past the initial *Shee-it*. Which was just as well, since he had more pressing things to tend to than gawk at a bunch of obviously fake hair. Wonder how much she'd forked over to get that look?

"Excuse me? How much is this? Colton! No! Don't touch!"

Dale turned to a shell-shocked woman, a newborn strapped to her chest, clutching the handlebar of an SUV-

size stroller that had been crammed to the gills with toddlers when she'd arrived a couple minutes ago. Well, only
two, actually; one about three and another one maybe a
year younger. The older kid, a boy, had immediately
screamed to get out, and was now tearing up and down the
aisles in a crazed euphoria while his mother shrieked,
"Don't touch!" every thirty seconds or so. Well, hell—let
a three-year-old loose in a toy store, what did she think was
gonna happen?

"It's okay, ma'am, it's not like he can hurt anything—"

Something crashed.

"—too badly," he finished, as the mother wailed, "Oh,
Colton…"

Dale peered over her head, refusing to frown. "It's just
a display of model cars. Uh, son? How about you come
over here and play with these puppets? Or the wooden train
set—"

"No!"

"—or maybe you'd like to go on outside to the Jump?"

Obviously intrigued, the child ceased his Godzilla im-
personation long enough to say, "The Jump?"

His mother, her voice tinged equally with hope and des-
peration, said, "Oh, he *loves* to jump."

"Me, too," Dale said, ignoring the mother's quizzical
expression as he led the child through the store and on out
back where Dale'd set up several wooden swing sets inside
the fenced-in area, as well as an enclosed, inflated castle-
shaped Moon Jump probably bigger than the kid's bedroom.

"Cool!" the kid said, and he was off like a shot.

"Is it safe?" his mother said, jiggling the baby who'd
just awakened and was making squeaky, fussy sounds.
From her stroller, the other toddler let out a single, ear-
piercing shriek, just for the hell of it.

"Oh, yeah. And tell you what, ten minutes in that puppy

and you won't here a peep out of him the rest of the morning."

"From your lips to God's ears," she said, then asked Dale again for the price of the toy. No sooner had she done so, however, than both babies started to howl in uncomplimentary keys. Judging from the look on Mama's face, she wasn't far from that stage herself. Unperturbed—it took a lot more than a couple of bawling kids to shake him up—Dale grabbed a hat out of a box by the counter, a new product he'd been in the process of marking when she'd come in, and plopped it on his head. Then he squatted in front of the older baby.

"Hey, Little Bit," Dale said softly, reaching up to press the button in the back of his hat. "Get a load of this!"

Tears spiking her lashes, both the baby's mouth and her big blue eyes popped wide open as she stared at the hat.

Then a soft chortle popped out of her mouth. Then another one, and another, until the store reverberated with the sounds of baby belly laugh. Dale chuckled right back as a pair of pudgy hands shot up toward the hat.

"Mine!"

"I want one, too," the boy said, staggering back toward them, out of breath and flushed. The littlest one was still squawking her head off, but Dale figured two out of three was pretty good.

Mama apparently thought so, too. She plunked down the educational game she'd been holding and practically twisted herself inside out to get her wallet out of her purse. "I'll take two of those hats."

"Don't you want to know how much they are?"

"Ask me if I care."

Dale slid behind the counter, grabbed a second hat from the box and took the woman's charge card just as the two gals he'd seen before barged through the door in a flurry of obvious agitation. At least on the younger one's part. In fact, that hair of hers seemed to fairly vibrate around her face.

He reminded himself he had customers to tend to, even as he quickly processed how that sack of a dress seemed to swallow up the redhead's little body. And this could be a long shot, but he was guessing that big shopping bag in her hand had something to do with the severely annoyed look on her face.

"It's not the end of the world, Jo," the older woman was saying, the softness of her tone at odds with her I-am-*somebody* attire. "You said yourself it wasn't a sure thing."

"*Before* I showed them the samples. Not after." Red glared down at the bag as if she wanted to smack it. Then she glanced around the store, huffed out a sigh and said to the other woman, "Look, you're the one who needs to shop. Why don't I just go back out to the car and wait for you?"

No, somebody shouted inside Dale's head just as the older woman—Red's mother, maybe?—grabbed her by the arm and pulled her farther into the store. *Bless you,* the somebody said as Dale went through the here-you-go-have-a-nice-day-now motions associated with sending the mother and her kids on their way. "No," the blonde was saying. "You need to get something for this baby, too."

Now that Dale was able to devote his entire attention to the drama unfolding before him, he could see the resemblance between the two women. They were both on the short side, kinda soft and bony at the same time, the way short women sometimes were, with similarly pointed chins and straight noses that curved up, right on the very tips. The older one seemed the type almost obsessed with her appearance in a classy, conservative kind of way, while the younger one—who Dale could now see wasn't all that young, maybe a few years behind him—looked like one of those women who threw on the first thing that came to hand.

"I'm sure the baby's nose won't be out of joint if you pick something out for me," she was saying. "I haven't even seen Aunt Barb in—what?—ten years."

"Twelve, but that's not the point. Oh, would you look at that adorable stuffed frog—"

"You look at the stuffed frog. I'm outta here."

But as she turned to leave, her mother once again grabbed for her. Only instead of getting her daughter's arm, she got one of the bag handles. The paper was no match for two equally determined women pulling in opposite directions, and the bag split in two, dumping out a pair of what looked like very fancy dolls or something on the floor. On a disgusted sigh—and what Dale surmised was a very unladylike cussword under her breath—Red squatted down to retrieve them, her hair billowing out around her shoulders. A silver comb popped loose and skipped across the floor to where he was standing.

Dale scooped up the comb and made his way over—not too fast—to help her, getting just close enough to notice her ringless left hand, to catch a whiff of her sweet, natural scent.

"Here, ma'am...let me get that—"

"It's okay, I'm fine..." She glanced up, those crazy curls quivering around her face like they were alive, and something about her—he had no idea what—just grabbed him by the throat and wouldn't let go. Except her gaze—clear and green, like pale jade—zipped right past his eyes and on up to the top of his head as a startled shriek of laughter fell out of her mouth.

Which was when Dale remembered the stuffed hamster in the hula outfit, perched on top of his head, shaking its booty like there was no tomorrow.

Chapter 2

The laughter had roared up from inside Joanna like flood-waters breaching a dam. And there wasn't a damn thing she could do to staunch it, even though her sides were killing her and she was perilously close to wetting her pants. Then she caught her mother's and this stranger's flummoxed expressions and collapsed cross-legged onto the floor, her howls now punctuated with the occasional snort.

An instant later she was sobbing.

Oh, Lord, just take me now, Joanna thought, vaguely aware of her mother's pleas to get hold of herself, for God's sake, before somebody else came into the store, and of the man's apparent decision to flee.

And Joanna tried, she really did. But no dice. Between Bobby's news and the gallery owner changing her mind and the generally crappy state of her life, she must have been more fried than she'd thought if all it took to send her over the edge was a gyrating rodent in a grass skirt.

She started laughing all over again.

Eventually the storm passed, both the sobs and the laughter subsided, and a paper cup filled with water appeared in front of her.

"Here," crooned a whisky-smooth, Southern-accented baritone beside her. She glanced up into a pair of eyes so blue and cool and clean she got shivers. Except then she remembered the way her face swelled up when she cried and she ducked her head, for once in her life grateful for her curtain of hair. She took the proffered cup and gulped the water in three swallows, thinking all she needed now was to choke.

"You okay now?"

"I...yeah. I th-think so." Joanna scrambled to her feet, dusting off her backside before digging a tissue out of her handbag, which gave her a convenient excuse for avoiding the man's gaze as he rose with her. "I'm so sorry—" She blew loudly into the tissue, figuring at this point a little honking was hardly going to hurt her image. "It's just—"

"No need to explain, ma'am. Sounded to me like you needed to get that out of your system. Here—you dropped this."

Joanna glanced down to see her comb gleaming in the palm of his hand. A nice hand. Strong-looking. Graceful fingers, for a man.

She was an artist. She was supposed to notice these things.

She was also supposed to remember she had a mother. Somewhere.

"The lady who came in with you's over in the back of the store, having a look-see," he said, as if reading her mind.

"That's no lady," she said, blowing her nose again. "That's my mother. Who's not real comfortable around melt...downs..."

Joanna had turned toward the back of the store and was now struck dumb at the child's wonderland before her eyes. Somehow wedged in among shelves of toys that reached clear to the ceiling of the tiny shop were any number of hands-on play areas—low tables overflowing with building sets and construction toys and tiny dishes set up for an impromptu tea party; an open closet burgeoning with flashes of shiny fabrics, feathers, jewels, shoes, hats; bins of stuffed animals and puppets, and easels and paints, and rocking horses and miniature drum sets and lions and tigers and bears.

Oh, my.

A chuckle, soft and sexy, winnowed through her entrancement and finally pulled her gaze to his. The hamster chapeau was gone, but now her attention glommed onto a grin blooming across a pleasant—very pleasant—face. Lean. Tanned. Just asymmetrical enough to be interesting but not worrisome, couple of dimples, a strong jaw. Laugh lines. A face that had ripened and sharpened well with age, even if she could have done without the surfer dude hairstyle—a little too blond, a little too long. Still, way down low, she felt a tiny prickle of something that definitely *was* worrisome. Like not knowing you were hungry until you smelled the French fries.

Still grinning down at her, he slid his hands into his jeans' pockets. "Actually, for a while there, it sounded like you were having a high old time. And I bet you feel a lot better now, don't you?"

"Other than the residual mortification?"

He shrugged underneath a bright red T-shirt with a glittering Playing For Keeps emblazoned across the front. "Didn't bother me any. Why should it you?" While Joanna stood there trying to think of a witty comeback, he retrieved the Santas, then glanced up, his eyes touching hers just long enough to set off a *zing*. A tiny one, nothing major. Along the lines of what you might get when you test a battery to see if it's still alive.

Well, hell. Where were the Pheromone Alert! signs?

"You make these?"

"What? Oh. Yes." Joanna stepped back, mentally shaking off all those pheromones clinging to her like burrs. "Clarence. And Stanley." At his questioning expression, she added, "Each one is unique. Well, I recycle the clothing patterns, but each face is carved freehand so no two are alike...."

She'd never been attracted to total strangers, no matter how appealing their laugh lines were. So it had to be her apparently fragile emotional state causing this current brain blip. Still, as she watched him take in Clarence's chubby, dimpled face, his curly white hair and beard, watched him finger the Santa's velvet robe decorated with dozens of pearl buttons and miniature metallic braid, she had to admit *something* about the man was making her blood...hum.

How totally bizarre.

The blue eyes met hers, clearly impressed. And clearly—whoa—interested. "You're good." Then he grinned in that way men do—or at least did back in the Dark Ages when she'd last dated—that sets off alarms.

"Is that a come-on?"

Which she wouldn't have said it if hadn't been for that Dark Ages business.

However his expression didn't change one iota. Well, except for the merest hitch of one eyebrow. "You want it to be?"

"No." She was almost positive she meant it, too.

"Then it isn't. And even if it was, that's got nothing to do with the fact that I think you're one helluva talented lady."

Okay, so that won the guy a point. Or two. "Thanks."

Still holding Clarence, he seemed to hesitate a moment, then offered his hand. "Name's Dale McConnaughy. The store's mine."

His handshake was the kind to make her really question that *no* of a second ago. Almost. "Joanna Swann."

"You were trying to sell these next door?" Dale went

on, now appraising Stanley, a Santa in denim overalls and a red-and-green-plaid workshirt. Striped stockings ended in open-backed bedroom slippers on his feet; through a minuscule pair of wire-rimmed glasses, he frowned down at a tiny teddy bear in his hands.

"More or less. They'd said they'd take two on consignment." Joanna stuffed her hands into the pockets on the front of her dress. "Then this morning the owner said she didn't have room."

"I'll take them."

"What?"

"I'll take them," he repeated. "I mean, I'll buy them from you."

She frowned. "Look, just because I broke down—"

"I don't want them because I feel sorry for you, okay? I want 'em because you do freakin' unbelievable work and because I've got customers who'd go nuts for something like this. So what's your price?"

Well, hmm. Certainly a change from Ms. Hoity-Toity-we-don't-really-have-much-call-for-*crafts* next door. However...

"Oh, that's really nice of you, but, see, I don't really have a wholesale price. Because I put so much work into them? I mean, the gallery would've taken a percentage, but—"

"How. Much."

She felt her skin warm. "Three hundred. Each. Including stands."

The little boy sparkle reasserted itself in his eyes. "*Thank* you. And you say no two are alike? Can you get me more?"

Joanna waited out the short surge of dizziness, then said, "Uh...yeah. Although I'm pretty booked up between now and Christmas with special orders—"

"You think you could do six more by Thanksgiving? I'll prepay," he said when she hesitated.

Was this guy totally off his nut or what? If this was how he ran his business, he'd be bankrupt within the year. "Yes, I could probably fit in another half dozen by Thanksgiving. But—"

"Good." He vanished into the back for a moment, returning with a large business-size checkbook, which he slapped open on the counter. "That was three hundred each, you said?"

"Um…Mr. McConnaughy?" Without moving his head, his eyes angled to hers. "These aren't toys, you know," she said.

"Yeah. I know. So?"

"So…this is a toy store?"

On a chuckle, he straightened, his arms folded across his chest. For some reason Joanna's gaze was drawn to the top of his left hand, to the patch of oddly smooth skin set in the midst of the sprinkling of light brown hair.

"You may be talented as all get-out, Ms. Swann, but your salesmanship sucks." Her attention zipped back to his face. "I don't think I've ever run into someone more determined to shoot herself in the foot before."

"It's not that. It's just—"

"—that these aren't meant for children, so why the hell am I buyin' them for a toy store?"

"Well, yes. There are a lot of small pieces on these a child could choke on. These are meant to be displayed, not played with."

The right side of his mouth hitched up. "I kinda figured that out."

"You…oh."

"Uh-huh. But then, how would you know more'n half my customers are adults comin' in to buy things for themselves?" He finished writing the check, ripped it out and handed it over to her, with instructions to get him an invoice whenever it was convenient. Then he capped his pen, tossing it back onto the cash register. "A person doesn't have to be a kid to still get a kick out of playing. And collecting's something anybody can do. Cars, dolls, model trains…'' He picked up Clarence. "Santas.'' He grinned down at the doll, then back at her. "Looking at this guy just makes you feel good inside, doesn't it? Like I want to laugh right out loud.'' He looked at her, something like wistfulness softening his features, making her insides jump. "Sometimes grown-ups need a little poke to make 'em remember what it was like to be a kid, when it was okay to believe in magic. And that's something most folks can't put a price on.''

Joanna stared at the check, shaking her head. "Even if they can get them for a fraction of the price at Costco or Sam's.''

"There you go again. Tryin' to talk me out of this.''

"But by the time you take your markup… I'm sorry. It's about this practical streak I have.''

"Which you put aside to make these, I take it.''

"No,'' she said, her brow puckering. "This is a business. My livelihood. I can't afford not to be practical…why are you laughing now?''

"Would you listen to yourself? I can't think of many things more impractical than making dolls that sell for three hundred bucks a pop.''

"Which is why I don't sell too many of them. I mean, I'll never get rich from these.''

"Then why do you do it?''

"Because…they feed something inside me.''

"Then trust me…they'll feed something inside everyone who buys one, too. Something none of that mass produced stuff can ever do. Sure, most folks are perfectly content buying what they're gonna see in half their neighbor's living rooms. But you and I know that's not enough for everybody.'' He leaned his hands on the edge of the counter, hooking her gaze in his. "Not for the fools who have the nerve to try to compete with Toys "R" Us and Target and

K mart, or the ones who spend hours making a single doll instead of holding down a regular job in some office with a guaranteed paycheck and a dental plan. Or for the ones who pay five, ten, a hundred times more for something than they have to, just for the satisfaction of having something that nobody else does…''

"Joanna! Come here!"

She jumped, tearing her eyes away from the crazy man and toward her mother, who was beckoning her to the back of the store. Joanna wended her way through the narrow aisles to look outside at a display of wooden play forts with attached swing sets, each one bigger and badder than the next and more expensive.

"Wouldn't the boys love one of those for their birthday?"

"Right. Honestly, Mom—I paid less than that for my first car."

But her mother, hanging on to the stuffed frog she'd apparently decided on for the new baby, had already turned to Dale, who'd followed Joanna. "My twin grandsons' eighth birthday is two weeks from today—can you have one of these delivered by then?"

"I can't let you spend that much on the boys—!"

Glynnie quelled her with a don't-be-rude look as Dale assured her that was no problem. Then another customer arrived and, with a "Be right back, ladies," Dale took off. Glynnie smacked Jo lightly in the arm.

"For God's sake, Joanna. It's just money. Loosen up."

"Been down that road already, Mother. I'm perfectly happy being my tight little self again."

"Happy? Hell, you haven't been happy in years."

"Excuse me?"

"Well, it's true."

"Is not."

"Is, too." Glynnie glanced over, presumably to make

sure they couldn't be heard, then lowered her voice anyway. "I saw him making goo-goo eyes at you."

"No, you didn't," Joanna whispered back.

"Don't tell me what I didn't see, young lady. I could
feel the buzzing from clear on the other side of the store."

"That's because you forgot to take your Prozac this
morning."

"Joanna Swann! You know full well I haven't touched
that stuff in years. And anyway, that has nothing to do with
the fact that your flirting skills could use a major tune-up.
And here's a perfectly good learning tool, tossed right in
your path. So what could it hurt to practice?"

"Oh, gee, I don't know. Maybe because he's a total
stranger? Because for all I know he's married? Because—"
this had just come to her "—I haven't got the time or
energy right now to start from scratch?"

"Honey, if you're waiting until they bring out the heat
'n' serve variety, you're outta luck."

"Mother. Even discounting his questionable marital
status or the fact that I've known him for, oh, five minutes,
the man is nuts."

"Why do you say that?"

Joanna showed her the check. Glynnie's eyes shot to
Joanna's. "And this is for…?"

"Eight Santas."

"Oh?" Glynnie frowned. "Oh."

"Yeah. *Oh.* What kind of crazy person gives a total
stranger a check for twenty-four hundred dollars, with no
paperwork, nothing, no assurances that I'll even deliver?
The man is not well. Or at least, not fiscally responsible."

"Okay, maybe you have a point," Glynnie said, her attention straying to Dale, helping the man who'd come in
to pick out a computer learning game. "But come on, admit
it…when was the last time you saw somebody that cute?"

"This morning," Joanna said. Glynnie looked at her.

"Your grandchildren's father? Dark hair, dark eyes, charming smile? Totally clueless—"

"Okay, ladies, I'm back," Dale said, making them both jump. "Now, which one of these would you like? I've got 'em all in stock."

"That one," Glynnie said before Jo could protest again, naturally pointing to the largest one in the batch. She whipped out her AmEx and smacked it down on the counter, dumping the hapless frog beside it. "And you said you can deliver it in time for their birthday?"

"Sure thing. If you'll just fill this out—" he handed her a clipboard with a form of some kind on it "—we can get it all set up for you." While her mother did as he asked, he turned his attention to Joanna. "So. You've got kids?"

Was it her, or did she detect just the slightest edge to that question? "Three," she said. "The boys and an eleven-year-old girl."

"Sounds like you've got your hands full."

Before Joanna could answer, Glynnie said, "Oh, it's not so bad." She handed him back the clipboard. "They're with their father every weekend. Are you married, Mr. McConnaughy?"

Dale dropped the clipboard, which clattered to the counter, while Joanna fumbled for her brain before it landed on the floor and rolled away. When he looked up, Joanna pointed to her mother behind her back, then mimed hanging herself.

Then he did this slow, lazy grinning thing, and Joanna felt her blood heat up a degree or two. "Why?" he said to her mother. "You fixin' to ask me out?"

Nice save, she thought as her mother—or the alien that looked like her mother—merely smiled. "Oh, I wasn't asking for myself. I'm happily married, thank you."

"Well, I'm glad to hear that, Ms. Swann. But you know…" Dale leaned forward, bracing his hands against the edge of the counter. Those nice, slender, sinewy hands.

"Maybe you should be careful who you ask that question. Some folks might take it the wrong way. Especially from a woman as attractive as yourself."

Glynnie laughed. "Boy, you really know how to lay it on thick, don't you?"

"Just speaking the truth, Ms. Swann," he said, ringing up the sale. "Just speakin' the truth. As a matter of fact, when you two first came in—"

"Please don't tell me you thought we were sisters."

Again with the loopy grin. And a noncommittal shrug. "A man can't help what he sees." He bagged up the frog, then handed it to her, along with the charge slip and a copy of the order. "Somebody'll give you a call before we come out, okay?" he said, and then a mini swarm of customers came in, affording Joanna the perfect opportunity to grab her mother's arm and drag her out of there.

"What were you *doing?*"

"Just having some fun," Glynnie said, wresting her arm out of Joanna's grasp. "Remember fun?"

Joanna stomped around to the driver's side of the van, unlocked the doors and climbed in. "Yeah," she said, slamming shut her door as her mother got in. "I remember fun." To her annoyance, her eyes burned. "I think."

"Oh, for heaven's sake—you don't think I really meant anything by that, did you?" her mother said. "I was just testing him. And you're right. That smile, that attitude… He *is* like Bobby. And God knows you don't need to go through *that* again."

Joanna twisted the key in the ignition, backing the van out of the parking space the instant the engine growled to life. "God knows," she echoed, probably shaving five years off her mother's life by darting across four lanes of traffic to make a left turn.

Two weeks later the roof still leaked, Bobby still hadn't reimbursed Joanna for his half of the plumbing bill and

Gladys, Henry Shaw's Great Dane, was still pregnant. On a brighter note, however—well, brighter for Joanna and the female canine population of Corrales—immediate and permanent sanctions had been imposed on Chester's wild oats. The dog seemed to be resigned to his fate, even if, judging from his actions, he was still a little fuzzy on the ramifications of his visit to the vet. But then, as long as Joanna knew he was shooting blanks, she really didn't care all that much what the dog knew.

So all in all—she steered the van into the pickup lane in front of the elementary school—things were about the same.

The bell rang. Joanna didn't bother looking for the boys in the blur of shrieking children disgorged from the sprawling series of buildings. A minute later, however, she picked out their shrill little voices like a mama sheep recognizing her lambs' bleats from all the others in the herd.

"I called shotgun!" Matt, the oldest twin by ten minutes and the image of his father with his dark eyes and straight hair, bellowed beside the van. The twins were fraternal, not identical, as different in temperament and personality as they were physically. Although they were extremely well matched when it came to fighting over something they both wanted.

"Nuh-uh, I did!" Ryder bellowed right back as somebody yanked open the passenger side door and a whirlwind of elbows and knees and backpacks flew into the front seat. "Mo-om! Tell him to get in the back!"

It never ceased to amaze her how they could have the same argument, day after day, over something neither one had ever won. "Both of you get in back and your seat belts on," she said mildly. "We're gumming up the works here."

"Aw, Mom...it's just to the house."

"Now."

With a lot of grumbling and shoving and one backpack

smacking Joanna in the face, they crawled through the space between the front seats and plopped into the back. "Didja bring any snacks?" Matt asked. "I'm about to starve to *death*."

"I imagine you'll survive until we get home," Jo said, pulling out into the single-file stream of minivans and SUVs and pickups leaving the parking lot. "Either of you got any homework?"

"Nope," Matt said. "Did it all in school. An' I got all my spelling words right on my pre-test, too, so I don't have to take the test tomorrow!"

Joanna's eyes darted to the rearview mirror to catch Ryder's sinking expression. Damn. For the millionth time, she tried to gauge how to respond to Matt's good news without further damaging her other son's increasingly fragile self-esteem. "Wow, Matt-o. You must've studied really hard."

"Nuh-uh. I just knew 'em without even looking."

Thank you, Matt. "How about you, Ry?" she said gently, wishing she could ruffle his cinnamon curls, which even as short as she kept them were every bit as obtuse as her own. "You have much work today?"

"I don't remember." His green eyes, a little darker than hers, flashed in the mirror's reflection. "I *think* I finished all my math in school, maybe."

"You did? That's wonderful!"

His mouth stretched into a thin smile and Joanna's heart cracked. The child had been tested every which way to Sunday, but there seemed to be no real reason why the very material that came so easily to Matt should be such a struggle for his brother. Joanna knew, even if she didn't find two or three unfinished papers in his backpack, there was still a good hour to hour and a half of spelling and reading and math fact practice, just so Ryder wouldn't fall more behind than he already was. It was hard on her, it was even harder on a child who'd already spent six and a half hours at school, but what was hardest of all was seeing the perplexed expression in Ryder's eyes at his brother's seemingly effortless success.

From birth, they'd been total opposites. Matt had come out protesting his confinement at the top of his lungs. Ryder had opened his eyes right away, calmly taking it all in, flinching only at his brother's raucous cries from across the room. Matt had been the first to roll over, the first to crawl and walk and talk, always barreling through life at full throttle. Ryder, however, had to be coaxed to go down the same slide his brother had just rocketed down ten times in a row. And then only if Bobby or Joanna went down with him. He was the one who'd patiently spend ages building the three-foot-tall tower of blocks, his brother the one who'd knock them down.

Academically, however, they'd seemed to be on a par with each other until last year. While Matt continued to gobble up new skills like the hungry little caterpillar, Ryder had begun to struggle. Although quiet and attentive in class, he was now almost a full grade level behind. What got Joanna, though, was that she would have expected the reverse to be true, that the one who'd spent the first five years of his life in perpetual motion, except when he was asleep, would have been the one more prone to learning difficulties, not the quiet, contemplative one.

The quiet, contemplative one whose self-confidence was beginning to leak at an alarming rate, no matter what Joanna did to caulk it.

Both boys were out of the car and into the kitchen before Joanna could close her door and drag her weary butt into the house. Dulcy, her middle-schooler, had already been home for a half hour. What passed for music blared from her room. Cats swarmed Joanna's ankles, begging her to make it stop.

"Turn it down, Dulce!" Joanna hollered automatically, hanging her car keys on the hook by the back door. The music dimmed from brain-numbing to merely irritating; a second later, the child stomped down the hall in her customary sexless hooded sweatshirt and jeans, brown eyes flashing behind wire-rimmed glasses.

"Okay, which one of you dorks was in my room?"

"Not me!" came out of two crumb-speckled mouths.

"Right." Dulcy held up The Evidence: a box of colored pencils. "This was brand new and full when I put it in my desk yesterday, and now half the pencils are either gone or broken. And I know one of you did it—"

The phone rang.

"—and now I have to use them for a social studies project and I don't have them and this like *so* pisses me off—"

"Dulcy! Hello?" Joanna said into the phone, glaring at her daughter. She couldn't hear whoever it was for the eruption of "I don't know where your dumb old pencils are!" behind her.

"Well, one of you does and I'm not leaving this kitchen until I get 'em back!"

"Sorry, hold on," Jo said into the phone, then slammed it against her sternum. "Kids! Take it elsewhere!"

"But, Mom, what am I going to *dooooo?* This is due *tomorrow!"*

"I. Am. On. The. Phone. I will take care of it *later.* Everybody *out."*

The boys trooped into the family room to watch TV; Dulcy thumped back down to her room, wailing about how much her life sucked. Joanna—who at the moment could relate more to her daughter's lament far more than she'd ever let on—sighed and held the phone back up to her ear.

"I'm sorry. Who is this again?"

"Dale McConnaughy, ma'am. From Playing for Keeps? Just calling to confirm that we're delivering that play set to your house tomorrow afternoon?"

The boys began arguing about something in the other room, Dulcy cranked up her music again and the dog began to hack up something in the middle of the kitchen floor.

And suddenly, because clearly she was closer to losing it than she thought, all she wanted to do was to wrap herself up in that Bourbony Southern accent and never come out again. Because, see, this was the one thing that *had* changed during the past two weeks.

Whether Joanna liked it or not.

Long-buried images came roaring to the surface of her desexitized brain, of hot bodies and cool sheets and endless orgasms. Preferably hers. Not that she'd ever had endless orgasms, but a girl can dream.

"Ms. Swann? Is everything all right?"

"What? Oh, yes… Sorry. I was…distracted," she said, her gaze wandering over to the cupboard where she kept the baking stuff. For the past week, in those scant milliseconds when she wasn't worrying about a kid or a roof or her work or her ex, and sometimes even when she was, thoughts of Dale McConnaughy had stormed her brain like a bargain hunter at K mart the morning after Thanksgiving. She didn't understand it, she sure as hell didn't like it, and there didn't seem to be a damn thing she could do about it. Other than taking the edge off the pain with chocolate. Which was why she was now yanking open her cupboard door, letting out a small sigh of gratitude that she hadn't been hallucinating the package of chocolate chips. She'd make cookies. Warm, gooey cookies packed chock full of hundreds of little orgasms for the taste buds.

One learned to adapt.

"So…we're on for tomorrow?"

Joanna ripped open the bag and tilted it to her upended mouth. Cookies, hell. Who had time for foreplay?

"Yes," she managed to get out around a mouthful of squished chocolate. Maybe not quite as satisfying as when combined with butter and brown sugar and…nuts, but sometimes, you just can't wait for the, um, full package. "Their…party is at five, so as long as it's…up by then, that should be fine."

She stuffed more chips into her mouth.

"No problem." A pause. "Uh, ma'am? You sure you're okay? You sound kind of funny."

"What? Me? No, I'm fine," she said, and he said okay as though he wasn't really sure and then they hung up—just as something crashed in the other room.

Joanna knocked back another handful of chips, thought about Dale's long, slender hands and orgasms for another twenty seconds or so, then went to clean up the dog's little present.

Chapter 3

Although Dale knew there were some pretty highfalutin homes in Corrales, a small, horsey community flanking the western edge of the Rio Grande on the fringes of Albuquerque proper, he still hadn't been sure what to expect from the address he'd been given. The mother clearly had money, but he got the feeling Joanna was one of those types determined to make it on her own if it killed her. So when Jose steered the store truck down the dirt road leading to the house, and the spreads kept getting bigger and bigger, he began to wonder just what the heck was going on here.

Especially when the house itself came into view. Like a large, odd-shaped bug hugging the landscape, the traditional earth-toned adobe, with its flat roof and portal stretching across most of the front, looked to be one of those that had been added on to as the mood struck over the years. The property took up a good three or four acres, he guessed, with an open horse shelter and paddock off to one side. Mature, drooping cottonwoods, their leaves mostly yellow this time of year, and gnarled, dusty green olive trees sheltered the house; a dozen or so terra-cotta pots in various sizes, spilling over with assorted late-season flowers, had been plunked in no particular order along the meandering stone walk between the driveway and the front door. And there were cats everywhere, three or four of which were now lazily making their way toward the truck like they had nothing better to do.

Except for the muffled barking of a dog inside the house, it was dead quiet. Peaceful. And had he been somebody else, Dale might have thought the place looked real inviting.

In a life filled to the gills with crazy doings, this had to be one of the craziest. When Charley had called in sick this morning, Dale could've gotten someone else to fill in. No reason for him to go getting it in his head that a little exercise and fresh air on this beautiful fall day was just what he needed. Except he knew damn well fresh air and exercise had nothing to do with it.

Like he said. Crazy.

Wasn't like the signals he'd sent out to Joanna Swann the other day had been exactly reciprocated. Even if they had been, she didn't seem the type, he didn't think, inclined to mess around just for the fun of it. Which was all Dale *was* inclined to do. And she had kids, to boot. Messing around and kids did not mix. Oh, he got a real kick out of talking to 'em and watching them play, the way their imaginations took flight from the simplest things. Yeah, kids were great. Long as they were somebody else's.

So, all in all, it was a damn fool thing, that he was here. Except it'd been a dog's age since some gal had riled up his curiosity exactly the way Joanna Swann did. Why, he couldn't quite figure out, although it was refreshing, her not knowing who he was. Or maybe it was because she didn't seem that all-fired concerned about how she looked, which set her apart right there from most of the women he'd known over the past little while. He just liked what he saw, was all. And whether it made sense or not, he wanted to get to know her better, at least before making a conscious decision about whether or not she was a lost cause.

He almost flinched when Joanna stuck her head out the front door and hollered that they should drive around to the back, which they did, parking on the dirt driveway that separated the stable/paddock from a parklike area that passed for a backyard. More cats—or maybe it was the same ones, Dale couldn't tell—swarmed them when they got out of the truck, joined by a fuzzy, medium-size brown-and-white mutt who acted like they'd just come home from the wars.

Dale waded through the furry bodies toward Joanna, now standing on her back patio. She was wearing worn jeans and a white, floppy sweatshirt, but even though it was kinda chilly out, she was barefoot. He wondered if the flagstone was cold on her feet. Which got him to wondering about other things he shouldn't.

The cats, having already lost interest, drifted off. The dog, on the other hand, was amusing himself by trying to shove a slobbered-up old tennis ball into Dale's hand. Joanna said, "Leave the man alone, Chester," but more like she figured that's what she should say than if she actually expected the dog to obey. Which he didn't.

Dale wrestled the ball out of the dog's mouth and lobbed it clear to the back of the yard. It felt good, throwing again. Even if he couldn't do it over and over the way he used to.

"I didn't expect you to bring out the set yourself," Joanna said. Dale turned, somewhat disappointed to note that her expression wasn't nearly as hospitable as the dog's had been.

"Somebody got sick. I'm filling in."

"Oh." She swiped at a couple of loose curls that were fluttering around her face, the rest of her hair being stuck up on top of her head with a pencil rammed through it, of all things. "You can just leave the store like that?"

She sounded kind of annoyed, for some reason. "It's my store. I can pretty much do whatever I want. But since you seem so concerned—" he turned and motioned to Jose to go ahead and start unloading the truck, then turned back to Joanna "—I've got a couple part-timers minding the place…"

His not-quite-full-out-flirting grin faltered slightly when a man a few years younger than Dale, shorter but more sturdily built—like a pit bull, Dale thought—came out of the house to stand behind Joanna. Despite sharp features that should have made him intimidating, the grin that split the man's features as he approached Dale, his hand outstretched, told a whole 'nother story.

"Bobby Alvarez," he said, his words tinged with that slight Spanish accent Dale had come to realize often clung even to Hispanics whose families had been in the area for generations. The grin widened. "Otherwise known as 'the ex.'"

Since this fact did not seem to particularly perturb Bobby, Dale figured he needn't let it bother him any, either. So he returned the grin, and the handshake. "Dale McConnaughy," he said, bracing himself for the reaction. Not that there always was one these days. But it happened often enough, especially with a mug that had adorned a million Wheaties boxes not all that long ago.

"Dale McConnaughy? Damn, I thought you looked familiar! Hey, babe—" he turned to Joanna "—you know who this is?"

"Yes, Bobby. Dale McConnaughy. We've already met."

"No, I mean, do you know *who* this is? Atlanta Braves? Pitched a shutout in the last game of the World Series against the Yankees a few years ago?" He let out a whoop of laughter, then took Dale's hand again and pumped it for all it was worth. "Man, I cannot tell you what an honor this is!'' Then he frowned. ''But what the hell are you doing setting up kids' swing sets?''

''I own a toy store now, since I retired. Bum arm.''

''Oh, yeah,'' Bobby said. ''I remember readin' something about that.'' He looked like he had more to say on the subject, but changed his mind when he saw Jose lug the first round of materials through the gate. ''Hey—you guys need some help?''

Dale felt a prickle of annoyance. An ex-husband did not fit in with his plans. Except then Joanna said, ''No, they do not. You told me you had a one-thirty appointment, remember?''

''It's that late already?'' Bobby said, checking his watch. ''Damn.'' He shrugged. ''Don't know why, but I can never keep track of time. Used to drive her nuts,'' he ended on a chuckle, fishing his keys out of his back pocket. ''Okay, I guess I'd better go.'' He leaned over and bussed her on the cheek, then said, ''You'll call me when it's time to bring the kids over, right?''

After Bobby left, Joanna stood frowning at the space where her husband had been until Dale said, ''So…where you want us to put this?''

Her head whipped around, her eyes a little glassy-looking. ''What? Oh. Over here.''

Still barefoot, she tromped toward the back of the yard, pointing to a spot underneath one of the tallest cottonwoods. ''I don't know if the roots might be a problem, though…''

''You got an ax?'' Jose said. ''We can take some of them out, it won't hurt the tree.''

Joanna told him there was one in the shed; with a nod, Jose loped off, the dog trotting along to keep him company. Dale was about to ask her which end of the set she wanted closest to the tree when she suddenly said, ''Honestly. I'm surprised he didn't pee around the perimeter of the property.''

"Who? Jose?"

She looked at him, eyes wide. Then laughed softly. "No. Bobby."

"Oh." Dale shrugged. "Maybe he still has feelings for you?"

"We've been divorced for more than three years. I somehow doubt it."

Her curls were bouncing in the breeze and her mouth did this cute, kinda three-cornered thing when she smiled, and because he was as territorial as the next male animal he thought about moving closer, staking his own claim. Maybe leaning one palm on the tree trunk, right over her head.

Oh, yeah, this was definitely a game to him. One of his favorites. One he hadn't felt much like playing in a long time. And wasn't all that sure he should be playing now.

Because, unless he was sorely mistaken, Joanna Swann played by a whole different set of rules than he was used to. If he wanted to set this one up to win—should he decide that's what he wanted to do—he'd best remember that. So he didn't move closer. In fact, he crouched by the pile of four-by-fours, going through the motions of checking them off on his parts list, even though he'd checked them three times before loading them into the truck. "Don't see as time has much to do with anything."

"Time?" She hooked her thumbs in her pockets in a way that managed to be sexy as all get-out and childlike at the same time. On closer inspection, she wasn't near as skinny as he'd first thought, although far as he could tell underneath the sweatshirt, she didn't have much in the way of breasts. But this was one instance where size did not matter. "Nothing," she said. "But I sure hope you're wrong. For his pregnant fiancée's sake, if nothing else."

"Oh. That puts kind of a different spin on things, huh?"

"That would be my take on it."

"Still and all, maybe he figured he made a mistake, walking away from you."

After a moment she said, "He didn't walk away. I did."

Dale looked up. That hadn't been regret in her voice, not that he could tell. But there was something that niggled at him, anyway. "Because?"

"Because I saw no point in sticking something out that wasn't working anymore."

"I see." A pause. "Don't take this the wrong way, but you got any idea why you're telling me this?"

Her gaze met his, cool as a freshly cut lawn on a summer's day. "None at all." Then she tilted her head. "So you were a ball player?"

To hide his smile, Dale got up and crossed to where she wanted the set, nudging the roots with the toe of his shoe. Nice tactic she had there: if the conversation wasn't going the way she liked, she just moved on to something else.

"Yep," he said. "My entire adult life, up until a nasty case of pitcher's arm ended my career a couple years back."

"I'm sorry."

He shrugged. "It happens. I...take it you're not a fan?"

"Of sports? No. Paying a bunch of grown men millions of dollars to chase, kick, bat or otherwise torture a ball never made a whole lot of sense to me."

"Don't hold back now, tell me what you really think."

She laughed. "Okay, so I'm not going to wet myself because you were a sports star."

"So why'd you say you were sorry?"

Her smile faded into a faint blush. "Because...I can imagine how hard it must have been for you to give up something you loved. Assuming you did."

It was the weirdest thing. With most women, he had no trouble keeping track of whether he was making points or not. Not with this one. Damn, it was unnerving, the way she managed to be aloof and sympathetic at the same time.

"Yeah. I loved it." Although not for the reasons she probably thought. The real motives behind his playing, for his determination to win at that game, too, weren't any of her business. Or anyone else's.

Jose and the dog finally returned with the ax. After telling them to come get her in the studio if they had any questions, Joanna called the dog and carefully picked her way back to the house in her bare feet. Dale noticed there were two little dusty butt-cheek impressions on the bottom of the long white sweatshirt, a detail that fueled his imagination. Behind him, Jose chuckled.

"Shut up," Dale muttered. Jose just laughed harder.

Could Joanna help it that her worktable sat at the perfect angle to see across the yard? Or that the play set really only worked in that spot? And was it her fault that stuffing Santa bodies didn't exactly require her entire concentration? She would have been looking out the window anyway, right? And it certainly wasn't her fault that Dale McConnaughy had taken off his shirt.

Or that he liked to wear his jeans slung low on his hips.

She was an artist, after all. Her perusal of Dale McConnaughy's naked torso was no different than all those life drawing classes she took. Muscles and sinews and shoulders.

Oh, my.

On the floor beside her, stretched out in a patch of dusty sunlight, Chester twitched, dreaming. One of the cats, who was just passing, smacked Chester's nose on general principles; the dog jerked awake, looked accusingly at Joanna, then crashed his head back on the floor with a beleaguered sigh. Joanna chuckled, then looked out the window again and gave a beleaguered sigh of her own.

Maybe Dale McConnaughy represented everything Joanna didn't want or need, but he was one fine specimen of human male. And Joanna was one fine specimen of pathetically horny female. That she should feel a twitch in her hoo-hah every time she looked at the guy was hardly a surprise.

What was a surprise was that, for all Dale McConnaughy's come-to-papa charm—yeah, yeah, she wasn't totally out of the loop—she'd bet her butt that charm was a cover for something that went far deeper. Oh, she had no doubt he was out for only one thing, but unlike most guys who saw sexual conquests as some sort of Holy Grail, she had the distinct feeling Dale McConnaughy used them because his real Holy Grail was out of his reach.

Which was certainly a presumptuous conclusion for her to have reached after—what?—two five-minute conversations. But she remembered vividly, from her stint as a part-time art teacher before the twins were born, seeing that particular expression in this or that student's eyes. The look that said, "I'm fine, don't dig, don't ask, don't make me think about things I don't want to think about." A look that asserted itself at unguarded moments, when buried or ignored pain dimmed even the brightest smile. After a dozen times of asking the kids' teachers what was up, and getting answers she didn't want to hear, she no longer questioned if she was seeing what she thought she was. She knew.

But reaching out, however subtly, to a nine-year-old was far different than reaching out to a grown man who would, in all probability, completely misinterpret her motives. Which, considering the way her nerve endings were shouting, "Hallelujah, I am reborn, sister!" would be a completely understandable misinterpretation on his part.

So she wouldn't reach out.

At all.

Ever.

"Hey, honey!"

Joanna jumped a foot, then turned to see her best friend, Karleen Almquist, click-clacking her way across the room in a pair of high-heeled ankle boots and designer jeans that could practically fit Dulcy. Karleen was not, and had never been, into the natural look. Karleen, bless her, not only believed comparing her to a Barbie doll was a compliment, but a reputation worthy of keeping intact at all costs...as long as she could pass those costs on to the Spouse of the Week.

They'd been best friends forever, although nobody, including Joanna and Karleen, could quite figure out why. Habit, most likely. And an ability to accept each other for who they were. But they'd been there for each other from the do-you-think-he-likes-me? middle school squealies to the breakups of their respective marriages, although Karleen's track record in that department was running three to one over Joanna's. The only good thing to come out of the last marriage—according to Karleen—was that, this time, she got the house. A house less than a half mile from Joanna's. So Karleen, who had turned an avocation into a career as a personal shopper for dozens of time-crunched professional women in town, popped over nearly every day, even if only for a quick cup of coffee. A nice diversion, frankly, since Joanna's work kept her more housebound than the kids ever had.

"Ooooh, I like this one," Karleen now said, running a finger down the front of a Santa in an ivory velvet robe on which Joanna had hand painted an ivy design, stitching on tiny red beads here and there for the berries. Then she looked out the window and gasped.

"Holy crap," she breathed, as artfully plucked sandy brows disappeared underneath artfully scraggly bangs that had been dark brown and lethally stiff in high school. "Is that *real?*"

"Couldn't tell you," Joanna said, deadpan. "He only has his shirt off."

"More's the pity." Then she smacked Joanna in the arm. "You've got all that right out your window and you didn't even call me? What kind of friend are you?"

"Hey. My eye candy. Go find your own. And don't drool on the velvet."

"So who is he?"

"Guy who owns the toy store where we got the play set."

"Does this toy store owner have a name?"

"Dale McConnaughy."

"The baseball player?" Karleen squeaked.

"Apparently so. And apparently this means a lot more to you than it does to me."

"You bet your ass it means something. He made All-Stars five years running, voted MVP the last year he played, pitched at least twenty no-hitters during his career—"

"Since when do you know so much about baseball?"

"Since Jasper."

Husband Number Two.

"And if I never see another game again," Karleen said, "it will be too soon. But I do remember not feeling too put out if the Braves were playing and Dale McConnaughy was pitching. The camera used to zoom in for closeups of his face, and those *eyes...*" She sighed, her own eyes glazing over. "And you know how baseball players grab their crotches?"

"I really don't want to go there, Kar."

"Sure you do. I mean..." She leaned on the table, her silicone-enhanced breasts immobile beneath her chenille sweater, and lowered her voice. "Took more than a single tug to rearrange himself, if you know what I mean."

"Oh, Lord," Joanna said.

"What?"

"You sound hornier than I am."

Karleen pouted. "It's been three *months!*"

"There are worse things."

"Name one."

"Starving to death."

"Honey, I haven't eaten a full meal since 1983. Food, I

can live without.'' She spared another glance outside, then brightened. ''Hey—sure looks to me like those boys are thirsty, don't you think?''

''No, they're fine. They brought their own water.''

''I cannot believe you're that dense.''

Joanna threaded a needle, biting off the thread with her teeth. ''I'm not—what the hell are you doing?'' she yelped as Karleen snatched the needle out of her hand, then dragged Joanna off the stool and out of the studio. Chester roused himself and followed, just in case all this activity had something to do with food.

''Either jump-starting your pathetic love life,'' Karleen said, once in the kitchen, ''or saving mine from an ignominious death.'' She yanked open Joanna's refrigerator door.

''I do not need my love life jump-started—''

''Good. You've got tea,'' Karleen said, hauling a plastic pitcher off the top shelf. ''And don't be ridiculous, of course you do.''

''Not today, I don't. I've got a party to give later, remember?''

The tea poured into a pair of plastic tumblers, Karleen gave her a bemused look. ''You've never heard of multitasking? So what d'you have they could munch on? Cookies or cake or something?'' She threw open another cabinet and grimaced at the array of Little Debbie boxes. ''What kind of domestic goddess are you, anyway?''

''The kind that doesn't have time to bake. Kar, I really don't think—''

''That's right, sweetie,'' she said, arranging a selection of the goodies on a plate. ''You just sit back and let little old Karleen do the thinking for once, 'kay?''

''The last time I let you do the thinking for both of us, I ended up grounded for a month.''

''Which is the number one perk of being a grown-up, honey. Nobody's gonna ground you this time.'' The cups balanced on the plate with the treats, she elbowed open the patio door leading out back, then turned and did the famous Karleen Almquist I-dare-you smile and said in the famous Karleen Almquist wispy little what-me?-get-you-in-trouble? voice, "You coming? Or you conceding this one to me?"

Joanna told herself she was only following so she'd be sure to get her plate and tumblers back.

"Hey, boss. Looks like we got company."

At Jose's heads up, Dale squinted over the yellow plastic slide he was bolting into place to see a pleasantly bosomy blonde in high-heeled boots mincing across the lawn toward them, having a devil of a time hanging on to that plate in her hands. Joanna followed, looking none too pleased about whatever was going on. When the women were still several feet away, one of the cats—Dale had long since given up trying to figure out how many there were—decided now would be a good time to launch himself against the blonde's ankles.

"For God's sake, Jo," the blonde said, wobbling for a second, the plate in a death grip, "call it off!"

Jo let out a single sharp "Git!" and the thing booked it. For about two seconds. But long enough for Blondie to scoot the rest of the way across the yard, grinning that careful way women did who were deathly afraid of wrinkles.

"Thought you boys might like some tea and a snack," she said, then seemed to realize there really wasn't any place to set down the plate. Jose took it from her; her hand shot out toward Dale as if sprung from prison. "Karleen Almquist," she cooed. "Joanna's best friend."

"I told her you'd brought your own water," Joanna, who clearly did not worry about laugh lines and such, put in. And Dale made a snap decision to take advantage of an unexpected opportunity.

"Ah, but nothin' beats a tall glass of ice-cold tea," he said, taking one of the tumblers and turning his smile on Karleen, who was doing her damnedest not to look awe-struck. He knew it wasn't fair, or right, to judge a person by appearances, but how many women like her had he run into over the course of the past several years? Pretty women who deep down didn't trust that they really were, who never really believed their God-given attributes were sufficient unto themselves, who measured success by whether or not men found them attractive.

Women who seemed to forget that the flower never had to chase the bee.

Deliberately, Dale let his gaze sidle over to Joanna for a moment—who, as far as flowers went, was probably more like a Venus's-flytrap—before returning it to her friend. "Thank you, Karleen," he said, taking great pains not to cross the thin line between being polite and flirting, trusting that Karleen would know the difference. And that Joanna, who was discussing the play set with Jose, wouldn't.

Of course, since she didn't seem the least bit interested in what was going on, it would appear he was wasting his efforts. A realization that annoyed him far more than it should have. So he inched a hair closer to flirting with Karleen, resurrecting one or two old lines he used to be able to count on to make a gal laugh, all the while keeping one eye on Joanna. And Karleen did indeed giggle when she was supposed to, although not in quite as airheaded a manner as he might have expected, and her smile really was very nice and her eyes really were very pretty and her perfume wasn't the kind that could knock a man over. So, all in all, he should have been enjoying himself.

Except the longer Dale stood there, drinking his tea and eating the little cakes and chatting up this pretty woman he didn't want to be chatting up while the flat-chested, hay-wire-haired woman he did want to chat up seemed hell-bent on ignoring him, the more annoyed he got. By the time Joanna turned to him and asked how much longer he thought they'd be, he was startled to find himself next door to mad.

Not that he had any right to be. After all, he was just playin' around.

"What do you think, Jose?" he said. "Another half hour, maybe?"

The older man nodded his agreement. "Good," Joanna said. "I'll call Bobby, let him know when to bring back the kids." Then she took their empty tea glasses, stacking them inside each other, said, "Let's not keep the guys from their work," to Karleen, and started back toward the house, giving the blonde no choice but to call, "Nice to meet you!" over her shoulder as she went.

Leaving Dale feeling like he'd just been issued a challenge.

One he had absolutely no business accepting.

Chapter 4

"**Y**ou are hopeless!" Karleen said the minute they were back inside. "Would another couple of minutes have killed you?"

Joanna shoved the patio door shut and marched her little overwrought self across the kitchen. "I never said I was playing along. Beside, I've got a party to set up," she said, yanking out bags of Bob the Builder plates and cups she'd stashed in the cupboard where she kept the extraneous kitchen crap she'd accumulated over the years. "I've got no time to waste standing around watching the man slobber all over you. Especially as I've seen that act before."

"You can't be serious."

"What? That I've never seen men drool over you? Not that it bothers me, I'm certainly used to it after all these years—"

"Oh, for heaven's sake!" Karleen grabbed a package of plates from her and attacked the plastic wrapping like a lion gutting a wildebeest. "Whose benefit did you think that was for? It wasn't *my* attention he was trying to get, you idiot!''

For the tiniest sliver of a second, something totally insane and irrational—hope, maybe?—shoved aside the annoyance that was even more insane and irrational. "You know, you really need to start eating more. I hear the brain's the first thing to go.''

Karleen grinned. "*Some*body's pi-issed.''

"I'd have to care to be pissed. Since I don't—'' she ripped open one of the other packages of plates and slammed them onto the counter "—I'm not. And wipe that smirk off your face.''

"Jo, Jo, Jo...don't you know that flirting with one woman in order to make the other one jealous is the oldest trick in the book? How many of these suckers you want opened?''

"All of them. Okay...just for the sake of argument, let's say that's what he was doing—''

"Aha!''

"That was hardly worth an *aha*. Especially as I was about to point out this oh-so-mature behavior would attract me why?''

"Because he's hot, he's giving out all the right signals—''

"To you,'' Joanna pointed out, unwrapping napkins.

"—and you're deprived. And I told you, the flirting with me business was just a ruse. Since you had your back to him the entire time, you couldn't see that he kept looking over to see if you were reacting.''

Joanna jerked up her head, which earned her one of Karleen's smug smiles. Okay, so she felt about twelve, but she felt...kinda tingly, too. Alive. Like maybe there was something to look forward to.

Damn.

"Sounds like a perfect fit to me,'' Karleen said, which effectively blew the tingly feeling all to hell.

"And in case you've forgotten—are there boxes of candles in one of those bags?—I was married to a man whose idea of a formal social event is a keg party. Why on earth would I be even remotely interested in somebody who would use one woman to get another one? Let alone someone who spent a good chunk of his life spitting, throwing a ball and adjusting his package? Activities, by the way, I don't find particularly endearing in males over the age of three."

"Never mind how incredible he looks without his shirt."

"Yeah, well, if memory serves, Bobby looks pretty damn good without his shirt, too." Joanna pulled the first of the two cakes Bobby'd dropped off earlier—one chocolate, one vanilla—from the bottom of the fridge and set it on the bar. "Trust me. After a while, it's not enough. Even you know that."

Marginally deflated, Karleen climbed up onto one of the stools flanking the bar and slit open a package of candles with one lethal hot-to-trot red nail. "Yeah, I suppose you're right. You care how these go on the cakes?"

"Not a bit. And I know I'm right. On this, at least. Next time—if there is a next time—I'd really like a man, you know? Not an overgrown boy."

"Aha."

"What now?"

Karleen waved a peppermint-striped candle at her. "You know what your problem is? You see every guy you date as potential husband material."

Joanna gave her a look.

"Okay, so I'm being theoretical. But I'm just saying, should the earth shift on its axis and you ever do date again, you've gotta go through at least one gap guy before you can even begin to think in terms of wedding bells."

"A gap guy."

"Sure. You know. Someone to bridge the gap between husbands."

"I take it we're talking about sex here?"

"Honey, I'm always talking about sex. Not that it's a bad thing if they can hold up their side of the conversation, as well as other things, for more than five minutes at a time. But it's not crucial."

Joanna laughed. "You're nuts."

"No, I'm perfectly serious. Think of it like…a sherbet to cleanse your palate between courses."

"You mean, something fruity?"

"Oh, for Pete's sake. Be serious."

"Hey. You're the one comparing men to sherbet."

"Something light," Karleen said, delicately inserting a candle into the frosting. "Insubstantial. A little tart, maybe, but nothing that'll ruin your appetite for the real thing. Listen, honey, I may not be any good at marriage, but I am an expert at surviving the wasteland between them. Hell, in three years? I'd've gone through three or four by now. Raspberry, lemon, pineapple…"

"Sounds exhausting."

"I take plenty of vitamins. Why do you think God invented pool boys?"

Joanna sighed. Notwithstanding that tingling business a few minutes ago, so Dale was good-looking. And, okay, he seemed like a nice guy. And maybe it had been a dog's age since one of those had crossed her path. Still…

"I don't know, Kar…" She moved on to making hamburger patties for the grill, kneeing aside the hopeful dog as she idly mused that, after three years, she still hadn't gotten used to not having to take off her wedding ring so it wouldn't get mucked up. "Someone to just…tide me over?"

"Is that a sparkle I see in your eyes?"

"Only reflecting the insane glint in yours."

"Look…" Karleen's lips moved, counting each candle before she turned her attention to the second cake. "Who told you to watch your back around Heather Sanchez our sophomore year, huh? And who made you let Eric Stone know you were available to go to homecoming? And what a night that turned out to be, right?''

''Never mind that I nearly died from embarrassment when my mother found the condoms in my purse.''

''And who told your mother they were hers so you wouldn't get in trouble?'' Joanna speared her with another look. ''Okay, so maybe she didn't believe me. But what I'm saying is, have I ever steered you wrong? I mean, yeah, we'll have to think of some reason for you to see him again, but that shouldn't be too hard. You have kids. He has a toy store.'' She shrugged. ''Not even you can deny how neatly everything's falling into place.''

Joanna slapped a meat patty onto the growing pile on the plate beside her. The dog whimpered and leaned heavily against the lower cabinet. ''Watch me.''

''For crying out loud, honey—the Olsen twins could be grandmothers by the time someone comes along who meets all your criteria. But hey, if you wanna sit around and watch your hymen grow back, what business is it of mine?''

''If that's supposed to cheer me up, you're failing miserably.''

''All I'm saying is,'' Karleen went on, ''if you deliberately pick someone you *know* is wrong for you, you won't be tempted to think of him as husband material. No pressure, no expectations…what could be better than that? So, here…'' She reached across the counter for her purse, pulling out what looked like a compact. ''You better take this.''

Joanna glanced over. ''I don't use powder…oh,'' she said when she caught sight of the glittering foil packets inside the now open compact. ''Jeez. You still carry them with you?''

''I still shave my legs every morning, too. A girl can never be too prepared. And the compact's nice 'cause you can sneak a peek at your makeup while the guy's…you know.'' She clicked shut the compact again, wiggling it in her hand. "Where should I put this?"

"Back in your purse."

"You haven't forgotten how to use them, have you?"

"Considering who taught me? Not bloody likely. It was years before I could look at a jumbo frank without blushing. But I can't—"

"It's not safe to expect the man to remember, you know."

"Yes, I do. But I'd rather take care of things on an as-needed basis, okay?"

"Okay," Karleen said at last, finally snapping open her purse and dropping the compact back inside.

"Karleen?"

"Yeah, honey?"

"I really do appreciate what you're trying to do, but did I ever tell you how much I hate sherbet?"

She shrugged. "Maybe you just haven't tasted the right flavor yet."

Joanna sighed.

A mile or so south, in the no-frills, three-bedroom apartment he'd been living in since his divorce, Bobby Alvarez leaned in the doorway to the master bedroom, trying to convince his stomach to unknot. Tori sat on the edge of the bed, her hands clamped on the mattress edge through the lacy white comforter she'd picked out, a tiny crease wedged between her brows. He'd seen that crease before. It always meant trouble.

"Hey," he said lightly. "Jo just called, said it's time to bring the kids back for the party. You about ready?"

Tori lifted her eyes, solemn and dark blue, outlined with some smudgy stuff that made them look even more solemn. She was almost as tall as him, but thin enough to look swallowed up in the baggy velour top she wore over a pair of jeans, an effect enhanced by her long, dark hair, which she wore loose and parted in the middle, like a teenager. "Do I have to go?"

This was no surprise. "What's wrong, sweetheart? Don't you feel good?"

"I'm okay. It's just..." The corners of her mouth twitched. "All those people, your family..."

Stifling what would have been a weighty sigh, Bobby closed the few feet between them, the mattress sagging when he sat beside her. "Aw, honey," he said, looping an arm around her shoulders and tugging her to him, her flowery-smelling hair slippery under his cheek. "They're gonna be your family, too, you know."

"The kids, yeah." She twisted the brand-new engagement ring—even getting it at Sam's Club, it had pretty much wiped out his Visa—around and around her finger. "Not your ex. Or her parents."

God, this sucked. The whole reason he'd fallen for Tori to begin with was because their relationship required little mental effort on his part. Not like him and Jo, who were like those two cats that still lived out in back of Joanna's house and couldn't cross paths without spitting at each other. And he was thrilled about the baby, even if he wasn't about to admit to Jo or anybody else that he'd nearly had a coronary when Tori'd told him she'd found a tear in her diaphragm. How they were going to manage, what with a good chunk of what he was making already going to Jo and the kids, he had no idea. So he figured he had plenty of worries without having to deal with pregnancy hormones, too.

But ready or not, he had to, didn't he?

"Hey. We talked this all through, remember?" And since talking things through wasn't exactly Bobby's strong suit, the prospect of tilling the same ground ad nauseum wasn't exactly giving him a big thrill now. "About how everybody being together is gonna be inevitable from time to time? That it'll be easier for the kids to accept you if you're included in family get-togethers?''

"I know. But this is just so...weird. Not what I imagined, y'know?''

Praying for the smarts to get through the minefield without blowing off his balls, he said, "You knew I had kids from the get-go, Tor. It wasn't like I sprung 'em on you."

"I know. But..."

He saw her hands slip over her tummy and something primitive and possessive shot through him. In a way, it was kind of sexy, knowing he'd put the baby there. But it also signaled the onset of what amounted to nine straight months of PMS. Hell, if you wanted teenage boys to abstain from having sex too early, just lock 'em up with a pregnant woman for twenty-four hours. Guaranteed to kill any chance of an erection for a good five, maybe ten years.

"It's just I watch you and Jo together," she was saying, "and all I can think is, I can't compete with that. With what the two of you still have."

He panicked for a second, afraid he wouldn't be able to keep up. "What are you talking about? All Jo and I do is fight."

"Not always."

"Okay, only like ninety percent of the time. And when we're not, we're either recovering from a fight or gearing up for one."

"Because you still care about each other."

"No, because we're from two different planets."

"But you have this...this history together."

"Well, yeah. We were married for nine years. We have three kids we're raisin' together. I can't change that, can I?"

She blew out a quick sigh through her nose. "No, I suppose not."

"But now it's time for you and me to make our own history, right?"

"And I'll always be second."

By his estimation, he had maybe ten seconds to defuse this bomb. "That's not how I see it, honey. Yeah, maybe you're…second, chronologically, but…okay—you know how a movie might be number one at the box office? But then, the next week another movie comes along and *that* movie is number one?"

She stiffened.

"Dammit, Tor…I'm lousy at this—"

"Oh, never mind," Tori said on another sigh. "I know what you're trying to say. It's just I keep thinking, if your marriage to Jo didn't work out, what's to say ours will? And it's not like I've got a whole lot of experience to fall back on. My mother's been married and divorced twice. I haven't seen my real father in years. So I'm not exactly feeling real secure. Especially as…"

"What?"

Tori gave him a look that scared the crap out of him, because she looked far too much like Jo did, there at the end. Still did, come to think of it.

"Look," she said, "I know I had nothing to do with you two breaking up, but still. I feel bad. That I'm in the middle. That *you're* in the middle. That I have you, and I'm so happy, and she has…nothing." Then she pulled her feet up onto the edge of the bed, toying with one of her toe rings, her mouth all funny.

"What?"

"I can't say it, it's too tacky."

"Tori, I'm not a mind reader. Whatever you're thinking, just say it."

After a moment she said, "It's not that I resent the money you give to Joanna for the house and stuff, and certainly not whatever you pay for child support, but somehow…well, I wish she didn't need to depend on you quite so much. And that really sounds selfish and stupid and horrible, but I don't want to start out our lives together wondering if every time we buy something for us, we're spending money that should go to your first family instead—''

"Dad?"

At the sound of his daughter's voice, Tori pulled away. Dammit, they'd been dating for more than a year, living together for three months. The kids spent every weekend with them. In other words, their relationship was hardly a secret—and would be even less of a secret once he told the kids about the baby—but Tori refused to show any affection toward him when they were around.

Dulcy stuck her head in the door, her dark, thick curls struggling to escape her ponytail. As usual, she wore some loose top, her long legs encased in a pair of bleached-out jeans. She was nearly as tall as Jo now. Way she was growing, she might even end up passing Bobby. He wasn't sure how he felt about that.

But he sure knew it scared the hell out of him to think there were boys just like he'd been out there, lying in wait....

"Dad? Hello? The boys are totally driving me nuts." She frowned slightly at Tori but didn't acknowledge her presence. "Can we *please* get going?"

"Sure. Just a sec, okay?"

With a huff, Dulcy stomped away.

"She hates me," Tori said.

"No, she doesn't."

"Right. She looks at me like I was something she found in back of the refrigerator."

"Honey, she looks at everyone like that. If this is a girl—" he laid his hand on Tori's belly and immediately felt stirrings that would do him absolutely no good right now "—she'll look at you that way, too."

Tori covered his hand with hers, which wasn't helping the stirrings any. "How come you know so much about teenage girls?"

"I've got three sisters, remember? First time a girl

looked at me like I *wasn't* something she found in the back of the refrigerator, I couldn't talk for three days.''

A small laugh bubbled out of Tori's mouth. Then she said, ''I'm sorry for what I said earlier. It's not my place—''

''No, it's okay, baby, I want you to feel you can tell me anything.''

Which wasn't exactly true. Frankly, half the time women told him what they were thinking, he only got more confused. Like now. He was pretty sure he was supposed to do something about whatever was bothering Tori. He just had no clue what that might be.

''I love you,'' Tori said, rubbing her cheek against his shoulder.

''Aw, I love you, too, sweetheart,'' he said, figuring he'd just hang on to that, for now. Then he kissed her, long and deep, deciding maybe all this communication garbage wasn't so bad after all, once you got used to it.

But during the fifteen-minute drive to Jo's house, the boys about to bust from excitement in the back seat of the Taurus—which made him realize he was going to have to go the minivan route, once the baby came, damn—he kept mulling over what Tori said, about Joanna's being alone, about how it would be nice if there was somebody else to help out financially, since she was never going to get rich off those Santas she made, that was for sure.

The fact was, he worried about Joanna. A lot more than he'd ever admit to Tori, who'd for sure take it the wrong way. But he didn't like the idea of Joanna being all by herself in that big house, when he had the kids. And he didn't like the idea of her being lonely, either. Oh, she could act as independent as she wanted, but Bobby knew her. Joanna was a woman with a lot of love to give. Hell, why else would she have stuck out the marriage as long as she had? So, yeah. Joanna's falling in love again, getting married again, would be a very good thing for everybody.

Somebody good at fixing things would be a bonus. Or well off enough to pay for somebody else to do it. Somebody to take the heat off of Bobby. One of those win-win situations, you know?

But who? He'd tried to get Jo to go out with some of his friends, but she'd never gotten past a first date with any of 'em. If only he knew somebody he could nudge in her direction, y'know? Like when he used to sell cars, before Joanna's father hooked him up with the advertising manager at the TV station. Somebody would come into the showroom and Bobby'd simply steer 'em toward the car he figured they'd like. Then, if they showed interest, he'd close the deal.

He really, really liked closing deals.

They pulled up in front of Jo's house, the house he no longer lived in but was still expected to help keep up, Bobby frowning when he saw Karleen's shiny white Expedition hogging half the driveway, parked behind the Playing for Keeps pickup. Huh. Guess they weren't finished yet.

Huh.

The kids and Tori got out of the car—Tori had to pee every five minutes these days, seemed like—but Bobby sat there, thinking. Shoving the puzzle pieces around to see if he could get them to fit. Thinking about how, when he'd come out onto the patio earlier, he thought he'd picked up on some pretty heavy-duty, who-the-hell-are-you? vibes from Dale. As if Bobby'd interrupted something.

As if maybe the dude was interested in Joanna.

Now if maybe Joanna was interested *back*...

Aw, come on...it couldn't be this easy.

Could it?

A grin stretched across his face.

Dale seemed nice enough, Bobby guessed he was okay to look at, and he probably had money. Hell, star players raked in serious bucks.

Of course, Joanna would probably have a fit if she knew what Bobby was thinking.

Which just meant Bobby'd better be good and sure she never found out.

Chapter 5

Great, Joanna thought. The kids were here, but the play set wasn't finished. Once again, a man had made a promise he hadn't kept. Except then Joanna walked out onto the back patio as the boys let out gleeful shrieks at their first glimpse of the set, and she thought, So what? What was important here? That her kids were happy, or that everything went according to *her* schedule?

And happy they were, bouncing around like a pair of fleas and bombarding Dale with a million questions. Neither twin had ever been the slightest bit shy about talking to strangers, which had been a constant source of worry to her when they were younger. That this particular stranger posed no threat to her sons was of little comfort, since she was the one in danger—from the way his expression lit up when the boys flew across the yard, his laughter as he hoisted them up into the fort.

Her stomach flip-flopped at the still-warm memory of her and Karleen's conversation.

Talk about the power of suggestion. Left to her own

devices, Joanna would never consider actually *doing* anything about her attraction to Dale. What would have been
the point? But then Karleen'd had to go and mess with her
head and make her think she needed something she didn't,
like the time she'd talked Joanna into buying a pair of boots
she'd ended up wearing exactly once.

What a perfectly good waste of lust that had been.

Just as this would be.

"You're staring," Karleen said behind her, making her
jump.

"Am not."

"Are, too."

"Go to hell."

That got what, from anyone else, would have been a
cackle. From Karleen, who still had smoker's voice even
though she'd given it up five years ago, the sound was more
like what an engine did when it didn't want to turn over.
"Looks like he's good with kids."

"I should hope so. Considering he owns a toy store."

"Yeah, well, remember Mr. Salazar? Our Driver's Ed
teacher? The one who hated to drive?"

"Karleen, you can't make opposing points in the same
observation."

"Speaking of points," Karleen said, nodding toward the
boys who were storming back toward Joanna at full tilt.
Grinning, they wrapped all four arms around Joanna's hips.
Matt muttered a quick, "Thanks," then took off again,
leaving Ryder still clamped to her.

"This is the best birthday ever! Thanks, Mom!"

If it had been up to her, she would have told the kids
outright the set came from her mother, but Glynnie had
insisted they think it came from Bobby and her. Why it
was okay for the kids to think their parents were spoiling
them, but not their grandparents, was something Joanna had
never understood. Especially considering the million and

one Christmas gifts that appeared under the tree every year clearly labeled ''From Geegee and Gramps.''

She smoothed back Ryder's wild hair, then looked up to catch Dale watching them and thought, *Oh, God, no. Not the lost-soul look.* A flush blossomed across her skin, from all sorts of things. Surprise and consternation and, yes, dammit, arousal.

''You're welcome, sugar pie,'' she said, unhooking both her eyeballs and hormones from Dale and hugging close the small body that belonged to her. A slightly let-down feeling that this would probably be the last ''little kids'' birthday trickled through. By next year, who knew what the boys would be into?

Ryder took off, leaving his warmth imprinted on her skin, underneath the cotton sweater she'd put on. Her arms folded, her gaze followed his path back to the play set.

And Dale. Who was still watching her.

Karleen sniggered beside her.

''What's so damn funny?''

''The way you two are playing pass-the-eyeball, for one thing. And if you dare tell me you're not enjoying having a hunk like that gawk at you, I'm calling the undertaker, 'cause you must be dead.''

A good three or four seconds later Joanna said, ''I'm not dead.''

Karleen let out a sigh of what sounded like relief, only to then mutter, as Bobby came around from the front of the house, ''That's my cue to make myself scarce before I say something I'll regret.''

With that, Karleen hustled back inside. Bobby waved to Joanna, but kept on toward the swing set and the kids— Joanna assumed Dulcy and Tori must be inside the house— where he and Dale exchanged handshakes and head nods and a short conversation she couldn't hear. Then Bobby turned to the boys and their mouths and eyes popped wide open as she heard excited babbling intermixed with,

"You'll have to ask your mother," and she thought, *Uh-oh*.

Dale glanced her way for a moment, then back to Bobby, who only laughed and shook his head. Then she saw Dale mouth the words, "You sure?" which is when Joanna decided it was in her best interest to go find out what was going on and how this affected her immediate future.

"Mom!" Matt yelled when she got a few feet away, "did you know this is Dale Muhconney an' he used to play baseball for the Braves an' he was real famous and Dad said if it was okay with you, could he come to our party, pleeeeease, Mom?"

Joanna's eyes snapped to Dale's face, hoping for a, "Sorry, guys, but I've already got other plans." Or something. When no such words came forth, Joanna took the rapidly retreating bull by the horns and said, "Guys, you know not all grown-ups get off on parties with a million crazed little kids—"

"I've got no problem with that," Dale said, and she felt defeat settle in for the night as the kids jumped up and down and yelled, "Yaaay!"

"But only if it's okay," Dale said, his gaze fixed on her in a way that no man's gaze had been fixed on her in many moons, and Bobby said, "Of course it's okay, she always makes too much food for these things anyway," and suddenly the air was filled with the acrid scent of conspiracy.

She didn't know what, and she sure as hell didn't know why, but whatever was going on here, she somehow got the feeling Dale's motives for accepting this invitation went beyond a penchant for cake and ice cream. Because of that many-moons-gaze thing and all.

The man wants to get into your pants, birdbrain.

She sucked in a breath, braced for the wave of outrage. She should feel…insulted. Denigrated. Incensed.

What she felt was…wet.

Karleen would be beside herself.

''Of *course* it's okay if you come. To the party,'' she hastily added.

''But…what about Jose?''

Five heads turned to the little man as if just remembering his presence.

''No, is okay,'' he said, waving, his grin revealing the hole where his front tooth should have been. ''My wife, she expects me home soon.''

So that was that.

A few minutes later, after all the bolts and fastenings had been checked and Dale had gone, promising to return in forty-five minutes or so, Joanna turned to her ex-husband and uttered a single, loaded word.

''Why?''

Bobby shrugged. ''Once I told the boys who he was, they naturally asked him to stay for the party. You know how you've always told the kids to feel free to invite their friends to come over. I guess Matt and Ry figured this fell into that category. It's no big deal, right?''

But it was a big deal. For reasons she could hardly go into with her ex-husband. Because she wanted to jump Dale McConnaughy's bones and she didn't *like* wanting to jump Dale McConnaughy's bones and the whole situation was making her very crabby.

''No, it's no big deal,'' she said, turning to go back inside the house just as she heard her parents coming in through the front door, Karleen complimenting Glynnie on an outfit Karleen had probably sold her. ''So where's Tori?''

''Bathroom, probably. Listen…'' Bobby glanced behind him, then lowered his voice. ''I know this is really crappy of me to ask, but do you think you could, like, be extra nice to her tonight?''

''And here I'd been *so* looking forward to making her miserable. Honestly, Bobby—when have I not been nice to Tori?''

"I know, I know…it's just she's kinda feeling a little sensitive right now, and she thinks…well, she's not real sure how she fits in, you know?"

"And somehow, it's my responsibility to make sure she does?"

"Dammit, Jo. Couldn't you just say 'sure, Bobby' for once and not make everything such an issue?"

"But torturing you is the only fun I have these days."

"Jeez."

"Bobby. I like Tori. In fact, I probably like her better than I do you. And I'd never intentionally do anything to upset her or make her feel like she doesn't belong. And yes, I'll go out of my way this evening to be 'extra' nice to her. But if by 'fitting in,' you mean she'd rather I wasn't in the picture at all…sorry, bub, but there's not a whole lot I can do about that. We were married. We have kids. We're still part of each other's lives. Them's the facts. So if she's feeling insecure about your relationship—"

"Hey, sweetheart," Bobby said as Tori entered the kitchen, looking a little wan, very pretty and painfully young. Like Johnson-era Cher, but without the edge. "You want something to drink?"

"Some juice or water or something, maybe?"

Joanna waited a moment—it wasn't as if Bobby didn't know where things were—then gave up and went to the fridge herself. From outside, one of the kids screamed, "Daaaad!" and he left. Terrific.

"So," Joanna said. "We've got apple, orange or cran-berry-grape."

"Orange, I guess. I read that folic acid is good for the baby?"

"Yeah. It is," Joanna said, chalking up the prick to her heart as something not worth considering. After all, she thought as she poured the young woman a large glass of juice, even if she felt a smidgen of envy because Tori was pregnant, that *was* Bobby's child she was carrying.

Jo handed Tori the juice. "So…congratulations. On the baby."

Tori regarded her warily over the rim of her glass, then nodded. "Thanks."

"How are you feeling?"

That got another should-I-trust-her? glance. "Fine, I guess." She sat at the dining table, twisting the glass around and around with the fingers of her right hand. "I just had no idea I'd be so tired all the time. It's like if I sit still for more than five minutes, I pass out. Work's been a real bear. And I can hardly get any studying done."

Jo leaned back against the counter next to the stove. "It'll pass. The tiredness. Until the last month, which makes up for the previous eight."

The grimace tightened. "Gee, thanks."

Joanna smiled. "It'll be worth it, though. Trust me—"

"You're being nice to me because Bobby told you to, aren't you?"

Of the many, many things Joanna could have said, the truth won out. "No. Even though he did. But I'm only telling you so you know he cares about you enough to make an idiot of himself."

The corners of Tori's mouth turned up before she took another sip of juice. "He can be sorta clueless sometimes, I guess."

Oh, honey, I could tell you stories….

"You know we're getting married, right?"

"Yes," Joanna said, biting her tongue to keep from mentioning that Bobby had a habit of marrying the girls he got pregnant.

"Does that…does that bother you?"

"That he's going to marry *you?* No. Am I concerned about his taking on more responsibility? I won't lie and say I'm not."

"You mean, that this baby might divert his attention from his other kids."

Joanna shrugged, then said, since she couldn't stand Tori's suddenly stricken expression, "I swear, I do not have a problem with Bobby's starting a new family. Not in theory, anyway. But it's not going to be easy, his trying to juggle all of this—"

"He's not stupid, you know."

Ah, but Tori's defense was admirable. Naive, but admirable. "Never said he was. And I honestly think, most of the time, he wants to do his best. I'm just not sure he's ever figured out how." She hesitated, then gently added, "All I'm saying is, be prepared to take on the bulk of the load for keeping things going. Because Bobby is one of those men who just can't."

"Then you really don't love him anymore?"

Merciful heavens. Joanna didn't know they made them this insecure.

"Let's put it this way," she said. "We had this big dog once, when I was a kid. In many ways, Dozer was a great dog, friendly and lovable and cuddly, but we finally had to get rid of him because no matter what we did, we couldn't housebreak him, or stop him from jumping up on people. But he went to a good home, and even though I'll always think of him fondly, no way did I want to live with him again."

Tori frowned.

"But hey," Joanna said, "we heard the people we gave him to worked wonders."

The young woman seemed to consider this for a bit, then extended her left hand. "Did you see my engagement ring? I just got it last night."

Her stomach jolting, Joanna leaned forward to dutifully admire the solitaire. It wasn't a huge ring, maybe a half carat. But even a half carat—set in platinum, no less—wasn't cheap, a knowledge gleaned from years of drooling over display cases. And in its facets, her new roof shimmered like a mirage.

"It's lovely," she said.

Smiling, even.

Joanna had been slamming things around in the kitchen for a good five minutes when her mother and Karleen came in, just in time to see her kick shut the oven door.

"She's wearing her Kill Bobby face," Karleen said to Glynnie, who nodded and said, "Things not going well, dear?"

It suddenly hit Joanna how much she'd really like, just once, to unburden herself to her mother. But she didn't dare. So with a "Later" glance at Karleen, she said, "Nothing that won't pass. Bad time of the month, is all."

"Sweetie, I hate to tell you this," Glynnie said, sliding up onto a stool on the other side of the breakfast bar, "but you've been having a bad time of the month for three years."

"I have not!"

Karleen raised one hand. "Uh, yeah. You have."

Joanna lifted her eyes heavenward. "Just one person on my side, God. Is that too much to ask?"

"But we are on your side!" Karleen said, then looked at Glynnie. "Aren't we?"

"Of course we are," Glynnie said as Joanna tromped across the kitchen and yanked open the refrigerator door, hauling out tubs of potato salad and coleslaw. "But then, maybe if you'd stop pretending things are always okay when they obviously aren't…"

"Everything's fine, Mom."

"Tell that to the innocent appliance you just kicked. Here I am, giving you an opening to tell me what the problem is, but you clam up…"

"Oh, goody," Karleen said, climbing up onto the bar stool next to Glynnie's and snatching a carrot stick off the veggie tray in front of her, stopping just short of cramming it into her mouth when she realized both women were staring at her. "This brings back so many memories, when Mama and I used to fight. It just hasn't been the same since she died. And besides," she added when Joanna gave her the don't-you-have-someplace-else-to-be? look, "if you tell Glynnie now, you won't have to tell me later."

"There's nothing to tell."

"Uh-huh," Karleen said. "And that little bauble twinkling on Tori's left hand has nothing to do with your foul mood, I don't suppose."

Understanding dawned in Glynnie's eyes. "Bobby gave Toni—"

"Tori," Karleen said.

"—an engagement ring?" Joanna glared at Karleen as her mother added, "Well, I suppose that's to be expected, if they're engaged. Or am I missing something here?"

"My guess is," Karleen said, carefully selecting a celery stick, "that our Joanna's prickly mood has something to do with Bobby's not having given Jo—"

"Karleen, that's okay—"

"—his half of the roof repair money. What'd I say?" she finished as Joanna shut her eyes.

Glynnie looked at Joanna. "Why didn't you tell me you needed help with the house?"

"Karleen?" Joanna said.

"Yeah?"

"You just reached the last stop on Memory Lane."

Karleen's eyes bounced between Jo and her mother, then her mouth fell open in a little *O*. "Gotcha." She grabbed a piece of broccoli for the road and click-clacked out of the kitchen. Joanna turned back to her mother. "Because I don't need help, with the house or anything else."

"But you just said—"

"Mom? This is between Bobby and me. We'll work it out."

Her carefully penciled brows drawn together, Glynnie reached over and selected her own celery stick, swiping it through the bowl of onion dip in the center of the dish. "What about the money you just got from that sale you made the other day?" she said, crunching.

Thinking about that sale led to thinking about Dale— again—which led to Joanna's wondering when everything had gotten so damned complicated. Okay, *more* complicated. In her next life, she was coming back as a sponge.

"It's already earmarked," Joanna said.

"You want me to do my lawyer thing?"

"I want you to stay out of it."

"And watch the house crumble down around your head?"

"See, this is why I don't tell you stuff. Because you hear I'm having a problem and you immediately want to jump in and fix things for me."

"That's what parents *do,* Jo. Which I would think you would understand, now that you're a mother yourself."

"My oldest is eleven, Mom. Not thirty-two."

"Since when is there a statute of limitations helping your kids?"

Joanna sighed. "That's not the point. Not completely, anyway. I appreciate your offer, I really do. But if I accept it, Bobby's off the hook."

"And maybe it's time you let him."

"What?"

"I'm serious. Maybe it's time to just chalk it all up to…experience and move on. Why beat your head against the wall?"

Momentarily forgetting who she was talking to, Joanna opened her mouth to defend herself, pointless though the gesture may have been since her mother kept going.

"And why do you think I don't know what's been going on? You may not say much, but I didn't get where I am today without knowing how to read between the lines. We've got the money, why not let us help?"

"Because I don't need—"

"Oh, Joanna—would you get over yourself? You're driving a ten-year-old car, you haven't bought any new clothes in a dog's age and now your roof is about to cave in. I mean, those Santas you make are wonderful, honey, they really are, but you clearly can't support yourself and the kids on what you make off of them. I just don't get why you're being so stubborn about this."

Joanna's stomach knotted. No, Glynnie didn't get it, didn't have an inkling how much baggage came attached to those offers of help. She could understand her mother's disappointment in some of her choices over the past twelve years. But what she couldn't deal with was the pity, that poor dear Joanna would probably never amount to much, that she was her parents' cross to bear, they'd probably always have to support her so they might as well be cheerful about it.

"Mom," she finally said, reaching across the counter and taking her mother's hand in hers. "I *like* my old car. I'm perfectly happy with my wardrobe—"

Okay, so that part was a lie, but it wasn't as if she had anyplace to wear fancy clothes, anyway, right?

"—and as soon as Bobby comes through, the new roof is a done deal. And I'm doing fine, financially. Well enough for me, anyway. Not everyone has to be wealthy to be happy, you know. So thanks for the offer, but no—"

Outside, male voices—one baritone, one tenor—rose in a fevered and not exactly pleasant duet. Dulcy pushed back the patio door and stood there, slumped against the opening, reeking of preadolescent disgust. "They're at it again," she said on a pained sigh.

After twelve years, one thing hadn't changed: Bobby and her father still couldn't agree on how hot the grill should be.

"I'll be right out," Jo said, thinking if Dale McConnaughy had a lick of sense, he'd stay as far away from this family as possible.

* * *

In the past forty-five minutes Dale had changed his mind no less than ten times about coming. But somehow, here he was, standing under the portal in a more or less new pair of jeans and the first clean long-sleeved shirt he'd come across, a whole new bunch of cats giving him the once-over as he contemplated the ubiquitous chile *ristra* hanging by the front door and inhaled the luscious tang of seared beef wafting from the back, and then Bobby Alvarez opened the door and it was too late to turn back. From behind the house, somewhere in the neighborhood of a hundred kids were yelling their heads off.

"Hey, man—glad you could make it." With the kind of grin that immediately made Dale suspicious, the other man stood aside to let Dale in. A couple of the cats darted inside, but the rest seemed content to stay out. "Party's out back," he said, leading Dale past the softly lit living room filled with mismatched overstuffed furniture, the scuffed wooden floor partially hidden under worn Oriental rugs. Looking forlorn, the dog lay on the sofa with his chin propped on the arm, thumping his tail in a halfhearted greeting when Dale passed.

"What's wrong with him?" Dale asked.

"The dog? He's ticked because he can't go outside. Last time we had a cookout, he helped himself to most of the main course." When they reached the eat-in kitchen, a spacious, cluttered space divided from the family room by a tiled breakfast bar, Alvarez said, "Something to drink? Tea? Soda? A beer?"

"A Coke if you've got it."

Curiosity flickered briefly across the man's features, but all he said was, "Sure thing."

Dale stood at the end of the bar, taking in the cobalt-blue and yellow Mexican tiles along the backsplash, the hanging baskets filled with potatoes and onions, the side-by-side refrigerator all but buried in bright drawings of toothy dinosaurs and construction vehicles, of photocopied directions and lists and notices overlapping each other in no apparent order, all precariously clinging to the dark brown surface by means of an array of magnets ranging from cats to boots to miniature frames with photos inside, to ads for Pizza Hut and various household repair services. The disarray of people who were busy, Dale thought, not lazy.

Of people with lives.

Everything fluttered when Bobby opened the refrigerator, but miraculously stayed in place. Joanna's ex handed Dale a Coke, then uncapped a Coors bottle, taking a swig from it before noticing the bag in Dale's hand. ''What's that?''

''Oh, right. Some stuff I had lying around. For the boys.'' He dug the *Captain Underpants* books, whoopee cushion, and baseball glove out of the bag. ''I brought another glove, too, in case they might want to play later.''

Alvarez looked dumbstruck as he picked up the glove. ''Damn—you even signed it? The boys'll be beside themselves. And this…'' With a huge grin he snatched the deflated whoopee cushion off the bar and blew it up, then squeezed it, letting out a bark of laughter when it blatted. ''I haven't seen one of these in ages!''

''Give it to me, lemme show you something.'' Bobby handed back the cushion; Dale blew it up, then pressed it this one certain way so the *fpfpfpfp* ended on a long squeal….

A girl about twelve or so came into the kitchen, let out a disgusted, ''*Dad*, jeez!'' then breezed out again, a bag of chips in her hand.

When they finished laughing their butts off, Bobby said, ''That was my daughter, Dulcy. She gets her sense of humor from her mother.'' He chuckled a couple more times, then said, ''I honestly didn't think you'd come back.''

Yeah, well, Dale still wasn't sure about that, although he supposed he could duck out pretty much anytime he wanted to. And do what? Go back to his empty condo and watch ESPN? Go bar hopping?

God knew, he'd done his fair share of carousing, if for no other reason than to keep from being alone. From thinking about things there was no sense in thinking about. But lately...

His tastes had changed, was all. Still, why had he shown up here tonight?

Maybe he didn't want to answer that one, he thought as Bobby led him out back, introducing him to Joanna's parents—her father, a tall, lanky man with a shock of silver hair and major eyebrows, looked vaguely familiar for some reason—and Bobby's fiancée, a pretty gal with long brown hair and enormous blue eyes who looked like she felt even more out of place than Dale did.

Then he caught sight of Joanna over on the far side of the patio, nearly blotted out by a swarm of little kids as she fussed with things on a long table covered in a fluttering checkered tablecloth, and he heard her laugh at something one of the kids said, and he remembered damn well why he'd accepted the invitation, even as it became crystal clear why he should have turned it down. Especially when she looked up, just for a second, and a flush washed over her cheeks when their eyes met.

Huh.

He also thought about going over and saying hi or something, but everybody's eyes were on him so he settled for lifting his Coke in a greeting and she nodded and mumbled something about being glad he could make it, then disappeared around the side of the house.

The boys discovered him right about then, dragging him away from the under-ten herd to see the rabbits they kept in a hutch at the far end of the yard, next to the empty stable. Two or three cats started to follow them, but their hearts really weren't in it. From beside the gas grill off to the side of the patio, Bobby yelled something to them about not being pests, but Dale waved away their father's concern. Besides, it was a relief having an excuse to get away from the adults, who he got the feeling were all looking to him for something.

"The bigger one's mine," the one with the dark, straight hair—Matt—said, and then went on about how they were both girls so they couldn't have babies together and what-all they fed them and how their father had bought the rabbits for them at the fair and that Mom had been kinda mad and how she'd told their father that if they didn't take care of the rabbits, she was packing them right up and taking them to his house. And all the while, the other boy, Ryder, had just stood there quietly, stroking his bunny, a black-and-white lop-eared, not saying anything. Now, unlike a lot of adults, Dale generally got off on rambunctious kids. But the quiet ones always stole a piece of his heart.

So he squatted by the cage and said to Ryder, "What's her name?"

"Emily," Matt said with a snort.

Dale looked over at Matt and said quietly, "Any reason why your brother can't answer his own questions?" The kid looked taken aback, but then he shook his head and Dale said, "That's what I thought," and turned again to Ryder.

"Emily's a real pretty name. What made you pick it?"

"She was my best friend in first grade." Eyes exactly like his mother's, just as intelligent but without the sass, met Dale's. "But she moved away."

Matt tapped Dale on the shoulder. "Hey, Mr....Mc..."

"Let's just go with Dale."

"Mr. Dale...I've read more Caldecott books than anybody in my class."

Now, Dale didn't have a clue what the heck a Caldecott book was, but he did know that one kid's boasting about his accomplishments around another kid, especially a sibling, was usually sufficient to provoke a rise to the challenge. But Ryder just stood there, petting his bunny, like he hadn't heard. But not like he didn't care. Like he was trying to pretend he didn't.

Luckily, though, before he had to figure out how to handle things, Joanna called for the kids, telling them they were about to eat soon, to come get cleaned up. The kids took off. Dale straightened, watching Joanna watch her sons as they ran toward her, the intensity of her gaze binding them to her as surely as if they'd been attached by a string. She touched each of them in turn when they reached her, her attention lingering a second or two longer on Ryder, who must've started talking about him, if the curious look on her face when she looked in Dale's direction was any indication.

Like dead leaves disturbed by a sudden breeze, old, dried-up feelings rustled inside him, leaving him feeling unsettled.

The boys went on in; Joanna stayed outside, waiting.

"You've made a big hit," she said, her arms now crossed. The pencil had been banished from her hair; instead, all those curls fought against a skinny gold headband that looked to be rapidly losing the battle. She'd put on some lipstick, too, a natural color that glistened softly on her mouth.

"They're good kids," Dale said. Except, when she nodded, he saw worry etched in the lines around her mouth, between her brows. "But then," he said, "that's probably because they've got a good mama."

Her mouth twitched. "And how would you know that?"

"Just a hunch. From what I saw just now. The way they went running off, soon as you called them. Like they wanted to go to you, not like they were afraid of what you might do to 'em if they didn't."

Joanna laughed. "Damn. There goes my reputation."

But there was a heaviness to her voice that disturbed

something inside him, enough to make him do something stupid and to ask if everything was okay with Ryder.

She flinched slightly, and he could tell she was about to say, "Of course," or some such, except a tear slipped out. Her arms tightened, like she wanted to wipe it away but to do so would only acknowledge its presence. "It's…none of your concern," she said softly, not in a way meant to make him feel he was butting in, but because she simply didn't wish him to worry himself. And Dale didn't wish to embarrass her by pressing the issue, especially since he wasn't all that sure himself of the motives behind his inquiry.

"You have kids of your own?" she asked, catching him off guard. Although it shouldn't have. Women like Joanna just naturally wondered about things like this.

"Hell, no."

Her head tilted slightly. "You sound like you'd rather eat slugs."

"No," he said with a smile he really didn't feel. "I just don't think I'd be much good at it. Not for the long haul," he added when she frowned at him.

"And you're basing this on…?"

"Gut instinct? The fact that, for all the kids I've seen and been around, I've never felt like I was missing out by not having any of my own?"

"But I was watching you with the boys—"

He held up one hand to cut her off at the pass. "Likin' kids and wantin' to deal with 'em on a full-time basis are two different things. I mean, look at you, all tied up about your boy. I have enough trouble worrying about how to take care of myself, let alone trying to figure out how to make anybody else happy."

She looked at him oddly. "You don't strike me as the selfish type."

"That's because you don't know me," he said, then thought, *Oh, yeah, that's a great way to get the woman into your bed.* Then he said, "And you don't strike me as the kind of woman who would judge somebody else by her own standards. Not everybody's cut out to be a parent…"

Shards of memories he thought he'd swept out years ago pricked at him, deep inside. He realized she was giving him one of those damned compassionate looks that gave him the willies.

"You're absolutely right," she said quietly. "Raising kids is hard, and messy, and usually thankless, and it's easy enough to lose sight of the joy of parenthood when you *did* want your kids. But just for the record? I'll gladly deal with being 'tied up' about my babies, as you put it, for the chance to see the world through their eyes on a daily basis. In fact, I'd have another one in a minute if I—" Her mouth clamped shut, then stretched into a tired smile. "Well. You might as well go mingle. Food'll be ready in a sec." Then she disappeared inside the house, hugging her burdens to herself like she was afraid of the mess they'd make if she dropped them.

When Dale looked up, he realized that Bobby Alvarez had been watching them. Not that Dale cared, not really, but antagonizing husbands, ex or otherwise, was not something he cared to do on a regular basis. So you could've knocked him over with a feather when Alvarez suddenly grinned at him, nodding in a way that Dale could have sworn was meant to be encouraging.

Chapter 6

"This means a lot to the kids, you coming to their party like this," Roger Swann, Joanna's father, said to him a minute or so later. Dale had duly reintegrated himself into the group, slipping easily into the good-old-boy charm he always used to mask a background that not even years of making obscene amounts of money could disguise.

So over the screams and laughter of more than a dozen little boys racing back and forth in the yard, he smiled at Roger, who looked laid-back enough in a long-sleeved denim shirt and blue jeans probably a size or two bigger around the waist than the man had worn ten years ago. That is, until you took a real good look at the silver-and-turquoise concha on the man's bolo tie, as well as the no-doubt, custom-made cowboy boots peeking out from underneath the jeans' hems.

"Thanks. It's my pleasure." Dale took another sip of his soda, then said, "You know, it's just bugging the life out of me, but you look familiar. We haven't met before or something, have we?"

Roger grinned. "You must've seen my last set of commercials." At Dale's frown, he said, "Mesa Lincoln-Mercury? Reassures folks, seeing the man behind the dealership. Or so I'm told." He laughed. "Besides, I'm just a big old ham at heart. Even if it does embarrass the life out of Joanna's mother."

Whatever Dale was about to say vaporized when Joanna came back outside, that blond friend of hers in tow, the two of them toting plates and utensils and things.

"That Karleen's sure a looker, isn't she?" Roger said.

"What? Oh. Yeah. I guess."

One bushy gray eyebrow arched speculatively before Roger dropped heavily into a nearby molded plastic chair, waving Dulcy over.

"Hey, baby...come on over here and sit beside your old granddaddy." After a cautious glance at Dale, she did, whiskey-colored eyes huge behind a pair of wire-rimmed glasses, her dark brown hair as wild and curly as her mama's. She was pretty, Dale supposed, in the way of girl children straddling adolescence, her top front teeth still a little too big for a mouth still the natural pink of a child's. Her smile in answer to Dale's flickered shyly, but her gaze was wide and clear and questioning.

"So what made you decide to go into retailing after your retirement?"

"A whim," Dale said mildly, settling into another chair. "Just something I always thought I'd like to try someday."

"You happy with it?"

"Pretty much, yeah."

"Heard you had all sorts of offers to coach."

"I did."

"But...?"

"Just wasn't something I could wrap my head around, is all."

Roger's intense scrutiny didn't make Dale near as uncomfortable as the unexpected sympathy he saw there. Just when he thought for sure his skull would pop from the tension, Roger waved his empty glass toward Dale's soda can. "You ready for another one of those?"

"No, no. I'm good."

Roger handed his glass to Dulcy. "Would you mind seeing if there's any more Sprite, honey?"

With a nod, the girl got up and started for the drinks table, only to have her grandfather call her back before she'd gotten very far. Glancing around before slipping a billfold from his back pocket, he removed a bill, quickly folding it up in his hand before slipping it into his granddaughter's. "Now don't you dare tell your mother I gave you that or she'll have my hide."

"I won't, Gramps." Grinning, she leaned over and kissed him on the cheek. "Thanks." Then she scurried away, her curls bouncing.

"I take it her mother would disapprove?" Dale said with a grin of his own.

"To put it mildly. Joanna's got a real bug up her butt about Glynnie and me spoilin' them. But what's the point of havin' grandkids otherwise?" He squinted at Dale, then said, "You're not from here originally, are you?"

"No, sir. Texas."

"So's half of Albuquerque," Joanna's father said on a chuckle. "What made you decide to settle here?"

Dale leaned forward, his hands clasped between his knees. "I spent a couple of years traveling after I retired. Landed here a few months back, decided to stay. Great weather, nice people, lots of sky…just hadn't found any place I liked better."

"No family left back in Texas, then, I take it?"

"No," Dale said, willing his mind to stay blank on the subject. "Not for a long time."

Their conversation was interrupted by Joanna's calling everyone to eat. As he and Roger got up and headed toward the food, Dale watched Joanna gently fussing over the kids, making sure they all took at least more than one thing, telling them she didn't care if this was a birthday party, there'd be no cake and ice cream if they didn't eat either some of the salad or some veggies from the dip tray. And no, she told Matt, a single carrot stick did *not* cut it. The kids all groaned, but they dutifully piled raw vegetables on their plates. Of course, no telling where those vegetables would end up, since Dale sincerely doubted whether many of them would actually find their way into little stomachs. But Joanna looked so damned tickled with herself, Dale could hardly stand it.

And he sure liked seeing her pretty face relieved of some of that worry, even if it was just for a few minutes.

Again he reminded himself that, up until now, nothing cut his libido off at the knees faster than discovering a woman's other name was Mom. So what the hell was going wrong this time?

He'd known she was a mother before he'd delivered the swing set…and he'd still flirted with her. He'd known she was a mother before her ex-husband and the kids had begged him to come to the party…and he'd still come. And now, even after seeing she was the kind of woman who'd put her kids ahead of everything, and everyone, else, he still couldn't keep his eyes off her. Or his thoughts from wandering down paths clearly marked Dead End.

"So, Dale…" Roger said, blowing Dale's thoughts to smithereens as they reached the table. "That your old Maxima out in the drive?"

The kids all tended to, Joanna apparently figured it was safe to leave the adults to their own devices, scooting back inside for whatever reason. Tamping down a quiver of disappointment, Dale forced himself back to the topic at hand, loading up his hamburger bun with three patties, a slice of cheese and plenty of lettuce and tomato. He passed on the onions, though. "It is."

"Plannin' on trading her in anytime soon? You know, for something a little flashier, maybe?"

"Hadn't thought about it, to tell you the truth. Figured as long as she gets me where I need to go, no sense giving up on her just yet."

"Huh," Roger said, about to pile a second hamburger on his bun until he caught his wife glaring at him from the other side of the table. With a sigh, he put it back. "Well, you ever decide you're in the market for a new vehicle, you just let me know. I'll fix you up with a good deal, and that's a promise."

"I'll be sure to keep that in mind."

"Speaking of the market…are you in it?"

"The stock market, you mean?" He moved on to the potato salad, wondering how he'd managed to get left alone with Joanna's parents. Where the hell was everybody else? "Some."

"I don't know about you," Roger said, "but our portfolio's taken quite a few hits this past little while."

"Yeah," Dale said. "It's been rocky, all right."

Then Glynnie picked up the thread of the conversation. "But with that salary you must've been getting, I'm sure you're sitting pretty, aren't you? And I hear pro players get *very* nice pensions."

What the Sam Hill was all this about? Still, wasn't like his earnings weren't a matter of public record. What he did with his money, however, was not.

"That's true, ma'am. But like your husband said, times've been rough this past little while."

Salad tongs poised over her plate, Joanna's mother said, "You mean to tell me there's nothing left?"

A deaf man could've heard the shock in her voice. Not to mention the disappointment. And suddenly Dale understood.

Warning, warning—gold digger dead ahead.

"Ma'am?" he said quietly, and with a smile—putting

folks in their places generally went down easier, he found, when you were pleasant about it. "I'm not one for discussing my finances with people I know, let alone perfect strangers. So pardon me if I find your questions a bit personal for my taste—"

"Mr. Dale!" Matt yelled from across the yard. "They're sayin' I'm makin' up stories about you being a baseball player!"

"Excuse me, won't you?" he said with a smile for the Swanns, then strode off toward the kids.

"Did you hear that?" Glynnie whispered to her husband the minute they got far enough away that Joanna wouldn't hear them. After a brief scan, Roger headed out to the other side of the yard. Right over the grass, naturally.

"Did I hear what, Glynelle?"

"He said he was broke."

"He did not say he was broke—"

If she broke off her heel on one of these damn tree roots, there was going to be hell to pay.

"—he said things've been rough."

"Same thing."

"No, it isn't. He's probably got most of his money sunk into that store of his. You know it takes years for a new business to turn a profit. And just like everybody else, his investments probably aren't worth what they used to be."

"Still and all, he must've made millions as a player, right? I may not know how much it takes to start up a toy store, but I somehow doubt millions. So where did it all go?"

"I don't know and I don't care and you're just P.O.'ed that he told you to mind your own business. Frankly, I'm impressed he showed as much restraint as he did."

"Restraint, my butt. He was next door to rude."

"Well, hell, Glynnie, you cornered the poor man."

"*Me?*" She stumbled over a root, fought to regain her

balance. Roger, naturally, didn't notice. "I wasn't the one putting out feelers about his old car!"

"Now that was just the salesman in me, you know that. Selling's as natural to me as breathing. And besides—"

Oh, for pity's sake. He would choose to sit at the picnic table, and here she was in a cream-colored skirt.

"—what do you care about Dale McConnaughy's financial situation?"

Glynnie spread a napkin on the bench, then tried to sit without getting it all crumbled up underneath her. "I don't suppose you've noticed the way he keeps looking at Joanna?"

"Of course I have. I'm not blind." Roger took an enormous bite of hamburger, seemingly unconcerned.

"And?"

"And what?" he said, chewing.

"And the last thing she needs is to get herself tangled up with somebody else who can't handle money."

To her consternation, Roger chuckled. After he swallowed he said, "You know, Glynelle, you jump to conclusions faster 'n anybody I know. Okay, so maybe the guy's got the hots for our daughter—"

"Roger!"

"Well, honey, you brought it up. But since I don't get the feeling it'd ever go any further than that, I think you're not only worrying prematurely, but unnecessarily." At her raised brows he added, "I somehow doubt he's the settling-down type, is all."

"And that's supposed to make me feel better?"

Roger frowned at that. Well, hallelujah. Glynnie leaned forward—carefully, so as to not smear ketchup on her sweater—and said, "He looks at her exactly the way Bobby used to, at the beginning."

The frown vanished, to be replaced with a gleam in his eye and that off-kilter grin that still stirred her blood after nearly thirty-five years. "Which happens to be exactly the way I used to look at you, too, petunia. Still do, if memory serves. So think about that before you start going on about how you want something better for her this go-around, okay?''

Frowning, Glynelle jabbed a plastic fork at her potato salad, thinking, *Men.*

Despite the financial inquisition from Joanna's parents, Dale had been doing fine up until the kids started opening their presents, when claustrophobia—or maybe it was Joanna's unamused expression when the boys went crazy over the whoopee cushion—sent him out for some fresh air. He and about a thousand cats ambled toward the stable, where he found Joanna's daughter perched on top of the post-and-rail fence.

After they exchanged a couple of tentative ''Heys,'' she said, ''How come you're out here?''

''My ears were beginning to ring,'' he said, and the corners of her mouth turned up. ''But if you want to be alone, I can just head back—''

''No, it's okay.''

''You sure?''

''Uh-huh.'' She waited until Dale got closer, then said, ''The swing set's pretty neat. I think the boys'll like it a lot.''

''You been on it yet?''

''Oh, I'm way too old for things like that.''

''I see.'' Dale leaned his forearms on the top rail, his hands clasped. ''There ever any horses here?''

''Not since my great-grandma was alive, nuh-uh. Mom said she rode a lot when she was a kid. I sometimes think it would be cool to have one, since we've already got a place to keep it. But Mom says they're too much work and too expensive to take care of.''

''Unlike all these cats.''

The girl giggled. ''Mom says there must be signs around

directing all the strays here. She doesn't have the heart to call Animal Control about them, so she gets them fixed and lets them stay. Most of 'em live outside, although we make sure they're in the tack room at night so the coyotes don't get 'em.''

Dale winced; Dulcy giggled again.

"How many are there?" he asked.

"Four inside and twelve outside. For now." She braced her hands on the railing on either side of her hips and looked down at him. "Mom told me about how you were wearing this hamster hat in your store the other day, that she started laughing so hard she couldn't stop."

"Yep. She sure did." The part about her mama's crying, though, he decided to keep to himself.

Dulcy looked down at her lap, plucking off a stray leaf and tossing it on the ground. "She hasn't laughed like that in a long time," she said, a little crease between her brows. Then she looked right at him and said, "I've got a whole bunch of your cards. You know, from when you were still playing?"

"You do?"

"Uh-huh. I started collecting cards when I was six. Mom thought I was nuts. But Dad and I used to watch baseball all the time, when he still lived with us. Then at his place, on the weekends, after Mom and Dad got divorced. Until Tori moved in. She doesn't like sports much more than Mom does."

"She seems nice enough otherwise, though."

"Yeah. I guess."

Dale decided to move on. "You play any?"

"Some. At school and stuff. I did Little League for a while—girls can play up until they're twelve here—but I could see it was really hard on Mom, trying to get me to practices and games when she had to work with Ryder on his school stuff and get her own work done, too. So I quit."

"That's too bad."

She shrugged, not looking at him.

"Wasn't until high school that I ever played with a real team, either," he said, "if it makes you feel any better."

"Really?"

"Nope."

"So how'd you get to be so good?"

"Oh, I don't know," he said, wondering why he was even *looking* down this road. "Lots of little things fallin' into place, I guess. Got an old glove from some kid I knew then I used to find balls in the woods behind the stadium where the high school kids played. So I'd take my glove and a ball or two and go off to this vacant farm not far from where I lived, and I'd spend hours pitching that da— that ball against the side of the old barn, getting so I could predict within an inch where it would hit." *Until there was nothing but me and the ball and the sound of it hitting that barn, over and over and over.* "Then, later, me and a few kids'd get together for informal games, now and again. That's when I learned to bat, too. Although I was always better at pitching. Anyway, my point is, you can still just play for fun, you know. Maybe you could get your mama to play with you. Or your dad, on the weekends—"

"Dulcy?" Joanna called over by the house. "It's cake time!"

"Coming!" The kid hopped down off the railing, unselfconsciously brushing off her butt. "Well, Mom's way too busy to play, even if she wanted to, so that's out. And there's no kids in the neighborhood my age. None who'd want to play, anyway. And we can't play at Dad's, 'cause he lives in an apartment complex."

"What about your brothers?"

"They're *eight*," she said, as though that explained everything. As they approached the house, she said, "Why'd you come to the party?"

"Well..." He scooped up one of the cats, a skinny gray

tiger who started purring to beat the band. "Because I was invited. And I thought it'd be fun."

She gave him a weird look, but kept whatever thoughts she had on the subject to herself.

Dale wasn't sure if that was a good thing or not.

Once the other parents began showing up to collect their kids, Tori started in on Bobby about leaving, too, since it was going to take her all weekend to write this paper for her sociology class, she said. But between the boys not being ready to go until they'd had a chance to try the mitt Dale'd given them and Bobby's not yet having had a chance to feel Dale out about Joanna, he wheedled another fifteen minutes out of her.

"Then we'll go, I promise," he said, and gave her a kiss, which seemed to do the trick. So she snuggled up on one of the chaises on the patio, wearing his Mariners jacket, and Bobby scrounged a couple of tennis balls off Chester and went out to watch Dale play catch with the kids. As usual, Matt was trying to hog both Dale's attention and the new glove.

"Let your brother have a turn, now," Bobby shouted to the boy from the picnic table, where he and the dog sat watching.

"But, Da-a-ad—he keeps missing!"

"Yeah, well, you're not exactly a threat to Mike Piazza yourself, buddy."

"Who?"

"Never mind. Give your brother the mitt. Go on."

Grumbling, Matt flung the mitt in Ryder's direction, who, yes, dropped it. But the look on his face when Dale carefully tossed the ball to him and he actually caught it…well, it made Bobby's heart swell. It pained him nearly as much as it did Joanna, the way the boy's self-confidence had gone to pot over the last little while, even if Bobby didn't say much about it. He didn't know what *to* say, to tell the truth. But he sure as hell knew what it felt like, having to struggle to be as good as the next guy.

It finally got too dark to play, so the kids trooped back inside and Tori hauled herself up to go pee again before they left. Dale walked over to the patio, dropping his own glove onto the glass-topped table to take a swig from the water bottle he'd left there earlier. "Guess it's about time I said my goodbyes," he said, and Bobby realized it was now or never.

"The kids really got a kick out of that. Thanks."

Dale shrugged. "I enjoyed it. There's nothin' like the look on a kid's face when that ball lands right in the glove, y'know?"

"I was just thinking the same thing. Watching Ryder, especially."

There was a split-second pause before Dale's, "Oh?"

"Yeah. He's havin' a lot of trouble in school. Learning to read and stuff. Then with his brother bein' the same age and getting good grades all the time…well, it's hard on the kid. You know what I mean? Which in turn is hard on Joanna. Especially with her being alone with them all week. I mean, I do what I can over the weekends, when they're with me, but five days is a lot more than two. I know she worries a lot about him."

Dale gave him a funny look.

"Not that I don't, don't get me wrong. But Joanna's the mother, you know? Women tend to get more balled up about stuff like this."

"I wouldn't know."

"Yeah. They do. And I can see where it's beginning to take its toll. You know what I mean?" Bobby hooked his arms together over his chest and leaned against one of the patio cover supports, hoping like hell Dale took the bait. "Hell, she never goes out, never does anything except work and take care of the kids. That can't be healthy, you know?

And then with Tori and me getting married…I feel bad about that.''

The bottle stopped halfway to Dale's mouth. "Why should you?"

"I suppose you're right. But Joanna and me, I guess we've kinda got a weird relationship. God knows, our marriage was a disaster waiting to happen. When she told me she wanted a divorce, I not only wasn't surprised, I was actually relieved, if you wanna know the truth.''

"Really?"

"Yeah. Crazy, huh? The funny thing is, though, it wasn't like we didn't care about each other, because we did. Still do. And I think we both wanted to make it work, for the kids' sake. Hell, for our own. But in the end, we just couldn't.'' He paused. "Anyway, so here I am about to start a second family and, well… I just can't help thinking about how she's alone and all, y'know?''

Dale looked at him for a good long time, then finally took a sip of that water, screwing the top back on when he finished. His mouth twitched. "You wouldn't by any chance be trying to sic me on your ex-wife, would you?''

"Hey, you weren't exactly keeping your interest a secret,'' Bobby said, grabbing his opportunity and running with it. "And all I'm sayin' is, the coast is clear on this end. If the interest is mutual. Which something tells me it is.''

That earned him another one of those looks. "Let me get this straight. You're telling me how much you care about Joanna and what happens to her, and yet you're trying to pair her up with somebody you don't know from Adam?''

Okay, so maybe when he put it like that, it didn't sound so good after all. Still, Bobby was in it this far, might as well see it through. "Maybe I don't know you personally. But I never once heard anything, y'know, when you were in the pros, that would make me worry. And besides, I've always had this sixth sense about people, from all the time I was selling cars? Ten minutes of observing somebody, the way they interact with other people, and I know exactly what kind of person they are.''

"You do, huh?''

"Yep.''

"And what kind of person am I?''

"Somebody I can trust.''

Dale took another sip of his water, then said, "And Joanna would have both our hides if she knew we were having this conversation, wouldn't she?''

"You got that right.''

That got a low laugh. Then, "Well, Bobby, don't think I don't appreciate what you're trying to do. But if you're looking for somebody to take up where you left off, to be there for your ex-wife for the long haul, I'm not your man.''

"Hell, I don't expect you to be thinking in serious terms before you even get to know her—''

"You're not understanding me. I don't do serious. Ever. With anyone. So if you want to take back your…magnanimous gesture, I'll completely understand.''

Not that this surprised Bobby, even if it did disappoint him a bit. "I see. Well. I appreciate your honesty.''

"Oh, I'm always honest. Even when it gets me in trouble.'' In the charcoal light, Bobby saw his lips curve. "Or keeps me out of it.''

Bobby grinned back, thinking no matter what, the seed had been planted. Given time, it was bound to sprout. Besides, all he needed was someone to keep Joanna—who he could tell was nurturing a nice little seed of her own—occupied until Tori's hormone-induced paranoia ran its course. With any luck, even a couple of weeks might be enough.

"I hear ya,'' he said. "But to tell you the truth…well, I'm not all that sure Joanna's in the market for another husband, anyway. Not right now, in any case," he added at Dale's raised eyebrows. "She even told Tori she doesn't envy her, so I'm thinking you probably don't have much to worry about on that score. But from here on out, it's strictly between the two of you. I won't say another word."

Dale gave him one of those hard looks again, then nodded and walked away.

That conversation with Joanna's ex-husband had distracted Dale so much, he was a good half mile away from Joanna's house before he remembered his glove. Since he'd pitched the World Series winning game with that glove, he wasn't keen on losing it. So back he went, hoping it was where he'd last seen it so he wouldn't have to bother anybody. Or, more to the point, bother himself more than he already was.

Bobby's Taurus was still there; Dale drove around to the stable, partly so he could get to the backyard, and the glove, easier, and partly because he did not want Bobby getting any ideas about why he was returning.

Soon as he got out of his car, however, he heard voices and car doors slamming out front, and he relaxed some: apparently Bobby and the kids were leaving. He quickly scanned the yard, frowning when he didn't see the glove right off, only to remember he'd carried it up onto the patio.

Where—yep—it still was.

He'd just grabbed it and was about to skedaddle when Bobby's and Joanna's voices, floating out from the high window looking out onto the patio, stopped him dead.

"...you're damn straight I'm angry, Bobby! You agreed to pay for half the repairs. Which you never have. So excuse me if seeing a diamond on Tori's hand upsets me a little."

"Jo, please...everybody's already out in the car...."

"I asked you for that money for the roof two weeks ago!

I'm getting real tired of putting out pots to catch the drips every time it rains.''

"Hey, this is New Mexico. How often does that happen?"

"Not funny. When am I going to see that money, Bobby?"

"God, Jo—I honestly thought you were above the first-wife-resentment crap."

"Don't you *dare* pull that on me! This has *nothing* to do with my being the first wife, or you getting married again, or anything except the fact that you're always crying poor when *I* need something, but somehow you had the money for *that*."

"I had to get her a ring, Jo! Otherwise she would've thought I was just blowing air up her skirt about gettin' married!"

"At the expense of my roof!"

"That's right! *Your* roof. *Your* house—"

"Where *your* children live most of the time, in case you've forgotten!" There was a pause, as if maybe she was trying to get control of herself. "And where I lived with nothing but a plain gold band for nine years because a diamond ring was a luxury we couldn't afford!"

"Oh, for God's sake, Jo…"

Then their voices faded out, like they were leaving the kitchen. Feeling like a spy or a burglar or something, Dale stayed out of sight on the patio, waiting until he heard Bobby's car leave before making a dash for his own. Only he hadn't gotten but two steps when he heard behind him, "What the *hell* are you doing here?"

Chapter 7

Since he was busted anyway, he figured he might as well turn around. She was standing there with the dog, looking more startled than mad, he thought. Hoped.

"I forgot my glove," he said, holding up the evidence. "I just meant to get it and get out."

"And I suppose listening underneath my window to a conversation that was none of your business was just a fringe benefit."

"I swear, I only heard a sentence or two—"

But she was waving away his apology like she didn't have the energy to listen to it, a conclusion borne out by her collapse into one of the chairs beside the table. "It's just not fair," she said, clutching the arms of the chair for dear life. The dog got up on his hind legs to lay his head in her lap. Distractedly, she started to pet him. "Not that I expect life to be fair," Joanna said, rousing Dale from some very frustrated thoughts, "because it never is, but honest to God—*why* do I keep expecting him to keep his promises when he never does?"

Dale wasn't sure whether this was a rhetorical question or not, but he figured since he was here and all, he might as well toss in his two cents.

"Because you're by nature an optimistic person?"

She grunted.

"And I also think you've got every right to be jealous."

A beat or two passed before she glared at him. "I thought you said you only heard a sentence or two?"

"I didn't say which ones."

Again, she waved away his comment. But she said, "I am not jealous because she got a diamond and I didn't. Pissed, maybe. But not jealous."

"Pardon me if I don't see the difference."

She bounced up out of the chair, knocking the poor dog on his butt, hit a switch on the porch that lit up most of the backyard, then took off toward the swing set. Since he couldn't think of anything else to do, Dale followed. So did the dog, who clearly didn't have anything else to do, either.

Joanna straddled one end of the two-person glider and pushed off like she was trying to get to the moon. Dale leaned against the cottonwood trunk, his hands in his pockets; the dog lay at his feet. "So what's the deal with the roof?"

"Okay, now you're up to at least five or six sentences."

"Sorry. But I thought maybe I should stick around to make sure things didn't get out of hand."

"Oh, for heaven's sake. Bobby's never laid a finger on me—"

"Wasn't you I was worried about."

"Oh," she said, followed by a harsh sigh. "Flat roofs are bitches, because the water can't run off as easily as it does off a pitched roof, *canales* notwithstanding. Those things that jut off the top of the house," she said by way of explanation when he turned around to see what the hell she was talking about. "If the roof isn't retarred regularly, it springs leaks. Many leaks. And no, maybe it doesn't rain a lot here, but when it does, it tends to rain hard. And last spring we had a couple of heavy wet snows, which didn't do it any favors, either. And the house—at least the original part, where the living room and kitchen are—is old, maybe eighty years.''

"So...how come you bought it, knowing it was only gonna have problems down the road?''

"I didn't buy it. I inherited it from my father's mother, who died right after Bobby and I were married. So technically, he's right. It is my house—I assume you heard that part, too—but since his kids do live here, is it too much to ask that he help keep it up?''

"No. But why not sell it and move someplace that's less of a hassle?''

She looked at him as though he'd suggested she eat raw liver. "Because it's my grandmother's house! She was born here. So was my father. So was Dulcy. Giving it up would be like giving up one of my children.''

It was hard for Dale to imagine being loyal to a few walls and a roof that leaked, never mind how many family members had been born here. But then, that could be because the concept of home wasn't something with which he was all that familiar.

"Look, if you need help with the roof—''

"Thanks, but I'm hardly going to accept help from a total stranger.''

"I wasn't offering.''

She stopped swinging. "You weren't?''

"Nope. Which you would've discovered if you'd let me finish what I was gonna say. Which was that I was wondering why you just don't ask your parents for the money. Assuming they have it,'' he said as her expression darkened.

"Oh, they have it, all right.'' She pushed off again, her feet dragging along the ground because her legs were too long. "And since I've already had this argument with one of the parents in question, let's not go there, okay?"

"I'm only sayin'—"

"I know what you're saying. Same as they keep saying. They're there, they're willing, why not? Because it's Bobby's responsibility, dammit. He never had to make a single mortgage payment, and I never asked for more than child support. Child support and half the repairs."

"No alimony?"

"When we split up, I was making more than he was. There didn't seem to be any point. And now he's got a new baby coming, and he's getting married again…"

"And you're ticked she got a diamond."

"You're like a dog with a bone, aren't you?"

"Takes one to know one."

"Why? Because I want my ex-husband to live up to his promises?"

"Well, that, too. Since you just admitted yourself he never keeps 'em. But what I'm wondering is why it's so hard for you to just admit what's really bugging you about this."

She stopped swinging, leaning her cheek against her hands, clasped around the glider's support. Then she shrugged, her sudden vulnerability stealing his breath. "Maybe because I don't really *know* what's really bugging me about this."

Lord save him, he wasn't used to vulnerable women. Dumb, helpless ones, looking to him to protect them, yeah. Or, at the other extreme, women who were so busy tryin' to prove they were equal to men, they could make a man's balls shrink just by looking at him. But this was a whole new breed, someone with enough guts to let her guard down, who wasn't afraid to show she was human and maybe just plain tired of trying to make all the pieces fit.

And that…genuineness scared the crap out of him. It was like stumbling across something you didn't even know you were looking for, yet knowing immediately you had to have it...even while knowing, just as strongly, you wouldn't know what to do with it if you got it.

"It's stupid, sometimes," she said, "the things we want. Like, just once, for a man to do something without being nagged about it."

Dale felt the muscles in his back tense. "And maybe it's not fair to judge the entire male population by your ex-husband's actions."

She didn't seem to notice the edge to his words, or care, sitting there in the chilly night, her breath frosting a little around her mouth. "My sons aren't much better," she said with a half smile. "Although I'll give them some leeway since they're only eight. But I keep my ear to the ground. I hear things."

"From a certain friend of yours who's been married three times in twelve years."

"Now how on earth did you find that out?"

"We met up outside the hall bathroom. I swear, I've met some yakky women in my life, but Karleen managed to cram more into two minutes than anyone I've ever known."

Joanna laughed, the sound rich and warm and making him more glad than he wanted to admit that he'd forgotten that glove. "Yep, that's Karleen. But I'm the only one allowed to say things like that about her."

"Oh, she's okay. Or she would be if she'd just stop trying so hard. She reminds me a little of my ex-wife—"

Damn.

"I take it that's not a good thing?"

"No. But we were talking about your problem with men."

"I'm bored with that," she said. "Let's talk about your ex-wife instead and why you think Karleen reminds you of her."

"Let's not. So what about your father?"

"My father? What about him?"

"Well, I don't know. I mean, we didn't talk all that much this evening, but still, he strikes me as the kind of man who keeps his promises."

"My father." Her eyes twinkled. "The car salesman."

"Oh. Forgot about that."

She laughed again. "Okay, so he's the exception that proves the rule."

"You don't concede defeat easily, do you?"

"I stayed married for nearly nine years to a man I shouldn't have married in the first place. So what does that tell you?"

"Off hand? I'd say that makes you the kind of woman who took the 'for better or worse' part of her marriage vows seriously."

She cocked her head at him, her gaze speculative in the harsh, weird light. "I take it your wife didn't?"

"You're bound and determined to talk about that, aren't you?"

"It's that dog-and-bone thing. And besides, since my own divorce, I've developed a morbid fascination for why other peoples' marriages fall apart."

"I had a real nice time tonight," Dale said, turning to go.

"She left you, didn't she?" she said quietly.

He could've kept going. Probably should've. But he didn't. Instead he turned back, expecting to see pity, which he was prepared to hate, but seeing understanding instead...which he wasn't prepared for at all.

"Yeah," he said simply, and then she shivered in the night breeze, and he said, "You should get inside, it's gettin' cold," at the same time she said, "Would you like to come in for coffee?" His "no" came out a lot quicker and a lot sharper than he intended, and he could see her flinch from what must have seemed like a rejection.

"What I mean is," he said, trying to gentle his voice

even though it was probably better letting her believe he was rejecting her, "my guess is it's been a long day for you. And I don't need to add to my list of sins by accepting an invitation only offered out of politeness."

She looked like she might argue with him for a second or two, then shrugged. "Whatever. You're right. I'm whacked."

"So I'll just say good-night, then," he said, making a beeline for his car.

"Don't forget your glove," she called.

Dale tried to take the ninety-degree turn back to the patio like that was what he'd meant to do all along, although she probably already figured he'd forgotten the damn thing, thereby proving her theory that men were basically helpless. So he got the glove and returned to the car, and she apparently waited until he was in it before she started back for the house, and he sat there and watched her go inside, his hand on the ignition key. When the patio and yard lights went out, he turned the ignition and gave it some gas…

Nothing happened.

So he turned it again and gave it some more gas.

Still nothing.

So after two or three additional attempts to start his piece-of-shit car, he strode back to the house and up onto the patio, rapping on the glass door rather than going all the way around to the front—which, since he could see her shadow moving around on the other side of the closed drapes, would have meant she'd've just had to traipse through the house anyway—feeling… Well, he wasn't sure what he was feeling. Although unbalanced would do, for the moment.

The drape twitched back. He thought she might have been frowning at him. Then she unlocked the door and pushed it back. Cats and dog exchanged places. "What's wrong?"

I'm losing my mind. "Car problems," he said.

"Oh?" She peeked out the door, like she expected the car to be behind him, then back at him. "What if I said I didn't believe you?"

"You think I'm pretending the car won't start?"

"Well, since I didn't hear the sound of a motor trying to turn over...yeah."

"Here," he said, tossing her keys. "Go see for yourself."

"Fine," she said, tromping past him, through the gate and out to the car. She yanked back the car door and, leaving it open, got inside, rammed the key into the ignition, twisted the key and gave it some gas.

The engine roared to life.

"How the hell'd you do that?" Dale said.

Joanna sat there for a moment. Or two. Then she cut the engine and swung one leg out of the car, frowning up at him.

"Why didn't you just come back and say you'd changed your mind?"

"Swear to God, that thing would not start up a minute ago."

"Uh-huh."

"I *swear.*"

She got out, slammed the car door shut, then just stood there, looking mightily perturbed, the breeze stirring all those curls. "You have apparently forgotten that I hear the words *I swear I didn't do it* at least twenty times a day?"

"Joanna, I know what it looks like..." Then he started to laugh, mainly because the whole situation was so damn absurd. After a moment she started to laugh, too. Not crazy laughter, but it's-okay laughter.

Then she said, "So you really don't want to come in?"

The laughter faded. "I didn't think I did. But maybe I've changed my mind."

Things got real quiet for a long time.

"I don't know," she finally said. "You sure you want

to risk it? What if I get it into my head to jump your bones?''

Hope leaped to life inside him. ''You planning on doing that?''

She did some more pondering…then shook her head. ''No. But I just think it's interesting that you'd take that chance. For all you know, I could be the clingy, desperate type. Glenn Close in *Fatal Attraction*.''

Dale crossed his arms, wondering if they were going to spend the entire night standing out here in the cold. ''My instincts tell me I don't have a whole lot to worry about.''

''Betcha that's what Michael Douglas thought, too.''

''Hey. You were the one who invited me in to begin with, remember? What if I try to take advantage of *you?*''

''You won't live to take advantage of anybody else,'' she said.

''Oh, yeah?''

''Yeah,'' she said. ''I got my brown belt in karate when I was eighteen.''

At that, Dale leaned forward to rest his hand on the roof of his car, close enough for their hormones to start cross pollinating, deciding it probably wouldn't be prudent to tell her he'd had his black belt for fifteen years. Any more than it would be to tell her exactly how much of a turn-on he found the idea of her pinning him to the mat. Or he, her. Either way was fine by him.

''Don't be so sure about that,'' he whispered because, suddenly, he was back in the game. And judging by the slight tensing of Joanna's mouth, he was on top of it, too…even if he was playing blind. He didn't know what he wanted beyond the moment. Beyond tonight. Wasn't worth thinking about, anyway, since in his experience, the future tended to do what it wanted irrespective of a person's druthers. But was it so wrong, to want to sample for himself something that other men took for granted?

She licked her lips and his interest kicked up another

several notches. Then she startled him by burying her face in her hands, a muffled, "What in God's name do I think I'm *doing?*" working its way out from behind her palms.

Dale reached out and lazily captured one of those wild curls, twirling it around his index finger. "You're inviting me in to make you the best damn cup of coffee you've ever tasted. And nobody's gonna jump anybody's bones. At least—" he lifted the curl to his mouth when she lifted those wide, questioning, fearless eyes to his, locking their gazes as he brushed the softness across his bottom lip "—not tonight."

"That a promise?" she asked.

"Only if you want it to be."

One eyebrow lifted. Then she tugged her curl from his grasp and started back to the house, clearly expecting him to follow.

Hot damn. There was a man standing in her kitchen. And he didn't even have a repair bill in his hand.

Even though, five seconds back in the glaringly lit room redolent with the fumes from her argument with Bobby, the erotic fog in which Joanna had allowed herself to drift into went *poof!*

Joanna wasn't sure whether this was good or not. On the one hand, erotic fogs not being exactly regular occurrences in her life these days, this one's premature dissipation had left her feeling a bit let down. However, smart decisions did not erotic fogs beget. Marrying Bobby, for instance. Not to mention her letting this six-foot-and-change stud muffin follow her home. Still, that thing Dale had done with her hair should keep a nice buzz going for weeks. Just think what might happen if he ever touched anything with nerve endings.

Bad Joanna. Bad, bad Joanna.

And, oh, wouldn't she love to be *bad* Joanna, just for one night?

And whilst she was pondering all this, Dale had begun cleaning her kitchen.

"What are you doing?"

"Helping."

"Why?"

Plates in both hands, Dale scanned the devastated kitchen, then looked at her. "What is this, a trick question?"

"Well, stop. I never let a man clean on the first date."

"Is that what you think this is?"

"As close as I've gotten to one in…a while." She sat at the kitchen table, waiting out the trickle of guilt about letting him do all the work.

"Don't tell me you haven't gone out with anybody since the divorce."

"Of course I've gone out since the divorce," she said, scraping together enough energy to sound huffy, even as her earlier conversation with Karleen neatly shoved aside the guilt. As a gap guy, Dale McConnaughy had definite possibilities. Try as she might, however, she just could not see him as sherbet.

Chocolate, maybe.

Bittersweet.

Solid.

Maybe laced with Grand Marnier.

But even Joanna knew you couldn't make a meal of chocolate.

Not that she hadn't tried.

"How many times?"

Her gaze snapped to his. "Excuse me?"

"How many times you been on a date since your divorce?"

Oh. "And this is your business how?"

"Humor me."

Would somebody tell her why she was finding the sight of a man loading her dishwasher so incredibly fascinating?

Oh, wait…nobody but her had loaded the dishwasher in about a million years. Hell, in her state Homer Simpson would look good. "You have to understand, I didn't date much before I met Bobby—"

"How many?"

"Twice."

"Two men, or two dates?"

"You know," she said, standing, "there's still tons of birthday cake left, which I certainly don't need and it'll just go stale before the boys come back on Sunday night—"

"You mean to tell me—" he clattered things around a bit, then grabbed the dishwasher stuff out from under the sink and filled the little dealie "—in three years, you've had exactly two dates?"

"I didn't *mean* to tell you anything. You dragged it out of me. And please, I'm dead serious about the cake. I'm gaining weight just knowing it's in the house."

"Jeez," he said, banging shut the dishwasher door.

"What?"

He studied the buttons a second, pressed the right ones, then looked at her. "Okay, can we get one thing clear right now? I don't know what parts of your anatomy you've got issues with—and don't bother telling me you don't because I've yet to meet a woman who doesn't—so if you're worried about the size of your butt? Get over it."

She automatically twisted around to look at it. Unfortunately, it was still there. "It's okay?"

"Honey, I haven't been able to take my eyes off of it all evening."

"Oh," she said, thinking maybe that erotic fog hadn't dissipated quite as much as she'd thought. Could be that this was one of those men who traveled in one all the time. And hot damn, he and his pet fog were standing *right here,* doing the hungry-raking-gaze thing over her body and looking all strong and solid and Grand Marnier-laced, and she said, "Oh," again, although she thought it might have sounded a little needy that time. Then Dale asked where the coffee was, which forced her out of her monosyllabic, fog-induced stupor.

While he went about making it, she allowed herself a little hungry raking. Fair's fair, after all.

"And I like flat-chested women, too, in case you're wondering."

Her gaze whipped to his, its appetite suddenly gone. "I am not flat-chested!"

Dale chuckled.

"Hey, buster—I nursed three kids. Including twins. So put that in your pipe and smoke it."

He raised one eyebrow.

Joanna blinked. "Are we on dangerous ground?"

"Honey," Dale said, leaning against her counter and crossing his arms as the coffee aroma began to suffuse her kitchen and make her feel safe. There was a false illusion for you. "I was *born* on dangerous ground."

She exchanged the next, "Oh," with, "Is that your way of warning me?"

His gaze was steady. "Pretty much. I'm not lookin' to get tangled up with anybody." One side of his mouth lifted. "On anything other than a temporary basis, at least."

"Why not?"

His eyes narrowed. "I've got my reasons. But considering what I just said, I don't think there's much point in goin' into 'em."

"Well. At least you're up front about it."

"I try to be. Saves wear and tear on the nerves down the road. Unless of course, the woman gets it into her head to change my mind."

"Which would be stupid."

"I've always thought so. Like I said, I've got all I can handle looking out for myself. Don't need any encumbrances."

"Is that what you think family is?" she said softly, not

believing the hard look in his eyes for a single minute. "An encumbrance?"

"For me, yeah."

"That's too bad. Because I don't feel that way at all."

"I kinda gathered that," he said with a half smile. "So I suppose that means this is dead in the water, huh?"

Joanna took her time gathering her thoughts before she spoke. "Well," she said at last, "I'm certainly not opposed to the idea of being married again, someday. Maybe having more kids. But this time with someone who understands you can't play at marriage, that half-assed doesn't cut it." She paused. "Someone who takes life, and its responsibilities, seriously."

"So I guess that leaves me out."

She was grateful she didn't know him long enough to be disappointed. "Of my long-term plans? Absolutely."

Understanding glimmered faintly in his eyes. "But…?"

She shrugged.

Dale watched her face for several more seconds, glanced at the coffee, which was ready, then his watch. "Okay. Here's the deal," he said. "I'm staying exactly twenty minutes, which should be long enough to drink one cup of coffee. Then I'm going home so both of us can think about where we want to take this…what's so funny?"

She raked one hand through her hair. "Oh, I don't know. Because I feel a bit like the last item left in the scratch-and-dent sale right now? Because I've got God-knows-what all over my shirt and I have a bad hair *life* and I've reached the point where the bag boys are calling me 'ma'am' and I have the horrible feeling if I tried to act sexy, I'd laugh. Or you would."

"You do tend to say whatever pops into your head, don't you?"

"It's a genetic curse."

Dale studied her for a moment or two, then got two cups

from the cabinet over the dishwasher and poured coffee into each of them.

"How do you take it?"

"Black," she said and he handed her one of the mugs.

"Believe me, I wouldn't laugh." One side of his mouth twitched while hers went dry. "Send up a prayer of thanks, maybe. But where is all this coming from? What the hell did you think was going on out by my car?"

"Um…flirting?"

"No, that was definitely me comin' on to you."

"Oh. I knew that."

He chuckled. "Joanna, nothing's gonna happen you don't want to happen, okay? So why don't you just relax and enjoy the moment?"

"I am enjoying the moment. I think. It's what comes next that rattles me."

After a slow sip of his coffee, he said, "Let me guess. Those two dates you had? They didn't involve getting naked, did they?"

"Hell, they barely involved dessert."

He lifted the mug to his lips again, obviously considering all this. "You know, I don't usually attract women like you."

Not what she was expecting. "Who says I'm attracted to—"

His laugh cut her off.

"Okay, forget that. What do you mean, women like me?"

"You know. Normal ones."

After her eyebrows returned to earth, she said, because she didn't think it was in her best interest to disabuse him of him rampant misconception, "So…you're in this for the novelty of it?"

"Aren't you?"

He had her there. "Let's take our coffee into the living

room,'' she said, because that was the best thing she could come up with on such short notice.

Tori sat up in bed, twisting her engagement ring this way and that to make it sparkle in the light from the bedside lamp, trying to distract herself from all the gurgling and spitting going on behind the bathroom door as Bobby brushed his teeth. In one of the two small bedrooms across the hall, the twins were already sawing logs; from the other, Tori could hear the clackety-clack of Dulcy's keyboard as she yakked with her friends online. It was totally bizarre to think that the girl would be a teenager in less than eighteen months when Tori had been one herself not all that long ago.

The ring glittered some more when she wiggled her fingers. She didn't think she'd ever get used to seeing it there. And for a couple of seconds, after Bobby'd presented her with it, she'd half thought about telling him to take it back since she knew he couldn't really afford it. She got over it, though.

It was the most beautiful thing she'd ever owned.

With a huge yawn, Tori sank into the pillows propped behind her back, letting her eyes drift closed. Her mother, a veteran of two lousy marriages and one good one—finally—had warned her about taking other women's leavings. Still, once she got a load of this ring, even Mama would have to admit that Bobby Alvarez was several cuts above her average ex-husband.

She heard the toilet flush; a second later, Bobby came out of the bathroom in his boxers, accompanied by a cloud of aftershave-scented steam. *Uh-oh.* Tori's stomach pitched at the strong scent, at what it signified. And when he crawled into bed, that hopeful look in his eyes, it was everything she could do not to cringe.

He lifted her left hand and smoothed his lips across her knuckles. The very move that had led to her current condition, if memory served. Tori let out a long breath, praying Bobby didn't take it the wrong way, and prodded the underside of the ring with her thumb.

"I don't think Joanna was any too thrilled when I showed this to her." She saw the muscles tense in Bobby's back, for a second, then he went back to his finger nibbling. "She'll get over it," he said, then added, "Speaking of which…I had a nice chat with Dale McConnaughy right before we left." He took her index finger into his mouth, gently scraping it across his bottom teeth. Tori tried to concentrate, but…nope. No reaction whatsoever. "I gave him the go-ahead," Bobby said. "About Joanna."

She didn't have the reaction she should have had to that, either. Oh, she'd caught all those sizzling glances between Dale and Bobby's ex at the party. And God knows she wouldn't mind seeing Joanna involved with somebody else so maybe Bobby could focus more on their relationship. But still. The whole thing made her feel like she had bugs crawling inside her.

"What'd he say?"

When he didn't answer right away, Tori figured he was being selective in what he told her. "Not much, actually. But I'm an optimist, what can I tell you?"

"I don't know, Bobby." By now, the bugs were doing a boot-scootin' line dance in her stomach. "Something about this just doesn't seem right."

Bobby stopped nibbling, his own frown matching hers. "I thought that's what you wanted? To get Jo interested in somebody else to get her off my case?"

She shrugged, twisting a piece of her hair around and around her finger, watching the black lace edging on the Victoria's Secret leopard-print nightgown he'd given her for her twenty-first birthday rise and fall as she breathed. It really wasn't all that comfortable—the damn straps would *not* stay up on her shoulders—but she didn't want to make him feel bad by not wearing it. "I don't know," she said again. "Doesn't it seem weird, the idea of her having sex with someone else?"

Bobby shifted to prop his head in his hand, looking more confused than usual. "Honest to God, woman. The questions you come up with. Honey, I haven't been with Joanna in more than three years. Statute of limitations ran out on that pull a long time ago. Besides, we weren't each other's first, we never thought we'd be each other's last. Speaking of which…" His hand inched up her thigh, underneath the nightgown.

Tori burst into tears.

After a brief what-the-hell? look, Bobby sat up and put his arms around her. "What is it, baby?"

"I j-just don't feel like fooling around t-tonight, okay?"

"Of course it's okay," he said, not doing a whole lot to mask his disappointment. But then he said, "I forgot, y'know, that sometimes women don't feel up to it when they first get pregnant," and when she twisted around to look up at him, he was grinning. "That'll change, you'll see."

Inside her head, her emotions collided. On the one hand she was thinking, How had she lucked out, getting a man this good on the first shot? On the other, though, there it was on the sidelines as always—his first marriage. It would never be just them, no matter how much Bobby insisted otherwise. Never. There were the kids, there was Joanna, there even were Joanna's pregnancies, used as a comparison to Tori's.

And this was nuts. She loved Bobby to pieces. And why not? Tori's stepfather had been cold, her own father a womanizer, and her mother's loser boyfriends in between not even worth thinking about. Not that Bobby was perfect by any means—Tori wasn't blind, for heaven's sake—but he loved his kids, he treated her like gold, he was funny and kind and never came home soused or raised either his hand or his voice to her. She'd be a fool to let him go, even if she had hoped to finish school before she got pregnant, since she didn't figure on being a receptionist for the rest of her life. And up until a few weeks ago, the only problem they'd ever had in the bedroom was not being able to get naked fast enough. But between work and school and the pregnancy, she just felt so damned wiped out....

The thought alone was enough to send her under the covers, scrunching the pillows under her cheek. "Maybe I'll feel more like it tomorrow night."

"Sure, sweetheart." He kissed her on her temple, then gently tugged the covers up around her shoulders. "You mind if I watch some TV, then? I'm like totally wired for some reason."

The pillowcase grazed her cheek when she shook her head. "No, go ahead. I'm just going to go to sleep."

Bobby was already out of bed and slipping into a pair of sweats. "That's a good idea. You get some rest, babe."

The instant he was gone, Tori started crying all over again.

Dale barely managed to hold in his laugh when Joanna flipped the light switch to her studio. Everywhere he looked there was fabric and thread and half-finished Santas and folders and papers and more fabric and bolts of trims and boxes and bins of...stuff.

"Kinda reminds me of my first apartment. Except it smells a whole lot better."

"Okay, so it tends to get a little untidy this time of year," she said. "But I can put my hand on anything I need in a second."

Thinking there were way too many ways to interpret that comment, Dale walked over to the huge worktable taking up a good third of the room, his thumbs hooked in his pockets. He wondered if she was as aware as he was that the twenty minutes had come and gone an hour ago.

And if she figured out why, he was dead meat.

He'd meant what he'd said out by the car, about this just being about coffee. But then they'd come inside, and there she was with all that incredible hair and those big green eyes surrounded by those fiery red eyelashes—he was guessing that was her natural hair color after all—looking like a woman determined not to let her neediness show. When he'd realized just how long it had been since she'd had sex, the old male drive to strike while the iron was hot kicked in but good.

But making the first move wasn't how he played the game. Making the first move—no matter how much he might want to—led to complications Dale neither wanted nor needed. And no, expressing an interest didn't count. That was just the coin toss to get things moving, to make sure both parties were paying attention. Whatever happened next was up to the woman. Always. No matter how much her laughter and her hair and that never-still mouth of Joanna's was making him ache, the idea was to make her ache more, to force her into letting him know, in no uncertain terms, she was ready to take things to the next level.

He slowly walked around the studio, the only sounds his boot heels clunking against the cement floor, the dog's tags jangling when he sat down to scratch. He took in the kiva fireplace in one corner of the room, shelves crammed with more bins or completed Santas in various sizes, the cobwebbed exercise bike by one of the windows. He could feel her eyes on him. Good.

See, it was a helluva lot easier to break things off when the woman couldn't say, "But you started it." So, technically, Dale never started anything.

Not that you could prove in a court of law, anyway.

"This here's a great room," he said, then turned to see how well he was doing.

Why the hell was Dale still here?

And why the hell, since he *was* still here, hadn't he made a move yet?

And—here was the Big Question—why did she want him to?

"The studio's one of the main reasons I won't give up the house," she said, thinking how long it'd been since she'd kissed someone taller than she was. And how selfish it was of him to keep that fine mouth of his all to himself. "Since I spend most of my waking hours in here...."

And then there were those very nice hands. Which was a really dangerous path to go down. Because she knew full well if he touched any number of her body parts that liked to be touched, she was doomed.

"...and I love how it's both part of the house and yet separate from it. My grandfather built this for my grandmother, who fancied herself another Georgia O'Keefe..."

Because she really didn't want to sleep with him. At least, not until she'd gotten a little more used to the idea of bringing her body out of retirement.

"Oh, yeah? Was she any good?"

"Depends on your definition of 'good.' I don't think she much cared whether she was or not. Or what anyone else thought. She just loved to paint. And my grandfather did everything in his power to ensure she got to." She nodded toward the far wall. "That's one of hers over there."

Dale turned to look at the painting—affording her a very nice view of a very nice butt—an explosion of color that, if you squinted, sort of looked like either a bouquet or the Sandias at sunset, Joanna had never quite been able to figure out which.

"It's really...bright."

Joanna laughed, hoping it sounded at least reasonably normal since she was having a really, really hard time concentrating on the conversation. "It's terrible. But I've got it in here for inspiration, not aesthetics. To remind me there's different ways of measuring success. And one of those is having the guts to do what you love, even if you're not very good at it.''

She could feel him studying her profile; need went merrily tramping across her traitorous skin. "But you *are* good at what you do.''

"Not at first, I wasn't. But if I'd given up just because my first few attempts looked like aliens…'' She took a step closer. He took a step away.

Again.

Okay, this was really beginning to tick her off. She wasn't imagining the heat in those blue eyes that, dammit, was making her hair stand on end. Yet every time she got close, he moved back. Just as he had earlier, over coffee, whenever she'd gotten tired of blabbing about herself and so had decided, for amusement's sake, to try poking around for a hidden panel that would lead her to the Inner Dale. But despite everything she'd heard about men getting off on talking about themselves, Dale had neatly steered her away, every single time.

Well, to hell with that. If he didn't want to talk about himself, fine. And damned if she was going to play the part of the desperate, sex-starved divorcée. Nobody'd twisted his arm to make him stay. If she was making him uncomfortable, he could leave.

But he hadn't, had he?

He slid onto a stool in front of a half-dressed grinning Santa. "This one of mine?''

"Maybe.'' At his questioning look, she said, "I've got a big show coming up right after Thanksgiving, so I'm making a whole slew of new things. When I'm done, I'll decide which ones are yours.''

"You care if I touch it?''

"Go ahead. It won't break.''

Neither will I, she thought, wondering why the heck they didn't give out updated rule books with the divorce papers.

Judging from the color in Joanna's cheeks, Dale surmised she was on the verge of either doing or saying something that would decide things one way or the other. He was only giving it another five minutes, though, since he wasn't sure how much longer he could hold out himself. As it was, his fingertips tingled up a storm as they followed the contours of the wrinkled Santa face, as he imagined Joanna's hands transforming the lifeless molding material into something so real-looking, Dale half expected it to tell him to quit messing with him.

He could imagine those fingers bringing him to life again, too. He'd been watching her hands all evening—well, when he wasn't looking at her hair or her mouth or her fanny—the way they never stopped moving when she was talking, the fingers slender and strong, no fingernails to leave marks on a man's back...even as they'd set a man's skin on fire, he bet.

"You make any money at these shows?"

He heard her sigh as she leaned her elbows on the table next to him, fiddling with a spool of silver trim. He caught her scent this time, an interesting mix of flowers and grilled hamburgers. And that certain something a woman gives off when she's aroused. Or getting there. "I can pull in half the year's profits with a really good show."

"And with a bad show?"

She turned to him, propping her chin in her palm, and grinned. "There are no bad shows."

Unless his radar was on the blink, one more move should just about do it. So he got up from the table and walked over to a set of what looked like architect's drawers. "What's in here?"

She took a little too long to answer. "It's easier to let you look than try to explain," she said stiffly.

Dale opened the drawers, which were filled with...stuff. Miniature toys. Odd scraps of lace and fabric. Fake jewels and buttons. Tiny wooden cutouts and beads. Feathers.

"Sometimes, being a pack rat isn't a bad thing," she said. He turned to her, snagging her gaze in his, watching the rise and fall of those cute little breasts underneath the soft sweater and mentally swearing at her for taking so damn long to take the bait. So here he stood, trying to look interested while she went on about how sculpting the faces and trimming the costumes were her two favorite parts of the process, about how she'd incorporate the customer's own fabrics into the doll if that's what they wanted, and just hearing the word *want* coming out of her mouth nearly melted his brain.

But he stood his ground. He was nothing if not patient.

And still she kept talking, faster and faster, something about this customer who'd wanted Joanna to use some of her dead husband's silk ties in her Santa's costume, only the roaring in Dale's ears had grown so loud, he barely heard what she was saying.

Then suddenly it was absolutely silent.

"Something wrong?" he said.

"Yeah," she said. "You."

"Me?"

"Oh, cut the crap, Dale. You've been watching me like a half-starved dog at a T-bone steak all night. But every time I get close to you, you move away. Why?"

It took everything he had in him not to smile.

Chapter 8

Joanna watched Dale amble back around the table, a smile playing across his mouth, and she thought, *Uh-huh. Just as I thought.* He stopped within easy touching distance, drawling, "I'm sure I have no idea what you're talking about."

"Sure you do," she said, deliberately stuffing her hands into her pockets, even though what she really wanted to do was to rip his shirt open and drag her hands across his chest. And how cheesy was that? But if it was one thing Joanna did not do, it was lie to herself. At least not on a regular basis. "You're deliberately provoking me."

"To do what?"

"See, that's the part I'm not real clear on."

He chuckled and stepped closer, his body heat practically shimmering off him. "I'm not backing away now."

Her butt bumped the edge of the desk. "I can see that."

"But just for the sake of argument, let's say I had been. Why was that bothering you? After all..." His next step brought their pelvises within nodding distance of each other, his breath close enough to graze her hairline. "I wasn't even supposed to be here by now."

"Yes, about that—" Something fell over behind her; she brushed it aside and somehow found herself sliding up onto the desk as Dale slipped neatly between her legs. She grabbed his shoulders to keep from toppling over. "Whatever happened to that twenty-minute thing, anyway?"

"I never have been real good at keeping track of time."

Oh, hell—another one? she thought at the very moment she realized his little maneuver had effectively trapped her. And since her only means of escape meant whacking Dale in the crotch as she swung her leg around...

"And then I thought," he said, "since you were giving me some pretty heavy-duty, dog-and-steak looks, too—"

"I was not!"

"—that maybe you'd changed your mind about jumping my bones."

So much for thinking she was being subtle. "And I suppose you were hoping I would?"

"Never said that."

"So...you were hoping I *wouldn't?*"

"Never said that, either."

Joanna shut her eyes again until the dizziness passed— no mean feat considering how good he smelled—remembering exactly why she hadn't bothered jump-starting her woebegone love life before this. She'd forgotten just how much energy it took.

And right now, most of that energy was gathering strength in a small, vital area between her legs.

"So. Are you saying you want to...?"

"Only if you want to," he said.

Not, she noted, *I want you so badly my teeth ache.* Or even a simple, *You bet your ass, sweetheart.* Either would have done nicely. Even so, however much she might be out of the loop, for damn sure she wasn't out of her depth.

"Does this mean we've changed our minds?"

"I won't tell if you won't," he said.

She shoved him aside—it was easier than she'd expected it to be, which she found mildly disheartening—and stomped toward the door. "Don't do me any favors," she muttered, thoroughly disgusted with, well, basically everything. Then a pair of hands grabbed her shoulders and twisted her around, and a hard, unyielding—but extremely talented—mouth fused to hers, and Dale kissed her in a way she hadn't been kissed in a very long time. The thought, *Yee-hah, I won!* whooshed through her.

Of course, *what* she'd won remained to be seen, especially considering the fierce look in his eyes when he broke the kiss.

"Trust me," he said in a low voice, "if we do this, the favor will be mutual."

When her heartbeat shifted down to something she could at least hear over, she said, "I see. So…what happened to going away and thinking about where we wanted to take this?"

"I'm done thinking. Your bed sounds as good a place to take this as any. Or right here might be fun."

Oh, dear Lord. Flashback to those long-forgotten days when any place you could manage it was fair game and locked doors were strictly optional…and then she tried to remember when she'd last changed her sheets and exactly what underwear she had on and thank *God* she'd passed up the onions at the party—

"Joanna? I appreciate that this is sort of a big step for you and all, but if you could get back to me on this sometime before I'm too old to care, I'd be real grateful."

She looked at him, thinking, *My first gap guy.* It was a landmark moment—

"*Joanna!* For the love of God—"

"Okay," she said, clinging to his shirt, really wishing he'd kiss her again so her brain would disengage and her body would take over, thus relieving her of any accountability for her actions. "I can do this."

"Oh, from the way you kissed, I have no doubt you can do this." He bent at the knees and looked into her eyes, and she saw a surprising amount of genuine concern mixed in with the heat. "The question is...do you want to?"

She nodded. "Except—"

"Oh, sweet Jesus—what *now?*"

"Well, I've never in my life slept with a stranger. I mean, you already know more about my life than my mother does, but I know virtually nothing about you."

His eyes narrowed. "You saying you won't have sex with me until you get to know me better?"

"That's about the size of it, yeah."

"Okay," he said wearily. "How's about, since it's real late and all, you ask me questions or something while we're working up to getting naked?"

"Kiss me again and I'll let you know."

So he did, one of those numbers that connected straight to her groin. Deep and thorough but not sloppy—he racked up mega points with that one—and within, oh, ten seconds, she wanted to crawl inside his skin.

"You're on," she whispered on a pant, and he grabbed her hand and hauled her down the hall, unbuttoning his shirt one-handed as assorted animals scrambled to get out of their way. Except halfway there, she came to a dead stop.

"Damn."

His look said his patience was clearly nearing its limit.

"Birth control," she said, pushing aside the sound of Karleen's cackle inside her head. "As in, I'm not on it."

"Not a problem," Dale said on what sounded like a relieved puff of air. "That naked, I'm not planning on getting."

She stopped again. "And if you think I'm going to do

this with some condom you've been carrying around in your wallet for God knows how long—''

"Lord Almighty, woman, no wonder you don't date much. I'm not an idiot, Joanna. And you can be damn sure I'm not gonna take any unnecessary chances when it comes to making babies." He grabbed her by the hand again, tugging her to the end of the hall. "This it?" he said at the doorway to her bedroom, a large addition tacked on to the original house some twenty years before.

As if in a dream, she blinked at the troweled walls and French doors leading to a private patio she'd seen every day for the last ten years, the antique Log Cabin quilt flung over the pine poster bed, the toy trucks and Lego and action figures scattered hither and thither over the scarred wooden floor, the towers of books—hers and the kids'—teetering on her nightstand.

"Yep, this is it," she said, wondering if her children's debris lurking in every corner might make it just a wee bit harder to banish them from her mind while she and Dale were—

He kissed her again, softly, his hands threaded through her hair, and then he was discarding his shirt and she thought, okay, maybe she could be persuaded to forget her kids. For a minute or two, anyway.

"You're shaking."

"No I'm not."

He frowned at her, his balled-up shirt clutched in one hand.

"Stage fright," she said. "I used to get like this when I did plays in high school. But I'd be fine once I was on stage."

One eyebrow lifted. "You want an audience?"

"No." She took a deep breath, releasing her inner goddess or whatever the hell it was called. "What I want is an orgasm. A five-alarm screamer, if at all possible. Preferably penis-induced."

One side of his mouth lifted. "Why limit your options?"

Oh, boy. "I'm not. That one just tops the list."

"Okay." Dale tossed the shirt on a nearby chair, then sat on the edge of her bed, removing one boot. "But I've got a condition, too."

"Oh?"

"Yep." He carefully set the boot to one side, started on the second one. "Once we get started, you can't change your mind."

"Hey. I thought a gentleman always gave the lady the option to change her mind, anytime along the way."

"Well, that might be true, except for two things. One—" he grunted a little getting the second boot off "—I never said I was a gentleman. And two—" he removed his socks, dropping them beside the boots "—I'm in no mood to be working at cross purposes." He stood, unzipped his pants, then pushed them and his briefs down at the same time. Economy of motion was a beautiful thing. "If you want an orgasm—although why you'd only want one is beyond me—I'll be more than happy to oblige. But that requires a certain…commitment on my part. You deciding to opt out halfway through is liable to tick me off, if you see where I'm going with this."

His comment only half registered, what with her being a trifle distracted by…things. If her excellent peripheral vision could be trusted.

"Oh. Yes. I suppose you do have a…uh, point."

She toed off her sneakers. Then stood there, rooted to the spot. Not staring. Dale sighed.

"Honey, I'm not sure my telepathic powers are sufficiently developed for me to give you that orgasm from clear across the room." He held out his hand. And grinned. "Come here."

So she did, somehow, feeling oddly like a sacrificial virgin despite the fact that virginity was but a distant memory.

She hadn't been exactly inexperienced *before* Bobby, a fact that she hoped to hell her mother never found out.

And being a mom herself definitely put things in a different perspective. Just the thought of some of her college escapades made her shudder....

"Okay," Dale said, tilting up her chin with his knuckle, his other hand teasing the hem of her sweater. "Ask. Now." His touch sent little shivers over her skin as he began to slide her sweater up, past her waist, her ribs... "Or forfeit your part of the agreement."

It took a second to click back in. "Oh, right..." *Think, think...* "Who's your favorite writer?"

"I don't really read—lift your arms, honey, that's it—all that much, so I'll pass. Black lace?" he said, but her head got lost in the sweater as he lifted it off, so her, "You wanna make something of it?" came out more like "Oounnaakeumfinovit?" and then there was light again and her sweater was sailing, and she was trying not to think too hard about his not-reading comment or why she seemed to be losing her grasp on her arousal.

"Okay. Um...what's your favorite—" he unsnapped her bra "—music?"

"Country," he said, skimming her bra straps down her arms, and she was thinking maybe they should go back to kissing or something because it sure felt as though steps were missing here. "Anything else gives me a headache. Hey. You're not nearly as puny as I thought."

"You're not real big on flattery, are, uh, you?"

"Not really, no," he admitted, but he'd gotten to his knees in front of her, palming her breasts as he kissed her stomach, and then he'd pulled her toward him to take one nipple in his hot, hot, hot mouth and things started to crank up again quite nicely, and, mmm, yeah, some things, a woman can do for herself, but this was not one of them...

Oh, hell. Just moan already.

"Favorite...time... of year," she got out as Dale did this

thing with his tongue that immediately catapulted him into the Foreplay Hall of Fame.

"Fall," he murmured, moving back down to her stomach. Which she was holding in for dear life while trying to will the stretch marks invisible.

"Mine...too," she said as he unsnapped her jeans, trailing kisses down her tummy as the zipper gave way.

"Your panties don't match," he said, putting a little more effort into getting her jeans down over her hips than a girl would like.

"Do you care?"

"Not a whole lot, no. Step out."

She did, then he kissed her, through her panties, and it was everything she could do to get out, "Favorite ice cream flavor?"

"Honey, they don't make the flavor I'm thinking about right now."

She heard her own startled laughter, and then they were at the bed and he was yanking back the covers and she was asking, "Political affiliation?"

"I tend to vote for whichever candidate pisses me off the least," he said as they tumbled onto the mattress in a tangle of arms and legs and kisses—

Joanna yelped, then reached underneath her to pull out the very Matchbox car Matt had been pitching a fit about not being able to find this morning, much more annoyed at feeling things slip away again than she was about the bruise she'd have the next day. The jettisoned vehicle clattered onto the bare floor, scaring a cat; Dale straddled her, thumbing her nipples so gently she sighed.

"F-favorite food?" she said, letting her eyes drift closed. Okay, this was good, this should do it, just a little more and...

"Anything I don't have to cook."

On another laugh, she opened her eyes again, seeing something in his that made her catch her breath, something undefined and yet sharp enough to lance through his what-me?-give-a-damn? veneer.

She grabbed his shoulders and pulled him down to her, wrapping herself around him, kissing his mouth, his face, his neck, whispering, "And just how often do you change those supplies in your wallet?"

The question sounded odd, she *felt* odd, not in her body somehow, even as he kissed her mouth, her face, her neck, whispering, "I tend to throw out a lot more than I use. But, shoot, honey—" more kisses, more stroking "—I've barely gotten started. You sure you're ready?"

"Yes," she said, because she really thought she was, or at least should be, even as she willed her body to *Get back here, now!* while he did what he needed to do and then returned to her, kissing her mouth to mouth and tongue to tongue, but not soul to soul because they were strangers and *this* was strange, this man she didn't know suckling and touching and stroking and doing things that by rights should have long since sent that inner goddess over the edge.

Frustration fueled her moans, then, although Dale wouldn't know it, how could he, he didn't know *her*...and she arched her back to bring her breast to his mouth, her pelvis to meet his searching fingers, desperately, desperately trying to squelch the qualms screaming, *But you don't do this kind of thing!*

The anticipation built, then faded, then built again and faded again, driving her crazy like the kids playing hide-and-seek at bedtime. She cried out, angry that scruples or whatever the hell this was should try to take this away from her, that women all over the world could hit the hay and have a grand old time without giving it a second thought, angrier still that Dale was so gentle and thorough and talented and they were both wasting their time.

And then she reached that point where a woman knows it ain't gonna happen, no matter what her partner does or how much she wants it, and since she couldn't get up and leave her body behind to go through the motions without her, she let him lift her hips and slide into her—slowly, thank goodness, three years was a long time—and basically gave up.

"What's wrong?" he whispered, and all she could do was shake her head, her eyes shut against frustrated tears.

He withdrew, taking a different approach, his lips and tongue soft on her stomach, her inner thighs, on that spot where, usually, results were pretty much guaranteed. And finally, *finally,* something flickered to life down there and she nearly cried out with gratitude that she hadn't died, that she was going to make it after all—which led to her having to banish an image of Mary Tyler Moore tossing her hat in the air—and then Dale was kissing her again and positioning himself and...

She silently wailed, a keening *Noooooo* as the flicker went *pffft* like a candle that hadn't really caught. But it was too late, he was inside and no way was she gonna stop him this time because that would just be mean. But she gave it the old college try, boy, shifting and wriggling and repositioning her legs, and once or twice, she felt something twitch, but then it died out for good and she just let Dale finish, getting nothing out of it herself except an acute case of regret.

Breathing hard, Dale hitched himself up onto his elbows, frowning into Joanna's eyes. "Where were you?"

With one hand, she shoved her hair off her face and said, "Cleveland?"

"Hold on a sec." Dale rolled away and took care of business, but by the time he'd turned back, fully intending to take care of *her,* she was out of bed and in her robe and halfway out of the room.

"Get back here. I'm not done yet."

"Yes, you are."

Cursing, Dale hauled himself out of bed and into his jeans, muttering to the dog who'd strolled in and was now looking at him with an accusatory expression in his eyes. The sound of the refrigerator door slamming shut called him to the kitchen, where she was cutting herself a piece of the chocolate cake large enough to choke King Kong, tears streaming down her cheeks. Angry ones, if the way she was wielding that knife was any indication.

"Hey. You were close."

"Trust me. I wasn't."

"Uh-huh." He counted off on his fingers. "You were flushed, you were wet, your pupils damn near swallowed up your irises—"

"And yet, no cigar." She yanked back the kitchen chair and crashed down into it, shoveling in cake like she was afraid it would self-destruct. All that writhing had done a real number on her hair.

"Okay, fine. So you didn't come. It happens. It's hardly the end of the world."

"No, but I think we can pretty much deduce from my lack of reaction that…this—" she pointed back and forth between them with the fork "—isn't part of *my* world. Flings and things. I clearly can't do this. Either that, or I've forgotten how to have sex."

Dale folded his arms across his chest. "Because you didn't have an orgasm."

"I'd say that was a pretty good indicator, wouldn't you?"

"Jesus. And they say *men* are performance oriented." He got a plate out of the dishwasher, then sat at the table, hauling over the cake. "Give me the knife. Handle first."

She smacked it into his hand, then went back to inhaling her cake. Dale cut himself a piece—he'd've preferred the white instead of the chocolate, but this one was here—and forked in a bite, chewing for a second or two before saying, "You know what I think? I don't think you've forgotten how to have sex as much as you've just forgotten how to enjoy it, is all."

She snorted and shoveled in another bite with all the finesse of a four-year-old, smearing chocolate all over her mouth. It was about the sexiest thing Dale'd ever seen.

"Okay, new tactic." He took another bite while she regarded him warily from across the mangled cake. "You usually get off during sex?"

Her fork pinged against the plate. Then she nodded, the hair boinging around her face. "If memory serves," she said. Lord, she looked so miserable, Dale thought his insides would melt. Never mind that he thought she was nuts for overreacting like this.

"Then maybe you just weren't ready and I misread your signals," he said. "Maybe it wasn't all your fault. Maybe if you'd stuck around I could've done something about it."

"If I'd thought you could have done something about it, believe me, I would have stuck around. I'm not the suffer-in-silence type."

"So I noticed."

Those wide, honest, vulnerable eyes met his, just for a moment, and he thought, *What the hell am I doing here with this woman?*

"But what would have been the point?" she said. "By then, it would have been like having somebody else's climax. A surrogate orgasm," she finished on a snort. "Totally mechanical and goal-oriented."

"Better mechanical sex than no sex at all," Dale said.

"For some people, maybe. Heck, for most people, maybe. But not for me."

Dale got up and stomped over to the refrigerator, more mad about not being able to figure out why he was mad than anything else. "You got any milk?" he asked, opening it. Five full-gallon jugs stared back at him. "Guess that answers that question."

"Three kids go through a lot of milk," she said.

"Figures you'd buy that one percent crap, though."

"Deal with it," she said, another bite of cake vanishing into her mouth. Then she slammed down her fork and buried her face in her hands. "I just don't get it," she said, shaking her head. "I wanted this." She moved her hands to the sides of her face, grimacing at him. "I was actually pretty excited there for a while."

"I know," Dale said, sitting down with his milk. "I was there."

"But it didn't seem to matter what you did..." She let out a sigh. "Nothing. Okay, maybe not *nothing*," she added when he frowned. "But not enough."

"Thanks for the ego boost."

"You're welcome," she said, reaching for the knife again and wielding it over the cake as if it were an executioner's ax. Dale lunged for her wrist before she could deliver the death blow.

"Hey!"

"You don't need that," he said. "You probably don't even want that. And you're gonna go through all kinds of recrimination shit tomorrow if you eat it. So save everyone who knows you the grief and stop yourself now."

A beat or two passed before she dropped the knife and folded her arms across her chest. "I wasn't exactly dopey in love with Bobby at the end. But we could still...you know. In fact, if the sex hadn't been so good, I probably would have dumped him a long time before I did." She looked up at him, pure exasperation in her eyes.

His cake finished, and feeling a little exasperated himself, Dale leaned back in his chair, his hands braced against the edge of the table. "You know what your problem is?"

She snorted again.

"Not that. You were just havin' a bad night, is all that was. And you think too hard about stuff. Analyze it to death."

"And you're basing this on...?"

"Well, for starters, I can't recall the last time I had sex and then spent this much time talking about it afterward. I mean, either it works or it doesn't. And afterward most folks either enjoy the afterglow, or else they shrug it off and go about their business. But I will say that, in my experience, ninety percent of the time when it doesn't work, means one or both parties was tryin' too hard to make it happen."

That got a shrug. "Okay, so maybe I do have this thing about figuring why things do and don't work. That's not exactly a character fault."

"Didn't say it was. Unless it borders on being a hang-up."

"Okay, that's it." She stood, crossing her arms. "I think you need to leave now."

"Fine," he said, bolting out of the chair and down the hall to her bedroom, yanking on clothing once he got there as if the place was on fire. As he was buttoning his shirt, however, he glanced up to see her standing in the door, looking a lot more confused than ticked, and his own consternation ran out of steam.

"Joanna, all I'm saying is, you're being too hard on yourself, okay? And you're too tired to be making any decisions right now."

Her brows lifted. "Don't tell me you want to do this again."

"You bet your sweet ass I want to do it again. I was having a pretty good time in here—" he patted the bed, which the dog took as an invitation "—until you started thinking too hard and got left behind." He hesitated, then said, "I don't do forever. You know that. Which is fine since I don't meet your criteria for forever in any case. But I don't fool around with women I don't like. Or respect. Leastwise, not anymore," he added at her skeptical expression. Then he blew out a breath when the skeptical expression didn't ease up any. "You're not just a body to me, okay?"

"How could I be anything else, Dale?" she said, smirking. "We don't know each other. At this point, I'm not even all that sure we like each other."

"Then I guess you didn't hear me two seconds ago when I said I didn't fool around with women I *didn't* like. And don't ask me why because I don't know, okay?" He tugged on first one boot, then the other, then rubbed the dog's upturned belly. Goofiest-looking mutt he'd ever seen, that was for sure. "Some people I take to right off, and some I don't. You're one of the lucky ones. Now if that's not enough for you, that's okay. But if it is…well, I wouldn't mind the chance to help ease some of those worries you haul around with you all the time."

He fully expected her to deny those worries—most women did, in his experience—so he was more than a little surprised when all she said was, "So what you're saying is, I should think of you like Calgon?"

"What the hell's that?"

But she flapped her hand and said, "Oh, Lord, Dale. I don't know…."

He stood, the floorboards creaking as he crossed the room. Then he took hold of her shoulders and looked into her weary face, wondering why on earth he didn't just walk right out of her life and not give her, or her life, another thought.

Why the thought of leaving her was bothering him so much when leaving a woman had sure never bothered him before.

He kissed her chocolate-smeared mouth, long enough to make his point but not get too worked up, and she kissed him back, but not like she was interested in getting things going again. Not right then, anyway. "Think it over, darlin', and let me know. It's up to you. Now go on back to bed, before you fall over,'' he said, which got a little smile. ''I'll just let myself out.''

But he'd only gotten a few feet down the hall when she said, ''Dale?''

He turned back. She was leaning heavily against the door frame with her cheek propped on one hand, the expression in her eyes far more naked than her body had been a little while ago.

''As it happens,'' she said softly, ''I like you, too.''

He was nearly back to his condo before it hit him that no woman had ever said those words to him before.

Chapter 9

For the rest of the weekend the memory of Joanna's little escapade with Dale lingered like shreds of a bizarre dream. Which was what came, she supposed, from not having had any sex, bad or otherwise, in forever. And from having nothing to talk to but cats, dogs and Santa Clauses, her parents and Karleen all being busy. Oh, there had been Mr. Your-Dog-Knocked-Up-My-Dog across the road, who'd accosted her when she'd finally dragged her fanny out to check her mail on Saturday afternoon—a sojourn that only added to her agitation when she discovered Bobby's last child support check had bounced, which in turn made two of hers bounce—but he didn't count. In any case, while she carved and stuffed and stitched, she replayed what Dale had said and she had said over and over and over until who said what got all smushed together like week-old stew.

She'd thought about calling Dale, although God knew what she might have said. To apologize? Maybe. Not to take him up on his offer, though. That was out of the question.

Even though... After three days, that look on his face when she'd said she liked him, too, still haunted her, translating into an unfinished sentence that began *I need...*

But trying to finish that sentence was driving her nuts. What did Dale McConnaughy need that she could possibly give him? Considering how well things had *not* gone on Friday night, it sure wasn't sex. Besides, she imagined he could pretty much get that whenever he wanted, without expending the energy it took to flick off a fly. So what was it?

She had no idea.

What she did know, however, she thought as she finished cleaning the kitchen on Sunday night and caught a glimpse of the clock, was that she was going to strangle her ex-husband if he didn't get the kids home within the next few minutes. He was already two hours late.

And right on cue, the back door popped open and kids and ex blew in on a gust of chilly wind, nobody seeming the least bit concerned about the time or her mood. Except Dulcy, who whispered to her that she'd been nagging her father since six o'clock to bring them back since she had a Language assignment due the next morning that the teacher hadn't given them until Friday, which she hadn't taken with her to her father's house since she'd thought she'd have plenty of time to do it that night and now it was late and she was, like, *totally* screwed.

Joanna assured Dulcy it would be okay, asked her to run the boys' bath, sent all three children away and turned on their father, who was standing there with one of his whaddidIdo? looks on his face.

"Dammit," she said wearily as water started thundering into the hall bathtub. "You know you're supposed to have them back by seven at the latest so I can get the twins bathed and into bed on time. And Dulcy says she had an assignment, which means she's not going to get to bed on time, either."

"I know, I know, but I got tied up and time just got away from me. It won't happen again, I promise."

Joanna waited out the sensation of her temples trying to meet in the middle of her brain. "Is it so terrible of me to want our children to get a good night's sleep on a school night?"

"Of course not, Jo. Stop being so dramatic. And anyway, so how much are they gonna miss? Maybe an hour?"

"Fine. So how's about *you* come over and try getting them up for school tomorrow? Especially now that Ryder's got that before-school phonics class on Mondays. Or did you forget that, too?"

"Look, you want me to take him to school, I'll be glad to—"

"Oh, and like I can really count on you to remember."

"So call and remind me."

"Oh, for God's sake, Bobby! If I have to call you, what's the freakin' *point?*"

"And maybe if you'd stop being so negative, you know, maybe stop expectin' me to screw up all the time, I wouldn't keep doing this shit."

She sank onto the nearest bar stool and let her head fall forward on top of her folded arms.

"By the way," he said, "I got your message about the bounced check."

Her head felt full of lead pellets when she lifted it, fully prepared for the latest recital of excuses. Instead, he was holding out a wad of cash.

"I'm really, really sorry about that. I forgot to make the deposit, still had the damn thing in my coat pocket."

Jo took the money and counted it, then frowned. "What about the fees for bouncing my checks? That's another fifty bucks."

"Jesus, that's highway robbery," he said. But he peeled off three more bills. "There's another thirty. I gotta gas up the car tonight. I'll get the rest of it to you ASAP."

Right. "And…the roof money?"

"Soon, babe, soon. I promise," he said, going over to the fridge and getting a Coke. Huh. Usually he did this dump-the-kids-and-run number on Sunday nights. Especially if Joanna wanted to talk about money. "So—" he pulled back the tab, leaning against the counter "—you have a good weekend?"

Uh-oh. "Since when are you asking me about my weekend?"

"What? I can't express a little interest in how you're doing? You know I still worry about you."

"Worry about your kids getting a good night's sleep," she said. "Or the roof. And I worked all weekend, as usual."

"No…dates or anything?"

Joanna somehow managed not to squirm in her seat. Her ex-husband might have been clueless, but he wasn't stupid. Or blind, she thought, praying the flush now prickling her cheeks wasn't nearly as noticeable as it felt. Not that she had anything to feel guilty about. She was free to do what she wanted with whomever she wanted, the same as he was. She was also under no obligation to discuss her sex life, or lack thereof, with anyone. Especially with suddenly, and suspiciously, nosy ex-husbands. "What's this all about, Bobby?"

"Nothing," he said with a shrug. "Just curious. Like I said, it bothers me, you know, the way you never get out or anything."

"Well, you can stop worrying. I'm fine."

"It's not like you couldn't get a date," he went on, typically oblivious. "Hell, you still look pretty good, when you fix yourself up. And Joey Walsh still asks about you. I never did understand why you didn't go out with him again."

"Because Joey Walsh is a crass, self-centered bore who treats wait staff like dirt and belches in public?"

"Hey. That's no way to talk about one of my best friends."

"Bobby. After *I* left the poor waitress a thirty percent tip to make up for *your friend's* rudeness, and we went back to his car—with me already thinking the ride back here from the County Line was going to be the longest one of my life—*your friend* had his tongue down my throat and his hand on my boob before I got my seat belt latched."

Bobby paled. "Crap. What did you do?"

"Channeled Bette Davis and smacked him. Then I got out and called a taxi."

Unbidden, a more recent memory elbowed past this old, putrid one, of the heat mixed with tenderness mixed with yearning in Dale's eyes, and bells went off.

Okay, so maybe Dale McConnaughy didn't do forever. But neither was he the loner he wanted the world to believe he was, was he? Why he'd picked her, God only knew. But boy, she could sure relate. Because here she was, too, a forgotten, moldy leftover in the cold, miserable refrigerator of *looove*.

And if the Santa business didn't pan out, she could always hire out to write lyrics for country songs. Yech.

"How come you never told me about Joey?" Bobby said, jerking her back to the present.

She sighed. "Because he might be the most obnoxious creature on the face of the planet, but he's basically harmless. And because he's your friend."

Bobby's expression darkened. "*Was* my friend. But what about Sam Gonzalez? Or Jerry Keller?"

"You really want to know?"

"Damn, I'm sorry, Jo. I had no idea. I was just tryin' to help—"

"I know that, Bobby. But you need to take a good hard look at some of the people you hang out with. Or at least, stay out of the dating service business until you get in some new stock."

"Yeah, yeah, okay, fine...but all I'm sayin' is, you should take a break now and then, y'know?"

"I'll take that under advisement. But my social life is my business."

"Now that's not exactly true, because what affects you, affects my kids. So if you're seein' somebody, I wanna know about it."

"Excuse me? I don't exactly recall your asking for my approval when you started dating Tori. Or any of the many others who preceded her. I didn't ask who you were sleeping with, I expect the same courtesy from you."

The shock in his eyes made her day.

"Are you sayin' what I think you're saying, Jo?"

She huffed a sigh. "I was speaking theoretically, for God's sake. And unless and until theoretical leads to adding a stepfather to the picture, I have no intention of telling you a blessed thing. Why are you looking at me like that?"

"Just thinking it's been a long time since I saw the woman who knocked me off my feet all those years ago."

More bells went off. At this rate, she was gonna be deaf before the night was out. "Hey," she said. "Is everything okay?"

"With what?"

"I don't know. You tell me."

"Like you give a damn."

"Believe it or not, I do. Even though you drive me totally insane, I haven't forgotten the early days, either."

His smile was a little wistful. "They were good, huh?"

"Yeah, Bobby. For the most part, they were good."

"Then...what d'you think happened?"

"We simply weren't right for each other. That's all."

He looked at her for a long moment, his fingers tapping against the side of the aluminum can. "You think Tori and me are right for each other?"

She nearly fell off the stool. "That's not a question I can

answer," she said cautiously. "Even if I knew Tori better than I do. Bobby? Are you two—"

"Mo-om!" Ryder called from down the hall. "C'n we get out now?"

Joanna tore her gaze away from Bobby and yelled back, "Did you wash your hair?"

"Aw, do we gotta?"

"Just a minute, I'll be right there—"

"No, no, you stay put," Bobby said, already halfway to the door. "I'll take care of it."

"No, that's…" She caught herself, remembering a soaked Bobby giving the twins a bath when they were toddlers, the three of them laughing their heads off as Daddy splashed just as much as they did. She also remembered the twenty minutes it would take her to swab the bathroom floor when they were done.

"Go right ahead," she said. The floor could stand to be mopped, anyway.

And when had she started substituting memories for living?

Ten minutes later the boys padded out barefoot in their jammies to kiss her good-night, to tell her Dad was putting them to bed, and she thought, *Whoa—what the hell is going on?* The contrition for his perpetual and never-ending sins of neglect and forgetfulness was nothing new. But his hanging around, the reminiscences, his putting out feelers about him and Tori—not to mention her love life—his helping out with the kids…

Okay, this was weird. Even for Bobby.

She jumped a foot when he suddenly reappeared.

"I went ahead and checked on Dulcy after I put the boys to bed," he said, slipping his baseball jacket back on. "I gave her some ideas for that assignment. And I told her, next time, to bring her work with her, that it wasn't fair to burden you with all of it. By the way, I had Ryder read to me a couple of times, over the weekend. I think he's getting better, don't you?''

Who the hell are you and what did you do with my ex-husband?

"Jo? You okay?"

"What? Oh…yeah, I'm…" She pushed her hair off her face. "I'm fine. Just tired."

"Maybe you should try to get to bed earlier tonight. You really look beat."

"Yeah. Maybe I should."

"Well, call me if you need anything. 'Night."

After he let himself out, Joanna sat staring at the door as if she'd just been struck by lightning, the odds of which were only marginally lower than what had just happened.

Whatever that was.

First thing Bobby saw when he opened his front door was Tori, sitting all curled up on the sofa in a big fluffy robe and slippers, watching something on TV. Her laptop lay closed on the coffee table, a shiny blue acetate folder on top. She looked up, frowning slightly.

"You were gone a long time."

"Sorry. I stopped to get gas and ran into Tony Eggleston. You remember him from the dealership? Anyway…" Bobby threw his jacket across the back of the tub chair his folks had given him when they moved out to San Diego and sank beside her, swinging one arm over her shoulders. She smelled all sweet, like she'd just taken a bath. Hope stirred. "We got to talking and I guess I lost track of time. He got married, did you know that? Last April."

"You should have called," she said quietly, focused on her program. "I was beginning to get worried."

"I'm sorry, sweetheart, you're right. I forgot." He hugged her to him and kissed the top of her head. "I'll remember next time. You get that paper done?"

After a moment she nodded, then pointed the remote at

the TV and clicked it off. "Well?" she said, twisting around to look at him, her curiosity apparently outweighing her irritation. "Did Joanna say anything?"

"Are you kidding? Not even when I gave her an opening. Of course, she doesn't know I saw his car there on Friday night when we left."

Tori relaxed into him. "That doesn't mean he stayed."

"No. But why else would he have come back? But I didn't figure it would hurt to play around with Plan B."

She tensed slightly. "And?"

He chuckled, even though the last thing he felt like doing was laughing. "She looked like she'd just landed in Oz."

Tori slipped one hand underneath his sweater and gently raked her fingers over his stomach, making his muscles twitch. "What if it backfires, Bobby? What if she thinks you really are putting out feelers about getting back together?"

The uncertainty in her voice tore at him, reminding him of how young she still was. Although he couldn't remember Joanna ever sounding like that. But then, Joanna had been born bossy. And since Miss Bossy would never in a million years take anybody's advice about anything, sometimes subterfuge was the only option. The way Bobby saw it, nothing would jump-start her own pathetic love life faster than thinking Bobby was interested in rekindling their relationship.

"Trust me, Joanna would rather drink used motor oil than get back together with me. Besides, I'm not *saying* anything to give her that idea, okay? So I can always say she misunderstood." He hugged Tori closer, ignoring the slight panic that never seemed to fully go away these days. "I wouldn't do anything to jeopardize what we have, sweetheart. I promise."

And he meant that, panic or not. The jitters were perfectly normal, he told himself, especially considering everything else that was going on in his life. But the thing was, he'd felt good, watching that stymied look on Joanna's face. Remembering the good times, when good sex and carefully timed gifts were enough to keep him out of the doghouse. Or at least, to get him out of it.

And even though Joanna drove him batty, with her constant harping about his responsibilities like he was a kid or something, that somehow everything bad that happened was his fault, he still admired her. She was a terrific mother, for one thing. And talented as all get-out. And he'd never seen anyone who could focus on something the way she could. That first year, she'd made peanuts from those Santas of hers. Two years later, she was earning enough to throw him out.

Well, okay, she didn't really throw him out. The divorce had been a mutual decision. But still—

"Hey. You up there," Tori whispered, cupping his face in her palm. "Where'd you go?"

He smiled down into her eyes, the panic subsiding somewhat in the face of all that trust and love and adoration. "I'm right here, honey." He kissed her, his erection going from zero to sixty in less than three seconds, then palmed her still-flat belly, where a new little life had taken root. *His* new life.

"I take it you're feeling better?" he asked, praying he didn't sound as desperate as he felt.

She smiled and let her hand drift south again. To, oh, about Florida, where things were hot and steamy. "I'm feeling just fine. But if you'd like to make me feel better, I wouldn't argue."

Grinning, Bobby kissed her again, banishing all thoughts of ex-wives and other annoyances. But just as things started getting interesting, he realized he'd forgotten to mention that he'd invited Tony Eggleston and his new wife over for dinner tomorrow night.

No matter. He'd tell Tori later. And anyway, unlike

Joanna, Tori'd always been cool with his bringing people home on the spur of the moment.

Hormones, that's all this was, Tori thought as she parked her aphid-green VW Bug in the driveway behind her mother's almost-new Honda Accord. Why else would she be feeling so on edge all the time? She hadn't meant to yell at Bobby for not telling her he'd invited those people over for dinner, but she'd had a rotten day at work and she was tired and she'd planned on going to the library, and then he'd shown up with company...well, it had just snapped her last nerve, is what. Oh, she'd held it in until after they'd left, but then she'd really let him have it.

Only then she'd felt bad, because Bobby had looked so awful and unhappy that he'd screwed up, and she knew he didn't mean to be so forgetful all the time, but honestly. Sometimes Tori wondered how the man had managed to survive as long as he had.

It was enough to drive a girl home to mother. Well, not home, exactly—the boxy ranch house in front of her belonged to her mother's new husband, Leo. In only a few months, Tori could already see her mother's influence, from the freshly painted dusty-blue shutters against the brickwork, to the clay pots filled with gold and rust and white chrysanthemums nestled here and there among the expanse of shade-dappled crushed white rock that made up the front yard, to the pretty little wind chime hanging by the front door.

She could just feel her mother's pride, having that house. Even one with a moonscape for a front yard. Leo had already put her mother's name on the deed—with his grown children's blessings, too—so if something should happen to him, she'd have a place to live in for the rest of her life, if she wanted.

Despite her own bad mood, Tori smiled: Mama had for sure gotten a good man this time, bless her heart. And nobody deserved it more. Growing up, Tori had gotten used to frequent upheavals in her life as her mother changed jobs, changed men, changed addresses...changed her ideas about what would be best for Tori and her. For the most part, though, each change had represented a step up, even if only a tiny one, so Tori learned early on not to regret leaving something that wasn't worth regretting to begin with. And as she grew older, she understood more and more how much her mother had overcome to get as far as she had.

So this house, and the man who came with it, represented a major victory for Edith Thompkins Medina—her maiden name and Leo's being the only two last names she currently used—an undereducated alcoholic who'd followed Tori's father to Albuquerque from Dallas only to dump him when she found out about the other women in his life. A woman with the courage to overcome an addiction that had robbed her of nearly two decades of her life.

Feeling almost ashamed of her current state of disgruntlement, Tori got out of the car, dragging a big Target shopping bag behind her. What was left of the ash tree's lemon-yellow leaves glowed in the late afternoon sun, vibrant against the cloudless blue sky. The front door wasn't locked, as usual for this time of day. An attendance secretary at one of the nearby high schools, Mama was usually home by three-thirty at the latest.

The combined scents of fire smoke, pot roast and Summer Breeze air freshener, just like Tori used, tickled her nose when she went inside. Like the outside, the interior was already beginning to reflect her mother's taste—a new pastel floral slipcover on the couch, a pretty fabric flower arrangement in pinks and soft blues on the glass-topped coffee table, the houseplants her mother had carted from apartment to apartment over the years. But nothing to announce she'd taken over the house. Mama respected the life Leo had shared with his first wife, who'd died of cancer five years before. And she was not the kind of woman to demand a man give up his memories, especially good ones.

"Mama? You home?"

Looking neat as always in a pair of beige pull-on pants and a rainbow-striped cotton sweater—her mother could not abide blue jeans, although she said she didn't mind if Tori wore them—Mama came around the corner from the kitchen, a smile on her carefully made-up face, her arms outstretched.

"Well, isn't this a nice surprise!" she said, pulling Tori into a hug. Then she held her away, curiosity glimmering in her pale blue eyes. She'd recently lightened and chopped off her shoulder-length dark blond waves, into a short, feathery style that softened otherwise pretty features made haggard from years of worry, overwork and alcohol. Tori thought it looked real nice, but she was still having some trouble getting used to it. "But why aren't you at work?"

"It's one of my school days, remember? But the class was canceled, anyway, so I thought I'd come visit with you for a bit." She held up the Target bag. "I bought you something. For the house."

Mama took the bag from her and peeked inside. "Oh, my goodness—isn't that beautiful!" Beaming, she removed the small, ornately decorated carousel music box from the bag. Ever since Tori could remember, her mother had been crazy for carousels. "I know exactly where I'm going to put it. Thank you, sugar! And it just so happens I've got something for you, too. I was going to bring it over later in the week, but since you're here…" She grinned, then motioned for Tori to sit. "Just wait here. I'll be right back."

The tiny woman scurried off only to return a few seconds later with a fair-size Mervyn's box. "I hope you don't mind that I went ahead and did this, but they were having this big sale and I'm afraid I kinda lost my head. Go ahead, open it."

Tori did, only to let out a small "Oh" at the array of tiny blankets and hooded towels and little sleepers and booties and undershirts inside.

"I got everything in yellows and greens, since we don't know what it is yet." When Tori couldn't say anything at first, her emotions clogging her throat, her mother said, "Oh, no…you're mad at me, aren't you?"

"Of course not," she said, leaning over to give her mother a hug. "It's just…so early yet, you kinda caught me off guard, that's all. My goodness…" She stroked a fingertip over a delicately woven baby blanket, white as snow, then held up a tiny pair of white satin shoes, still in their box. "Everything's so…tiny."

"I know. Hard to believe you were that size, once upon a time. I think this one's my favorite," she said, pulling an itty-bitty sleeper with teddy bears all over it out of the pile. "So…you and Bobby set a wedding date yet?"

The floodgates opened.

"Honey! Ohmigosh!" Her mother pulled her into her arms, patting her hair. "What is it, baby?"

"H-hormones," Tori managed to choke out, but her mother took her by the shoulders and looked into her eyes, her mouth turned down at the corners.

"And?"

"A-and everything's just happening so fast."

"And?"

Tori managed a little gurgly laugh, wiping her tears away with the heel of her hand. "That's not enough?"

"You never could lie to me," Mama said. "And you're doing a piss poor job of it now." She frowned. "Bobby been treating you okay?"

At that, everything spilled out, about how in spite of her loving Bobby more than anything, there were all these…little things he did that were driving her crazy, and she kept thinking she should just keep her mouth shut, not make trouble. Otherwise, she was scared to death she'd drive him away. Just like Joanna had.

"His first wife?" Mama asked.

Tori nodded.

Mama handed her a tissue, set the box of baby clothes on the coffee table, then went to the kitchen. A few minutes later she returned with a cup of peppermint tea, like she used to do when Tori was little and Mama would let her stay up past her bedtime and they'd watch a movie together, waiting—often in vain—for Tori's father to get home.

"Now," her mother said after Tori had taken several sips of the tea, "start at the beginning."

So she did, going on about how Bobby could never seem to remember anything, such as calling her when he was going to be late or telling her about something the kids needed—which would then get her in trouble with Joanna—or, like last night, not bothering to tell her he'd invited this couple over for dinner.

"And there I was with a panful of Tuna Helper!"

"What did you do?"

She smirked. "Threw together a salad and tried not to look embarrassed. But it was so...*lame.*"

"I'm sure it was fine. But did you say anything to Bobby later?"

"Of course I did. And like always, he just about wet himself apologizing and saying it would never happen again. And then..." She blushed.

"He made love to you and suddenly you didn't care anymore."

Tori nodded. Mama sighed. "Oh, yeah. I know how that goes." Then she picked up Tori's left hand. Fingering the engagement ring Tori had shown to her over the weekend, her mother said, very gently, "You having regrets?"

"No!" she said. Too quickly. "I love Bobby. And I know he loves me. He's nothing like—" She ducked her head, staring hard at her tea.

"Nothing like any of the bozos I kept bringing home."

"I don't mean to sound like I'm criticizing you—"

"What it sounds like, is that you learned a thing or two from my mistakes. And thank God for that. You've got a lot more on the ball at twenty-one than I sure did," Mama said on a sigh. "And from what I've seen, I don't doubt that Bobby loves you. He just needs a little fine-tuning, is all. Like they all do," she added with a soft laugh. She settled back into the corner of the sofa, her arms crossed over her middle. "But what's really bothering you is Joanna, isn't it? That you keep feeling like there's an extra person in your relationship."

Tori let out a long sigh. "I can tell Bobby feels like he's being pulled in two different directions. Except I don't feel like he's the one in the middle." She met her mother's gaze. "I feel like I am."

"Which you knew going in."

"Knowing something isn't the same as understanding what it means. I even...well, I kinda put a bug in Bobby's ear about how maybe if Joanna had someone else to turn to other than him all the time, she wouldn't be so... clingy."

"Oh, Tori...you didn't!" Mama laughed. "You of all people should know life doesn't work that way."

"I do know that. And actually, as soon as I made the suggestion I realized how dumb it was. Except before I could call Bobby off, there he was trying to fix her up with some ex-baseball player, of all things. Dale...Mc Something, I can never remember his name. That pitcher for the Braves you used to be so crazy about?"

"He's...he's here in Albuquerque?"

Tori laughed. Her mother sounded about the way Tori would if Brad Pitt walked into her Title Company one day to close on a house. "Can you believe it? Turns out he owns the toy store the boys' swing set came from." She went to take another sip of her tea, only to realize it was gone the same time her mother did.

"Here, honey, let me get you some more—"

"Oh, no, that's okay—"

But her mother had taken her cup and was gone. Feeling a little revived for having unburdened herself, Tori got up and walked over to the fireplace, surveying the photographs on the mantel. Mostly Leo's first wife and children, she guessed. "So what was his name?" she called to her mother, still in the kitchen.

"Who?"

"That baseball player. It's driving me nuts that I can't think of it."

She heard the microwave ding. "Dale McConnaughy," came the reply over the soft clanging of a spoon against earthenware.

"That's right. McConnaughy. Thanks," she said when her mother returned. "He's even better-looking in person than he is on TV." At her mother's odd look, she laughed. "I didn't get struck blind when I got engaged, you know."

"No, no, it's not that...I'm just...you actually met him?"

Tori took a sip of the tea, then picked up one of the photos. "Yeah. He came himself to put up the swing set and Bobby just went on ahead and invited him to stay, bold as brass." She chuckled. "He may be forgetful, but one thing I'll say for him, he has no problems going after what he wants. Who's this?"

"What? Oh, Leo's oldest girl, June. When she graduated from college. And that one there's of his boy Steven, taken last year. Imagine that...Dale McConnaughy here in Albuquerque." She nudged Tori. "He as *skinny* in person as he is on TV?"

Tori laughed. "Actually, no. Although there's not a spare ounce of fat anywhere, far as I could tell. And his eyes are bluer, too."

"Was he...nice?"

"He seemed to be, the little I was around him. And he got on great with all the kids."

"Well, that's good," her mother said, picking up the carousel Tori had brought and carrying it over to a display case on the other side of the room. "You know how you build up these images in your mind about what somebody might be like. Then there's nothing worse than finding they're turkeys in real life. This look okay here? I don't want it to get lost in the shadows."

"No, it's good. You really like it?"

Mama turned to her, one of those sappy mother looks on her face. "Even if it wasn't beautiful, which it is, I'd love it anyway, just because you gave it to me." She crossed back to the sofa and picked up the empty Target bag, carefully folding it into quarters. She'd never known Mama to throw away a bag. "So where's this toy store of his? Oh, don't give me that look—you've got a baby coming, right? So what's wrong with grandma scoping out the toy possibilities?"

Tori laughed. "Mama, you are too much."

Her eyes twinkled. "Honey, trust me, if George Clooney opened a toy store here in town, I'd want to know where that was, too! You know, I've got enough food in that Crock-Pot to last Leo and me a week. Why don't I give you half of it, just in case that fool boy you're gonna marry decides to bring company home again tonight?"

Chapter 10

Knowing he had some major kissing up to do with Tori—and being big on killing as many birds with one stone as possible—Bobby took off from work a little early to go to Dale's store. Even though he had no idea what he would say or do once he got there. Or even, for that matter, if Dale would be working today.

But picking out something for the new baby gave him the perfect excuse to go to a toy store. And this one happened to be close to work. If he happened to find out anything about what was—or wasn't—going on between Dale and his ex-wife while he was there…well, that was just icing on the old cake.

And he'd bet his butt something was going on. Aside from seeing Dale's car at the house, there was Joanna's evasiveness when he'd questioned her the other night. Funny thing was, though, now that things looked like they might be falling into place exactly the way he'd hoped, he wasn't all that sure how he felt about it. About thinking of Joanna with another guy. If that's what was happening here.

And it might not be, he knew that, for any number of reasons.

Still, he had to know. Even if it wasn't any of his business.

He didn't see Dale's car parked out front, but the minute he walked inside he spotted his shaggy blond head darting back and forth in a forest of hanging monkeys and lemurs.

Momentarily distracted from his mission, Bobby slowly panned the store, almost unable to take it all in. He'd never seen so many toys crammed into such a small space. It was like walking into the playroom that every kid dreams of having, a combination of Santa's workshop and Planet Fun.

"See you tomorrow!" a middle-aged woman called to Dale, waving toward the back of the store as she hot-footed it out the front door, which whooshed shut, jarring the bell.

"Hey, Bobby…" He whipped around to see Dale grinning at him, a question or two lurking in his eyes. "What brings you here?"

Hoo-boy. "I thought it might be nice to surprise Tori with a gift for the baby. Women like that kind of stuff," he added with a smile.

Dale nearly choked when he saw Bobby Alvarez standing there, as if his wandering thoughts about Bobby's ex-wife had somehow conjured up the man. For five days the memory of Joanna's big green eyes had plagued him, in his dreams, at the store, at home in front of his computer, during meetings with manufacturers' reps and Web site designers and photographers as he prepared to launch Playing for Keeps into cyberspace in a major way.

If he didn't know better, he'd say he was smitten.

But he did. So he wasn't. Obsessed—a little—maybe. In any case, he figured he might as well get over it, since he pretty much figured she wasn't going to call. Not that he should be surprised—going after someone like her had been a long shot at best, even if he had kept enough brain cells functioning when they'd been in bed to realize he was losing her.

He glanced at Bobby, standing there with his hands stuffed in his pants' pockets as he looked around, and thought it must take a lot to keep from losing somebody like Joanna. Not that Dale wanted to keep her or anything.

"What did you have in mind?" he asked Bobby.

"I have no idea."

"Well, the baby toys are over along that wall. Why don't you give them a look-see? Of course, you can't go wrong with a stuffed animal."

Bobby nodded and wandered off, and Dale's thoughts wandered back to Joanna and how the idea of never seeing her again was sitting like a rock in his gut. And didn't that just beat all? There'd been women who'd come on to him, and women he'd gone after, and some he'd gotten, and some had told him to shove off. And he'd never had any regrets, one way or the other, not when the ones who'd said yes drifted out of his life, or when he'd been rejected outright. Oh, he'd felt like crap when his wife walked out, but that was more his ego taking it on the chin than anything else. Once she'd gone, he hadn't missed her nearly as much as he'd thought he would. But after only a few hours with Joanna…

Which was all the more reason to be just as glad she hadn't called and given him a second chance. Now he remembered why he didn't form attachments, especially to women: you can't miss what you never had.

Dale heard a whirring sound that told him Bobby was playing with the remote control construction vehicle set on display in the center of the store. A few seconds later, the dark-haired man returned to the counter.

"This is some place you got here. Makes me feel like a kid again, y'know?"

"That's the idea. After all, it's generally not the kids who buy the toys."

"Guess you got a point there. Most places, they're so, I dunno, impersonal or something." He drifted over to the floor-to-ceiling shelves filled with stuffed toys, chuckling as he picked up a two-foot-long anteater. "But I could stay in here for hours." He turned, squinting up at the dozens of monkeys hanging over Dale's head. "Hey, one of those might work. Tori's got a real thing for monkeys."

Dale got several down and spread them over the counter; Bobby took his time making his selection, finally settling on one of Dale's favorites, a gray rhesus with a startled look on its face, like it had just been goosed. But the monkey was the only thing Bobby seemed settled about, Dale thought as he rang up the sale.

"That's $25.40 with tax."

Bobby handed him a charge card, then leaned heavily against the counter, looking like a man who wanted to talk but didn't know what to say.

And Dale, for reasons he never clearly understood, had always been the one people talked to. Not that he ever had much to say back, although maybe that was the appeal—a person could spill their guts knowing Dale wouldn't come back with a bunch of advice they had no intention of following anyway. He'd learned enough about his teammates' personal lives to write one hell of an exposé, if he'd had a mind to. But to a man, they knew he wouldn't do that. Dale had never divulged a single secret to anybody about anything, not since he was a kid. So Bobby's intuition happened to be right on the mark in this case: Dale was a man folks could trust. Something, at least, he could justifiably be proud of.

But whatever Bobby wanted to get off his chest—and judging from the troubled look on his face, something was definitely eating at him—it was highly doubtful Dale wanted to hear about it. So he stuck the monkey in a plastic bag, handed Bobby his receipt to sign and played dumb. Only then Bobby said, "Tori and me, we had a fight," in that way most men did when they knew they'd screwed up, big-time, but couldn't for the life of them figure out why.

"So you're bringing her a monkey?"

Bobby pulled it out of the bag again, almost mimicking the thing's goofy expression. Then, grinning, he turned it around, its limbs flapping. "Tell me how she could possibly look at this and stay mad at me."

"And here all these years I thought flowers were the get-out-of-jail-free card of choice," Dale said.

"Oh, I'll get her flowers, too. I'm not stupid. That stupid, anyway." He stuffed the monkey back into the bag and rubbed the nape of his neck. "You'd think I'd know by now how touchy pregnant women got—"

The bell over the door jangled irritably as a harried-looking woman rushed in. "Are you still open?" she said, her eyes wide with panic.

"Sure are," Dale said. "Something I can help you with?"

"I forgot my daughter's got a birthday party to go to tonight! And it's for a boy!" she said on a near wail. "I have all girls! I have no idea what to get a boy!"

"That's easy," Bobby said with a shrug. "Wheels or weapons."

"Or anything gross," Dale added as the woman's horrified gaze *boinged* from Bobby to him.

"Absolutely. Especially if there's blood involved."

"I've got something even better than that." Dale pointed toward the back wall. "You see that slime-making kit over there?"

Bobby twisted around. The woman didn't.

"Oh, yeah, I see it." Bobby walked over and picked one up, making a face of approval as he checked it out. "This looks awesome."

"It is. I took one home and tried it myself. It's really great when you add green food coloring, so it looks like this huge ball of—"

"I think I'll stick with wheels," the poor woman said, looking like she couldn't get out of there fast enough. Dale reached up to yank down a package of six miniature construction vehicles from a hanging display over his head.

She didn't even look them over. "How much?"

"Six ninety-nine. And by the way," he said as she yanked a ten out of her wallet. "Boys also like building and construction sets, art stuff and puzzles—"

"Things that fly," Bobby added. Dale noticed he still had the slime kit in his hand.

"And dinosaurs. Just in case you have to buy something for a boy in the future."

The woman looked only marginally relieved. But on her way out, a fully furnished, four-foot-high Victorian dollhouse snagged her attention and Dale watched the way her whole expression changed, how the knotted muscles between her brows relaxed as she let out a soft "Oooh" of wonder. Then her gaze skittered around the store, from the display of Madame Alexander dolls to the shelves of brightly colored toddler toys, to the open, old-fashioned cupboard chock full of dress-up stuff, to the window seat crammed full of storybook characters—Madeleines and Peter Rabbits and the whole cast of Maurice Sendak's *Where the Wild Things Are*. She slowly picked up an Angelina Ballerina doll, all tulle and roses and satin, and smiled at the wide-eyed mouse face grinning back at her.

Then she hugged it to herself.

A second later she plopped it down in front of Dale. "I'll take this, too."

"For one of your girls?" Dale asked as she dug out her checkbook.

"Maybe," she said, her eyes sparkling.

Bobby chuckled after she left.

"What's so funny?"

"Just thinkin' that if I brought that doll home for Dulcy? She'd look at me like I'd left my brain someplace." He thunked the slime kit down on the counter. "She'd get much more of a kick out of this, believe me. So," he said, pulling out his credit card again, "you take things home to try 'em out?"

"Now and then," Dale said, thinking about the train sets and model cars and things that took up most of his apartment.

Bobby grinned, dumping the slime kit in the bag with the monkey. Dale wondered if Dulcy would ever see it. Especially when Bobby said, "Joanna always used to get on my case about playin' with the kids' toys more than they did."

"What about Tori?"

The grin collapsed. "We haven't gotten that far yet." Then he let out a huge sigh. "I used to think I understood women. But you know something? The older I get, the more I realize I don't know jack."

"I think God planned it that way on purpose," Dale said, walking over to the door to flip the Open sign to Closed. "Otherwise, what man in his right mind would get anywhere near 'em?"

"That's for sure." Still leaning on the counter and clearly not in a hurry to go anywhere, Bobby looked over at Dale. "But what's the alternative? Being lonely sucks."

Dale waited out the twinge around his heart and said, "Oh, I don't know. There's a lot to be said for never having to give up the remote."

Bobby wagged his head in a there-is-that gesture, then said, "You ever been married?"

"Once. Years ago."

"Bad breakup?"

"About average, I suppose." Then he walked over to the same construction set Bobby had been playing with earlier to rescue a couple pieces that had landed on the floor, unable to resist picking up one of the controls and setting things in motion. Bobby joined him.

"Damn thing's as bad as a video game," he said.

Dale nodded to his right. "There's another control over on your side, for the forklift. I can dump, you can pick it up."

"Cool."

They played in silence for a minute, then Bobby said, "You know, it really gets me the way women think they have the market cornered on feeling bad about stuff. Like we don't hurt, too, when a relationship goes sour." He made the forklift pick up a stack of logs Dale dumped out, then glanced over at Dale. "I'm not real interested in screwing up a second time. With Tori."

Dale had nothing to say to that. But he was picking up undercurrents to the conversation that were making his skin itch.

"And now that we've covered that ground," he said mildly, "you mind telling me why you're really here?"

After a moment Bobby blew out a sigh, then set down the control and shoved his hands back into his pockets. "Okay. I saw your car parked over by the stable when we left Friday night. So I was curious, y'know. About what was going on. Between you and Jo," he continued when Dale refused to react. "And…you're not gonna tell me, are you?"

Dale continued playing. "I went back to get my glove," he said. "Even so, setting aside your go-ahead to pursue her if I liked, it seems to me you gave up the right to pry into her personal life the minute you signed those divorce papers."

A second or two passed before the man smiled. "My own family's scattered all over the country, so Jo and the kids are the only family I've got. Well, and Tor, of course. I guess it's harder for me to let go than I thought."

"I can understand that," Dale said, but of course he didn't. Frankly he couldn't imagine feeling that attached to another human being. Nor did he want to. Sounded uncomfortable, to say the least.

Bobby walked back to the counter and picked up his bag. "Like I said, I'll always care about Jo. What happens to her. And I do want to see her happy. But how she gets there—and who she gets there with…I guess that's totally up to her, whether I like it or not."

"I certainly think the lady would appreciate that sentiment," Dale said, trying to keep his face from revealing too much.

"Damn," Bobby said, looking mildly stricken. "You don't suppose that means I might be growin' up, do you?"

"Happens to the best of us, I hear."

Bobby chuckled, then finally started for the front door. Before he got there, though, he turned and said, "Listen…me and a couple of other guys get together for poker once a month. Nothing heavy duty, just for fun, y'know? So I was wondering, if you weren't doing anything next Thursday…maybe you might like to join us? Unless you're good. If you are, I take back the invitation."

Dale was torn. On the one hand, it had been a long time since he'd been a part of something. With rare exception, the few real friendships he'd made while playing were beginning to fade like photographs left out in the sun. And he liked Bobby. It took a lot for a man to admit he was flawed, especially to another man.

But it was Bobby's very openness that challenged Dale to dig up a bunch of fears and doubts and feelings Dale didn't want to dig up. Because he knew if he dug too far, he ran a damn good chance of hitting the past, buried even deeper than the fears and the doubts and the feelings.

"I know how to play," he said at last, "but I don't know if I'd go any further than that."

Bobby's eyes lit up. "So you'll come?"

What were the alternatives? Another night alone in his condo, watching videos or going over the books or placing orders? Or hitting the bars, which he found even more meaningless than he had when he was younger?

It's just a lousy game of poker, for God's sake.

"Yeah," he said. "I'll come. You want me to bring anything?"

Bobby looked like a kid who'd just found out he was going to the circus. "A bag of chips or somethin' would be great. Or a six-pack, if you want. Somebody's sure to be a designated driver."

After scribbling his address and cell number on the back of a business card, Bobby left, looking much happier than when he'd come in.

"Well, that makes one of us," Dale mumbled, annoyed to discover some of those buried feelings had wormed their way to the surface anyway.

Not that he was *un*happy, exactly. He knew only too well what unhappy was. And it had been a long time since his life had qualified for that particular status. But if he were being honest with himself, he had to admit that this sense of being…unsettled, had been brewing for some time. Like what he imagined homesickness was, even though he'd never been homesick in his life. You gotta have a *home* for that to happen, he thought sourly. And none of the condos and apartments he'd lived in since his first stint in the minors even came close.

But there'd been times recently he'd been so lonely, he hurt. Not that it made a lick of sense—considering what he'd been through, especially with Meredith—but there it was. It was like nearly thirty years of looking only to himself had knotted inside him like some cold, black hole.

He'd only meant to protect himself. Not to hate what he'd let himself turn into.

An easy evening playing low-stakes poker would be good for him, he decided. Even if it meant possibly becoming closer to Joanna's ex-husband and all that potentially entailed.

Which, dammit, led to thoughts of wild, curly red hair and a gutsy green gaze that could jar a man's brain loose if he wasn't careful.

So maybe Dale was tired of being careful. *As* careful, anyway. And while he still wanted Joanna to make the next move, what could it hurt to jostle the pinball machine a little?

Dale found his attention meandering over to his window, all done up in pumpkins and skeletons and what-all for Halloween. Soon as that was over, though, it'd be time to set up his Christmas display. And what would be just the thing for the middle?

That's right. A Santa.

Still, as he closed out the two registers and prepared the bank bag, he knew deep down that what he was about to do had nothing to do with Santa Clauses. Or even sex, not really, although he wouldn't turn down the opportunity to make things up to her, should the occasion present itself. What he wanted right now, so badly he ached, was to see that three-cornered smile. Hear her laugh. Share the company of a woman who'd said *she liked him*.

Even if that meant venturing onto dangerous ground.

"'Do you…see the mon…mon…'"

The fire flickered in the studio fireplace as Joanna concentrated on the laugh lines in the face she was sculpting, waiting to see if Ryder could figure out the word on his own. She preferred to sit and cuddle with him during his reading time, but one of her customers had called this afternoon and asked if she could get her order a week earlier since her husband was suddenly being transferred back east and she didn't want to pay shipping charges if it was at all avoidable. Since no was clearly not part of Joanna's vocabulary, she'd agreed. Therefore, being Queen of the Multitaskers, she was running a load of laundry through the wash, keeping an eye on the clock so she could toss the cut-up potatoes into the stew at the right time, listening to her son read and—oh, yeah—*working*.

Polishing the stool seat with his butt, which Ryder tended to do whenever he got frustrated, he blew out a sigh and started the sentence over. For the third time. "'Do you see the mon...' It's too hard! I don't know what it is!"

Joanna glanced at the word. "What's the *s-t* sound?"

Ryder frowned, then looked over at her. *"Monster?"*

"See? You did know what it was!"

He gave her a holey smile, then continued. "'Do you see the m-monster with the gr...gr...'" He held the paper out to her.

"Great," she said. Sometimes it was easier to just give him the damn word.

"But I thought *e-a* made an *ee* sound?"

"Not in this case."

"That's dumb."

"You're right, it is," she said, frowning at the uncooperative face in her hands. Right now it looked more as if *Where's the Pepcid AC?* was going to come out of its mouth than *Ho, ho, ho.* A suspicious sound across the room caught her attention. "Hey, cat! Cut it out!" Joanna snatched up a wooden stuffing tool and lobbed it across the room at the cat who had decided the new bolt of red velvet standing on its side would make a perfect scratching post. The tool bounced off the fabric, a good foot over the cat's head, but close enough to send the beast flying across the room.

Ryder slammed his elbow onto the table and his head into his palm. "'Do you see the monster with the greet—'"

"Great."

"Mo-om! Don't tell me!"

"But you said the wrong—"

"Okay, okay, *great.* Jeez... 'Great big...nose? Color his...fur...blue.'"

God, this was torture. Although she wasn't sure which

one of them was suffering more. Joanna glanced over at the worksheet as Ryder picked out a blue marker to color the overly probosciscized monster's fur. There were a helluva lot of monsters to color. And they hadn't even started on his math worksheets yet.

But at least it took her mind off Dale, right?

"Mom!" Dulcy bellowed from the living room, making Joanna jump a foot. "That man's here!"

"Could we have something a little more specific?" Joanna yelled back.

"You know, the guy who was here for the birthday party?"

Ryder was gone in a flash, leaving Joanna sitting frozen on the stool, her heart ramming frantically against her ribs, like a bird trying to escape.

Then she came to with a little gasp, taking two seconds to brush most of the crud off the front of her sweatshirt. Somehow, though, she doubted that was sufficient to pass the fashionista litmus test, a fear confirmed by a glance in the smudged black glass of the upper oven as she zipped through the kitchen. She briefly considered hightailing it down the hall to change. Letting a man see you naked was one thing; letting him see you in the ratty lounge pajamas you only wore when you were doing laundry was something else entirely.

But, oh, well.

She was the last one to reach the front door, including the dog and two of the cats. Not that it mattered, since the boys were both chattering at him nonstop. Of course, had it occurred to any of them to let him in?

"Honestly, guys—don't leave the poor man standing outside..." Jo shoved assorted children and beasts out of the way so Dale could enter, commending herself for acting so blasé about the whole thing, a task made just a hair more difficult when he smiled at her and she remembered where his mouth had been the last time he'd been here.

"Hi…" she said, trying to send what-does-this-mean? signals over several dark-haired heads.

"Hey," he said softly, grinning as he took in her charming ensemble. He, natch, could have stepped right out of a Calvin Klein ad, with his perfectly broken-in jeans and his white cotton sweater and that leather jacket. He smelled like cold and fire smoke and leather and whatever aftershave he wore and where on earth did she get the idea that Friday night had just been a fluke? Maybe she hadn't made it to the finish line, but there wasn't a damn thing wrong with her engine.

"Nice pants," he said, the grin spreading.

Joanna rolled her eyes. "So," she chirped, her arms crossed over, hopefully, the worst of the stains. "What's up?"

"Well, actually, I came to ask a favor. About my order?" he said, and her heart stopped its desperate escape maneuvers and instead sank like a rock, *thud*. Since nothing was guaranteed to bore her children faster than that thing Joanna did to keep them fed and clothed, they wandered off to undoubtedly inflict more damage to her poor house. "Oh?"

"Yeah." He rubbed his mouth. "I know this is really last minute and all, but I was wondering…if maybe one of the Santas was ready so I could use it in my window? I'm thinking about setting up the Christmas display this weekend."

Only he kept his gaze hooked on hers the whole time. Hmm. Call her crazy, but somehow she had the feeling they weren't really talking about Santa Clauses. Her heart got up, dusted itself off and tested its wings again.

"You could have called," she said.

"I don't live all that far away. It was no big deal to stop by. And I thought I could save you a trip."

Then he grinned in that way that every woman since time began knows means *uh-oh*.

"What's going on, Dale?" she said softly.

Chester waddled over and flopped onto his back at Dale's feet. Dog had no shame whatsoever. Taking his cue, Dale squatted to rub Chester's belly. "I'm not sure," he said at last. "But I think we got off on the wrong foot. Or something. The other night, I mean." He looked up. "Am I confusing you?"

"To put it mildly."

"Well, good." He got to his feet again. "Because God knows I'm probably more confused than you are. And I'll totally understand if you say no. And I'm not talking about the Santa Claus, although I'll understand if you say no about that, too."

"I see." She listened to herself breathe for a couple seconds. "Whatever happened to leaving it up to me?"

"Be honest, now. Would you have ever called?"

She thought, then said, "Probably not."

"That's what I figured. That you'd let that pride of yours prevent you from doing something you know you want to do." He shrugged. "I just decided I didn't want to take that chance."

"There you go with the charm again."

"Figured right now you'd probably appreciate forthrightness more than charm. Since you strike me as the kind of woman who wants to know where she stands with a person. I'm right, though, aren't I? About you wanting to try this again."

Funny thing. She still didn't know this guy, not really. Yet she suddenly realized she'd never met anyone she could trust more. Maybe he'd never totally open up to her—forthright? Uh-huh. Who was he kidding?—but she'd lay odds he'd never lie to her, either. The question was, though…could she trust herself?

"Yes," she said. "You're right. But—"

"Oh, Lord. Why do there always have to be 'buts'?"

"The 'buts' go with the territory, Dale. Deal with it. Hey,

maybe, even after everything that happened, I do still want…you know. But I'm also still not the type who can…you know. And I'm really not up for making both of us feel like horse pucky again. At least, not this soon.''

"Yeah, I figured that's what you'd say."

Down the hall, war broke out. Yelling, insults, something thudding hard enough to shake the wall. The usual.

"Then…?" She lifted her hands in a so-explain-it-to-me gesture.

"I'm not asking…" His gaze darted past her to where her kids were now doing their damnedest to break the sound barrier, then back to her face. "They always like this?"

"No. Most days are much worse."

He smiled at that, then took a single step closer. Which still left a good five or six feet between them. "It's your company I want, Joanna. More than…the other. At least, that's what I'm thinking right now, so that's what I'm goin' with."

"My…company?"

Half his mouth quirked into a smile, as if it took too much effort to engage both sides at the same time. "What? You don't believe me?"

"In a word…no."

"Well, believe it. Oh, I'm not saying I'm closed to the idea of us getting cozy again, somewhere down the road. When the time's right. Which it clearly wasn't before. But…" He scratched his neck, then let out a sigh. "But you're different from any other woman I've ever known. So it occurs to me that maybe this calls for a different kind of relationship."

She tilted her head at him. "But still temporary."

"You asking or you telling?"

"I'm just…curious."

He walked over to the entertainment center, staring at the last family photo they'd had taken before the divorce.

To look at that picture in its sleek silver-toned frame, no-body would suspect that she and Bobby'd had a rip-roaring fight not an hour before. Or that the very next morning, she'd tell him she thought maybe it would be better if they separated.

For better or worse, she'd promised. For richer or poorer. She frowned.

"I don't make promises," he said quietly, almost as if he'd been listening to her thoughts. "I find it makes for a lot less pain in the long run. Except for one thing—I don't two-time whoever I'm seeing." A rueful smile played across his mouth. "Had it done to me, once or twice, but I've never given a woman cause to call me a cheat."

"But if we're not—"

"Doesn't matter. Loyalty has nothing to do with that. So whaddya say?"

She sat there, listening to the kids tearing through the house and the dog yapping, and Dulcy's music pulsing from down the hall and how her life was made up of nothing but her work and her kids and her kids and her work, with the occasional load of laundry thrown in for fun, and how all the adults in her life were always either after her about something, or she was after them, and how before she and Dale gave in to their impulses she'd been thinking how nice it was, having a man around she didn't have to nag about something.

Or who wouldn't nag her.

"About the Santa," she said, almost wincing at the flash of disappointment in his eyes. "I had a cancellation. It's a bigger one, though, than the ones you ordered—"

"I'll take it," he said.

Instead of saying, "Great!" or "Would you like to see it first?" or something that might actually have made sense, she heard herself say, "Would you like to stay to dinner?"

Once again, one of those slow, lazy grins spread across his face. "I'd like that fine, Miss Swann," he said.

Chapter 11

Dale finally swallowed the hunk of beef he'd been working on for what seemed like five minutes. Okay, so cooking wasn't her strong suit. Not that the stew was bad, exactly—he discreetly added salt for the third time—but he almost envied the boys their corn dogs.

"Are you kidding?" Joanna'd said when he asked her how come they weren't eating the stew, too. "Everything *touches*. Anyway, they both scarfed down raw carrots earlier, so I don't feel like a total washout as a mother."

The canned biscuits were okay, though. And for sure it beat whatever he would've come up with. Except then she said, "Sorry about the beef. I should've started the stew at least an hour earlier, but I got carried away in the studio and I forgot," and of course he smiled and assured her it was fine.

"Somebody's mama raised him right," she said with a grin.

Fortunately the boys picked that moment to start in about

wanting to carve their pumpkins after dinner, which saved Dale from having to respond.

"Ohmigosh, you two…it's already seven-thirty. And Ryder, you still haven't done your math homework—"

"That's not due until Friday!"

"And Halloween's the day after tomorrow," Matt pleaded. "If we don't do it now, when're we gonna?"

"Tomorrow after school?"

"But David Montoya's having that party tomorrow at his house!"

Joanna slumped back on her chair. "Drat. I forgot about that."

"So can we? Pleeease, Mom?"

"Guys, I just can't deal with it tonight. I've got a ton of work to do yet, and it's late, and I'm already pooped. But I tell you what," she said over their *It's not fair*, "I'll get everything set up so you can work on them right after you get back from the party tomorrow, okay?"

"But Mo-om…"

"Ryder, why don't you go get your math?" she said, rising from the table. "I'll help you with it while I'm cleaning up the kitchen."

The kids all exchanged disgusted glances, then trooped out of the kitchen. Dale stacked the rest of the bowls, grabbed a couple of glasses and followed Joanna over to the sink.

"Tell you what," he said. "Why don't you go do whatever you have to do, and I'll handle the pumpkin-carving detail?"

"That's very sweet of you—or very crazy—but I already said—"

"I know what you said. But this way, they get to carve pumpkins, *I* get to carve pumpkins, and you don't have to worry about it. We'll even clean up," he added when her mouth popped open.

She closed it again, took the bowls he was holding and stacked them in the dishwasher. "It's too late," she said. Again.

"Oh, come on, Mama. One late night isn't gonna kill 'em."

She slammed shut the dishwasher, then stood there, one hand parked on her hip. Damn...those pants she was wearing were big enough to stick a whole other woman in there.

"Why is it that every man I know seems hell-bent on undermining me?"

"Maybe it's because you say 'no' too easily," Dale said, mildly irked.

Her eyes flashed to his. "Oh, yeah? Well, it's just like I told Bobby the other day—who gets to deal with a pair of sleepyheads tomorrow morning? And it sure as hell won't be you."

"I understand that. So when's their bedtime?"

"The boys? Nine. And no later."

"That's an hour and a half. How many pumpkins we talking?"

She crossed her arms. "Three."

"So how hard can it be?"

Her eyes narrowed. Then a half smile flickered over her lips. "Okay, Mr. Know-it-all. You're on. But if I find so much as a single pumpkin seed..."

"You'll what?"

"I'll...think of something. And you promise they'll be in bed by nine?"

"Hey, kids," he yelled as he backed away, holding her gaze in his and grinning like a fool. "Who wants to carve pumpkins?"

Bobby stood in the doorway, watching Tori sleep on top of the bed, fully clothed. Judging by the textbook abandoned at her hip, he guessed she'd conked out while reading. Joanna hadn't slowed down much during her pregnancies, but Tori's mom had told him she'd wanted to sleep twelve hours a day when she was carrying Tori, so he guessed this was normal for a lot of women.

He tiptoed over to the dresser and carefully laid the rustling bag from the toy store on top of it. But not carefully enough, apparently.

"Hey," Tori said on a yawn behind him. He turned around to see her glowering at the clock on her side of the bed. "I only meant to close my eyes for—" she yawned again, rubbing her bare leg where it peeked out from beneath the hem of her stretch pants, the rest of her swallowed up inside one of his old red-and-white U.N.M. sweatshirts "—a minute. Jeez, I'm turning into a total slug."

"You need your rest," Bobby said. "It's okay."

The ring sparkled when she covered her mouth to hide yet another yawn. "I guess," she said, then added on a sleepy smile, "You smell like a hot dog."

"Lots of fireplaces going. Guess I picked up the scent."

She pulled herself upright and tucked her knees to her chest, looking at him for a long time before saying, "I'm sorry for getting mad at you."

Bobby felt something warm inside him as he walked across the room and sat on the edge of the bed. "That's okay, too. I didn't take it personally. Hey—I got you something. For the baby."

"Yeah?" She brightened. "What?"

"Close your eyes." He got up and retrieved the monkey, hiding it behind his back until he got back to the bed. "Tadah!" he said, whipping it in front of him.

She opened her eyes and gasped, then burst out laughing. "Oh, Bobby! He's *wonderful!* Give him to me!" Now sitting cross-legged on the bed, she giggled down at the toy on her lap. "Where on earth did you find him?"

"Dale's store." When her eyes shot to his, he continued,

"I wanted to check it out, anyway. For the kids, y'know. He's got some place there, you gotta go see it sometime—"

"You went to ask him about Friday night, didn't you?"

Bobby let out a sigh. "That'd been the plan."

"So what happened?"

"Let's put it this way. I don't know any more now than I did before. But the difference is, I don't care so much. Dale's okay, y'know?"

After a moment she nodded, then clambered out of the bed. "I stopped by Mama's today," she said, going to the closet and pulling out a large box. "Look what she gave us for the baby."

She dumped the box onto the bed, then tore off the top, plucking a bright yellow sleeper off the pile. "Can you believe how tiny this is?"

Bobby took the soft garment out of her hands, shaking his head. "Funny how you forget. When Dulcy was born, she was so small, I nearly wet my pants at the thought of holding her. Or worse, *dropping* her."

Tori's silence made him look up; he sighed at her crestfallen expression. "I can't help that I've done this before, baby," he said. "That this isn't new for me the way it is for you. Doesn't make it any less special."

She didn't say anything, just put the sleeper back on top of all the other things and closed the box. "Well. Are you hungry? I stopped by Mama's and she gave us pot roast and potatoes—"

"This is real scary for you, isn't it?" he said, his heart turning over in his chest as her eyes filled with tears. After a second she nodded, then cleared her throat.

"Sometimes I feel…like I'm riding my bike down a really steep hill, and I'm going faster and faster, but I can't stop and I don't dare try to jump off—" she wiped a tear from the corner of her eye "—so all I can do is hang on and pray I get to the bottom without killing myself."

Bobby reached over and took her hand. "That pretty much describes how I've felt for most of my life."

A short, panicked laugh hopped out of her mouth. "So you're saying it doesn't get any better?"

"Not that I can tell. But the thing you gotta remember—" he got up from the bed and hooked his hands at the back of her waist, pulling her to him "—is that you're not going down that hill by yourself. I'm right there with you."

Her mouth quirked. "So we can crash together?"

He laughed and kissed her lightly on the lips. "You worry too much, you know that? Now, what was that you were saying about pot roast?"

She smiled, and kissed him back, and they went to the kitchen where she served up pot roast and potatoes and green beans. But every time their gazes met, he could see worry in her eyes, like a stray cat that wouldn't go away.

For the past hour or so Joanna had felt like a little kid forced to stay in at recess while all her classmates were outside whooping it up and having a high old time. All that giggling…honestly.

Then she heard Ryder shriek in mock fright, Dale's low voice rumble, "Okay, buddy—you're in for it now!" and she mumbled, "To hell with it," tossed down the half-stuffed Santa body and went to save her kitchen, and probably her sanity, before it was too late.

The shrieks—Matt's as well as his brother's—had reached the skull-splitting level when she barreled into the kitchen. "Okay, guys, what's going o—"

A glob of seed-studded pumpkin slime hit her square in the face.

Except for the occasional dog snuffle at her feet, there was absolute silence. Then, "Oh, hell—I mean, heck—Joanna, I didn't mean…here, let me get that…"

Joanna slowly fingered the goop out of her eyes, blinking at the red-faced, paper-towel-wielding man in front of her trying his damnedest to keep from laughing. Somehow she managed to keep a lid on it as she glanced around her kitchen, her eyes saucering as she did. Although they'd spread newspapers over the kitchen table, it looked more as though they'd blown the pumpkins up rather than carve them: there were slivers and chunks of orange *everywhere*, including her children's—and Dale's—hair.

And—she lifted one hand to confirm—hers, as well.

"Now that was an accident, I was aimin' at the kids," he said—she allowed a glance at the co-culprits, huddled together wide-eyed and slack-jawed near the dishwasher, before venturing farther into the room. "And I said we'd clean up, and I meant it, so—here, honey, this towel's damp—" he pressed a towel into her hand, moving backward as she moved forward in a sort of bizarre dance "—so please don't be too mad, okay?"

She stopped in front of the table, noticing they'd used every mixing bowl she owned to collect pumpkin gook. Distractedly, she wiped at the worst of the mess on her face with the damp towel, staring.

"What's going on?" Dulcy said, coming into the kitchen from the living room side, only to stop dead in her tracks. "Oh. Wow. I knew there was a reason I didn't want to do this." Then she apparently caught sight of Joanna. *"Mom?"*

"I'm really sorry, Jo," Dale said, taking the dirty towel from her and handing her a clean one. "Honest to God...hey!"

Dale nearly tripped over one of the cats in his split to get away from Joanna, who had scooped up the biggest, nastiest, stringiest handful of pumpkin pyuck she could hold and was now out for revenge.

All three kids started shouting and laughing as Joanna

chased Dale around the table—twice—through the patio door and out into the backyard, running faster than she knew she could and having more fun than she'd thought a person her age could have fully clothed.

She heard her own laughter, blending with the sounds of her children—bless their sweet little hearts—cheering her on with taunts of, "Get 'im, Mom! Get 'im good!" and Dale's entreaties to remember it had been an accident—

"Head him off, guys!" she yelled to the kids when he neatly dodged her, as she realized the pumpkin innards were rapidly becoming cold and gummy in the chilly night air. Ah, but revenge was definitely sweet, she thought as the kids headed Dale off, trapping him just long enough for Joanna to aim and let loose.

Yes!

The kids still clinging to his arms—as well as they could, at least, considering how hard they were laughing—Joanna wiped her hand off on her butt and slowly approached Dale, his grin flashing through strings of pumpkin.

"You play dirty," he said. "Usin' your kids to take me down."

"And don't you forget it," she said.

Chuckling, he worked a hand loose to wipe pumpkin off his face, letting it drop to the ground. The dog started to eat it, seeds and all.

"That is one dumb dog," Dale said.

"This is not a news flash. Okay, guys," she said, feeling a pang of genuine regret as the Real Joanna Swann asserted herself. "Time to get ready for bed."

Both boys started in with the "Aw, Mo-om" routine, but Dale cut them off with, "You heard your mama. And believe me, I do not wish to have her ticked off with me anymore tonight."

"C'n we show you our pumpkins first?" Matt said, fusing their slimy hands together and hauling her inside.

"Sure. Dulce, make sure the cats are all in, okay?"

Once back inside—Joanna tried not to wince as three pairs of male feet indiscriminately ground pumpkin residue into her floor—they all manned their pumpkins. Dale was the first to turn his around for her approval.

"Whaddya think?"

Of course, since he was using one of those intricate patterns from the book that came with the carving tool set, she had no idea what it was supposed to be. But he looked so pleased with himself, she just made appropriate oohing sounds and left it at that. Then there was Ryder's, which, though simpler, was no less identifiable, while Matt had opted for the traditional triangles-for-eyes-and-a-row-of-jagged-teeth approach. Thank heavens.

"You guys did a great job, but it's now fifteen minutes past your bedtime and you still have to get cleaned up."

"Can't we skip baths, just for tonight?" This from Matt, who looked downright jaundiced.

"If you think I'm letting either of you in bed that dirty, you're nuts."

"Aww-ww, Mom…" they both said.

"Aww-ww, Mom," Dale echoed. She gave him a dirty look.

"C'n we at least light them for a minute to see how they look?" Matt said.

"Okay," Joanna said, no more resistant to the sight of three pairs of pleading eyes than the next woman. "But just for a minute." The cats safe from the coyotes for one more night, Dulcy returned to the kitchen as Joanna rummaged in the kitchen drawer for candle remnants. Finally candles were in and lit, lights were out, and everybody let out an ooh of wonder at something they'd seen every Halloween of their lives. Well, she didn't know about Dale, Joanna thought, stealing a glance at his face and thinking how sexy eerie candlelight could be. Even if he did have a pumpkin seed hanging off his left earlobe.

She focused again on the pumpkins.

Matt's classic jack-o'-lantern face was startlingly effective in its simplicity; Ryder had done a trio of sinuous ghosts; and Dale, who'd inherited Dulcy's pumpkin—she'd apparently pronounced the whole idea "gross," bailing before they'd gotten started—had carved out an entire haunted house, complete with a full moon, bats and a witch flying by.

"Wow," she said in genuine awe. "These are really impressive."

"You like them, Mom?"

"I really do. But now it's *really* time for a couple of little goblins to get their behinds into the shower. So come on."

Fifteen minutes later the boys settled down—and moderately less diseased-looking than they had been—she returned to the kitchen to find it already halfway cleaned, even though she had no doubt she'd be sweeping up pumpkin seeds for months. Shoot, she was *still* pulling the occasional strand of Easter basket grass out of gee-if-it's-on-the-ground-it-must-be-food-Chester's butt.

"See?" Dale said, folding up the paper with most of the pumpkin gunk trapped inside. "The boys are in bed by nine—"

"Thirty."

"—and I'm cleaning, just like I said I would. So it all worked out, didn't it?"

Joanna swallowed down the sickening sense of déjà vu, thinking, like the kids, *Not fair.* Granted, Dale was taller, blonder and his voice as at least a full octave lower, but otherwise this could be Bobby standing here with that goofy gotta-love-me grin on his face.

"You sure look cute with pumpkin seeds in your hair," he said.

As she was saying.

"Are you always so sure of yourself?" she said.

She saw his movements hitch as he stuffed the pumpkinized newspaper into a black garbage bag. "No, ma'am," he said quietly, tying up the bag. "There are some things I'm not sure about at all. You got a mop?"

"That…wouldn't be the sound of you opening up, would it?"

"No, that would be the sound of me asking if you've got a mop." He looked at the dog, who was frantically licking the floor. "Then again, maybe you don't need one."

"He is good for something," she reluctantly admitted, hauling a squeeze mop out of the broom closet and swishing it at the dog, just because she could. But instead of taking the mop, Dale walked over to the sink to wash his hands, then his face, saying they should probably put the pumpkins outside where it was colder, so they wouldn't shrivel up so fast.

The chilled air felt good on her heated face, the woodsmoke smell as comforting as childhood as they carted the pumpkins out to the picnic table in the back—she didn't trust leaving them out front, not since the one year some creeps had smashed all their jack-o'-lanterns. "Dulcy had spent more than two hours carving hers," Joanna said, heaving her pumpkin up onto the table. "She cried for nearly as long. And she's never carved one since."

"Ah, hell. If I'd known that—"

"It's okay," Jo said. "I buy her a pumpkin every year. I figure when she's ready, she'll do one again."

Dale nodded and walked backward in the direction of the empty stable, his head back, a faint breath cloud hovering around his mouth. "I've been here for nearly a year," he said, "and I still can't get over how many stars there are."

"They don't have stars in Texas?"

"Yeah, they've got stars," he said, cautiously dragging out the words. The few dried-up cottonwood leaves left clinging to the trees rattled softly in the breeze. "But I don't recall telling you I lived in Texas."

"Somebody mentioned it. My father? Dulcy?" Joanna climbed up to sit next to the pumpkins, her feet on the bench. "She said you and she talked, at the party."

"Oh. Yeah, I suppose we did." He looked toward the stable. "So your grandmother used to have horses?"

"A couple, when I was younger. I used to spend a lot of time out here riding."

"You miss it?"

The simple question shook awake dusty memories of hours spent riding the trails along the *bosque,* free to do nothing but think. And dream. But that was a long time ago.

"Not really," she finally said, her hands linked in front of her knees. "But I don't tend to think much about things I can't have."

"Obviously."

It took her a second to catch his innuendo, then she picked up a small branch that had landed on the table and threw it at him.

"Hey. I think about that. A lot, actually."

"You just don't act on it on a regular basis."

"I also contemplate devouring entire cheesecakes. On a regular basis. It's called controlling my life. Not letting it control me."

"Honey, I hate to break it to you, but if this is what you call having a handle on your life..."

"Just imagine what it would be like if I *didn't* have some control over it."

"This from the woman who actually wants more kids."

"Okay, so the plan is flawed," she said on a sigh. "But I don't know, maybe because I had the first ones when I was so young, I'd kinda like to try it again. Now that I have some vague idea of what I'm doing."

"So if you want another kid so much, why not go to some sperm bank and have done with it?"

She laughed. "Because going about it the old-fashioned way is a lot more fun. Besides, I can't see me purposefully having a child without a father."

"Because it's immoral?"

"Because it's too damn hard. And it's far easier on the ego when the kid has two parents to hate instead of just one."

After a second Dale walked back over to her, the night breeze ruffling his hair. "You cold?"

"No. It feels good."

He nodded, then sat on the bench, facing away from her, his elbows propped on the table. "Somehow I don't think your kids hate you."

"Says the man who's never lived with a teenager-in-training."

"Dulcy doesn't hate you," he repeated, then added after a pause, "She worries about you, though."

"What makes you say that?"

"Just a feeling I got from talking to her. If you ask me, I think she thinks you work too much."

She shivered a little as fallen leaves chased each other across the driveway, snickering and whispering. "Well, nobody asked you, did they? Besides, what's wrong with demanding the best of myself?"

"Nothing. Unless you lose sight of the bigger picture." Chester brought him one of his scuzzy tennis balls, pestering Dale until he threw it out into the yard for him. "Or forget how to have some fun, every now and then." The dog brought back the ball, thrilled to bits when Dale played tug of war for a second, then tossed it back out. "See, old Chester here has the right idea."

Joanna sighed. Dale turned back around. "What was that for?"

"You don't take anything seriously, do you?"

"Shoot, there's too many serious people in the world as it is," he said evenly. "Gotta have somebody to provide comic relief. And there you go, sighing again. Now what's wrong?"

"Other than the fact that you sound exactly like Bobby, nothing. But then, I tend to forget the rest of the world isn't as anal as I am."

"Oh, don't feel so bad. If it weren't for you anal types, the rest of the world would always be wearing dirty socks."

"Oh, *there's* a bright spot."

He chuckled, then said, "Besides, I got no problem with demanding the best of yourself. I wouldn't have had a career if I hadn't had the same attitude. But I'm just wondering if that's got something to do with why you won't let your parents help out more? With the house, for instance?"

"We've already covered this, Dale. And anyway, would you let yours, if you were in my shoes?"

A pause. "That's neither here nor there, since my parents haven't been in the picture for years."

"Oh. I'm sorry."

"It's okay," he said, but somehow Joanna didn't think it was. "In any case," he continued, "it just seems to me it would be easier to seek help from someplace you'd be more likely to get it, rather than harassing your ex-husband to death."

Joanna shifted to give the blood in her butt a chance to circulate. "Now you sound like my mother. Which, in case you're wondering, isn't racking up the points."

Dale laughed softly, then said, "Something tells me, though, Bobby's not as terrible as you're making him out to be. I mean..." He hesitated, then said, "He never hit you or the kids, did he?"

"Ohmigod...no! Never! Criminy, he hardly even loses his temper." She slid down off the table to sit beside him on the bench. "The thing is, I *don't* think Bobby's a bad person. I never have, or I wouldn't've stayed married to him as long as I did. He just refuses to grow up, to take his responsibilities seriously. For Tori's sake, I hope he comes to his senses sometime soon."

Dale threw the ball for the dog again. "Maybe he has."

Instantly suspicious, she looked at the side of his face. "What does that mean?"

"He came to the store this evening."

"Who? Bobby?"

"Yeah. To get a present for Tori. Well, for the new baby. He didn't go into any details, but I gather they had a fight about something, and Bobby had accepted the role of the guilty party." Joanna snorted. "Isn't that a step in the right direction?"

"If that *were* a new direction, yeah."

"Oh." A pause. "He invited me to his poker game next Thursday. And I thought I might go." He looked up at her again. "I take it by the size of your eyes this bothers you?"

She forced her eyelids back down and shoved, "Why should it?" past the high-pitched *What?* lodged in her throat.

"Oh, I don't know. Because maybe this is sorta weird? Your new lover becoming friends with your ex-husband, I mean."

"You are *not* my lover."

"I think technically, I am."

"Only if we have sex again. Which is not a given."

Dale just chuckled.

"In any case," she went on, refusing to spend a second longer wondering how on earth a chuckle could turn her inside out, "I don't give a flying fig if you play poker with him or not. Although I will warn you—he cheats."

"So do I, so we're even."

Joanna opened her mouth, shut it again, deciding against telling him who else was likely to be part of the game. Like her father. Then she said, "In any case, none of my feelings about any of this have anything to do with my feelings about not letting Bobby off the hook—"

"You know, I think you're the only person I know who could come up with a sentence like that stone-cold sober."

"—because," she continued, ignoring him, "we made the decision to get married, to have a family…" She shut her eyes for a moment, took a breath. "Okay, so maybe we did things backward. I got pregnant, we got married. Still, we did make that commitment, to bring these kids into the world and take care of them. My parents had nothing to do with that. And…" She looked at him. "You really want to hear all this?"

"I don't exactly have any pressing engagements. Except maybe with that mop and your kitchen floor, but I suppose that can wait a few minutes."

"Okay. Well, up until I met Bobby, I was the quintessential good girl, following in exactly the footsteps my parents wanted me to take. It was okay to dabble in art, but nobody with a grain of sense tried to earn a living at it, you know? And I was bright—well, I suppose I still am, although sometimes I wonder if my brain has atrophied— bright enough to get into pre-law at U.N.M. on a full scholarship, even if I didn't need it. I was one of those little suckups who firmly believed my own happiness was tied to making someone else happy. Even to the point of dating a son of a family friend all through high school, and then getting engaged to him the beginning of my junior year of college. Not that we planned on getting married right away, but I guess everyone wanted to make sure we were both taken off the market."

"Let me guess. Then you met Bobby."

"Then I met Bobby. And it all fell apart. Although I didn't see it that way at the time. I was living off campus— which was rebellious enough—and Bobby was my roommate's brother's best friend. And he was the antithesis of everything my parents represented. He wasn't into drugs or anything like that, but I'd never known anyone that free from life's constraints. And it was a revelation. He was always laughing, always ready to have fun, always seemed to get by without driving himself crazy, and I looked at my own neatly ordered life and thought, Jeez Louise—is this boring or what? And I just...snapped."

"I can't imagine you snapping," Dale said.

"Think back. Friday night. My studio."

"Oh, yeah."

"Anyway, I *meant* to change my major to art and break off my engagement to Tom. Who seemed more relieved than I was, actually. However, I *didn't* mean to get pregnant. Not right away. But Bobby and I thought we were so much in love, and we really were excited about the baby, and too young to know—or believe—how hard it was going to be down the road."

"And your parents had a cow."

"More like an entire herd."

"Even though you didn't really want to do law. And what's-his-name wasn't right for you."

"True. But then, neither was the man I did marry. I just couldn't see it at the time. However, while they certainly weren't thrilled when I told them I was pregnant, they eventually got past it for the baby's sake. And eventually, they even came to like Bobby. Well, my father did. You know, the son he never had and all that. Which made it even harder…''

''For you to admit you'd made a mistake.''

''Bingo.''

''And that's why you won't let them help you now. Even if they want to.''

''I'm not an idiot, Dale,'' she said, starting to shiver in earnest. ''I certainly wouldn't let my kids go hungry or homeless, if it came down to that. Of c-course I'd accept their help under those c-circumstances.''

''You're freezing,'' he said gently, watching her, and she thought, between that voice and those eyes, not hardly. But she took the hand he held out to her after he stood, letting him yank her to her feet and lead her back inside.

Only she'd no sooner gotten used to the warmth of his hand wrapped around hers when he dropped it as though he'd been zapped. An entirely understandable reaction, since Dulcy was right there in the kitchen, making herself a sandwich.

Chapter 12

"What were you guys doing out there?" she asked, all innocence.

"Talkin'," Dale said in the same tone. "Freezin'. Playin' with the mutt."

Dulcy and Dale regarded each other for several seconds while Joanna silently cursed the complexity of life. Chester—for whom life could be broken down into three or four basic components—woofed and deposited the slimy tennis ball at Dale's feet.

"Oh, yuck! Get that disgusting thing out of here!" Joanna soccer-shuffled the ball over to the patio door to boot it outside. "And he's not a mutt, by the way. He's a P.B.G.V."

"What the heck's that?" Dale said, mop in hand, staring at the dog staring mournfully outside. "Sounds like some kind of home shopping network."

Dulcy giggled, jostling Chester's attention away from the exiled ball and back to the prospect of food.

"It stands for Petit Basset Griffon Vendeen," Joanna said.

"You're makin' that up."

"Wanna see his papers?"

"Good Lord. No wonder the dog's got problems."

"Oh, it gets better. He's being slapped with a paternity suit. Great Dane across the road," she added before he could ask.

"How the heck—"

"Back porch steps."

Dale laughed, then shooed all of them behind the counter with the mop. "Okay, you two, over there. Don't need no womenfolk a'gittin' in my way."

That got another giggle from Dulcy. Joanna climbed up onto the stool beside her daughter and snitched a corner of her sandwich. Pretty soon, she was going to have to do some serious thinking about all of this. Because, as much as she hated to admit it, there were certain aspects to Dale McConnaughy's personality—not to mention his person, she thought, contemplating the way the muscles bunched and strained in his forearms as he mopped her floor—that were making her just a little loopy.

Okay, so he was fun to be around. He got on great with the kids, although ironically enough, their no-big-deal acceptance of this man's sudden presence in their lives, when there had been no such animal since the divorce, made her more uneasy, not less. Weren't kids supposed to get all bent out of shape about this stuff? Did this mean hers weren't normal?

And maybe she should try worrying about one thing at a time, just for novelty's sake.

So back to Dale, who was actually doing a fairly decent job of cleaning her floor. Not to mention scrambling her brains, which hadn't exactly been any too stable to begin with. Anyway—over Dulcy's squeal of protest as Joanna grabbed another piece of sandwich—it would seem she was back on square one. Whether or not to go the Gap Guy route, that is. Because that's all this could be. And not only because Dale's refusal to talk about himself took "reticent" to a whole new level, but because that reticence left her nothing to go on but the surface stuff. And unfortunately, an awful lot of that surface stuff reminded her an awful lot of Bobby.

To hell with the sandwich. Time to haul out the big guns.

"Hey!" Dale said when she tromped across the wet floor toward the cupboard. "I just cleaned there!"

Ignoring him, she fetched down her bag of Ghiradellis and tromped back across the floor, resettling herself on the stool. Dulcy, who was truly her mother's child, held out her hand, eyes alight.

"What is it with women and chocolate?" Dale grumbled, wringing out the mop in the sink.

"It completes us," Joanna mumbled around a full mouth.

"Yeah," Dulcy agreed. Chester looked hopeful.

"You can't have chocolate," Joanna said to the dog, trying to work up a little sympathy and not getting very far. "It'll make you sick."

"This to a dog who eats raw pumpkin," Dale said. "Seeds and all."

"And dirty socks," Dulcy added. "And G.I. Joes."

Chester shifted on his bottom to assume his "starving" pose. And whined.

"Yeah, but there's a chemical in chocolate that's not good for them," Joanna said, a trifle surprised that she actually cared.

"But plastic's okay?" Dale asked, washing his hands.

"Since he's eaten—I'm guessing here—twice his weight in plastic since his arrival and is still alive and kicking, apparently so. We will, however," she said around another mouthful of chocolate, "undoubtedly have a bunch of pumpkin plants sprouting in the yard next spring."

Dulcy frowned. "Why...? Oh. Ewww."

"We'll have to call you Chester Pumpkinseed," Jo said to the dog. Chester flicked his gaze to Joanna for half a second, then back to the bag of chips. Dale reached over and snatched a few chips from the bag, tossing one to the dog.

"Hey! I just said—"

"I know all about dogs and chocolate, Joanna. I also know he'd have to eat like a whole pound or something to get sick. One little old chip isn't gonna hurt him. He's probably eaten more than that when your back's been turned."

She could have sworn Chester gave her a sly grin.

Then she looked up at the clock and let out a gasp. "Oh, my word—I had no idea it had gotten that late! Dulce, you should have been in bed ages ago!"

Her daughter shrugged. "I wasn't sleepy."

"Well, you better *get* sleepy. Go on. I'll come in to say good-night in a minute."

Dulcy made a face, but she reached up to give Joanna a hug anyway before shuffling off to her room.

Announcing it was time he got going, as well, Dale set the damp mop up against the sink. They walked out to the living room, where he shrugged into his jacket. His scent suffused the room, stirring a sweet longing inside Joanna even worse than whatever that had been on Friday when she'd been at the mercy of her starved hormones. A longing intensified when, once outside, he said, "You've got some great kids, Joanna."

She leaned against the doorjamb, her arms crossed against the rapidly dropping temperature. "You do realize that saying stuff like that is a surefire way to make serious points with a mother?"

"I had an inkling, yeah," he said with a half smile. "But do you give Bobby any credit for that?"

"Of course I do. And the kids adore him. With good reason."

The smile turned pensive. Frowning slightly, he reached out to barely touch her hair; she held her breath. "Don't go getting mad at me, okay? But I think it's time you stop beating yourself up for ticking off your parents all those years ago. Seems to me things might've been a lot worse if you'd followed the paths they wanted you to take." He lowered his hand, stuffing it into his pocket. "And something tells me they know that."

Then, while she stood there, too flabbergasted to think of a comeback, he said, "I've maybe got an idea about something to help Ryder, but it's too late tonight to discuss it. I'll call you."

Then he turned to go, leaving Joanna not sure what to think anymore.

She'd no sooner shut the door than the bell rang. When she opened it again, Dale's mouth was set in a rueful grin. "The Santa?"

"Oh. Right. Hang on." Not sure she could trust herself if she let him back inside, Joanna made tracks through the house, quickly wrapped up the Santa in an oversize plastic bag, and hurried back out to the front.

"You might want to look him over—"

"I'm sure he's fine," Dale said, taking the Santa from her. "Well. Good night."

"Wait…" She grabbed the front of his jacket, yanking him down just far enough to kiss his cheek.

He looked as though he couldn't decide whether to be startled or pleased. "What was that for?"

"For being my Calgon," she said with a shrug. He shook his head, then strode off into the night, leaving her feeling exhilarated and achingly empty at the same time.

Remembering the pumpkins were still lit, she returned to the backyard to find Dulcy standing on the patio in her nightgown and robe and panda bear slippers. Joanna lifted an arm and tucked her firstborn against her side, inhaling what the boys called her "girly" scent.

"It's after eleven, sweetie. You're going to have a terrible time getting up tomorrow."

Under her arm, Dulcy shrugged. Chester yapped at the largest pumpkin, just to let it know he was on the case, then came to flop down at their feet. And Joanna thought about what Dale had said earlier. Was he right, that Dulcy worried about her?

Or was her daughter worried about herself, about the future?

Her heart *ka-thunking* against her ribs, Joanna squeezed Dulcy's thin shoulders. "Should...I save myself the trouble of wondering when you're going to bring the subject up and just assume you have questions about me and Dale?"

A second or two passed before Dulcy slipped away and plopped down on the porch swing, making it shudder and creak. "It's okay, Mom. I mean, you and Dad have been divorced like forever." She stuffed a mass of curls behind one ear, the lit pumpkin faces reflected in her glasses. "Most parents start seeing other people like five seconds after they're divorced." She made a face. "If they bother to wait *that* long."

"So...you really wouldn't mind if I...dated another man?"

"No-o," she said, as if Joanna had just asked the dumbest question in the history of mankind. "Well...as long as it wasn't somebody who wanted to be like this second father to us or something. Sarah Romero really, really hates the way her mom's new boyfriend acts like her real father doesn't even exist. But I don't think Dale would do that.

He's cool. So it's okay with me if you wanna go out with him and stuff.''

Joanna blew out a breath, then joined Dulcy on the swing, praying the bolts were strong enough to support both their weights. "We're not actually…dating."

"Oh. Then…what are you doing?"

After a silent prayer of thanks for the darkness, she said, "Thinking about dating?"

"But you like him, right?"

"Yeah. I do. I'm just not sure *how* I like him."

"Oh. Okay.''

They swung in tandem for a few moments, then Joanna asked, "Does Dale remind you of your father?"

"Mom—Dale doesn't look anything like Dad."

"I don't mean that. The way he acts.''

Dulcy tucked her feet up underneath her, which made the swing wobble dangerously until she finished wriggling and had settled against Joanna. "Maybe, a little. You mean because he gets all goofy and stuff?"

"That's it.''

"Then, yeah. I guess he does. But—" a huge yawn interrupted her "—that's what I like most about Dad, too." She yawned again. "I guess I'm finally ready to go to sleep now.''

"I should hope so," Joanna said, gently easing them both off the swing, then guiding her very sleepy daughter back to bed. She tucked her in, a luxury she hadn't been allowed since Dulcy turned eight and announced she was old enough to put herself to bed now, thank you, then tiptoed out of the bedroom and back down the hall to the kitchen to close up the house.

And as she did, her daughter's words—that the part of Dale that reminded her of her father was the part she liked best about both of them—laughed at Joanna from every corner of her mind.

* * *

Dale didn't know why, but there was something about being inside the blindingly illuminated Wal-Mart when it was pitch black outside that seemed almost obscene. What was even more obscene, though, was hearing some poor little kid screaming its head off from somewhere in the depths of the store. His first thought was to wonder who on earth would drag a baby out at this time of night, only to catch himself, thinking maybe whoever it was didn't have a choice.

Then again, he thought as the kid took it up a notch, maybe they did and were just being stupid. Dale wasn't usually prone to judging people—especially considering his own roots—but he had to say, the folks he'd seen in the store so far weren't exactly the best examples of God's handiwork around. Which got him to wondering, as he contemplated whether a four- or a five-foot tall artificial tree would work better in the store window, what that said about him.

He decided on the five-footer, hefting the ungainly box into his cart with a crash. It felt kinda strange, buying all this Christmas stuff when he'd never so much as put up a wreath in any of the places he'd lived. He'd been in and out of his marriage between Valentine's and Independence Day—which was actually pretty fitting, if you stopped to think about it—so if Meredith had been the type to go all out with decorating for the holidays, he wouldn't know. And Dale himself had never seen much point.

Man. It'd been more than five years since his divorce, but he'd been thinking about Meredith and his marriage more in the past week than he had in that whole time. And he knew exactly who to blame for that.

Here he'd been so proud of himself, not giving in to the impulse to kiss Joanna good-night when what does she do but up and plant that kiss on his cheek. And it had thrown him for a loop, is what. Come-ons, he knew how to handle, how to react to. But this...this...well, hell, he didn't even know what to call it, let alone what to do with it. All he knew was, for a couple of minutes there—okay, okay, a few hours—he'd felt more peaceful than he'd been in a long, long time.

Until the pessimism moved in, like it always did.

He loaded five times more stuff than he could possibly use for the window into the cart, then figured he may as well pick up some coffee and milk and cereal while he was at it, since he couldn't remember if he was about to run out or not. Room service was pretty much the only thing he missed about being on the road. That, and being too busy thinkin' about the game coming up, or the one he'd just played, to spend much time ruminating about his sorry excuse for a life. Except, he never used to think of his life as being particularly sorry. For the most part he liked living alone, being alone, having nobody to answer to but himself. Nobody to worry about, or to worry about him.

Except now it was as if some big old voice had boomed inside him, *Who the* hell *are you kidding?*

And right alongside that, softer but no less insistent, another voice whispered, *So maybe it could work this time, bonehead.*

With Joanna? Right. Sure, he liked being with her, getting her to laugh. The way she made him feel, as though he belonged. But even if he discounted the fact that they really didn't have a whole lot in common, she had kids. And wanted another one.

And not even he was fool enough to believe that was the real problem.

He shook his head, like he could jostle the thoughts loose, only to find himself flung back twenty-some years, when he was one mad, scared-shitless little kid who was sure he only existed to make other people feel better about their own lives, and that county-appointed shrink telling him he wasn't being punished, he hadn't done anything wrong and that he deserved the good things in life, just as much as anybody else. Including, the woman had said, the right to be loved.

After all this time, that still hurt. That some stranger would look him in the eye and give him false hope like that. But the kicker was that he was enough of a chump to still cling to that stupid hope, even though he'd had the opposite proven to him, over and over and over.

And yet he thought about Joanna giving him that kiss, and he felt a good chunk of the tightness loosen inside him.

There weren't a whole lot of lanes open at this hour, although it was surprising how many fools were in here. As he unloaded his cart, the cashier, a young man with a dark ponytail and several earrings, was having an animated conversation in Spanish with a guy about his own age ahead of Dale. A buddy, Dale gathered from what he could decipher from the rapid-fire and heavily slanged exchange, punctuated with lots of laughter.

With a, "See ya, man," the cashier sent the customer on his way, then looked over at Dale with a big grin. "Danny" his name tag said.

"Man, you're plannin' on doin' a lot of decoratin', huh?" he said, quickly scanning the items and dumping them into bags faster than Dale could get them reloaded into the cart. "I love the holidays, y'know?" he went on, scanning and dumping with an odd kind of grace. "The way it smells, an' all the lights. And my mother and grandma, they makes the *tamales* with the real corn husks…" He laughed, showing off a gold bicuspid. "I'm gettin' hungry jus' talking about it. Okay, that's…one hundred, twelve dollars and fifty-two cents."

Dale swiped his charge card, which was the first time the clerk had a chance to get a look at him. "You look familiar, y'know?'' he said as the register spit out the receipt, then the charge slip. ''You been in here before?''

''Not this late, no,'' Dale said as Danny handed him the receipt without asking to see the card—how the place managed not to get stiffed a thousand times a day only went to prove how honest most people were when it came down to it—but did happen to look at the receipt after Dale signed it. Then his head whipped back around.

''Dale McConnaughy? Like, the pitcher for the Braves?''

''That's me.''

The kid grinned from ear to ear, then reached across the counter and pumped Dale's hand. ''This is so freakin' cool! And *damn,* Joey Armijo is gonna piss his pants when he finds out! Jerk practically begged me to take his shift tonight! Hey—'' Danny frantically patted all his pockets. ''Damn—I don't have nothin' you can sign to prove I saw you—hold on!'' He snatched up a photography studio flyer and thrust it into Dale's hand, along with the pen. ''This okay?''

''It's fine,'' Dale said, hoping this wasn't what the shrink had meant about his deserving to be loved. He'd certainly never gone into pro sports for the celebrity aspect of it, or because he was looking for public adoration or anything like that. Hell, he still hadn't quite come to terms with how simply doing something well, something he loved—something he'd taken up simply as a means to keep from losing his mind—had somehow made him famous, for lack of a better word. Not that he minded giving the kid an autograph, for God's sake. But this fame crap was definitely getting old.

''So…you don't play no more?''

''Nope,'' Dale said, handing Danny back his pen and the signed flyer.

''That's too bad. You were, like, the best.'' The kid grinned down at the autograph, like he couldn't believe it.

"Oh, wow, you just made my day! Hell, you just made my year! Thanks, man!"

"You're real welcome," Dale said, then wheeled his laden cart out to the brightly lit parking lot, inhaling the crisp, dry air. There weren't too many cars in the huge lot, most of 'em huddled toward the front, his own about half-way down.

Dale grinned. Then, when he figured nobody was look-ing—not that he really cared—he shoved off and jumped on the back of the cart, free-riding the length of the lot, the breeze whistling in his ears.

Chapter 13

Karleen showed up on Halloween night in a black fright wig, green skin, purple lipstick and a witch's costume that practically revealed her drawers. And not from the hemline, either.

"Honestly, Kar," Joanna said, "what are you? An extra in *Haunted 'Hos.*"

"Nah, they were all redheads," Karleen said, snitching a bite-size Special Dark from Joanna's trick-or-treat bowl. "So where's the kids?"

After Joanna hopped back on Karleen's train of thought, she said, "Bobby came over to take them out trick-or-treating, so I'm on door duty. And why are you dressed like that anyway?"

"Going to a party later." She eyed Joanna, whose orange-and-black sweatshirt announced, *This* is *my costume.* "A grown-up party."

Joanna poked through the candy, selecting a Hershey's kiss. "I think I remember those."

Eyebrows twitching, Chester mournfully guarded the

bowl. Karleen took pity on him and gave him her candy wrapper. He ate the paper but spit out the foil. "So why don't you come, too?" she said. "Bobby's taking the kids back to his place after they go trick-or-treating, right?"

"Oh, no, Kar. My party days are o*ver*."

The doorbell rang. Karleen opened the door. Six little boys of assorted ages and sizes opened their mouths to scream "Trick or Treat," but nothing came out except the eyes from their heads. Especially when Karleen bent over to drop three pieces of candy into each bag.

"They were so cute!" she said after they'd gone.

"Which is probably about what they're saying right about now, too," Joanna said. "Here." She handed Karleen a sweater. "Put this on before you launch half the neighborhood kids into premature puberty."

Karleen slipped on the sweater, leaving it unbuttoned. "Oh, come on! It'll be fun!"

"The party, you mean? Right. I'll have one glass of wine and fall asleep in the corner somewhere. Besides, what on earth would I wear?"

That got another appraisal. "That's it?"

"Well, there is Ryder's Brussels Sprout costume from the school play, but that's probably not what you had in mind."

"Which is why it's lucky for you that I'm not only your friend, but that I share—"

This did not sound good.

"—and that we're the same size."

"I'm not going to this party." Joanna looked at Karleen's chest. "And we are *so* not the same size."

Karleen looked at Joanna's. "You may have a point there. But whatever." She thrust a Macy's shopping bag into Joanna's hands. "Go. Transform yourself. I'll man the door."

"With those boobs, you won't *man* anything." She

shoved the bag back at Karleen. "And I'm not going anywhere."

The doorbell rang again. Only when she opened it, her own kids screamed, "Trick or treat!" loud enough to deafen people three states over. Then, giggling hysterically—as if they didn't do this every single Halloween—they all scrambled inside, the boys taking off for various bathrooms while Dulcy went to dump out her loot on the kitchen table.

"Potty break," Bobby said, his baseball jacket reeking of woodsmoke and Tori's too sweet perfume. "Hey, Kar," he said, taking in her outfit. "Nice...costume. Don't think I've ever seen green ones before. But your makeup's smudged right...there..."

"Aunt Karleen!" Dulcy called as Karleen smacked Bobby's hand before he could make contact. "Come see what I got!"

Muttering something to Bobby about "in your dreams," she traipsed off in search of Dulcy. Bobby chuckled, then turned to Joanna. "The kids are wearing down, but they want to go to another ten houses or so. Then I guess we'll head back to my place." He paused. "Tori rented *The Nightmare Before Christmas* and made up some spiced cider or something."

They exchanged knowing glances.

"You couldn't talk her out of it?" Joanna asked.

"I tried, believe me."

"But the kids hate apple juice. And they've seen that movie like a million times."

"I know, I know. But..." He let out a sigh and rubbed the back of his neck. "She's really trying, Jo. She wants the kids to like her."

"Then maybe she needs to think about listening to their father when he tries to avert a disaster," she said gently.

"She won't listen to me," he said, almost whining. "Maybe if you called her—?"

"Oh, no. No way am I getting in the middle of this. Or pulling the 'I'm their *real* mother' number. No matter what I say," she went on when Bobby opened his mouth to protest, "she's only going to see it as interference. You two—or five, actually—will have to work this out on your own. Besides, Tori's a sharp cookie. She'll figure it out."

He rammed his hand through his hair, then let out another sigh. "But…well, what if you said something to Dulcy, y'know? About not being too hard on Tori?" He bent at the knees and caught her eyes. "Please?"

Damn him and that puppy-dog look. "Oh, all right," she said on a rush of air. "Although if the kids can't be honest with Tori, it seems to me she'll just keep on making the same mistakes."

"Just for tonight, Jo. I'll work on the other, I promise. By the way…" He fished in his pocket for what turned out to be a folded check. "It's not the whole amount, but this should help, right? For the roof?"

She glanced at the check, which was for less than half what she'd asked him for, then looked up at Bobby at the precise moment their sons roared back into the room, eyes bright and bladders emptied. A grin split his face, and it hit her like a ton of bricks that everybody was right—expecting Bobby to live up to his promises was a waste of time, energy and emotion. Always had been, most likely always would be.

Bobby was doing the best Bobby knew how. Maybe that hadn't been enough to warrant staying married to him, but it was stupid to keep expecting him to be someone he wasn't, to be more than he could. Child support was one thing—Bobby owed that to his kids, and it'd be a cold day in hell before she let him off that hook, no matter what. Other than that, though, she was done with it. If she wanted her parents to see her as a grown-up, if she wanted to see *herself* as a grown-up, and if she wanted to keep living in this money pit she loved so damn much, then she'd have to figure out a way to handle it all herself. No Bobby, no parents, no nobody. It was time to let go. To let *him* go.

And maybe by doing that, he'd figure out how to let go of her, as well.

She reached over and grabbed his jacket, tucking the check back inside his front pocket. The look on his face was priceless.

"What—"

"You've got a new baby coming. You need this more than I do."

"But the roof—"

"Is my problem. Not yours. Consider this my engagement present, okay?"

He blinked several times, then grabbed her in a silent, one-armed hug. She saw his Adam's apple convulse when he let go and called Dulcy, who called back she didn't want to go out again.

"I'll have a word with her while you're out with the boys," Joanna said. "About Tori."

"Damn, lady," Bobby said, shaking his head. "What got into you tonight?"

She smiled. "Tell you what—I won't try to figure it out if you don't."

"Deal," he said. But after he'd opened the door and the boys had scampered back outside, he added, "You're really somethin', babe, you know that?" Then he closed the door behind him before she had a chance to reply.

Feeling relieved and a little sad at the same time—and borderline reckless, which was probably not good—Joanna picked up the Macy's bag and peered inside. From what she could tell, there wasn't enough fabric to cover an anorexic gnat.

"Does this mean you've changed your mind?" Karleen said from the doorway.

"God help me, I think maybe it does," she said.

* * *

Two hours later Joanna wriggled and squeezed herself through a sea of James Bonds (two) Spider-Men (at least three), and the usual assortment of sexy cats, witches, mummies, Draculas and clowns (oh, yeah, there were a lot of those, and not all of them in costume) to find Karleen and tell her she was leaving.

"But things are just getting started," her friend shouted over music so loud, Joanna wouldn't have been able to tell what group it was even if she had cared. "You can't leave now."

"Watch me," Jo shouted back, immensely grateful she'd insisted on taking her own car. She yelped as, for at least the tenth time since she'd arrived, someone's hand landed someplace it did not belong. "I'll call you tomorrow," she mouthed, then wriggled back through the throng to get to the front door and freedom.

Once in the car, she rolled down all the windows, both because she was about to burn up and to—hopefully—dissipate at least some of the cigarette and alcohol fumes clinging to her clothes and hair, thanks in no small part to an inebriated hot dog ("Hey, honey, I'm Wiener Man. Get it? *Wiener* man?") spilling his beer all over her. Praying she wasn't harboring an inadvertent secondhand buzz from the smoke that definitely was not from cigarettes, she started the car and pulled out into the street, wondering how on earth she'd ever actually thought these things were fun and instantly fearing for her children, who would undoubtedly be attending soirees like these in the not-too-distant future.

"I'm way too old for this," she muttered to herself, cautiously navigating the treacherous curves. The party had been at a house in Sandia Heights, close enough to be considered the same general neighborhood as her parents' but far enough away to be totally unfamiliar. So, using the bowl of glittering city lights below her as her compass, Joanna kept steering west until she eventually ran into a street she recognized. A street that, to get to the east-west route that would take her back across the river, went right past Dale's store.

Which, she saw as she passed, was all lit up.

And she was feeling just sorry enough for herself, and ornery enough, and pissed off enough for having let Karleen drag her to some stupid party she'd known from the get-go she wasn't going to enjoy, that she pulled into a Chevron station, turned around and backtracked to the shop, completely forgetting she smelled like she'd been on a three-day bender.

Dale's arm flew across his eyes in the glare of headlights, his heart momentarily stopping when it looked as though the car was coming straight through the glass. But then the engine stopped, the lights went off—although now all he saw were two huge red spots—a car door slammed and someone was approaching the window. A woman, he thought, the red spots bouncing as he blinked. A woman tapping on the glass and going, "What the hell are you doing?"

Joanna?

"Hold on," he said, willing his heart to get going again as he unpretzeled himself from the floor, then limped out of the window and around to open the door for her. Except the minute he did, the stench of stale beer nearly knocked him over.

"It's not me. It's the shirt," she said, her mouth twisted as she flapped the hem of a sweatshirt that proclaimed itself her costume. "Maybe I should stay outside. This probably isn't exactly the smell you want lingering in a toy store."

He pulled her inside anyway. "It might help if you stopped stirring things up like that."

"Oh. Sorry." She folded her arms across her chest, then seemed to notice he was staring at the sweatshirt. Only it wasn't really the sweatshirt he was staring at. It was her.

The way all this energy seemed to vibrate from someplace inside her.

"It was either this or three scraps of silk and a couple of chains," she said.

He grinned. "That shirt would not have been my first choice, trust me."

"Somehow, I think you would have looked even sillier than me in three scraps of silk and a couple of chains. God, I stink. Some bozo tripped in front of me and it was all over. All over me, actually."

"Hold on," Dale said. "I might have something in back you can put on."

He strode off through the darkened store, still curious about why she was here, when she called, "In case you're wondering... Karleen dragged me to some godawful party in Sandia Heights."

"So *that's* why you're so dressed up," he said, flicking on the office light.

"That wouldn't be sarcasm I hear in your voice, would it?"

"No, ma'am." He pawed through the pile of clothes on the back of the extra chair by his desk, yanking out the two items that smelled the cleanest.

"Hey," she called. "I'm wearing makeup. *And* earrings. You're giving me a choice?" she asked when he came back with both a flannel overshirt and a gray sweatshirt.

"The way I'm going, I could probably sell men's clothes on the side. I'm always wearing extra stuff when it's cold in the mornings, then taking the top layer off when it warms up later and forgettin' about it. Once every two weeks or so I gather everything up and cart it back home to start over."

He saw a flash of teeth in the dim light as she chuckled—indulgently, he thought—before grabbing the sweatshirt and ducking behind the puzzle-and-games aisle to change. "Anyway, I escaped. From the party. Such as it was."

"With your virtue still intact?"

"I'm assuming so," came the voice over the stacks of boxes. "But there were so many hands on so many places on my body—that I did *not* invite, trust me—" her curls bobbed around her shoulders as she came back into view, looking about her daughter's age in the huge sweatshirt "—that I can't be entirely sure. You got a bag or something I can put this disgusting thing in? Or maybe two?"

He grabbed a pair of plastic bags from behind the counter; she put one inside the other, the sweatshirt inside that, then tied the top closed, making a face the entire time. "Anyway, I was on my way home and happened to pass by, saw the lights and wondered what you were doing here so late. So here I am. Stinky, probably sporting a mild secondhand high, and inordinately curious."

"I'm doing my Christmas window."

"Oh." She walked over to the window, standing on tiptoe to peer over the low wall separating the display area from the rest of the store. "Doesn't look like you've gotten very far."

"I just started," he lied.

"I see." She swiveled her head from side to side, her curls bouncing as she took in the naked tree, several boxes of lights and decorations, some pretty foil giftwrap he'd bought but had no idea what to do with, and her Santa, propped up against one wall.

"Tell you what." She turned to him, the three-cornered smile out in full force. "For a box of Dunkin' Donuts, I'll stay and help."

"Honey," he said. "You're on."

She'd only meant to stay for a minute. At least, she was pretty sure she'd only meant to stay for a minute. But the instant she saw that take-pity-on-the-clueless look on his face when he mentioned the window, she knew she was doomed.

Although that was nothing compared with how doomed she felt when she put on his sweatshirt and that male-right-outta-the-shower aroma smacked her right in the libido. Man, if she could bottle this, she'd make a fortune.

But that had been two hours ago and things had settled down a little since then.

Okay, so she was lying. Not only was nothing settled down, but with every silvery foil snowflake she cut out and every ornament she hung on the little tree and every fake present she made up and every snippet of conversation they had, she felt as though bits of her brain were floating away. Mostly the bits from the bins labeled Logic and Caution and This is How Grown-ups Do Things. But then, she'd pretty well emptied those bins when she'd turned the van around and come back here, hadn't she?

Then—*then*—he'd told her, finally, his idea about Ryder: that he'd noticed his drawings on the refrigerator, and how good he was at carving his pumpkin, and seeings as he was thinking of doing some how-to crafts classes for little kids on Saturday mornings—he'd rented the vacant storefront next door and was going to turn it into a combination play-room/classroom kind of thing—and did she think maybe Ryder might like to be his assistant? And she thought, damn—at this rate she'd be lucky to scrape together enough brain bits to find her way home again.

Other than that, though, he seemed content to listen, laughing at her stories about the party from hell and letting her prattle on about the kids and even about what had happened with Bobby earlier.

"So…how you feel about that?" he asked.

"I'm not sure," she said. "Good, I think. Like maybe I can move on now?"

"With what?" he said, those blue eyes about to burn right through her.

"I'm not really sure. But it's nice to have options."

"Sounds to me like you've had options for some time. You just haven't chosen to exercise 'em."

"Having them and being ready to act on them are two different things. It's like…I don't know. Trying to fit in new furniture before you've gotten rid of the old stuff. Either the new stuff doesn't fit, or the old stuff looks so tacky next to it, it doesn't work anyway." She leaned over to select her sixth donut of the evening. Or morning, actually. So she could count this as breakfast, right?

"So what are you gonna do about your roof?"

"Dunno," Joanna said around a full mouth. "I'll figure something out. Hey, maybe my show will be a sell-out."

"You ever sold out before?"

"No. But one can hope—"

She froze as he leaned forward and touched the corner of her mouth with the pad of his thumb. More brain bits floated off into the mist.

"That drop of chocolate's been bugging the life out of me for the last fifteen minutes," he said. Licking his thumb.

Joanna swallowed. "You know, you really shouldn't do things like that if we're not supposed to be getting down to brass tacks here."

A smile flickered across his lips. "That doesn't sound very comfortable."

"You know what I mean."

"Yes, I do," he said, suddenly serious. "You got any idea how much I'd like to kiss you?"

"I do now." Inside her tummy, donuts and anticipation started doing the cha-cha. "Are you? Going to kiss me?"

"No."

"Oh." She frowned.

"I take it that frown means you'd like me to kiss you?"

"I wouldn't be adverse to it, no." When several seconds passed and nothing happened, she said, "And you're still sitting over there because…?"

"It's not time yet."

"I don't suppose you'd be interested in letting me in on when that time might be?"

"I would if I knew. At least, I think I would. Maybe not. But in any case, since I don't, I can't."

She shifted from her rump to her knees and started arranging the fake gifts underneath the decorated tree. They'd posed her Santa—one of her largest, nearly three feet high in a traditional red velvet, fur-trimmed suit with black leather boots and belt—in a child-size rocker with a checklist in his hand, grinning out over what would be a batch of toys.

"I don't think I've ever met a man whose thought process was as convoluted as mine."

"That's because I've never met a woman who's ever tangled up my thought processes as bad as you do," he said behind her.

She twisted around to catch the soulful expression in his eyes, and she thought, *Damn.* This was someone she liked. And someone she was attracted to enough to risk making a fool of herself in bed again. But this was not someone she could afford to lose her heart to. Even if he was interested in taking it. Because when you added her newfound sense of self-preservation to Dale's own admission that he didn't want the responsibilities of adulthood, didn't want to be serious about things that she had no choice in being serious about, there was no doubt in her mind that falling in love with Dale had disaster written all over it.

So sue her for not wanting to go through that particular hell again.

"You know," he said, setting down his coffee cup to crawl out of the window, "you're much scarier when you're quiet than when you're talking. And that's damn scary."

She tried to smile, only to yawn instead. "Even I start to wind down by 2:00 a.m."

"You ready to go home?"

"Soon," she said. "When we're done. So tell me," she said when he thunked the first batch of toys into the window, "what made you decide to open a toy store?"

He was quiet for a moment, opening up a box. "You know how kids are always dreamin' about havin' their own candy store or whatever? Well, this was my dream. All the toys I could imagine, all in one place. Everything I'd ever dreamed of playing with at my disposal."

She futzed around with a couple of the ornaments, not looking at him. "But most kids outgrow that fantasy."

"Guess I didn't."

He began setting up an elaborate wooden train set under the tree; Joanna sat back on her haunches, watching his features soften as he hooked section after section of track together.

"Okay," she said, picking up one of the brightly colored cars. "So this says to me you were either a greedy little brat who never *thought* you got enough toys at Christmas…" She hesitated. "Or a kid who really didn't."

Except for the soft clacking of the wooden pieces as Dale fitted them together, the silence was so heavy she thought she'd choke on it.

"Dale?"

"Let's put it this way," he said. "It was one of those two." His head swiveled around as she clumsily got to her feet. "Where are you going?"

"My legs are cramping," she said, hearing the irritation sharpening her words. But she no sooner got out of the window than Dale was behind her, turning her to face him.

"I don't talk about the past because it's not worth talkin' about, okay? Not because I'm trying to shut you out. I'm not…trying to hide anything. And even though there's things about my life I'd prefer to let lie, that doesn't mean I'm not honest about my life now. Keeping my own counsel means no disrespect to you."

"Will you just answer one question, then?"

"Depends on what it is."

"Did you have a crappy childhood?"

"And why is it so important to you to know what kind of childhood I had?"

"Because it would help me understand who you are now."

He let go of her shoulders, only to take her by the hand and lead her through the store and out the back door.

"Hey! It's cold out here!"

"You won't be cold for long," he said, holding open the flap to the huge inflated jumping...thing that reminded her of that cheapo blow-up chair she'd had in her dorm room her freshman year. Only a hundred times bigger. And hopefully sturdier.

"You're way too tense, lady. So take off your shoes and get inside."

She looked at him. "Is this going to get kinky?"

"I doubt it. Come on," he said, getting rid of his own shoes.

Too tired to care, she ditched her sneakers and climbed up the stairs, feeling as though she was about to jump off a cliff into the raging Colorado.

"You're wearing pumpkin socks?" Dale said, climbing in behind her...and pushing her inside.

Joanna shrieked, lost her balance on the undulating surface and fell on her can. Ohmigod, this was the waterbed from hell. "In...keeping with...the seasonal...theme," she said, unable to get her bearings enough to stand. Dale reached over and hauled her to her feet, hanging on to her hands until they were jumping together.

"Just pretend...you're a little kid...jumping on...your parents' bed."

"I never...did that!" she said, landing on her butt again. And again, he yanked her upright, only to immediately let her go. And suddenly she knew what a baby bird must feel like, taking flight for the first time.

"Neither did I," he said, now hopping all over the thing like a crazy person. "Which is why…I do it now. Especially…*this*."

He started jumping higher and higher, bringing his knees up to his chest each time, his hair flying, his arms flapping, making the surface *boing* so she couldn't find her balance for the life of her. Being halfway to slaphappy anyway, she burst out laughing…and then she simply gave up and gave in, sliding and bouncing and falling and laughing and *laughing* and laughing until her sides hurt and she couldn't get her breath. Then she somehow *boinged* over to Dale and shoved him so he fell, sending a tsunami rolling through the Jell-O-like floor and Joanna down again, too, howling with laughter.

And he caught her in his arms as they both lay there, gasping for air, winnowing his fingers through her hair as their laughter gradually died away, giving her an imploring look that would have stolen her breath if she'd had any left to steal.

She lifted her hand to the back of his neck, encouraging him. But he reached up and grabbed her wrist, gently pinning it to the floor beside her head.

"This is who I am now," he said softly, his breath puffing across her face. "Who I was before doesn't matter. And until you decide you can live with that, until I can look into your eyes and not see those million and one questions burning a hole in your brain, there's no point in taking this any further."

"I see. You give that ultimatum to all the women you sleep with?"

A shadow scuttled across his features. "I never had to. Because nobody ever cared enough to ask before."

She shut her eyes, thought, *Oh, God*, then opened them again. "But you still want to kiss me, right?"

His smile was so sad, it broke her heart…even as it made

her want to swat him one. "Oh, honey," he said, "I want to do a helluva lot more than that."

"But only on your terms."

"It's gotta be that way, Joanna. For both our sakes."

She struggled to get up—no mean feat when the ground won't stay still—then wobbled out of the jump, grabbed her shoes and made shaky tracks back inside. She sank onto the floor, shoving her feet into her shoes.

"You got any idea why you're so mad?" Dale said above her.

"I know exactly why I'm mad. It's you who doesn't get it."

"No, it's *you* who doesn't get it." He crouched beside her, but she refused to look at him. "You know as well as I do that whether we go back to being lovers or not, this isn't something meant to last. You want a baby, I don't. You get bent out of shape if somebody's ten minutes late to dinner—"

"I don't—"

"You do. I know the type, okay? You don't like sports, we don't like the same music, and we probably don't even see eye to eye on political issues. So what the hell difference does it make to you whether or not I do the whole connect-with-my-inner-child crap?"

"That's just it, you big dope," she said, getting to her feet and smacking the heel of her hand into his chest, biting back a growl when he didn't even flinch. "It doesn't make a shred of difference to me! But maybe, just maybe, it would make a difference to *you!*"

She snatched up the double-bagged sweatshirt, which she'd probably toss in the trash when she got home anyway, and hotfooted it to the front of the store.

"Joanna?" he said when she got to the door.

She whirled around. "What?"

"Thanks. For the window."

"You're welcome," she said, then did the best job she knew how of storming out.

Chapter 14

"But, honey, if you don't decide on a wedding date soon, you're going to be showing."

Across the table at Papa Felipe's where they'd met for lunch, the worried expression in her mother's eyes made Tori cringe. "I know, I know," she said, picking at her chicken enchilada. "But with the holidays coming and all…"

"Don't be silly! People are already up for a party, anyway! And I told you, Leo said you could have the reception at our house. It'll be tight, but at least you wouldn't have to worry about trying to find a hall or someplace on such short notice. And it's no big deal for me to make up some of those appetizers you can get at the Sam's Club, you know. So all we'd have to get is the cake and flowers. And a wedding dress, of course."

"Oh, Lord." Tori sank against the padded booth back, idly watching cars whiz past outside. "It makes me tired to think about it."

"That's why you need to leave it all to me. Now, you're

probably tall enough that you won't show for several more weeks yet...so why don't we say..." Clicking her tongue against the roof of her mouth, her mother pulled her checkbook out of her handbag and checked the calendar. "How about the second Saturday in December?"

"Mama, I can't set a date without Bobby. And what if the kids have something planned for that day?"

Her mother gave her one of her looks. "Well, you won't know until you call him up and ask, will you?"

"I don't know..." Tori sighed, halfheartedly taking another bite of enchilada while flipping through the pages of one of the bridal magazines her mother had brought along. But it was like going grocery shopping when you weren't really hungry. Nothing looked good. And some of the prices! She slapped the magazine shut. "Maybe we should just wait until after the baby comes."

"Oh, no, we shouldn't."

Tori looked across the booth, nearly laughing at her mother's horrified expression. "If all those Hollywood people can do it, why can't Bobby and I?"

"Because people like us can't get away with the same things they can. Nobody's gonna call Catherine Zeta-Jones white trash, believe me." She waved her cell phone at Tori. "So call Bobby. Ask him about the date."

You know, it would probably be less stressful in the long run to let her mother have her way. Besides, the longer she put off the wedding, the longer she'd have to deal with this awful jittery feeling. Only she just did not feel like talking to Bobby right now.

"I've gotta pee," she whispered, sliding out of the booth. "Why don't you call him while I'm gone? It's 555-0300."

So when Tori returned after her twentieth trip of the day to the john, she had a wedding date: December 13th. She tried to take a breath, she felt like her lungs had frozen up.

"Honey...are you all right?"

"Yeah," Tori said, pasting on a smile for her mother's sake. And hers, too, she supposed. Hadn't she read somewhere that just the act of smiling was supposed to make you feel better?

"Anyway, Bobby said having the reception at the house was fine with him, as long as it was okay with you. And that later, after the baby came? The two of you could still do a big wedding, if you wanted."

"No. This is fine." She picked up the five-pound *Modern Bride* and opened it at random, telling herself she didn't really have to throw up. "Guess that means I have to think about a dress, huh?"

"I thought we could go looking Thursday night, during the poker game. How's that sound?"

"Whatever," she said, telling herself it was only natural that all this talk of weddings and babies—hers, especially—should make her feel a little on the emotional side.

Joanna was standing at the kitchen sink eviscerating a chicken—or at least removing the little paper packet of innards—when the boys started yelling, "He came! He came!" in unison and hopping around like a pair of fleas.

"What on earth are you talking about?" she asked no one in particular, since the kids had already stormed down the hall to answer the front door. The damn packet tore, oozing entrails all over her hands. Blech.

"It's just Dale," Dulcy said mildly as she came into the kitchen in search of something to keep her from starving until dinner—a good two hours away yet—as if his appearance had been expected.

And about the time Joanna wrapped her brain around the fact that, for the second time in a week, Dale McConnaughy had shown up out of the blue, there he was, just a'grinnin' to beat the band.

And, as usual, there *she* was, hair a wreck, covered in velvet lint and up to her wrists in chicken guts. Charming.

"You look surprised to see me," he said.

"That might be because I am?" She dumped the guts into the sink.

He frowned. "The boys didn't tell you I said I'd come over and teach 'em how to pitch?"

"No, they didn't. But then, telling me things isn't their strong suit."

"Oh. Well, I said I'd come over today. So here I am."

"I can see that."

"It's okay, isn't it?"

She looked at him then, thinking, *Who the hell knows?*

Joanna shoved her hair off her forehead with the back of her wrist. "Yeah, yeah, it's fine. Although..." She glowered at Ryder. "Did you get all your homework done?"

Several worksheets appeared about five inches in front of her face. She didn't dare touch them, but she did back away far enough to see that, yes, it would appear he'd gotten it all done.

"Okay. Looks good. So go. Live."

The boys took off out the patio door, Dale following. Only he stuck his head back inside and said, "This doesn't mean I'm expectin' dinner again."

"Good," she said, and he disappeared. Only to reappear a second later.

"I mean, I wouldn't want to impose myself or anything."

She threw a chicken liver at him, which the dog intercepted before Dale could get back outside.

A few minutes later, bird in the oven, hands dechickenized, sweatshirt changed and hair somewhat combed, she slipped on her ancient Peruvian sweater and went outside, Chester squeezing out of the sliding door seconds before his tail got docked. The light was fast waning, that heavy, liquid gold of late fall afternoons gilding the bare cottonwood branches. She sat on the patio step, hugging her knees as she watched Dale patiently play with her sons, and thinking, *You know, mister, if you don't want to see a thousand questions in my eyes, then quit doing stuff to put them there.*

Questions such as, *Why are you here, considering the way we left things on Friday night?*

And, *Why is it you don't want kids again?*

And, *What am I supposed to do about you?*

Matt cheering him on, Ryder wound up and let the ball fly. Except the stupid dog intercepted that, too, zooming across the yard, the boys and Dale all in hot pursuit, yelling and flapping their arms like a bunch of nuts.

And the million dollar question. *What do you want from me?*

Joanna plonked her chin in her hand, the scent of garlic and onion from the baking chicken leeching through the slightly open window behind her, mixing with the invigorating, comforting smell of moldering leaves and woodsmoke. And wondered…could she squelch her natural inclination to heal the hurts of the world and simply have an affair with him on his terms? Even if none of those questions ever got answered?

He looked over at that precise moment and gave her one of those oh-Lord-save-me smiles, and she thought, *Hell, yes.*

Of course, just because *she* thought the time was right didn't mean *he* thought the time was right.

The boys came bounding over, out of breath and red-cheeked; she grabbed each one as he flew by and wrestled him down for a quick kiss before swatting his bottom and sending him into the house. Dale sank onto the step below her, breathing hard, the last rays of the sun kissing his hair, the fine planes of his face; and he leaned back on his elbows and looked over at her, and she saw the reason for his showing up, time after time, like a damn stray dog who didn't want anybody to put a collar on him and call him theirs, but who kept coming around for the food, anyway.

She told herself again, as her heart ached for all he wouldn't admit to, that she didn't dare let herself get too close, that it was already dangerous, what she was doing, what she was thinking. But dammit, she was lonely, too, and hungry—no, ravenous—for a man's touch, this man's touch, even if only for the moment…and he lifted a hand to the back of her neck and pulled her mouth to his and all she could think of was *yes* and *yes* again when his tongue touched hers like a question, and how different it seemed this time from the last and how she didn't want this to end, not ever—

Joanna pulled away, flushing like a fourteen-year-old, and Dale laughed and slipped his hand underneath the heavy sweater, skimming a knuckle down the side of one breast through her sweatshirt, so slowly, then over her nipple, more slowly still, as if everything of importance in the entire universe was concentrated in that one…spot, back…and forth…and back again until she had to bite her tongue to keep from crying out.

"I'm thinking it's time," he said softly. "What about you?"

She thought of asking why he'd changed his mind, only to decide who the hell cared. So instead she said, "How will I ever make it to Friday night?"

He said, "I have no intention of waiting until Friday night."

She choked on her own breath and said, "The kids—"

"They do go to sleep, don't they?"

She nodded, wondering how on earth she was going to get through dinner.

But she did. They all did. And, eventually, the dishes got done and the kids went to sleep and the dog went out and the cats came in, and she closed up the house and took Dale to her bed, again, praying nobody woke up anytime too soon.

And this time, by golly, they got it right.

* * *

The moonlight struck Dale in the eye, waking him from an unbelievably peaceful sleep. Deep and dreamless, for a change. The night had turned cold enough to pull Joanna's comforter over them, under which she now stirred, murmuring something that sounded like, "What time is it?"

He glanced over at the clock by her side of the bed, reaching for her at the same time. She was all warm and soft, smelling of sleep and sex and cherries, weirdly enough, and the thought of leaving this bed, leaving her, chilled him to the bone.

"Twelve-thirty. I should probably go soon."

"Not yet," she murmured, molding all that sweet-smelling softness to him, pressing her lips to the hollow of his throat, his chest, his nipples, her tongue hot and delicate against his sensitive skin. And he knew it would be more than her warmth, her kisses, even her sweetness, that he would miss. He'd left those behind before, with varying degrees of regret ranging from mild to medium, depending on his mood at the time. But Joanna's openness, her generosity, her willingness to give him everything she had while asking nothing in return...

He didn't deserve her. Even temporarily.

And he'd never craved anything more.

He wrapped an arm around her bare back, his breath catching at the gentle friction of her body sliding up his as he pulled her up to join their mouths. Hers met his already open, ready to receive, even more ready to give, unashamed of her hunger.

"Why do you smell like cherries?" he asked, and she laughed.

"I grabbed the kids' shampoo instead of my own this morning when I was in the shower." Her hand strayed down to cup him, fingers teasing, stroking. Provoking. She yawned. "You like?"

"Oh, yeah."

"I was talking about the shampoo."

"I wasn't." He shut his eyes, savoring, then said, "Again?"

"Please?"

"You're half asleep."

"Sleepy sex's the best," she mumbled, wriggling back down, her hair whispering over his chest as her mouth found its way to his navel. At least most of the scars were on his back. And if she'd noticed them, she hadn't said anything. Maybe she was learning. "Can't think," she said, "only feel. No inhibitions."

"None?"

Eyes still closed, she lifted her head, her brow puckered like she needed to think this over. A second later she shook her head, all those crazy curls dancing around her face, tickling him. "Nope." Then she went back to kissing his belly. In slow motion.

"So the first time—"

She held up two fingers, still kissing. Actually, more like nibbling.

"—*times* weren't enough?"

"Nope. Wan' more." *Nibble. Nibble.* "Three years is a looong time, buddy."

He chuckled and flipped her over, sending the covers flying, returning the favor, shoving aside regrets about what he couldn't do for her to concentrate on what he could. At his age, three times in less than two hours was pushing it— why any woman would have penis envy was beyond him, he thought as he moved lower, hoping to hell she had a good lock on her door and the kids were heavy sleepers— but if the lady wanted more, the lady would get more.

So he teased and nuzzled and did some serious nibbling of his own, changing his angle of attack from time to time just to keep things interesting for all parties concerned, until her breathing hitched and all these cute little sounds started up again in her throat and he said, "Like this?" and she hissed, "Yessss, oh yessssohpleaseohdon'tstop" and he whispered, between kisses, "Now?" and she tangled her fingers in his hair and held him to her, her last *"Yessssss!"* standing in for the cries she didn't dare let go, even as she did.

He held her afterward, as long as he dared, as if trying to somehow absorb her aftershocks. And her contentment.

"All better now?"

"Oh, yeah," she said on a long, breathy sigh.

"Good." Then he kissed her, on the mouth, her eyes, tonguing her nipple one last time before forcing himself out of the bed to find his scattered clothes.

He heard her roll onto her side, her soft laughter drifting to him like a caress.

"What's so funny?" he said, zipping up his jeans.

"Oh, nothing. Except why does the phrase 'I hate to eat and run' come to mind?"

He yanked his sweatshirt over his head, poking his arms through the sleeves. "And here I thought you were a lady."

"What on earth gave you that idea?"

"Damn. I don't even get credit for corrupting you."

Once again, her quiet laughter reached out to him, threatening to pull him under. Tempting him to forget all the *this-is-why*s and *because*s and *it-has-to-be-this-way*s that had become second nature by this point.

He sat on the edge of the bed to put on his sneakers, feeling the mattress shift as she scootched across to him. "The bed's already getting cold without you," she said, raking her fingertips up and down his spinal column and he thought, almost angrily, *Not nearly as cold as mine's gonna be.*

"I know." Shaken by his reaction, he bent to tie his shoelace, yanking it so hard he nearly broke it. "But it's probably not a good idea for me to be around when the kids get up."

Her hand dropped to the mattress. "You're right." After

a pause she said, "But that's not why you're leaving, is it?"

He twisted around to her, for the first time in his life regretting the answer he had to give.

"No." When all she did was brush her hair out of her face, he said, "That bother you?"

"A little, maybe," she said after a moment. "But not for the reasons you probably think. And it certainly doesn't surprise me. Not after—" she lifted one hand, tracing her fingertips over the most prominent of the scars "—our conversation the other night." Her hand dropped. "But I'll get over it. As long as we can do this again." He saw her smile flash in the half light. "Soon."

"I'm thinking…"

You're getting too close, I can't do this, I'm out of my mind for even thinking *about doing this.*

"…Friday."

"Took the words right outta my mouth."

"Good." He leaned over and gave her one last kiss, whispered, "Go back to sleep," then left through the French doors that led outside from her bedroom…out of her room, out of her house, and out of a life that could only be his every now and then.

And only for a little while at that.

Go back to sleep. Right.

Joanna got up, yanked on an old flannel nightgown and tromped into the bathroom. In the midst of trying—with little success—to unsnarl her hair, she grimaced at herself in the mirror. "You're an idiot, Joanna Swann, you know that?"

An insomniac idiot, at that. Now in her robe and antique-but-still-relatively-intact sheepskin slippers, she shuffled out to the studio, figuring if she was going to be awake for the next couple of hours, she might as well work. Every year she'd make up a batch of ornaments and Santa puppets from scraps so she'd have some less-expensive items to sell at the show, fun, brainless work she'd always been able to count on to soothe her frazzled nerves when the rest of her world went to pot.

Until tonight, when not even the plushness of satin and velvet against her fingers could erase the memory of puckered scar tissue.

She shut off the Pfaff and tromped back out to the family room, folding herself onto the old couch. Chester climbed up beside her, rolling over so she'd scratch his chest.

"It's not that I don't understand why he had to leave," she said to the dog, who groaned. "It's just…I don't think he *wanted* to." Chester groaned again. "What on earth is he so afraid of?"

The dog rolled his eyes backward to look at her, baring his tiny bottom teeth. Joanna sighed and got up. "Come on, you sorry bag of fur," she said, heading back to her bedroom. Once there, she patted the mattress. Chester sat on one hip on the rug, eyebrows twitching as he looked from her to the bed, then back to her.

"No, it's not a trick. I swear. Just don't hog the pillows, okay? And for God's sake, don't tell the cats. I'd never hear the end of it."

The dog jumped up after she got in bed, circling three times before flopping down with a weighty sigh, his head on what had been Dale's pillow.

"So Edie tells me you and Tori finally set a date?"

At Leo Medina's comment, Bobby glanced up from the cards Joanna's father had just dealt him—could be worse, a trio of diamonds and a couple of oddballs—to the heavyset, balding man who would be his stepfather-in-law in less than six weeks. He told himself the spurt of acid he'd just felt was because of Tori's salsa (great stuff, but hot enough to etch glass) and had nothing to do with his *ex*-father-in-law sitting right next to him. Or that he hadn't been sleeping so good lately. Man, he'd been having some strange dreams over the past week, the kind he'd wake up from with his heart racing. Except he could never seem to remember them. Which was probably just as well.

"Yeah," he said, taking a swig of his Coors, his heel bouncing against the carpet. "Second Saturday in December." He glanced across the table, saw Dale studying his own cards, frowning. Except Bobby now knew Dale's expression usually had nothing to do with the cards in his hand. A learning curve that had already cost him twenty bucks.

"You gonna open?" Leo said to him.

Bobby tossed in a couple of chips. Enough to get things going, not enough to give anybody a clue about his hand.

"I'll see your two bucks…and raise you another two," Leo said, adding four chips to the pile. "And the kid's due when?"

"June." Bobby shifted in his seat. Maybe he should switch to nachos, coat his stomach with some cheese.

Joanna's father folded; Dale saw Leo's bet and raised him another buck. Hmm. Bobby discarded his crappy cards and pulled two more from the deck. Aw, man…what the hell good was a three of clubs and a deuce of spades gonna do him?

"Edie's about to drive me nuts," Leo said good-naturedly, exchanging a couple of cards. "She's worse than my first wife was, wanting to be a grandmother. Maybe because Tori's her only kid and all."

"Tell me about it," Roger Swann said, leaning back in the dinette set's swivel chair, his hands linked behind his neck. Bobby noticed Dale kept his entire hand. "Glynnie spoils those kids rotten."

Bobby chuckled. "Like I don't see you slip 'em cash every time you're around 'em."

Dale's chair creaked when he leaned forward to shove a

couple chips to the center of the table, upping the ante a little more.

Leo scratched his round belly, saw Dale's two bucks and raised him another two. What the hell? "And you better believe that's exactly what I'm gonna do with this one of yours, too," he said to Bobby.

At Bobby's puzzled expression, the older man's heavy black eyebrows shot up. "What? You think just because Tori's not my flesh and blood, I won't see this baby as my grandkid?" Without waiting for an answer, Leo turned to Dale. "By the way, I gotta tell you—Edie's gonna wet her drawers when she finds out you're here tonight."

"Oh?"

"Oh, yeah. She's a big fan of yours. I'm talkin' serious groupie," he added with a rumbling laugh. "I always said the main reason we hit it off was because I had ESPN and could get all the Braves' games. And God forbid I needed to talk to her about anything when you were up on the mound, boy. 'Course, don't let it go to your head. She's got quite a thing for Barry Bonds, too. And the way she used to go on about Nolan Ryan's damn blue eyes…" Another laugh. "Let's just say it's a good thing I'm not the insecure type. But boy, is she gonna be ticked that she took Tori shopping for wedding gowns instead of hanging out with us like she usually does. She keeps saying she's gonna go over to that store of yours, but I guess she's been too busy to get there yet. Guess you must get a lot of that, though. Fans wanting your autograph and all."

"Not so much anymore," Dale said with a shrug, like he didn't want to talk about it. "But if your wife and I miss each other tonight you tell her to come over to the store anytime to say hello. Just be sure to have her call first, since I'm not always around."

"Well, that's mighty nice of you, Dale," Leo said with a grin. "I'll be sure to tell her. Thanks."

A minute or so later Bobby heard Tori's key in the front

door. Eyes bright and cheeks flushed, she popped into the apartment, a large dress box clutched in one hand. She'd pulled her long hair back into a clip, but strands of it stood up around her face, all staticky.

"No, no, don't get up, y'all. I'm just gonna put this away before ol' big eyes sees it."

"I take it you found a dress?" Bobby called as she disappeared into their bedroom.

"You take it right," she called back. "And no, you can't see it before the wedding, so don't even think about it."

Bobby looked around at the other men. "Am I the only man on the planet who doesn't *care* what the damn wedding dress looks like?" All three assured him he wasn't.

"Shoot," Roger said. "The only reason I even remember Glynnie's is because I've been looking at our wedding photo on the mantel every damn day for the last thirty-four years. Although don't ask me to describe it. White and lacy, that's all I can tell you."

"Bet you remember how hard it was to get off afterward, though," Leo said, chuckling.

"Lord, yes. What kind of sadist puts a hundred satin buttons on the back of a dress?"

Bobby thought better of contributing any more to the conversation, but he remembered all too well he never got the chance to remove Jo's wedding dress, some simple, slippery thing that came to her ankles—no lace or pearls for her, boy—because she was out of it practically before they got the hotel door locked. He smiled at the memory, noting with something like relief that that's all it was—a memory. And a slightly faded one, at that, not provoking much feeling one way or the other. Not like, say, when his kids were born. Both of those events were as clear in his mind as the day they'd happened.

Tori reappeared, a sliver of midriff teasing him above the waistband of her hip hugger jeans, looking smug as could be. Hard to believe she was pregnant, flat as her stomach still was. Joanna hadn't been able to get her jeans zipped at six weeks, and Tori was approaching—what?—two months or something. She slipped a hand onto his shoulder, seeming to notice Dale for the first time.

"Oh, shoot! Bobby, why didn't you tell me you'd invited Dale? Mama will have a cow when she finds out!"

"Wasn't I just sayin' that?" Leo said.

"And I would've invited her up," Tori said, "but she said she was tired and went on home." She looked over to Leo. "She said to tell you, by the way, and I quote, 'If he's not home by eleven, he loses out.'"

"Okay, okay," Leo said as the men all laughed. "But that is not an idle threat. I'm telling you, the man who invented Viagra must've been married to a woman like your mother."

"And what makes you so sure a *man* invented it, huh?" Tori said.

The others hooted with laughter, and Bobby thought, as Tori trailed her fingers across his back before heading into the open kitchen to make her nightly hot chocolate, *Yeah, that's my girl.* And when he looked over at her, her eyes met his and she gave him a wink and one of her sassy grins, and some of the anxiety that had been eating at him for the past week eased up. Not all of it, not by a long shot, but enough to make him think he was worrying over nothing.

It was nuts, sitting here feeling jealous of somebody who hadn't been married to Joanna for more than three years. But when the men had started talking about wedding gowns and the removal thereof, Dale had seen the look on Bobby's face that told him clear as day—just as he could pretty much figure Bobby was holding a halfway decent hand right now—that he was remembering his own wedding night.

Dale wasn't sure what he found more annoying—

Bobby's expression or his reaction to Bobby's expression. He'd never given a damn before about who his lovers had slept with. Of course, there was a difference, he supposed, between knowing a woman had slept with other men, and knowing who the other men were. That made things much more personal. One thing he did know, though: two men in the same room thinking about the same naked woman at the same time—unless she was a *Playboy* centerfold— was one man too many. He half wanted to say, *Hey—you had your turn. Now move on, buddy. She's mi—*

"I'll see you and raise you two more bucks," he said, shoving the unfinished word out of his mind before it had a chance to take root. And while he was shoving things out of his head that didn't belong there, he might as well clean out the part about his missing Joanna so much these past two days, he nearly hurt with it; the way he was about to go crazy with anticipation, knowing he was going to see her again tomorrow night; how he jumped every time the phone rang, scared it was gonna be Joanna calling him to say she'd changed her mind.

And the worst thing of it was, he had no right to feel any of it. If she was smart, she *would* call it off.

If he was smart, *he* would.

"I'm out," Leo said, slapping his cards on the table. Roger looked at Dale—and if Bobby had told him Joanna's father was one of his poker buddies, for sure he wouldn't't've come tonight—a half smile on his lips, and said, "You must be pretty sure of yourself," and Dale thought, *Like hell.*

As it was, he'd thought about backing out of tonight's game at least half a dozen times. But he hadn't, partly because he'd promised he'd be here, and partly because, oddly enough, he really did like Bobby. Weird though it was, he could understand why both his former and his future fathers-in-law liked him enough to play poker with him on a regular basis: Bobby Alvarez simply didn't have a devious bone in his body. And the two older men were okay, too. Even Joanna's father. The naked-Joanna-in-his-head problems aside, it was kind of nice to hang out with a few guys, none of whom were trying to prove anything to anybody else.

All of whom seemed perfectly content to be yoked to their particular women, he noticed. Joanna's father, married for thirty-five years to the same woman, and clearly happy. Leo, falling in love again after losing the woman he'd married when he was twenty. And Bobby, whose smile for Tori when she came through the door a little while ago sent a stab of envy through Dale so strong his heartbeat got off track for a second.

And that was not good. Not good at all. His survival depended upon certain things, not the least of was never, ever, letting himself feel envious of another man's love life.

But then, he'd never missed a woman this way before, either.

"I'm out," Bobby said, and Dale grinned, laying out his cards.

"Aw, man…" Bobby shook his head in disgust, half laughing. "I can't believe all you had was two lousy pairs," he muttered, displaying his Three of a Kind. "I was *sure* you had something good." He leaned back in his chair, arms folded across his chest, one side of his mouth pulled up. "So you lied. Again."

"Hey, now…" Still grinning, Dale leaned over to gather his chips. "It's not lyin' if you choose to believe I have more in my hand than I do."

"I'm not talking about that. I'm talking about you telling me you're a rotten player."

"I am. Not my fault if you're worse than I am."

The men all laughed, then got up to replenish their beers, relieve themselves, scavenge for more food. Bobby headed for the kitchen, looping an arm around Tori's shoulders. "One more game before we call it a night?"

The others said, "Sure," so Dale figured he could probably get through another twenty minutes or so. "Gotta go right after that, though," he said. "I'm in early at the store tomorrow."

He grabbed a Coke and returned to the table, sinking into the deeply cushioned swivel chair with a sigh. Bobby abandoned Tori to her stepfather in the kitchen and followed, a crease between his brows.

"Hey, man—you okay?"

Dale looked up. "Me? Yeah. Why?"

"I dunno…you look a little uncomfortable or somethin'."

"Long day. That's all."

Bobby nodded, took a swallow of beer, his eyes on Dale's Coke. "I know this is none of my business, but you don't drink, do you?"

A question Dale was more than used to by now. "Nope."

"Mind if I ask why?"

"Just don't have the taste for it, I guess," he said, giving Bobby his and-that's-where-this-conversation-ends look.

After a moment Bobby nodded, then said, "So…Jo tells me you suggested maybe Ryder could do this art class at the store or something?"

"Yeah. I'm thinking getting the kids to actually use some of the arts and crafts supplies we stock might be a good way to sell 'em, y'know? Not that I'm trying to get you and Jo to buy stuff for Ryder," he added with a laugh. "But I thought he might get a kick out of the class, since he seems to be takin' after his mama. And being as a lot of the kids would probably be younger, he could act like my assistant."

"He would get a kick out of that, you're right." Bobby took another swig of his beer, then said, "But I guess you haven't said anything to him yet. Since I talked to Ry tonight, before you came over. And he told me you were over to the house on Tuesday to play ball with them.''

Dale froze. Bobby leaned over and said in a low voice, ''And then he told me he woke up sometime in the middle of the night, just in time to see you drive away.''

Damn.

''So you're better at bluffing at cards,'' Bobby said with a shrug. ''But it's okay, man. It's not like I wasn't gonna find out sooner or later.''

''No, I suppose not.''

''Just one thing, though.''

''And what's that?''

''I know this was my idea. You and Joanna, I mean. But so help me God, you don't treat her right, I'll break every bone in your body.''

And what was Dale supposed to say to that? *It's not like that—it's just a temporary…thing.* Yeah, right, that'd go over big. Especially when Bobby added, ''See, no matter how hard I tried, I could never be what Joanna needed. What she deserved, you know? I know she never felt she could count on me, but it was like I couldn't get the hang of whatever it was I was supposed to be doing. She just doesn't need to go through that crap again, you know what I'm saying—?''

''Okay,'' Roger said, rubbing his hands in glee and settling back in his seat. ''Who's up for winning his money back from the new boy? Dale, why don't you do the honors?''

Dale took the deck and shuffled it in what felt like slow motion, beginning to think he was the most screwed-up bastard on the face of the planet.

Feeling better than she had in weeks, Tori carried her hot chocolate into the bedroom, setting it on the nightstand so she could sneak another peek at the dress while the guys were still playing. Mama had been right—she'd needed to move forward, was all, and things would start falling into place of their own accord. And the minute she saw the dress, all her fears melted away.

She shut the bedroom door and locked it, just in case, then held the cream-colored panne velvet dress up in front of her, sighing at the way it shimmered in the light. With its wide scoop neck and simple lines, it was the most sophisticated dress she'd ever owned. She'd wear her hair up, she thought, the way she'd seen Ashley Judd wear hers at some awards ceremony or other recently. No veil, just some pearl earrings, maybe the locket Bobby'd given her for Valentine's Day. And that pair of satin shoes she'd seen at Macy's with the strap across the instep.

What Joanna had looked like on her wedding day, Tori had no idea, since it wasn't like they still kept their wedding pictures up or anything. But somehow she had the feeling that once Bobby saw her in this dress, he'd never even think about Joanna in hers again.

And if that was childish of her, tough patooties.

She heard sounds from the other room that told her the others were getting ready to leave; she quickly tucked the dress back into its opaque cover in the closet and changed into her prettiest nightie, the red one with all the lace, then remembered to unlock the bedroom door. Keeping Bobby out was not on her agenda now, she thought with a smile.

She was nearly finished her cocoa when Bobby finally ambled down the short hall and into the room, his eyebrows lifting when he saw what she was wearing.

"Somebody must be feeling frisky tonight," he said, unbuttoning his shirt.

"Uh-huh. It was the strangest thing, though. The last thing I felt like doing tonight was going to look for a wedding dress, but we walked into Dillard's and there it was, and it was like everything just clicked. Like with the baby coming and all, I hadn't had the chance yet to feel like a bride."

"And now you do?"

"I guess so."

Bobby shucked off the shirt, then his jeans, and crawled over the bed to her on his hands and knees, growling, the tiny cross he always wore dangling from his throat. Giggling, she wriggled onto her back as he attacked her neck and breasts, kissing her nipples right through the lace, which really, really turned her on.

"Will you still want me when I look like an elephant?" she said.

He laughed. "I think the question is, will you want *me* when you *feel* like an elephant?"

Then, suddenly, she got this weird, kind of icky feeling, as if somebody was stepping on her chest so she couldn't breathe properly. She cupped Bobby's jaw in her hands and looked right into his eyes, almost afraid to ask what she needed to ask, right now, or go crazy with wondering.

"You didn't just ask me to marry you because of the baby, right? I mean, you really do love me, don't you?"

He got that funny look on his face, the one she could never quite figure out, then laughed. "Hey. If I didn't love you, there wouldn't be any baby, okay?"

"So everything's gonna work out? The baby, our getting married, all of it?"

"Of course it is, sweetheart," he said, kissing her lightly on the lips. "I promise."

Chapter 15

Friday morning dawned bright and clear and cold, with a sky so blue it shimmered. One of those days guaranteed to make a person glad to be alive.

Unless the person—in this case, Joanna—felt like death warmed over.

By the time she got Dulcy and Matt to school and Ryder—who, bless him, was the source of her feeling like death warmed over—reasonably settled down, it was nearly ten. Cursing the gods and anybody else responsible, she dialed Dale's number at the store. Some irritatingly peppy young thing chirped, "Sure thing—just a minute, 'kay?" when Joanna asked to speak with Dale.

"I'm so sorry," she croaked the minute he answered. "But I don't think tonight's in the cards."

Silence. Followed by a rather pithy obscenity.

"This is how you talk in a toy store?"

"I'm in my office. With the door closed. I can say anything I damn well please."

"This mean you're disappointed?"

More silence. Then, "Yeah."

"You know, that almost makes me feel better."

A heavy sigh shuddered through the silence. "And I'm being a jerk. You sound terrible."

"Which would be pretty much how I feel." She stopped to blow her nose. "It's just a cold, nothing life-threatening. Unfortunately, since being alive doesn't hold much appeal right now. But Ryder was home all day yesterday, so I got behind in my work. And I was up most of the night with him because he couldn't breathe. And now I've got his crud, and I'd better keep the other two here with me tomorrow at least, because they'll probably get it, and I can't in good conscience send them to their dad's with Tori being in her first trimester—"

"Mo-om!"

"I'll be right there," she called to Ryder, then said, "Anyway. There's no point in your coming over tonight." She started to cough, wincing as it scraped her throat. "I'm sorry."

"Not half as sorry as I am."

"I'll make it up to you, I pro—"

"Mo-om!"

"Go take care of the kid," he said and hung up.

Well, excuse me, she thought, dragging her sniffling, coughing, bedraggled body down the hall to the boys' room. Other than a weekly sweep to change sheets, collect laundry and ferret out substances that could become toxic if left to breed, she came in here only to dispense good-night kisses or in cases of dire emergency. Which this was. Ryder was lying on his side in the bottom bunk, red-nosed and watery-eyed, one arm hanging off the edge of the mattress. Oughtta be a rule that mothers and kids couldn't get sick at the same time.

"I don't feel good..." Much pointless sniffing. "My node is all 'tuffy."

"I know, baby. So's mine."

"Yeah?"

"Uh-huh. You hungry?"

"Uh-uh."

"Not even for some chicken noodle soup?" She brushed his hair off his head, which was cool. "And some Coke?"

He nodded. Whatever worked. If she could just get him to sleep for a while, then maybe she could get a nap and get back to work. With orders to ship and the show in less than two weeks, she could *not* afford to be sick. Literally.

Of course, ten minutes later when she brought him a mug of soup, he was out like a light. Joanna put it in the fridge, then lay on the couch in the family room, praying for a whole half hour of quiet.

The phone rang. Joanna stiffened when she heard her mother's voice on the answering machine. And oh, the temptation to ignore it was strong. However, there was something to be said for facing up to your fears, too. She grabbed the cordless from the coffee table in front of her, plastering it to the ear not buried in the sofa cushions.

"'Lo?"

"Joanna? What's wrong, honey ? You sound awful."

"Just a cold. I'll live. What's up?"

"You sure you're okay…?"

"Mom. I'm fine. Although if you don't tell me within the next three seconds why you called, I won't be."

"Well, you know how I told you about the new hot-shot attorney from Dallas who just joined the firm?"

"Uh-huh," Joanna said, not having the slightest clue what her mother was talking about, but also not having the strength to find out. "What about him?"

"Well…he happened to see a picture of you on my desk, and I think he might be…interested."

Joanna pinched herself. Nope. Not a dream.

"Mom—" She covered the mouthpiece and let out a sneeze powerful enough to scare the dog. "Momb, please…led's nod go there, okay?"

"Now hear me out, honey. He's in his mid-thirties, an excellent litigator…" She lowered her voice. "His billable hours are *extremely* impressive. And he's not bad to look at, either."

"Fide. You go oud with himb."

"You need to blow your nose."

"Believe be, if I could, I would. A'd don' change the subject. I don' wanna be fixed ub with eddybody."

"You're just saying that because you're not feeling well."

"No, I'mb saying thad because I don' wanna be fixed ub. I'mb thirdy-two…hold on…" She let out another killer sneeze, then said, "I'mb perfeckly capable of finding my owd man."

There was a pause. Joanna shivered, and not because she was cold.

"Whad?"

"Matt told me that Dale McConnaughy's been there a couple of times."

"Wheddid you talk to Matt?"

"The other day. I called and you were in the tub or something. Really, Jo…you couldn't possibly be serious about him, could you?"

Her head suddenly felt as if it weighed approximately five hundred pounds. Even though her mother's words were nothing more than a dim echo of the very thoughts trapped inside Joanna's stuffy head, the anger that flashed through her was downright startling.

"But it *would* be okay if I got serious with a *clone of the mad I dumped* twelve years ago, right?"

"No, of course not. But, honey…well, I wasn't going to say anything, since it's really none of my business…but Dale said some things at the party that corroborate what we thought, about his not being fiscally responsible." While Joanna sat there being stunned, her mother added, in a whisper for some reason, "He more or less indicated he has virtually *nothing* left from all that money he earned as a player. Can you imagine?''

"You know what, Momb? You're right. It is none of your business. Now if you'll excuse me, I need to go steam my head open. I'll talk to you later. 'Bye."

Then Joanna hung up before her mother could figure out a new angle of attack.

Not surprisingly, by the time she picked Matt up from school, he was coughing and sneezing, too, although his biggest worry seemed to center around whether or not this meant his weekend was toast. Dulcy, however, not only swore she was feeling okay, but tried valiantly to get Joanna—who, determined to be productive, had once again propped herself up in the studio, armed with tea and Halls—to go to bed, declaring she could handle things just fine, Mo-om, sheesh, she wasn't a little kid, for crying out loud.

"You're only eleven," Joanna said, willing her watery eyes to clear up long enough to stitch a pair of Santa pants without sewing her fingers to the fabric. "Besides," she said, honking into the sodden tissue she'd been keeping tucked in her sleeve. "I'm fide."

"Mom, your eyes are the same color as your hair. So's your nose. I still think we should go to Dad's so you can get some rest—"

"No. I mean, that's very sweet of you, but Tori does not need to catch a cold right now if she can possibly help it. I already called your father, told him to stay a—" she sneezed "—way."

"Wow."

Tissue to nose, Joanna looked at her daughter through a scrim of cold tears. "Wow?"

"You're, like, being really nice to Tori."

"You think I should be mean to her? And if you're gonna sit here and talk to me, make yourself useful. All those pants need the threads clipped on the seams."

Dulcy's brows went up at the pile of pants in all different colors and sizes, but she grabbed a pair of trimming scissors from the tray by the sewing machine and started clipping as instructed. Joanna was a firm believer in child labor, even if guilt impelled her to pay the child highway robbery wages.

"It's not that," Dulcy said, clipping away. "It's just...I don't know. She's so different from you, that's all."

"I think that was the idea, honey. Since your dad and I couldn't make our relationship work, it wouldn't make much sense for him to marry someone just like me, would it?"

"But she's like, practically *my* age!"

Joanna croaked out a laugh. "She happens to be the same age I was when I had you. Or had you forgotten that?"

Dulcy pulled a face. "It wouldn't be so bad, maybe, if she didn't keep coming up with all these dorky things for us to do that she thinks will be fun. And they're not. They're just stupid."

Oh, brother. Joanna blew her nose for what seemed like the thousandth time that day. And not only did her ears pop, but one nasal passage opened up. Yee-hah.

"That's because Tori really wants you guys to like her. You can't hate her for that, for goodness' sake."

"I don't hate her..."

"But?"

"It's just weird. That's all."

"I know it is, sweetie. But think how she must feel, trying to figure out where she fits in. It probably wouldn't hurt if you tried to meet her halfway instead of making her do all the work." As she watched Dulcy make another face, it occurred to Joanna, with a dull and somewhat sickening thud, that the last thing she'd expected when she signed those divorce papers was to find herself championing her successor. "Besides, aren't you at least excited about having a new baby brother or sister?"

"Mo-om."

"What now?"

"In case you haven't noticed? I'm not exactly into little kids?"

"Oh. But your brothers…?"

"—are *why* I'm not into little kids. So what are we going to do about dinner?"

Hell. She'd rather stick up for her ex-husband's pregnant girlfriend than think about that. Another wave of self-pity washed over her: bad enough that not only had her planned evening of sex and no cooking fizzled out because she had two sick kids and a nose that only worked on one side, now she had to think about dinner, too? As Dulcy would say, this was so not fair.

"I have no idea. But it's early yet. Maybe by six I'll think of something."

"How about pizza?"

"Maybe. We'll see." Unfortunately, ever since Pizza Hut started taking plastic, she could no longer use "I don't have any money" as an excuse. "You finished with those pants?"

Nodding, Dulcy handed them back to her, then frowned as she scanned the studio, which seemed about to burst at the seams with half-finished, half-naked Santas. "Wow. You think you'll get these all done in time?"

"I don't have much of a choice, do I? Is that the doorbell?"

Dulcy hopped off the stool and went to look. Ten seconds later Dale appeared in the studio doorway.

"Go away!" Joanna shrieked, mortified. Shocked. Thrilled. "We're disgusting and contagious."

"I'm not," Dulcy contributed as Dale said, waltzing on in as if he owned the place, "Believe me, I've seen disgusting. You're not even close. And I don't get colds. Here," he said, handing a lumpy plastic bag to Dulcy. "This needs to go in the freezer, thanks."

Dulcy scampered off; Joanna pulled her attention away from the mysterious grocery bag and asked, "What do you mean, you don't get colds?"

"Just what I said."

"And what are you doing here, anyway?" she asked, watching him scan the studio, frowning much the same way Dulcy had a minute before. "Don't you ever—" she sneezed "—work?"

"I closed up early. I was bored, anyway." He reached over, plucked a half-stitched Santa coat out of her hands and yanked her to her feet.

"Hey!" she said when he not-so-gently pushed her toward the door. "What the hell do you think you're doing?" She whirled around to head back to the sewing machine, only to yelp when his hands landed firmly on her shoulders, rewhirling her. Joanna dug her feet into the cement floor like the dog did at bathtime. "I've got too much work to do—"

"Which you're not gonna be able to do at all if you drive yourself into pneumonia."

By this time he'd successfully manhandled her into the family room, where he pointed to the couch. "Sit."

"I told you, I can't—"

He got right in her face, whacking her already iffy balance and sending her crashing backward into the cushions. "You look like hell, Joanna. And you sound worse. One night off ain't gonna kill you. But not taking it off might. Now, I'm gonna build a fire, then see about dinner—"

"We were thinking pizza," Dulcy, who had returned, put in. Joanna glared at her.

"Pizza is good," Dale said. "Since as we all know, I don't cook much. Or if you don't feel like pizza, we'll figure out something else. I can handle grilled-cheese sandwiches and scrambled eggs, but judging from the look on your daughter's face, that's not high on the list. Now, from what Dulcy told me when I came in, the boys probably aren't on death's door. You, on the other hand, are looking like a pretty good candidate.''

Joanna turned her glare on him. And sneezed so loudly the room echoed. "It's a cold, Dale," she said, then blew her nose. "Unlike some of us in the room with overachieving immune systems, whatever the kids get, I get."

"Yeah, but they're eight years old and aren't stressed out."

They stared each other down for several seconds until Joanna's nose started to drip. She blew, then said, her head tilted, "Is this some kind of knight-in-shining-armor rescue thing?"

"Yeah. You wanna make something of it?"

"Heck, no."

"Good. Because you wouldn't get very far. Dulcy, why don't you make your mother a cup of tea while I go check on the boys? Then I'll get the fire going and call for the pizza."

"I thought we were still discussing dinner?"

"Not any more." He pointed one finger at Joanna. "And don't you dare move your butt from that sofa, you hear me?"

"Can I get up to pee?" she called after him as he strode down the hall.

"Only if you check with me first," he called back, and she thought, *Uh, no...this is definitely* not *Bobby*. And maybe, when her head felt a little less as though somebody'd stuffed it with socks, she'd think about why Dale was here. And how she felt about that. Until then, she decided as she tugged the crocheted throw from the back of the sofa and stretched out, right now it made more sense to go with the flow than fight it.

She did, however briefly, wonder what was in that bag. Although it was probably indicative of how sick she really was that she didn't care enough to get up to find out.

* * *

"You think we should wake Mom up?" Ryder whispered to Dale, who was standing with two Pizza Hut boxes in his hands.

He knew she was miserable. And to tell the truth, while he wouldn't go so far as to call her disgusting, appealing was not the first word to come to mind when he looked at her, either, with her red nose and open mouth and her hair matted to kingdom come. And then there was the snoring to consider. But damn, if she didn't look cute, all curled up under the afghan or whatever it was, dead to the world.

"No way," he said, spinning around and leading the kids, the dog, and any number of cats back out into the living room. Lord, you couldn't walk anywhere in this house without a herd following you. "We can eat out here, I suppose," he said, plopping the pizza boxes on top of all the stuff on the coffee table. "Matt, why don't you go get the milk and a coupla cups or something?"

"Nobody drinks milk with pizza," the boy said, wiping his sleeve across his nose.

"You are tonight, buddy," Dale said. "And get a tissue, for the love of Mike. That's gross."

"Told you," Dulcy said, removing a curious orange cat from the table.

"C'n we play video games when we're done?"

"That okay with your mom?"

They all exchanged glances. "Sure," the boys said at the same time.

Dale looked at Dulcy, who sighed as she removed the cat again. The dog, who apparently knew better, decided to use the look-pathetic-and-whimper approach. "It's Friday. It's what they would do at Dad's anyway, probably. But Mom only lets them play them for a half hour at a time."

"And your dad?"

More conspiratorial glances.

"Should we all forget I asked that?"

Everybody nodded.

"Okay, then. After dinner, we'll play—"

"*You* like to play?" Matt asked, all big brown eyes.

"You bet. But if your mom wakes up and has a fit, no layin' the blame on me, got it? And where's that milk?"

Matt tromped off to the kitchen, only to return a few seconds later. "All we got are full gallons. I can't lift it."

Figured. Dale unfolded himself from the sofa and went back to the kitchen, unable to resist another peek at Joanna. Yep, still asleep. Still snoring. Still cute as a bug.

Dale had no idea why he was here. Nothing that went past the surface, at any rate. It was just one of those things, y'know? Like a voice said, *Do this,* so he did. What was scary was how loud the voice had been.

What was scarier, though, was how little he'd fought it.

It'd been a long time since he'd wanted to be somebody's hero. Even if only for a little while. Which was probably selfish and undoubtedly stupid, but it wasn't often he got the chance to be the good guy, to actually take care of somebody else. Not so anybody would know, at least....

"Dale?"

His thoughts scattering to kingdom come, he looked down at Ryder, who was clinging to the other side of the counter like he had suckers attached to him. With those curls of his, he looked a little like Frodo from *Lord of the Rings.* "You get lost or somethin'?" the kid asked.

"No. Why?"

"That's what Mom always says when she asks us to get something and we don't come back as fast as she thinks we should."

Chuckling, Dale grabbed the milk from the refrigerator and three plastic tumblers from the cupboard, thinking he could count on less than the fingers of one hand the number of women's houses he'd been in where he knew where they kept the glasses. And how it was kinda nice and kinda weird at the same time, knowing something like that. So, no, he most certainly was not lost.

Except then he glanced over at Joanna one last time before heading back to the living room and the kids, and the voice said, *Don't be so sure about that.*

The phone rang. Dulcy picked it up in the living room.

"Oh, hi, Grandma…yeah, she is….no, Dale's here," he heard her say as he came into the room. "You wanna talk to him?"

Great.

Dulcy handed him the phone, which he cradled between his neck and shoulder while he poured the milk. "Hey, Mrs. Swann, how's it going?"

"Uh, fine," came the somewhat perplexed-sounding voice through the line. "Although, well, I wasn't expecting to find you there."

"It was one of those spur of the moment things, you know?"

"I see. And how did you know Joanna was sick?"

He handed the first cup of milk to Ryder; all three kids' eyes were riveted to his face.

"We'd sorta had plans for tonight," he said, pouring another cup of milk. Keeping cool. "She called to cancel."

"I see," she said again, which was beginning to get on his nerves. "So the two of you really are…seeing each other."

"I'll tell her you called," he said, sliding right past that one.

"The kids are listening?"

"Yep, they're right here. We're about to have pizza."

"Oh. I see. I could come over. If you need me to."

He looked at the kids, all chowing down pizza and looking pretty damn happy. "Your grandma wants to know if she should come over?"

"Why?" Matt said. "Are you leaving?"

"Not plannin' on it."

"Then tell her we're fine," Dulcy said.

"No, Mrs. Swann—"

"I heard." A pause. "Kids can form strong attachments very easily, Dale," she said softly. "Just remember that."

Then she hung up, and Dale looked over at the kids chomping away, Ryder giggling because the dog was on the sofa trying to lick the cheese off the kid's chin, and panic swept through him. And not because the kids might become attached to *him*.

"Glynelle? Something wrong?"

Still clutching the phone, Glynnie looked over at her husband, molded to his leather recliner in the family room, highball in one hand, the *Albuquerque Journal* in the other.

"Dale McConnaughy's over at Joanna's house, that's what wrong."

"Oh? Huh," he said, and went back to reading his paper.

"That's all you have to say? 'Huh'?"

"What else do you want me to say?" Roger said, more to the paper than to her. "Although I suppose, if it makes you happy, I could add *that's nice.*"

"*Nice* is one thing it's not."

Roger lowered the paper. "And why is that? I told you he was over at Bobby's the other night for the poker game and—"

"What do you mean, he was over at Bobby's for the poker game?"

Roger frowned. "Didn't I tell you?"

"No, you did not. How on earth did that happen?"

"I don't know, exactly. I think Bobby said something about going down to Dale's store to get something for Tori, and they got to talking…and what does it matter, anyway, how he got there? The point is, he was there. And I like him. I think he'd be good for Joanna."

Glynnie huffed. She hadn't meant to, but it just sort of slipped out.

"Oh, hell…now what?"

"May I remind you that you still like Bobby, too."

"Why shouldn't I? He's crazy about those kids and from what I hear, he's doing a bang-up job at the TV station. And I thought we were talking about Dale."

"We were. But doesn't it tell you something that talking about Dale naturally led to talking about Bobby?"

"A path taken by only one person in this room," came floating over the sports section.

"But, Roger—"

"Glynelle." The paper snapped down. "Joanna is a grown woman. If she wants to keep company with Dale McConnaughy or the Pillsbury Doughboy, there's nothing we can say about it. He's polite, he doesn't drink, and he plays a mean poker hand. Let it go."

Glynnie was hard put to see how the last thing qualified the man as a prospective boyfriend or husband or anything else for her daughter, but there was no use arguing with Roger when he got like this.

"And by the way," Roger said from behind the paper. "I invited him for Thanksgiving."

"You did *what?*"

"You heard me. Boy didn't have anyplace else to go. And I figured, since he and Jo are an item anyway—"

"They are *not* an item."

Roger's expression softened when he looked up this time. "Denyin' it isn't going to change what is. And before you say anything else," he said when her mouth dropped open to protest, "even if he wasn't over there when Joanna's sick, I overheard Bobby tell Dale that Ryder told him he'd heard Dale leave real late the other night. Yes, after they'd been put to bed."

Glynnie sagged against the cushions of her ridiculously expensive, down-filled, silk-covered armchair. What Matt had told her was bad enough, but this…*this*…

"Oh, God," she whispered.

Roger shrugged, which prompted Glynnie, who had pretty much had all she could take, to tell him he was just about the most infuriating man on the face of the planet, not caring one whit what happened to his daughter, and how could he bear to watch her make the same mistake she'd made twelve years ago?

"And just maybe," Roger said in the irritatingly calm way of his, "you should give the woman some credit for having learned a thing or two in the last dozen years."

"I can't stand the thought of her getting hurt again."

"Neither can I, honey," Roger said gently. "Believe me. But you know, maybe it's time we faced up to our mistakes, too."

"What on earth are you talking about?"

"Maybe if we hadn't pushed her into all those directions she never wanted to go in the first place when she was younger, maybe she wouldn't have rebelled the way she did."

Glynnie felt every muscle in her back seize up. "If *I* hadn't pushed her, you mean?"

"Now, Glynnie, I never said that—"

"You didn't have to." She bounced up off her chair and started down the hall to her office. "I've got work to do before dinner," she said, making her pique known. "The roast will be done in a half hour."

"Let it go, Glynnie," Roger called after her, but she pretended she didn't hear him.

Chapter 16

Joanna woke up with a start, confused and disoriented until she finally recognized the vaguely familiar, rhythmic drumming overhead as rain. She nearly broke her neck bounding from the couch, the throw dragging behind her like a half-shed skin as she stumbled into the kitchen…where the drips lazily *plink-plonked* into assorted bowls and pots, thank God. Dulcy's doing, she supposed.

Or Dale's.

It was dark, she now realized. And very quiet, except for the drumming and the *plink-plonking*. She took a few tentative breaths to see if her nose was working, deciding sorta-kinda was about the best she could manage, then made her way out to the living room, yawning and huddling underneath the throw.

Engrossed in some cop drama on TV, Dale jumped a little when he noticed her standing there. ''You're up,'' he said.

''The rain woke me.''

''That leak is bad,'' he said, and she grunted. Then he

smiled. The kind of smile to make a woman's heart go pitter-patter, even if the woman herself felt like crawling into a cave until spring.

"You know what I really like about you?" he said.

"What?"

"The way you don't give a damn about how you look."

She sniffed, then reached inside her sweater sleeve for her tissue. "You know, as compliments go, that one really sucks toads."

"No, I mean it. Most every woman I've ever known would die rather than let a man see her without her makeup. But you've got this whole take-me-as-you-find-me thing going, y'know?"

"You're still not making any points here."

He grinned, cocked one eyebrow and said in a low voice, "How about if I say I find it really, really sexy?"

"Oh." She thought a second, hitching the throw up around her shoulders. "Okay, that might be worth a point. Or two."

He laughed, then said, "You hungry? There's still pizza."

She made a face, shook her head and yawned again. "Where're the kids?"

"Boys conked out about a half hour ago. Dulcy's in her room." He frowned. "You wanna sit? You're kinda weaving."

She stood there, staring at him. "Is it me, or is this a very strange relationship?"

"Guess that depends on your point of view. You gonna sit down or what?"

She did, plunking into the rocking chair across from the sofa, feeling muddle-headed and confused, as if she was having one of those dreams where she was in math class but knew she hadn't done a bit of work all semester and there was a test coming up and she was screwed.

"Why did you come over here tonight?"

He looked at her, his expression unreadable in the flickering light from the TV screen. "Because I wanted to," he said. "And I don't think it's in either of our best interests to take it any further than that, okay?"

"You do know what this means, though, don't you?"

He sighed. Loudly. And clicked off the TV. "What?"

"That this is about more than just sex."

A pained expression crossed his features. Then he waved her over to the couch, like an attendant at the fairground parking lot. "Come here."

"Can't. I'm in quarantine."

"And I already told you, I don't catch colds. And if I don't get to feel you against me at least once tonight, I'm gonna lose my mind. So get over here and quit bein' difficult."

Well, what could she say to that? Nor was she quite able to staunch her sigh when he put his arm around her shoulders and pulled her close. Heck, she didn't even bother to fight all the little *this is nice* thoughts scampering through her head.

"Comfortable?"

She nodded.

"Good. Now listen to me. Far as I'm concerned, this never was just about sex. And if that's all this is to you, then we are definitely not on the same page."

"Fine." She twisted around to look at him. "So you got any ideas about what this *is* about?"

"One or two, maybe."

And again, the void.

"Care to share with the class?" Joanna finally prompted.

"I'm thinking…friendship. How's that sound?"

Her first thought was that this was like finding out you were one of those hundred-dollar winners in a sweepstakes where the grand prize was a million. Nothing wrong with a hundred bucks, especially since you hadn't really expected to win anything to begin with, and you could certainly put it to good use...

But it wasn't a million, was it?

"Friends," she said. "Who just happen to sleep together."

"Okay, I can see how that might seem a little weird. But..." He rubbed her shoulder and said into her hair, "Finding a sex partner's easy. Finding a friend's a whole 'nother matter."

Then again, maybe she'd won more than she'd thought.

Joanna cuddled closer, wishing the fog would lift in her head enough for her to decide how she felt about any of this. Her oldest cat, Big Mama, jumped up on the sofa beside her, testing Joanna's thigh with her paw to make sure it was stable enough to take her weight. "Can I ask you something without you going nuts on me?"

"Guess that's a risk you'll just have to take."

She sighed mightily, then asked, "Were you friends with your ex-wife?"

He stiffened, a little, but she took it as a good sign that he didn't rocket from the sofa, dumping her and the cat in a heap.

"No," he said at last. "Meredith and I were never what you'd call friends."

Wow. First time he'd used his ex's name. Two good signs in as many seconds.

"But you loved her?"

"I think...I wanted to. Maybe I even thought I did. But in the end..." Underneath her cheek, she felt him shrug. She tilted her head back to look up at him. Yep, there was the clamped jaw.

"Let me guess. I'm getting too close?"

"Closer than I'd like, yeah."

"Just tell me one thing, and then I'll shut up, I promise. You said she left you?"

Another long pause, then a cautious, "Yeah..."

"Why?" she asked.

His mouth pulled into a tight smile. "I'm not sure," he said, then segued right into, "Your mother called. While you were sleeping."

Joanna sucked in a breath, which made her choke. She pulled away to sit cross-legged beside him, hacking like an eighty-year-old emphysemic, thinking Bobby would have taken off for the next county by now. Dale handed her his mug of what turned out to be cold, black coffee—yuck—then waited patiently until she'd finished coughing up her lungs. "Oh, God, I'm sorry," she finally said, now overheated and sweaty and more bleary-eyed than ever.

"Because you're coughing?"

"No. About my mother."

"I take that to mean I'm not off base in thinking she's not exactly wild about me?"

"No, no, it's—"

He laughed. She sighed.

"Trust me, this is about me, not you. No, I swear," she added at his disbelieving laugh. "She's only being a mother, Dale. Protective and all that fun stuff."

"Okay. If you say so."

A funny tightness in his voice made her glance over at him, but as usual, she couldn't tell a damn thing from his expression. "You'll be thrilled to know she tried to fix me up today. With somebody from her office."

Ah, *that* got the raised eyebrows. "She do this often?"

"Actually, no."

Now a squint. "So why didn't you tell her to butt out?"

"I did. But I doubt it took. She just wants to see me happy, that's all," Joanna said when he snorted. "Unfortunately she's yet to figure out we don't define happiness the same way." Cooling off now that the coughing jag was over, she wrapped the throw around her shoulders again and scooched her back up against the arm of the sofa, her feet on the cushion. "And I seriously doubt she'd understand...whatever this is we're doing."

He leaned back, one foot hooked on the edge of the battle-scarred coffee table, and looked at her, hard. "And what is it she wouldn't understand...that we're together, or that we're not together forever?"

Joanna fiddled with a clump of cat hair on the back of the sofa until the wave of disappointment—*Stupid, Joanna...stupid, stupid, stupid*—passed.

"Either one, I imagine."

"So don't tell her."

She let out a you-poor-deluded-creature laugh. "Oh, Dale...even if she didn't already know there's something going on, defined or not, this is my *mother*. More to the point, this is *my* mother. Resistance is futile."

"That mean you tell her everything you do?"

"Like hell! But I can't stop her from caring. Any more than I'd ever stop caring about my kids. Just as I'm sure your mother cares about—" She shut her eyes. "Damn. I'm sorry. I forgot—"

His precipitous rise from the sofa cut her off. As he gathered his cup and a few stray bowls left over from dinner, she imagined, he said, "Can I get you anything before we turn in?"

"Turn in?"

"I'm sleeping out here on the sofa. The kids said it pulls out, right?"

"Don't be ridiculous. You don't have to stay."

His brows crashed together. "I know I don't have to. But maybe I *want* to, okay?"

"You know, if I didn't know better, I'd say you were angry."

"Maybe I am."

"About *what*, for God's sake?"

"Quit pushing, Joanna."

"Hey." Clutching the throw, she stood as well, praying

her legs didn't give out since that would really take the edge off her reaming him out. Of course, so did whispering when you really wanted to yell your head off. "*You* push your way into my house, into my life, feed my kids and get in my face about my mother and generally come this close to pissing me off, and then *you* get pissed about God knows what and I'm supposed to ignore it? That's not the way it works, Dale. At least, not for me."

"We had an agreement—"

"Screw the agreement. You care about me—or at least, I assume you do, or why would you be here?—I care about you. Deal with it."

"Says the woman who'd rather let her damn roof keep leaking rather than borrow a few bucks from her parents!"

"That's...different! And lower your voice, the kids'll hear."

Dale let out a long, weary sigh. "Good God Almighty," he said in a hoarse whisper, "you are without a doubt the stubbornnest woman on the freaking planet."

"*I'm* stubborn! I'm not the one who refuses to let another human being peek inside his deep, dark past! Because, oo-ooh—" she made her voice go all creepy-crawly "—maybe somebody might discover you're a real human being after all!"

He glared at her for a long moment, then snatched his coat off the arm of the sofa. "You're right, there's obviously no reason for me to stay. But if you need me, dammit, you call. Got that?"

Then he was out the door.

Then he was back again.

"And by the way, folks're falling over themselves about that Santa in the window, so the sooner you can get the other ones to me, the sooner I can get you some business. Or does that compromise that dumb-ass pride of yours, too?"

This time the house shook when he slammed the door.

Joanna shut her eyes, only that made her dizzy so she opened them again. But honestly—did she hear what was happening? Was this some sort of Dante-esque scenario she was doomed to repeat throughout eternity, having the same arguments with men over and over without ever getting a clue that they don't change? Why couldn't she simply accept the fact that if she wanted to be with Dale—which she did, she did—she had to quit provoking the man?

On a sigh, she turned around to find Matt and Ryder standing at the entrance to the living room. Terrific.

"I thought you two were in bed."

"We couldn't sleep," Matt said, glowering. "Why were you and Dale arguing?"

Ears like beagles, these two had. "We weren't—"

"He sounded like he was scared," Ryder said, flopping onto his stomach on the floor to pet the dog.

"Don't be stupid," Matt said while Joanna just stood there and blinked at Ryder. "Why would Dale be scared of anything?"

"I'm not stupid," Ryder said, twisting around. "And I just said he *sounded* like he was scared."

"He is not!"

"I said *sounded like!* Jeez…"

"Okay, cut it out, you two. Get up off the floor, Ry, you'll get fur in your bed. And for the record, Matt? Everybody's afraid of something sometime. Yes, even big people."

Matt gave her one of those where-does-she-come-up-with-this-stuff? looks as Ryder asked, "C'n I have some ice cream?"

Talking to twin eight-year-olds was like trying to watch two TVs at once. "Nice try, but I already saw the dirty bowls. And you need to get back in bed."

"Aw, Mom…we're feeling lots better."

"Yeah, well, I'm not. So trust me—argue with me tonight and you *will* regret it."

She got the boys tucked in again and was on her way back to the living room when she heard Dulcy call her from her room. Joanna peered inside to see her sitting cross-legged on top of her bedspread in her jammies, petting Bones, a skinny little marmalade tom who could eat rings around Chester.

"What is it, Dulce?"

"You're gonna get mad."

"Dulce, for heaven's sake…" Joanna came into the room and plopped beside her on the bed, wrapping her up in the throw like a mama bird her chick. "If you've got something to say, say it. I promise I won't go off the deep end."

Her daughter kept stroking the cat until he was purring so loud the bed vibrated, then said, "I know what I said about how I didn't care if you want to date and stuff. And Dale's pretty cool. But…" She looked up, her eyes shiny behind her glasses. "But if the two of you are going to fight all the time like Dad and you used to…" Her face crumpled. "I don't want to go through that again, Mom, I really don't."

"Oh, honey…" Joanna grabbed the poor girl in a fierce Mama-hug, resting her cheek on her hair. "Neither do I, believe me."

"So…does that mean you and Dale aren't getting serious?"

A tiny, unpleasant knot formed at the back of Joanna's throat. "We're not planning on it, baby. I mean, we like each other and we can have fun together—" she actually said that without blushing "—but when all's said and done, I don't think we want the same things."

Dulcy stayed huddled against Joanna for a minute or so, then pulled away to pluck a dog-eared Harry Potter book off her nightstand. "I'm gonna stay up and read for a while, if that's okay."

"Sure, sweetie," Joanna said, knowing a royal dismissal

when she heard one, even as she knew there was a slew of unanswered questions pinging around inside her daughter's curl-topped head. Questions that would stay inside that head until Dulcy was good and ready to let them out. So Joanna hugged her not-so-little girl and left her to her book, only then remembering she hadn't eaten. Not that she wanted dinner now. What she wanted was—

Her pace sped up as she got closer to the rainforest of a kitchen, where she whipped open the freezer. And there it was, a lovely little pint of chocolate-chocolate chip ice cream with—literally—her name on it.

Damn him.

"You know something, Mr. McConnaughy," she muttered to herself as she ripped the top off the pretty gold container. "If you're really serious about keeping this *not* serious, you seriously need to stop doing stuff like this."

Dale clicked the remote, banishing Will Smith in mid-sentence. The big-screen TV was one of his few indulgences, even though he rarely had time to watch it. Besides, especially on nights like tonight, it was like sitting in a movie theater all by yourself.

The rain had stopped. He got up and went to the kitchen, blinking in the flash of light from the refrigerator when he opened it in the dark room. Not that there was much to choose from. Unlike Joanna's refrigerator which was so full you needed a road map to tell what was what.

Glowering, he grabbed a bottle of juice and let the door slam shut, plunging him into blackness again.

Maybe he should just tell her the truth, already. Get it over and done with. Even though her first reaction would undoubtedly be pity, which he could not abide and was why very few people knew. And of those who did, none of them were privy to the whole story.

But it wasn't Joanna Swann's pity holding him back. On the whole, he didn't figure her for the pitying type. At least, not for long. It was the look he knew he'd see in her eyes when the truth sank in, the reason he was determined to keep this relationship with Joanna short and sweet and out of deep waters. The reason he hadn't given Roger Swann a definite answer about coming to Thanksgiving, either.

Who the hell was he kidding, telling the woman he wanted to be friends? Because he could never be the kind of friend she'd expect him to be. Because even he knew real friends, true friends, didn't keep secrets from each other.

It wasn't supposed to happen this way, since it never had before. Not even with Meredith. Meredith, who'd worn him down at a vulnerable point in his life when he knew the arm was beginning to go. With his career coming to an end, marriage had seemed as good a way as any to stave off the years of emptiness yawning in front of him. Only, foolishly believing it wouldn't matter to her, he hadn't been honest about his future, at first. When he did come clean, the whole thing blew up in his face. And that had hurt.

Hurt almost as much as all the other times, as a kid, when he realized just how few people really wanted to know the truth.

So Dale had stopped being completely open with folks a long time ago, figuring he'd dispense information strictly on a need-to-know basis. And frankly, most times, people needed to know a lot less than they thought they did. And if that meant his relationships tended to be on the shallow side, well, that couldn't be helped, could it?

Swilling his juice, he walked into his office, clearing some new building set away from the answering machine. Which was blinking, as it happened. Since people rarely left messages, he never felt impelled to rush right in and check. A slight shiver of panic slicked over his skin, that it might be Joanna, that maybe something had happened—

"Hey, man, where the hell are you?"

It wasn't Joanna. And the mellow, if somewhat agitated,

voice on the tape made Dale smile as his unfounded anxiety limped away.

"Looks like I might be out your way a couple weeks from now, if that's okay with you. Prelims on those places seem fine. If they check out in person, something before Christmas is a definite possibility. So give me a call, let me know. It'll be great to see you, man."

Dale thought about calling Ben back right away. Might be nice to talk to somebody who wouldn't give him any B.S., you know? Somebody who didn't know Joanna and who consequently wouldn't have an opinion on the subject. Except Ben would see right through him. Seeing through people was what Ben Jamison did best. And Dale did not want anybody seeing through him tonight, messing with his already messed-up brain.

So he went back to the living room, falling onto the sofa, stabbing Play on the remote. Will popped back up onto the screen and continued with what he'd been saying, not in the least perturbed at having been so rudely interrupted. Not that Dale could hear Will—and now, Tommy Lee Jones—over the roaring inside his own head.

The woman aggravated the life out of him, and that was a fact. So why didn't he just call it quits?

Because sooner or later it was bound to run its course, anyway, whether he did anything to speed that up or not. Stubborn as Joanna might be, how many more nights like tonight would it take for her to get tired of fighting? For her to realize he was an extra burden she did not need in her life? So why not stick it out as long as it lasted, get some good lovin' and a meal or two out of the deal, right? As for what Joanna'd get out of it...

Well, he supposed he could reciprocate the lovin' part of things without straining himself too bad. And he hadn't been kidding about the interest people were expressing in her Santas, which probably would bring her more work.

Then he laughed out loud, struck by an idea so obvious, so perfect, his ornery mood lifted for the first time since walking out of her house earlier that night.

Oh, yeah. This oughtta frost that pride of hers, but good.

Chapter 17

At seven-thirty Monday morning, Joanna's doorbell rang. Before she could get out, "For God's sake—I'm still in my robe!" some child answered it, which meant she had all of ten seconds in which to throw on some clothes and groan at her hair before shoving said child out of the way with a bright, "Yes?" as if receiving visitors at seven-thirty in the morning was something she did every day.

A small Hispanic man of indeterminate age, holding a clipboard and dressed almost identically to her in jeans and a gray sweatshirt, flashed a whiter-than-white smile. Behind him, parked in front of her house, a white pickup proclaimed "Torres Contracting—Roofing/Remodels/Gutters/Siding/No Job Too Large or Small/Flat Roofs Our Specialty/Family-Owned and Operated/*Se Habla Español*.". Inside the cab sat three more men, their faces expectant. And hitched to the pickup, like a large, unkempt black bull, was one of those tar-making jobbers.

"We come to do the roof?" the man said. Somebody Torres, she guessed.

"The roof? There must be some mistake—"

"Miss Swann, right?"

"Yes, but—"

"Flat roof? Leaking over kitchen?" He backed up and squinted at the top of the house. "*Canales* need fixing, too?"

"Yes, but—"

"If we start now, we can be done by end of day."

"But I don't understand. And I can't pay—"

"Is already taken care of, no problem. If not good today, I can come back another time. But I was told not to leave unless roof was fixed or another time arranged to fix it."

Joanna crossed her arms. "Who told you not to leave until the roof was fixed?"

Another blinding smile. "Sorry, I don't know. My wife, she took the call and booked the job. So is okay? We start now?"

"Could I see the work order?"

"Sure, sure…" He handed over the clipboard. And, yep, there was her name and address.

And Dale's cell number.

Joanna sighed.

"Would you and your guys like some coffee? I need to make a phone call."

"*Sí, sí,* that would be great. Is *muy frío* today, yes?"

She told Dulcy to pour four mugs of coffee, then shoved her way through boys and animals to grab the nearest cordless and duck into the bathroom, closing the door behind her.

"What the hell do you think you're doing?" Joanna said when Dale answered.

"Not sleeping, obviously," came over the line, followed by a yawn. "Joanna? What the hell are *you* doing calling me at this godforsaken hour?"

"Maybe you should've thought about that before you sicced the roofers on me."

"Roofers? Hey—they're there already?"

"Dern tootin'. And what's the big idea? I don't want—"

"You know, I just heard somebody say the other day about how the longer you let a bad roof go, the worse it gets and the more expensive it is to fix."

"But—"

"—and I got to thinkin'—" another yawn "—that it seemed just plain stupid to let the thing continue to deteriorate when I could do something about it. But how pointless it would be for me to try to talk you into it. So I decided to skip that part."

"The talking-me-into-it part?"

"That would be it. And besides, I figured this was a good way to suck up—" another yawn "—after the way we left things on Friday night. How're you feeling, by the way?"

"Much better. But I can't accept this."

"Seems to me you don't have any choice. Seeing as they're already there and all. Now just say 'thank you' like the well-brought-up lady I know you to be so I can get back to sleep."

"You're not listening to me. I cannot accept this."

"Okay, okay, fine. I'm not awake enough to argue with you, that's for damn sure. But you're gonna have to tell Mr. Torres the job is canceled. Which seems a shame, you know? I mean, you needed a roof, he needed work—did I tell you he and his brothers are trying to go on their own after ten years of working for somebody else? But I'm sure he'll understand."

"And I suppose he's got five children to support?"

"Six, actually. And number seven on the way."

She sighed. "You are evil, Dale McConnaughy."

He chuckled, a slow, sexy laugh that made her mouth go dry. And then said, in a voice so low, so velvety smooth, that she very nearly lost it right there in her bathroom with her kids and four roofing guys standing all of fifteen feet away, "Oh, you ain't seen nothin' yet. Because I imagine, once you get out of that snit you're in, you're gonna be *real* grateful for that roof. And that you're gonna think of some real inventive ways of sayin' thank you.''

"Oh?" she said. On a squeak.

Dale laughed again. "You have a good day now, y'hear?"

Joanna hung up and walked back out to the living room, where Dulcy was doing the charming hostess bit with the four men, three of whom spoke virtually no English which gave Dulce a chance to practice the Spanish Bobby's grandmother had taught her before she passed away a couple years ago. Everyone looked expectantly at Joanna when she appeared.

"Is all cleared up, *sí?*"

"*Sí,*" she said. "It's all yours."

The men all trooped back outside, laughing and chattering as they began removing ladders and things from the truck to do whatever roofers did to make the leaks stop. And way down deep, past the annoyance and the pride and the aggravation, she was grateful. Actually, she was very grateful. Actually, she felt like crying, that here was one less thing she had to worry about. Hell, she'd been happy with the ice cream. But this…this was something.

This was…going to be real hard to explain to her mother. Or for that matter, to herself. But then, unless Glynnie took it upon herself to hoist her little Anne Klein-skirted fanny up onto the roof, how would she know? And should the subject come up, what was wrong with simply saying, "The roof? Oh, didn't I tell you? That was taken care of some time ago."

And then Joanna would cleverly change the subject to avoid perjury charges.

"You do realize what this means?" Karleen said a few hours later over the din of eight work-booted feet tromping around overhead, mingling with lots of loud, roof-fixing noises.

Joanna glanced up from the coat patterns she was pinning onto layers of suede cloth for her Western Santas. "That I'm now trading sexual favors for home repairs?"

Karleen's eyebrows lifted. "No, but let's get back to that in a sec, okay? This is guilt money, sweetie." More stomping, more unidentified noises. "Or in your case, guilt roofing. As in I'm-not-going-to-stick-around-but-please-take-this-as-a-token-of-my-esteem guilt. Believe me, I know. Only I usually got jewelry or cars."

"Kar, remember? Gap Guy? Isn't 'not sticking around' kinda a major part of the job description?"

"Uh-huh. And you should see your face when you say that."

After schooling her features, Joanna said, "Please. I give it two weeks, roof or no roof. A month, tops, before we drive each other crazy."

"I thought you said the sex was good?"

"I never said the sex was anything."

"Well, now's your golden opportunity."

Joanna thought about his hands on her skin and his mouth on her *everything* and jabbed herself with a pin. Now talking around her bleeding thumb, she said, "Okay, the sex is good. But this is strictly playtime. I mean, I can't even invite the man for Thanksgiving."

Karleen frowned. "Because?"

"Because no way am I sitting there watching my mother trying not to say what she's really thinking and Dale checking his ankles every ten seconds to make sure there aren't any shackles."

"And inviting him might mean you care more than you want to admit."

"That's not true!"

"Then do it. All he can say is no, right?"

Overhead, something thudded.

"And from where I'm sitting," Karleen added, "it's a small price to pay for a new roof." She leaned over, grinning. *"Dare ya,"* she sang softly.

Joanna threw a Santa head at her.

The phone to his ear, Dale slumped back in his desk chair in the store office, masking his eyes with his hand. Three days ago, when he'd sent the roofers over to Joanna's, he'd been feeling pretty damn good about his life, for a change. Now, however… "You sure about this?"

"Yep," the P.I. said on the other end of the line. "Just don't ask me how."

"I wouldn't dream of it." Dale glanced up at the bulletin board in front of him, obliterated under seventeen layers of memos and product info and scribbled notes to himself to take care of things he'd either long since taken care of or forgotten so long ago it didn't matter anymore. "But from what you could tell, you don't think she's here because of me?"

"Like I said, she's been in Albuquerque for years. You sure you don't want her new name and address?"

Just for a second, temptation speared through him. But just for a second. "Yeah. I'm sure."

"I dunno, Dale. If it was me, I'd want to be the one makin' the preemptive strike, you know what I mean? Get to her before she gets to you." He paused, then said, "If she needs money—"

"She wouldn't get it from me, in any case. Besides, it's been too long. Especially considering the way we left things. I just wanted to make sure I wasn't hallucinating, is all."

"Where'd you say you saw her again?"

"Raley's. In the checkout."

"And she didn't see you?"

"Not that I know of."

"Well, if you're sure—"

"I'm sure. Thanks."

"So…we're done, then?"

"Seems so."

"Then I guess I'll be sending you the bill. Let me know, though, if you need anything else, okay?"

"I'll be sure and do that. Thanks."

Dale had no sooner hung up the phone than a knock on the door made him jump. He got up and jerked open the door, nearly bowling over Alicia, one of his employees.

"Oh, I'm sorry," the blonde said, brown eyes supersize in her long face. "But there's a lady named Joanna here to see you."

His heart still pumping overtime from the phone conversation, Dale weaved through an amazing number of bodies for a Wednesday afternoon to find Jo, and the kids, standing in front of the counter, all of them laden down with shopping bags. Her face lit up when she saw him, making something thunk in his chest, that somebody should smile for him like that. And for a second that smile banished all thoughts of phone calls and certain discoveries he now wished he hadn't made, even if, a second later, the dread prompted by that phone call threatened to choke him.

"Hey," she said, the smile crashing into a frown. "You okay?"

"What? Yeah. Yeah, I'm fine." He forced a smile. "Distributor can't get me some of the stock I'm gonna need for Christmas, that's all. Whatcha got there?"

She gave him one of her I-don't-believe-it-for-a-minute looks, but mercifully only lifted the bags in her hands. She was dressed in sweaters and denim and those godawful clogs of hers, her hair yanked off her face by a clip of something, no makeup that he could tell, not a curve in sight, and he wanted her so bad it hurt to breathe. He wanted to bury himself in her, in her softness and generosity and honesty and goodness, and to forget about the past for a few goddamn minutes….

"The elves came," she said.

"Huh?"

"Your Santas," she said with a laugh. "I figured, since you got my roof fixed and all, the least I could do was fill your order. Besides, the kids haven't seen the store yet."

"What kids?"

She glanced behind her at the abandoned shopping bags lined up on the floor like drunken soldiers. "The ones I could have sworn I brought with me—"

"Mom! Mom! C'mere and look at this—"

"You gotta see this, Mom! This is so cool!"

Joanna turned back to him, grinning. "Those kids—"

"Dale?" Alicia interrupted. "Sorry," she added with an apologetic smile for Joanna, "but the guy's here to pick up the stuff for Toys for Tots? It's those six boxes stacked outside the office, right?"

"Right." Alicia scooted off; Dale turned to a pair of raised eyebrows. But before Joanna could ask whatever it was she was gonna, Dulcy, dressed a lot like her mother, reappeared hugging the same plush anteater her father had admired a few weeks back.

"Wouldn't this look great on my bed?"

Looping an arm over the kid's shoulders—why Dale hadn't noticed before that the girl was nearly as tall as her mother, he didn't know—Joanna beamed up at him, mouthing, "Christmas." She gave her daughter a squeeze and said, "Guess you'll have to ask Santa, huh?"

"Mo-om," Dulcy said, and Joanna told her to go keep looking, only keep an eye out for her brothers, too.

Then they were alone again. Well, as alone as they could be with a couple dozen bodies of various sizes swarming around them. Joanna hauled the bags up onto the counter, one by one, freeing the Santas inside, which got his employees to oohing and aahing and immediately talking about the best places to put them.

"I still think you're nuts, you know," Joanna said when they'd carted the Santas away to their new homes.

"Don't think there's ever been any question about that." Dale leaned back against the counter, his arms crossed over his chest, unabashedly gawking at the woman like he couldn't get enough of her. "How is the roof, by the way?"

"Settling in quite nicely," she said, folding up the bags. A marine in fatigues passed by, carting a large box. Joanna looked at Dale.

"And there's six of those?"

He shrugged. "All old inventory. And it's a tax write-off."

"Uh-huh. Anyway, about the roof...I intend to pay you back."

"I thought you just did."

"I'm serious, Dale. I can't stand feeling obligated."

"For what?"

"I'm not sure. It's just something I need to do. Act like a grown-up, you know?"

"Where's the fun in that?"

She blew out a short laugh, then stuffed the smaller bags into the still open larger one. Feeling better, Dale leaned over and said in a low voice, "This mean I can't come collect tomorrow night?"

Shew-*eee,* that blush was sexy. "As if I've been able to think of anything else all week," she said.

He moved even closer, taking advantage of the din in the store to whisper, "And I thought this was about more than sex."

Eyes bright, she opened her mouth to reply, only to jump when Ryder yelled, "Mom!" right behind her. They turned to see the kid holding a three-foot-long plastic diplodocus in his hands. "Look! An' there's a whole wall full of dinosaurs back there! This is like the neatest store in the whole world!"

Joanna bent to duly inspect Ryder's find, her eyes fixed

on the child's animated face, her love for the kid so obvious she practically hummed with it. Oh, Dale'd heard her fuss at the kids enough to know she wasn't cowed by them, even if, by her own admission, they drove her batty from time to time. But one thing was for sure—they always knew they were loved, by Joanna, by their father, by their grandparents.

And because they were loved, they'd be able *to* love.

Wasn't until he caught Joanna looking at him funny that he realized Ryder'd gone. "You *sure* you're okay?" she said.

"Just got to thinking, is all. Always dangerous," he said with a smile, then added, because he needed to change the subject, "How's he doing? In school?"

Three neat little wrinkles settled between her brows. "Hard to tell. Some days good, some days…" She let out a sigh. "Total loss. All we can do is take it one step at a time. Which reminds me—is the crafts class still on for Saturday morning?"

"You bet. Looks like there's gonna be about twenty kids or so."

"Great. Bobby'll bring him over, then." She tilted her head. "About tomorrow night…I was thinking maybe I could come to your place, for a change. Or…maybe not," she said, her brows dipping again at what must have been his poleaxed expression. "Okay, what is it? Afraid I might find some other woman's panties in the sofa?"

"No! It's just—"

"Oh, for heaven's sake—what *am* I thinking?" she said, banging the heel of her hand off her forehead. "How can you flee if you're at your own house, right?"

Dale's face warmed. "I almost think I like the panties-in-the-sofa excuse better."

She gave him a rueful look and said, "Well. See you at my place tomorrow about seven?" which should have made Dale feel relieved, only it didn't for some crazy reason. And after she'd gathered her chicks and ushered them out the door, even though the place was still filled with customers, Dale felt like he'd been stranded in the middle of nowhere without a compass or map or anything to tell him how to get back where he was supposed to be.

The next night, he was still looking for that damn map.

Joanna assured him going to Sizzler for dinner wasn't a date, since—she said—she refused to equate any place she'd take the kids with the word "date." Or where it was okay to wear whatever you had on when you decided to eat out.

Then she'd blushed, seeings as they hadn't been wearing much of anything when they'd made that decision.

She'd taken him right there on her living room floor before he'd even had a chance to say hello. Celebrating going back on the Pill, she'd said. And so they wouldn't fight, he imagined. And now she sat across from him in a dark booth, chowing down on some chocolate dessert that made Dale's teeth ache just to look at it, while the rest of him ached just to look at her, the way all those curls never stopped moving, the way every thought she had showed up on her face like a damn billboard, the way she smiled... Lord Almighty, the woman's smile was enough to break a man's heart. Or heal it, one.

Maybe they could keep it going for six weeks, if he could keep her fed and regularly orgasmic.

Of course, then she had to blow the moment all to hell by saying, "How come, if you're so dead set against having children, you never...you know. Had things taken care of."

He nearly choked on his coffee. "For God's sake, Joanna—"

"Nobody's listening, believe me. But I mean it. Why haven't you?"

That he couldn't come up with an immediate answer was somewhat troubling. That being with Joanna made him think about things he'd been perfectly content to let slide by all these years was even more so. Oh, yeah, the last thing he needed was some woman who made him *think*.

Yep, what he had here was one of those ironic situations: the one thing that most attracted him about Joanna—the way she was all open and honest about everything—was exactly what most scared him about her, too. It was easy to pretend, to hide, to keep secrets, when the woman was pretending, too. Or was so wrapped up in herself she didn't give a flying fig about what was going on inside anybody else's head.

He watched her watching him, her eyes big and calm and expectant, and shook his head. "I don't know. I mean, I've always been careful, so I never thought about it."

"Dulcy happened with a condom," she said. "So did the twins. You might wanna remember that the next time you're being *careful*."

Then, for the next few minutes, she concentrated on her dessert and he concentrated on his coffee until he noticed she'd started that fiddling thing with her fork she did whenever she got nervous.

"What is it?" he said quietly, figuring whatever it was, might as well get it over with.

Her mouth contorted into about six different expressions before she finally said, "Well, I've been thinking about something for a while but I couldn't make up my mind about it—I mean, how you'd feel or if you'd take it the wrong way, whatever—and believe me, if you say no I'll understand completely, so please don't feel obligated to say yes because you're afraid of hurting my feelings, but..." She actually cringed before saying, "Would you be even remotely interested in coming to Thanksgiving at my mother's house? Oh, God, I'm sorry. Forget I asked, okay? Let's just go back to what we were doing before—"

Dale reached across the table and grabbed her hand. "Okay, before your yammering uses up all the available oxygen in the restaurant—'' he swallowed, wondering how she was going to take this ''—your father already invited me.''

She blinked three times before responding. ''When did he do that?''

''When I was over at Bobby's, playing poker.''

''I see.'' More blinking. ''Why didn't you say something?''

''I forgot?''

That got a sigh. Then, ''So? Did you accept?''

''I hedged, actually.'' At the confusion in her eyes he added, ''Seemed to me if anybody should be inviting me, it would be you. Which to tell you the truth, I didn't realize until just this minute.''

''Oh. Well, I've asked you now.''

''Yep. You sure have.''

''Aaaand?''

He leaned back in the booth, one arm stretched across the top of the seat. ''I don't know. On the one hand, I don't want your family getting any wrong ideas.''

''Which could definitely happen.''

''That's what I figured. On the other hand, since they know about us, I'm thinking it might look even odder if I'm *not* there.''

She poked at the dessert, frowning. ''I hadn't thought about that.''

''And now this friend of mine's gonna be in town that weekend. Which could give us both a legitimate out,'' he added, watching her face, not quite sure what he was hoping to see.

''Is that a good thing?'' she said to her mushed-up dessert, then lifted her eyes to his. ''That you have an out?''

And he heard something he'd never heard in a woman's voice before. He didn't know what you'd call it, but he suddenly understood better what made men do some of the stupid things they did, just for a woman's smile.

"Your mother wouldn't get bent out of shape about another guest?"

And there it was, lighting up the whole damn booth. Hell, half the restaurant, seemed like. "Oh, probably," she said. "But then, I live for bending my mother out of shape."

"Well, then, honey…I guess I'm coming to y'all's Thanksgiving," he said, wondering how a person could feel like he'd just made the best and worst decision of his life at the same time. "And if your mama gives you grief, I'll be there to whup her butt."

Joanna burst out laughing, and Dale leaned forward to wipe chocolate off her mouth with the pad of his thumb, thinking she was about the sloppiest eater he'd ever known past grade school, and her breath caught, and he whispered, "Let's get out of here and go back to your house and forget about everything that's making us crazy," even though he knew he was telling a big fat lie because making love to Joanna didn't make him forget *anything*.

"Deal," she said.

Chapter 18

While Bobby generally liked most holidays, Thanksgiving ranked right up there with New Year's and Super Bowl Sunday. Food and football...what more could a man ask for, huh? Well, besides a fiancée who hadn't been glued to her computer all day. Tearing himself away from the game he'd been forced to watch on the little TV in their bedroom so he wouldn't disturb her, Bobby followed the sound of long nails clicking on the keyboard to find her still in her robe, madly typing away on her laptop on the dinette table.

"Hey, bookworm," he said, buttoning up his flannel shirt. "Didn't you tell me we were supposed to be at your folks' by three?" When she lifted her head with a vacant expression, he laughed. "Don't tell me I actually remembered something you forgot?"

Glowering at the screen, she shook her head. She clicked the mouse a couple of times before shutting the lid, then gathered up the books and note cards scattered to kingdom come all over the table. The neckline of her robe gaped open, giving Bobby an eyeful.

"Sorry," she mumbled, carting everything clumsily back to the bedroom as Bobby trailed behind. "It's just this paper's due early next week," she said, dumping everything on the dresser top, "and I just got a couple of the books I need for research yesterday. Give me five minutes, okay?"

Chuckling, Bobby sank into the club chair stuffed in one corner of the tiny bedroom as Tori hustled into the master bath. Five minutes? In his dreams.

"By the way, did you get some kinda hostess gift for Joanna's mother?"

Her toothbrush clutched in her hand, Tori stuck her head out of the bathroom door, a crease between her brows. "Why would I get a hostess gift for Joanna's mother?"

"For when we go over to her and Roger's place after we leave your folks?" At her rapidly deepening frown, he sighed and said, "I told you, I know I did. That we're goin' over there for dessert, since I have to pick up the kids for the weekend anyway?"

She glared at him for a second, disappeared for two, then came flying back out, creating a draft as she whizzed past him on the way to the closet. Still in her robe, she wrestled with the mirrored sliding door for a moment—he really did have to do something about that—before it groaned open. That she hadn't yet said anything worried him, a little.

"No, Bobby," she said, pulling her black suede miniskirt out of the closet and shoving the door shut again. She tossed the skirt onto the bed, then tromped over to the dresser, pulling out underwear and that short black sweater he liked so much. "You didn't tell me." To his disappointment, she turned her back to him, slipping on her panties, then a pair of patterned black panty hose, with the robe still on so he couldn't see anything. She spun back around, the robe clutched to her front, still glaring. "And you *certainly* didn't tell me about the kids coming over tomorrow."

"I'm sure I did," he said as she snatched the bra, sweater and skirt off the bed and headed back to the bathroom.

"No, you didn't," sailed out from behind the half-closed door. "And you say one word about mood swings—" she flew back into the room, fully dressed, combing her hair one-handed while tugging on one of her spike-heeled boots with the other "—you will never see these breasts again. Dammit, Bobby—I've got a ton of studying to do with finals coming up. And you're working tomorrow. The least you could've done was warn me I was going to have the kids!"

"I told you, thought I did," he said quietly.

She tugged on the other boot, not saying anything, then got up and grabbed her purse off the dresser. "Let's just go," she said. "I'll do my makeup in the car."

He followed her through the apartment and on outside. "Babe? Hey—" He grabbed her arm before they got to his car, turning her to face him. "I'm really sorry, I swear."

"You always are," Tori said, sounding as if she was pushing the words out. "But I am so tired of having things sprung on me because your memory sucks." She pulled away from him and strode to the car, her legs long and gorgeous under that short skirt, and Bobby got that awful mixed-up feeling again.

After they were on their way, Bobby finally realized it was up to him to get the conversation going again, even if that meant shoving aside the million and one doubt demons stomping on him with cleated boots.

"Okay, so you got every right to be mad at me, okay? But I'm only tryin' to keep things as normal as possible for the kids, honey. You know, so they can spend at least part of the holiday with both Joanna and me? And I'd promised Jo I'd take 'em since she's got that show all weekend. And don't go getting all thin-mouthed on me, for God's sake. I know how you feel about Jo's still bein' a part of my life—"

"You really don't get it, do you?" Tori said, facing him at last. "This has nothing to do with Jo or the kids. It has to do with your refusing to do something about this problem you have with remembering things. About caring enough about other people's feelings once in a while to *want* to do something about it. Between school and work and the pregnancy, I've got enough to deal with without constantly having to deal with your curve balls, you know? I mean…'' She looked back out the windshield, shaking her head. "Why can't you keep notes or something?"

"Okay, okay…I'll try harder to remember. I promise," he added when she snorted. "So remind me to get a notebook tomorrow so I can write things down, like you said."

Her head dropped back onto the rest, her eyes closed.

"What?"

"Nothing," she said on a sigh.

They drove in silence for a couple minutes, but it didn't seem quite so brittle now. Then Bobby said, "The kids'll be visiting friends and stuff tomorrow, so you should have plenty of time to study. And I'll take 'em down to Jo's show on Saturday, okay?"

She grunted.

"Y'know, with the baby coming and all, why don't you take some of the pressure off yourself and quit school for a while? It's not like you need to do it right this second or anything, is it? Why are you looking at me like that?"

"I can't believe you just said that. You really don't have a clue how important this is to me, do you?"

"Of *course* I know your education's important to you, sweetheart. I'm just saying I'm here, y'know? To take care of you and the kid? To be the man?"

Well, hallelujah—she didn't have anything to say to that. Bobby let out a slow breath as they turned onto the freeway ramp, the Sandia and Manzano mountains shouldering the cloudless, deep blue eastern sky. See, Joanna wouldn't've let it drop like that. Oh, no—she would've driven home her point, again and again and again, until he felt like his brain was leaking out of his ears. But not Tori. Tori knew when to back off, to let him win every once in a while. Which was the way it was supposed to be, right?

He glanced over to see her staring out the windshield, her hands tightly folded in her lap, then looked away again, his mouth turned down at the corners.

"Well, for goodness' sake, Jo—if you didn't have time to make the pies, why didn't you just say so? I'd've been happy to do it."

Refusing to take the bait, or to look at her mother, Joanna flipped open the flimsy cardboard-and-cellophane container and carefully lifted out the first pumpkin pie. She was in a good mood, dammit, and nothing or nobody was going to ruin her Thanksgiving. Least of all her mother.

"You told me to bring pies. You didn't say from where. And besides, not only are these cheaper than homemade, Sam's Club probably uses the same Libby's recipe the rest of the country uses. And—most important—neither one of us had to make them."

"But it's just not the same—"

"And did you raise the turkey yourself? Or grow the green beans in your own garden? Or milk the cow to get the fresh whipped cream to put on top of the pies?"

"Well, of course not, but—"

"Then trust me—nobody's gonna care that the pies aren't homemade but you. Great sweater, by the way. Is it new?"

Not being the most graceful loser in the world, Glynnie pursed her lips at the turn in the conversation. But then, apparently deciding to let it go in the interest of holiday harmony, she said, "Yes, it is. And it's nice to see how much use you're getting out of that one I gave you...how many years ago was it now?"

"Let's see..." Joanna went over to peer at the sacrificial fowl through the oven window. "I think this is from Christmas the year the twins were born. So see? You were right."

"About what?"

"About how the smart woman buys a few good, classic pieces that won't wear out or be unfashionable in a year."

Glynnie's mouth twitched. "Oh, so this is my fault, is it?"

"Of course. When in doubt, blame Mom. It's the American way. As traditional as turkey and store-bought pumpkin pie at Thanksgiving."

From down the hall, she heard the doorbell ring, her father answer it, the sound of two male voices—one Dale's, one presumably his friend's—nearly drowned out in the boys' screeches of glee. She and Dale had decided, since he'd be bringing his friend, not to go to her parents' together. Now she wondered, however—judging from her mother's expression—if what had seemed like a perfectly logical plan at the time was only going to make things weirder than they already were. Oh, well—she snitched several miniature marshmallows for the sweet potatoes from the bag—nothing to be done for it now.

"The kids like him, then?" Glynnie said quietly.

Joanna launched a couple marshmallows into her mouth and said, "Nearly as much as I do. And yes, we're having an affair. And no, I don't see much of a future in it," she added when her mother's mouth popped open. "And you know what? This really isn't any of your business—"

"There you are!"

They both turned at the sound of Dale's voice, and okay, so maybe her heart jumped a little when his eyes locked on hers. Like pretty much out of her chest. And maybe she itched to touch him, for him to touch her. It wasn't as if she wasn't going to admit her total infatuation with the man. Or that, after three years of celibacy, her erogenous zones were now on twenty-four-hour call. But that did *not* mean she wasn't keeping her head about her this time.

Not to mention her heart.

After they'd gone back to her house the other night, he'd

made love to her with an urgency that almost seemed like panic, as if…well, almost as if he were using her like a drug, to drown out whatever was going on inside his head. And while she had no longer had any complaints about the sex, as a primary means of communication it left a lot to be desired. Something was troubling him, she could tell. And whatever it was, she'd picked up on it when she'd delivered the Santas to his store the other day. That he couldn't—or wouldn't—tell her about it hurt more than she'd ever admit. But the thing was, the ache was more for *him* than it was for her.

As she said. This time she was hanging on to her heart. Even if only by a thread.

And while all this was shuffling through her head, he'd introduced his friend, a gorgeous African-American man named Ben Jamison, who had a sweet smile and thick, curly eyelashes to die for. Then Dale was plying her mother with flowers *and* candy *and* compliments on how wonderful it smelled, and both he and Ben were thanking her up one side and down the other for letting them crash her party, and Joanna thought, *Dammit, Dale, you're not helping things any,* because never in her life had she met a man as thoughtful and giving and decent as he was and if it wasn't for this little problem about his keeping a large chunk of himself to himself—and, okay, his not wanting to commit and/or have kids—he was, well, perfect.

Rotten creep.

Then, clearly taking advantage of her mother's flabbergasted state—a rare occurrence, indeed—Dale looked over at Joanna and gave her a smile and it hit her that the likelihood of her sharing next Thanksgiving with this man was slim to none, a thought that was not sitting well at all.

But not to worry, because then Karleen arrived with about a dozen bottles of sparkling cider, which she nearly dropped when she caught sight of Ben, and Joanna nearly burst out laughing at Karleen's expression.

"Ben Jamison," Dale said. "Karleen…?"

Joanna looked over at her friend, who'd apparently stepped out of the building for a minute.

"Almquist," she filled in.

Then everybody looked at Ben, who'd apparently stepped out right behind Karleen.

Dale leaned over to his friend and whispered, "It's nice to meet you, Karleen."

Everybody laughed, Karleen and Ben looked appropriately embarrassed, the kids all trooped in to find out what was so funny and Joanna's sons commandeered anybody they could get for an impromptu football game out in the minuscule plot of turf that made up the so-called backyard. Dale followed the boys, Ben followed Dale, Karleen followed Ben, and Joanna would have followed the devil himself rather than get stuck with her mother in the kitchen, only Glynnie said she could use some help. Rats.

"Well," Glynnie said, hauling the roasting pan out of the oven and thunking it onto the stovetop, "talk about being unsubtle."

"Oh, you know Karleen," Joanna said. "Never one to keep her feelings under wraps—"

"Oh, for crying out loud, I wasn't talking about *Karleen*. Now get over here and help me get this damn bird onto the serving platter."

Joanna obeyed, although she wasn't sure she wanted to get any closer to her mother than she already was. But she dutifully grabbed one end of the net thingy her mother put under the turkey and hefted it up and onto the Lenox platter that had long since replaced the grocery-store-issue Blue Willow. Only after the roasting pan was returned to the stove so Glynnie could make the gravy did Joanna say, again, "I know what I'm doing, Mom."

In the midst of siphoning off excess turkey fat, her mother looked over at her. "Gee. And where have I heard that before?"

"Could you please trust me, just once, to make the right decision? Or if it isn't the right decision, could you at least trust me to live through it?"

"Even if it means you get the short end of the stick again?"

"Yes," Joanna said over the twinge in her chest. At her mother's pained expression, she turned to look out the breakfast nook window, down on the raucous football game below. "I appreciate your concern, I really do," she said, watching her lover pretend to fumble the ball when Matt tackled his knees, the way Dulcy—far more weighted down with the complexities of human relationships than Joanna would have liked—hesitated when he waved her over to join them. "But maybe it takes some of us longer to figure things out, okay? Maybe some of us didn't have our lives all mapped out by the time we were sixteen. Maybe some of us are still works-in-progress."

She looked back at her mother, irritation and confusion making her eyes sting. "So my choice is either to do nothing at all or to resort to trial and error. Even if it means I constantly seem to do things the hard way."

Glynnie swore as she dropped the spoon into the bubbling gravy, then yanked open a drawer, rattling everything inside it as she said, "I'm not trying to upset you, Joanna. I swear." A pair of tongs now in her grasp, she added, "I just want you to know I'm here for you, that's all."

Joanna snorted.

The spoon apparently forgotten, Glynnie lowered the tongs. "What on earth is that supposed to mean?"

"Nothing. Forget it. Let's not get into this on a holiday okay—"

"Joanna. Now." Glynnie brandished the tongs. "And you don't want to mess with an armed woman."

Joanna glanced out the window again, for the moment wishing she could bury the past as neatly as Dale seemed to, then said softly, "Don't you think it's a little ironic your wanting to 'be here' for me now that I've muddled through the first thirty-two years of my life, including eleven years of motherhood, when you were never around when I was a kid?"

The shock and hurt in her mother's eyes when Joanna looked back made her cringe. Only Glynnie immediately rallied with, "That's not fair, Jo. It's not as if I was literally *never* around."

"Mom, I was lucky you had ten minutes for me at bedtime, when you were obviously exhausted and irritable and I knew you didn't really want to hear my problems. And when you were home, you were usually working. Do you know what it's like to feel you come in second to your mother's career?"

"But you didn't! I swear to God, I never felt that way!"

"And how would I have known that at four? Or seven? Or twelve?"

"But I was doing it for you—"

"No, Mom. You were doing it for you. You weren't even married when you went into law, let alone knew you'd have a kid someday. And I actually admire the hell out of you for being as devoted to your work as you are. It's just...what you needed and what I needed when I was little didn't jibe." She shrugged. "That's all."

Glynnie sagged onto a bar stool by the island. "Why...why on earth didn't you say something sooner?"

"Because what would have been the point? You can't help being who you are, even if I didn't understand it then. By the same token, though...I can't help being who *I* am. Even if *you* don't understand. You didn't mean to neglect me, I don't mean to disappoint you."

The shouts and laughter from outside battered the silence hanging between them before Glynnie said, "I may not have understood some of your choices, honey, but believe me...I've *never* been disappointed in you." Then she laughed. "Oh, Lord. Here I thought I was setting such a good example, showing you how to balance motherhood and a career. Because I couldn't stand the idea of being married to my house, the way my mother was. God, I'm such an idiot." Before Joanna could respond, she added, "Is that why you changed your major, then? And broke off your engagement to Tom? To get back at me?"

Joanna walked toward the island, shaking her head. "No. Well, not exactly. What I mean is, I wasn't thinking of you when I did those things. For the first time, I was thinking of me. What I wanted. Or more to the point, didn't want. And what I didn't want was to follow in your footsteps. So when I met Bobby—"

"—you grabbed at an alternative you hadn't considered before."

"Yeah. I did. And I know you still think I made a terrible mistake, marrying him. But you know what? Maybe our marriage didn't work, but we've got three terrific kids. And I found a way to support us and still be around for my kids that I might not have done if I hadn't been shoved up against a wall. Although," she added with a strained smile, "if the pattern holds, Dulcy will probably twist herself inside out to avoid doing things the way I did."

Her mother looked at her a good long time before finally returning to the stove to fish out the gravy-marinated spoon. "Considering the hardheaded stock from which she hails," her mother said, the words clipped, "I'd say that's inevitable."

"I'm sorry," Joanna said on a rush of air, "I probably should've kept my big mouth shut—"

Glynnie whipped around so fast, gravy splattered half way across the room. "And if you had, I *would* consider myself a failure. We may not be even remotely alike, but at least you inherited my balls."

After a moment Joanna grinned. "And your hair."

"Genetic curses, both of them. Here," Glynnie said

nodding toward the pot of steaming boiled potatoes. "Why don't you start mashing those?"

After several minutes of mashing had apparently jarred loose some of Joanna's thought processes, she said, "You know, maybe we don't toss out everything from the previous generation as much as we think we do."

"What do you mean?"

"Well, I can't exactly deny I owe everything I learned about determination and perseverance and attention to detail to you. And you learned how to cook a mean turkey and stuffing from Granny Frannie. So whatever kind of life Dulcy chooses for herself, maybe, just maybe, watching her mother go through her own torturous learning curve will teach her something about not depending on a man."

"And...about falling for the wrong ones?"

"I haven't fallen for anybody," she said, her words barely audible over the maniacal laughter thundering inside her head. "Believe me, after my experience with Bobby, there are certain mistakes I do not wish to repeat. But..." Frowning, she salted the potatoes. "Why *are* you so dead set against Dale?"

"If you already know there's no future in your relationship," her mother said behind her, "what difference does it make what I think?"

Joanna twisted around to meet her mother's troubled gaze. "Humor me. Although I can't believe you're still miffed about his comment at the boys' birthday party."

Her mother laughed. "Even if I hadn't had that coming, he more than made up for it today, in any case. No, it's not that. It's..." Her brow puckered, Glynnie wiped her hands on a dish towel, then climbed onto the stool beside Joanna. "Look, after more than thirty years of practicing law, I've gotten pretty good at telling when somebody's putting on a front of some kind. When they're...hiding something. I'm not clairvoyant, I couldn't begin to surmise what it is that Dale's not being honest about, but there's something…oh, I don't know, honey. My antennae's just up, that's all. And judging from your expression, I hit the nail on the head, didn't I?''

Joanna went back to her mashing. "He refuses to talk about his past, it's true. Which is a big problem for me, no matter how much I keep telling myself I could ignore it, if I had to. Except…''

"You can't ignore it because you care about him.''

She looked at her mother. "There are times I catch this look on his face that just rips me apart inside. He's hurting, I *know* he's hurting, and it's killing me that I don't how to help him.''

After a second her mother reached over and squeezed Joanna's wrist, a startling gesture for a woman not prone to shows of affection, then she got up to put the rolls in the oven.

"Mom?''

"Yeah?''

"If you want to be there for me now, it's okay. I mean…'' She swallowed, then said, "Any and all advice gratefully received.''

Glynnie turned again, one eyebrow raised. "And what makes you think I've got anything to say you don't already know?''

Joanna thunked the masher into the pulverized potatoes and buried her face in her hands. "I'm so freaking *confused*,'' she pushed out through her fingers.

Her mother's lack of a response only confused her more.

Chapter 19

Dale's patience was in shreds by the time he finally grabbed Joanna's hand a good half hour after they'd eaten and dragged her into the hall bath, a room fancier than any hotel he'd ever stayed in, even there at the end of his career when money was no object.

"What are you doing?" she said on a gasp when he locked the door.

"Getting you all to myself for a couple of minutes," he said, and kissed her, and she laughed and kissed him back with an eagerness that made him realize that the warmth he craved from her went beyond the sweet-tangy heat pulsing off her body in the tiny room. Then they got to touching each other the way they always did and he could tell how turned on she was getting, and he sure as hell knew how turned on *he* was getting, so he whispered, "You think we could manage it in here?"

"Buddy, I could manage it anywhere," she whispered on a little moan when he nibbled at that soft spot behind her ear. Which he might have found encouraging had she not picked that precise moment to push away, as far as she could, anyway, and not hit the door. "But my mother would know and there is no way I'm going down that path right now," she said, which confirmed the suspicion he'd been nursing for the better part of the last hour and a half, which was that she and her mother had had words. And most likely, about him.

He palmed her warm, smooth cheek, ducking his head slightly to look into her eyes.

"You want me to do that butt-whupping thing?"

Joanna gave kind of a snuffling laugh, then shook her head. "Actually, no. Thanks to you, we…worked out a few things that should have been worked out years ago."

"Thanks to me?"

"Yeah." She linked her hands behind his neck and smiled for him. "I realized I had to stop hiding behind presumptions and face a few things head-on. So I'm actually feeling pretty dang good right now." Which he might have almost believed if it hadn't been for that troubled look in her eyes. Then she angled her head and said, "Sorry you came?"

A question he couldn't've answered if somebody'd put a gun to his head. But what he said was, "Are you kidding? You're very entertaining in a large group."

A wicked smile stretched across her face. "Not nearly as entertaining as I can be in a small one. Like, say, you and me."

"Now that's just mean. You know I've got company for the rest of the weekend."

"Well, since I have to get up with the chickens tomorrow for this show, and you have to open the store at eight, Ben's being here is probably a blessing in disguise."

"If you say so."

She smiled at that, then removed her hands from behind his neck to link them around his waist instead, laying her head on his chest. And it occurred to him it probably wasn't real fair to her, him playacting like this, pretending to be part of something he could never really be part of. Only thing was, it didn't feel as much like playacting as he'd figured it would.

"Ben seems like a good friend," she said.

"And his being here has relieved your mind about me being a total recluse, right?"

She laughed. "I was beginning to wonder."

"We've been friends for a long time," he said, stroking her back, thinking he could almost get used to this, just standing here and holding her like this, thinking he'd give anything to be able to be honest with her about why Ben was here, if he could figure out a way to do that that wouldn't open up one big old can of worms. "Like me and Karleen?" she said, and he could hear the smile in her voice.

"Lord, no. *Nobody* has a relationship like you and Karleen."

She laughed again and looked up. "They seem to have hit it off. Ben and Kar."

"Yeah. I noticed that."

"But?"

"Ben lost his wife about a year ago in a car crash. Even if he didn't live in Boston, I'm not sure he's ready for anything serious."

"Oh," she said, more genuine sympathy in that one tiny word than most people could fit into a half-hour eulogy. "I'm so sorry. You think I should say something? To Kar, I mean?"

"I think Ben's perfectly capable of handling Karleen. And vice versa."

She regarded him steadily for several seconds, then said, "I know Karleen comes across like a ditz at times, and she doesn't exactly have the greatest track record in the world when it comes to choosing husbands, but Ben could do a lot worse, you know? Because after all's said and done,

Karleen's one of the most generous, loyal people I've ever known.''

Nearly overwhelmed with an emotion he couldn't even identify, Dale gathered her close, placing a kiss in the midst of all those crazy curls. ''She's not the only one,'' he whispered. From what sounded like a hundred miles away, one of the kids yelled for her.

She snuggled closer, even as she murmured, ''I suppose we've got to get out of here.''

''Oh, I don't know. I was thinking of staying until everyone else left.''

''Not that it's not tempting, believe me. But unfortunately, my kids are great trackers.''

She twisted herself around right as the doorbell rang. Cracking open the door about a hundredth of an inch, she whispered, ''Sounds like Bobby and Tori. Which means I have to go play the gracious first wife. For the children's sake. Better wait a minute or so before following me,'' she said, but he grabbed her hand before she could make a dash for it and said, ''I'll call you tonight,'' watching as her expression changed from surprised disbelief into delight as she grinned and nodded and darted back to give him a quick kiss before finally making her escape.

Leaving Dale sorely tempted to flush his head down the pretty pink commode.

Honestly, Glynnie thought when Dale zipped past the kitchen door not a minute after Joanna had. Did they think she was blind? Or stupid? There was nothing down that hall *but* the powder room. Did they have to behave like…like a pair of horny teenagers right under her nose for crying out loud?

She plopped the freshly whipped cream into a serving bowl…and started to laugh. Only one reason why she was getting her panties in a bunch about this, and it wasn' because she was ticked. Hell, she envied them so much she could hardly stand it. Oh, she had no complaints about Roger. And there was a lot to be said for the comfort and security of old love, and of familiar lovemaking. But there was nothing like that heady rush of a new relationship, the way you couldn't get enough of each other, when every touch, no matter how innocent, set your heart to racing.

Glynnie slammed a knife through the first pumpkin pie. Maybe she hadn't been the kind of mother Joanna had wanted, or needed, but she sure as hell was enough of one to worry about her only daughter. Except...how could she fight against that look in her baby's eyes when she talked about Dale? The woman was in love, whether she admitted it or not. Which meant, Glynnie thought on a heavy sigh, about all she could do now was pray her brains out.

"You need any help with that?" Dale said behind her, scaring her out of her wits. Clutching her chest, she turned to him, realizing with a spurt of annoyance she was no less immune to that grin and those eyes than the next not-dead-yet woman.

"No, thank you," she said. "Everything's under control. And you wouldn't be sucking up, now would you?"

Dale laughed, leaning against the counter with his arms loosely crossed over his chest. "Depends. Is it working?"

"I haven't made up my mind yet." She set the stack of dessert plates on the serving tray, then figured she might as well say what was on her mind. Except Dale beat her to the punch.

"Mrs. Swann," he said in that soft, country-boy drawl. "I know you have reservations about me and your daughter. And I don't blame you. I wish I could give you the kind of reassurances I know you want to hear, but I can't. I can tell you, though, that I've been totally up-front with Joanna from the beginning, about what will—and probably won't—happen between us. That's the best I can offer. And since Joanna seems to be okay with our arrangement, I would hope—for her sake—you could be, too."

Glynnie gave him her best make-the-witness-squirm stare. "I don't want to see her hurt. Again."

A half smile flickered around his mouth. "Believe me...neither do I."

She lowered her voice. "Then why don't you leave her now, before that happens?"

Roger, damn him, picked that moment to amble into the kitchen. But in the split second between her question and her husband's untimely entrance, she saw her answer in Dale's anguished eyes.

"Bobby and Tori are here," Roger said, nodding to Dale as he left the room. "And judging from both their faces, I'm guessing they had a fight. So what were you and Dale talking about?" he asked, scooping up a dollop of whipped cream out of the serving bowl with his finger.

Glynnie smacked his hand when he went for a second helping, then sighed, smoothing over the cream to mask Roger's assault on it. "One guess. I swear, I wish I knew what that boy was thinking."

She looked over at her husband, still as long and lean as he ever was, his eyes still as blue and full of the devil, and remembered that life didn't often give you a say in who you loved. Or why.

Roger's bushy brows dipped. "Why are you looking at me like that?"

"I was just remembering the first time we kissed."

"Huh. That was a long time ago."

"Yes, it was. Do you remember it?"

Grinning, he picked up the tray with the pies and plates. "Like it was yesterday, petunia," he said, and Glynnie thought about how her parents had thought her several bricks shy of a load for wanting to marry a used car salesman whose mother painted the world's ugliest pictures. And how nothing they said could budge her one single, solitary inch. Still...

"Is it so wrong of me to want good things for our daughter?"

Roger favored her with an indulgent smile. "Of course not, honey. But it is wrong for you to think you're the only one who knows how she's supposed to get those good things. And don't go getting that look on your face, Glynelle."

"What look?"

"The one you get when you're in the midst of getting your facts lined up for a legal battle. Raising a kid isn't like manipulating a jury—"

"I do not manipulate anybody!"

"—or even like selling a car. And yes, you do. Shoot, Glynnie, you know as well as I do that neither of us would be as good at what we do if we didn't know how to pull people's strings from time to time. But like it or not, our daughter's not fair game. Now how's about we let life take care of itself while we get in there and serve up some dessert? Because the sooner we get all these people fed and out of here, the sooner I can have my house back to myself." He winked. "And my wife."

Glynnie watched her husband leave the kitchen, actually considering what he'd said about letting life take care of itself.

Only then she thought, *Well, hell—where's the fun in that?* and felt very much relieved, as though some major disaster had been averted.

"You've got it bad for Dale, don't you?"

Still groggy from yesterday's turkey-and-pumpkin-pie overindulgence, Joanna glanced across her booth in the exhibition hall where Karleen sat at the sales table in a vibrant Grinch-green, cowl-necked sweater. In her denim jumper and white turtleneck, Joanna felt—as usual—like the dowdy third cousin. Although, out of concession to the holiday season, she had donned the gayest apparel she owned, a pair of candy-cane-striped socks and red clogs. Since Santas had been fairly flying off the shelves from the moment the doors had opened, by all rights nothing should be able to puncture Joanna's whooee-I-am-cleaning-*up* high, carb overload notwithstanding.

Except, of course, that particular subject.

Taking advantage of the momentary lull in traffic to rearrange and restock, Joanna pulled two small Santas out of a box stuffed behind the shelves and plunked them under the Limited Edition sign, keeping an eye on the elderly woman poking through the ornaments on the artificial tree set up in one corner.

"We've been here for four hours and this just now pops into your head?"

"No. But it's been too busy before this. Will that be all?" Karleen said with a charming smile as the woman tentatively set down a handful of ornaments, even more tentatively handing Karleen her charge card.

Joanna dug out replacement ornaments from another box she'd stashed underneath the skirted card table. "This wasn't supposed to happen," she said after the customer left, savagely hooking new ornaments onto the shivering tree. "Gap guy, my butt."

"Oh, honey," Karleen said, "That was just a ruse to get you off that butt and *out there*. You know as well as I do that you don't do 'gap guys.'"

Joanna stared at the blonde for several seconds. "You do realize this means I have to hurt you?"

"And sit here by yourself for the rest of the show? Like I'm worried. So it's going well, huh?"

"I don't think I've ever had a show start off this strong—"

"I'm not talking about the show, birdbrain."

"You know," Joanna said, nodding toward the booth across the way from theirs and lowering her voice, "I could have *sworn* I saw frames exactly like that in Pier 1 the other day. Yeah right, handmade originals—''

"So what you're saying is, your feelings aren't being reciprocated?"

Snatches of last night's phone conversation filtered through her thoughts as she monkeyed with the ornaments. She and Dale had talked and joked and laughed for more than an hour…about everything but his personal life. It was like existing in parallel dimensions—the closer they got in one, the more the gap yawned between them in the other. And it was driving her totally nuts.

"It doesn't matter," she said, kicking the ornament box back under the skirted table. "Since it would never work anyway."

"Why?"

"Well, let's see…his not being even remotely interested in anything long term is kind of a biggee. But even if he were…" Desperate to remember why Dale Was No Good For Her, she dug around in her brain for a second, unearthing an item she'd already bagged up to give away to Goodwill. "The man doesn't have a serious bone in his body, for one thing. All he wants to do is have fun."

"Oh, for God's sake, Jo…" Joanna looked at Karleen to find her doing that squinchy thing with her mouth Joanna hated with a purple passion. "I can't believe you're still harping on that. What is it with you and having fun, anyway? I watched the two of you yesterday. So the man acts like a goof sometimes. He makes you *laugh.* Just like Bobby used to, in the beginning."

"Did you hear what you just said? *Just like Bobby used to.*"

"I also said *in the beginning.* Before you got all stuffy and decided the only way to do something was Joanna's way."

"That is so not true!"

"Yes, it is. Honey, you know I love you, but your marriage didn't go belly-up just because of Bobby."

"I never said it did! But you know as well as I do that somebody had to be the responsible one, or everything would have fallen apart. Since Bobby clearly didn't want the job, it fell to me. And whose side are you on, anyway?"

"Oh, ditch the wounded look," Karleen said, unfazed. "But, honestly—you do have a tendency toward extremes. Yes, you do. You went totally flaky when you met Bobby. When you got disenchanted with the Free Spirit thing, you did a one-eighty right into tight-assdom. Nothing in between. No compromise...well, hey, Glynnie!"

And there her mother was—oh, joy, oh, joy. For the next few seconds Glynnie and Karleen oohed and aahed over each other's attire, Glynnie asking Karleen if she thought the Grinch green would work with her hair, and Karleen said she didn't see why not, which naturally led to the pair of them tsking over the sorry state of Joanna's wardrobe and how they really had to get her to the mall one of these days. And right when Joanna thought the conversation couldn't get any more depressing, Karleen said, "Jo and I were just talking about Dale."

Clearly the woman had a death wish.

"And Jo was listing the reasons why Dale wasn't right for her."

A very large death wish.

Her mother turned to her, eyebrows poised for flight. "Oh, really?" she said, and something about that "Oh, really?" made the hair stand up on the back of Joanna's neck.

"Yep. In fact, Joanna was just complaining about how he makes her laugh."

"I was not complaining about how he makes me laugh! I was complaining that he never seems to take anything seriously...oh, hell." She turned to her mother. "You didn't hear that."

Glynnie set down assorted shopping bags underneath the covered table—clearly she hadn't exactly made a beeline for Joanna's booth—and floated to the back, where she proceeded to rearrange Joanna's display.

"It is good to hear you laugh again," her mother said, then turned to Karleen. "But don't you think he seems a bit…pushy?"

Karleen leaned back in her chair, her legs crossed, rotating her high-heeled, black suede boot. "I don't know. Maybe. But after all those years of listening to Jo bitch about how Bobby never did a damn thing on his own steam, it's kinda nice for her to have someone who's actually self-propelled, don't you think?"

"You may have a point there—"

"Hello?" Joanna interrupted, thinking this was getting a little too surreal for her taste. "Remember me?"

"Don't be silly, dear, of course we remember you," Glynnie said. "Why would we be having this conversation otherwise?"

"And you know," Karleen said, "you can jump in anytime you like. We don't mind, do we, Glynnie?"

"No, we don't mind at all. So did you have something you wanted to add, sweetie?"

She blinked. "Beats the hell out of me. I mean, I thought I knew my place in the conversation, but now I'm not sure which side I'm arguing on."

"Then why don't you just say whatever's on your mind," her mother said with a smile, "and we'll figure it out for you."

Still confused, especially in the light of yesterday's conversation with her mother—or had she dreamed that?—Joanna looked from one to the other. "O-kay. Picking up on Karleen's self-propelled comment earlier…I want somebody who can take care of his own life, yes. Not mine. Besides, I'm not sure how well Dale does take care of his own life. I get the feeling the toy store is little more than a hobby. As far as I can tell, he has virtually nothing left out of all that money he earned as a star player, so where did it go?''

"Excuse me?'' her mother said as Joanna caught Karleen's sudden exaggerated interest in the hem of her sweater. "How come when I brought this up, you bit my head off? I thought you didn't care about the money?''

"I don't care about the money! It's what happened to it I find worrisome. And…and then…well, in all this time, the only friend he's ever mentioned is Ben. Doesn't that seem strange? For somebody so otherwise outgoing?''

"Oh, I don't know,'' her mother said. "If the guy played ball all those years? I mean, they move around a lot, don't they? Maybe he just never had a chance to make any real friends. Besides, you remember what your grandmother was like, the way she'd strike up a conversation with anyone who crossed her path, yet she had this thing about not wanting folks to know her business, so she never let anybody get close, never invited people over to her house, never socialized—not that I ever remember, at least. So maybe Dale's like that. And maybe you're worrying about nothing.'' She got up to help a kid poking through the Santa puppets. "Not that you've ever done that before. What are you doing?'' she said, jumping slightly when Joanna started sniffing her hair.

"Just trying to figure out what you've been smoking.''

"Really, Joanna…'' But Glynnie's attention had been snagged by the extremely well-heeled woman fingering the coat of one of the larger Santas, who now looked over at the three women, smiling.

"Are these made by the same person who has them in that toy store up in the Heights?''

"They certainly are,'' Glynnie said, preempting whatever Joanna was about to say. "You know, each one is unique.''

"I can see that,'' the woman said, glancing around a

the other Santas for a second before refocusing on the one in front of her. "The faces are really quite marvelous, aren't they?"

"All hand carved," Glynnie said.

"That's what the man at the toy store said. I could have kicked myself, though, for not buying the one I saw when I was in there. Because it was gone when I went back. Although…" Biting her lip, she looked at the price tag, then sighed. "I don't know. I mean, it's exquisite, but kind of pricey…"

"Oh, yes, it seems expensive now," Glynnie said, "but what a marvelous heirloom to pass down to your children. And their children after them. Besides…" Glynnie lowered her voice. "You never know when the artist might retire. If you don't take it now…" She shrugged. "Well, you know what the collectibles market can be for items like these."

"Oh, my, yes. Why, just the other day, one of my neighbors paid some exorbitant price at auction for a puny little piece of crockery I wouldn't have paid twenty-five cents for when we were young."

"Crazy, isn't it?"

Once again, the woman looked at the Santa.

"Just feel that velvet," Glynnie said. "It's real silk. And each one of those leaves is hand painted."

The woman let out another sigh. "I'd really be nuts to pass this up a second time, wouldn't I?"

"Would you like to think about it for a while?" Glynnie said. "I mean, it's probably unlikely someone else would come along in the next hour or so and buy it…."

"No, no…I'm not going to take that chance again." She turned to Karleen. "Do you take American Express? And can you deliver it, since it's so big?"

Somehow, Joanna managed to hold in her laughter until the woman was well out of sight. "Oh, my God…that was phenomenal!"

"Well, shoot, honey—all those years of living with your father have to count for something."

"But to tell her the artist was thinking of retiring..."

"Uh-uh, I never said that. If you recall, what I said was, 'you never know when the artist will retire.'" She batted her eyes, and Joanna cracked up all over again.

"Thanks, Mom."

"Are you kidding? That was almost as much fun as winning a case. And besides, that Santa was worth every single penny she paid for it."

"Amen," Karleen said, as Glynnie said, "Now. About Dale," and Karleen "Amened" that, too, while Joanna thought seriously about crawling under the table with the boxes and not coming out until both Karleen and her mother got bored and went away.

"He came to talk to me yesterday," her mother said.

"Who? Dale? When?"

"When I was in the kitchen, getting dessert ready." She took a deep breath. "Said he understood my objections, but damned if he didn't stand up to me. Not to mention for your right to live your own life. I was annoyed at first, until I got myself out of the way long enough to really hear what he was saying." She paused. "And I'll bet my ass the man's in love with you. He may not know it yet, and I'm sure he doesn't know what to do with it, but the look in his eyes when he defended you...well, I guess I finally realized I need to want the things for you that make *you* happy. Not what I think will make you happy—"

"But Dale *isn't* making me happy, he's making me frustrated and miserable and confused," Joanna said. "And I'm scared to death of getting too attached to a man I can't figure out and who's not the least bit interested in giving me all the puzzle pieces so I can. And your about-face, Mom, isn't helping me any."

"Actually," Karleen said, "I might have at least one of those pieces." Only the next wave of customers picked that moment to swarm through the exhibit hall, so it was another twenty minutes before anybody could find out what the heck she was talking about.

Lowering her voice as though the Santas might be bugged, she said, "I probably shouldn't say anything, since I'm just surmising, but long story short, Ben's a fund manager. You know, somebody who invests the money for foundations and stuff like that?"

Joanna frowned. "I thought he and Dale were teammates?"

"In the minors. Ben never made the cut, so he got out some years back and went into finance. Anyway, when he came over to my place last night—"

"Oh, yeah?"

Karleen glared at Joanna. "For coffee, gutter brain, since nothing was open on Thanksgiving, okay? And yeah, I know all about his wife's death a year ago, so believe me, coffee is *all* it was. Now do you want to hear this or what?"

Joanna motioned for her to continue, and she said, "So. I weaseled out of Ben that he was here to meet with a client about his fund's performance—"

"Over coffee."

"Yes, *over coffee*. So naturally, I asked him who and, naturally, he said he couldn't name names, although he could tell me it was a celebrity who anonymously funnels most of his earnings into a charitable trust."

"Must've been some coffee," Glynnie muttered.

Joanna said, "That's what I'm thinking."

Karleen ignored both of them, saying, "So I'm figuring it's Dale."

Joanna laughed, even as she got this weird little tingly feeling in the pit of her stomach. "As if he's the only celebrity in New Mexico."

"True. But when I came right out and asked if it was Dale, Ben took too long to say it wasn't. God, men are such lousy liars."

"Did Ben say what kinds of charities the fund supports?" Glynnie asked.

"Yeah." Karleen looked from one to the other. "Programs for victims of domestic violence."

Chapter 20

"**Y**ou *told* Karleen about the trust?" Dale stared at his friend, hoping like hell he'd heard wrong. Outside his office, the store was crammed with crazed customers who seemed to have forgotten there were four more weeks until Christmas. Inside his head, all hell had just broken loose.

Ben didn't look anywhere near as contrite as Dale might have liked. "I didn't tell her, I swear. Your name never even came up. But we got to talking and I'll admit I said more than I probably should have. And my guess is she put two and two together on her own. The woman's not stupid, Dale."

"Aw, hell, Ben..." Dale dragged a palm down his face. "You know she's gonna go straight to Joanna about it, don't you?"

"And you know what? Somehow, I can't get too worked up about you being upset because she found out you give all your money to charity. I never did understand why you kept it such a secret. But to hide it from somebody you're involved with—"

"I'm not *involved* with Joanna."

Ben had the nerve to laugh. "Aw, c'mon, man—you don't think everybody can see how you feel about her? And it's not hard to see why. Shoot, I was only around her for, what? A couple of hours? And I thought, damn, finally somebody ornery enough to deal with your crap—"

"Hey!"

"Well, it's true. She's perfect for you and you know it. And don't go giving me some lame shit about being in it just for the sex."

"Nobody's perfect," Dale muttered, yelling, *"What?"* at the knock on his office door. Brittney, one of his new sales assistants, came just far enough inside to hand him the mail, took one look at his face and darted right back out again.

As Dale halfheartedly shuffled through the envelopes and flyers, Ben said gently, "Look. I don't know what's behind your setting up the trust, although I have my suspicions. And up until now, I respected whatever your reasons were for not telling me. But I'm just saying, if…those reasons are personal, maybe you could use those to the trust's advantage. Celebrity causes always rake in the big bucks."

Dale looked up, his insides churning. "And for the sake of this friendship, I strongly suggest you back off."

To his annoyance, Ben simply shrugged. "Okay, man, it's your call. But just so you know? Your life-is-one-big-funfest attitude isn't fooling anybody. And it never has. You're one miserable bastard, and I guarantee you that woman you're 'not involved' with sees straight through you, too. And let me tell you something else…you don't come clean soon about whatever it is that's kept you from acting like a real human being all these years, you don't let somebody, *anybody,* inside to help you clean up the mess you call a brain, all that charity work you're funding won't mean jack."

Glowering, Dale leaned back in his desk chair, his arms folded across his chest. "You done?"

"I don't know. Did you hear anything I said?"

"Yeah, I heard."

"And?"

"And I think from now on, I'd prefer it if you remembered you're my financial advisor. Not my therapist."

The look in Ben's dark eyes pretty much said he wanted to knock Dale's lights out right then, but all he did was shake his head, muttering something about needing to get to the airport to catch his flight before striding out of the office.

Glowering even harder, Dale looked down at the pile of mail to see an envelope with Tori and Bobby's return address on it. He ripped it open, letting out a weighty sigh when he saw the flowery wedding invitation. He hoped to hell the tension between the two of them yesterday at the Swanns' was due solely to pre-wedding heebie-jeebies. Otherwise…

Damn. Why on earth had he thought he could somehow hover at the edges of these people's lives without getting sucked in?

Joanna's mother was right. Why hadn't he walked away? *Why?*

Sunday night, the changing of the parental guard. As part of his determination to turn over a long-overdue new leaf, Bobby got the kids back to Joanna's at seven on the dot. *And* gave her December's child support check, three days early. She looked like she might keel over from the shock.

"And I swear it won't bounce this time," he said. After Ryder had proudly shown Joanna the painted clay bird he'd made in Dale's art class at the store yesterday, Chester and the boys had run outside to the hutch to see the rabbits and Dulce had gone to her room, leaving Jo, Bobby and a half dozen cats in the baking-scented kitchen. Spotting the heaping plate of chocolate-chip cookies by the stove, Bobby pilfered one before Joanna could come to.

"Tori read me the riot act," he said, chewing and looking at his ex-wife. "About the way I keep forgetting things?" Joanna lifted one brow. Bobby grinned and kept chewing. Damn, the woman made the best chocolate-chip cookies in the world. "I know what you're thinking—so how come it didn't take when *you* kept hounding me?"

"No, what I'm thinking is more along the lines of *You go, girl.*" Then she squinted a little at him. "You look tired."

His shoulders hitched. "Things've been a little on the tense side with this wedding coming up and all. Although for some reason, once the invitations went out, I finally relaxed. Like the decision had been taken out of my hands or something, so I no longer had to think about it. Now all I gotta do is show up and say my vows, and I'm done. You get yours, by the way?"

"Uh…yeah," Jo said, sounding distracted, still squinting at him. That ugly old tom with the chewed-up ear jumped onto the counter; Joanna swept him off without even looking. "You're nervous about the wedding?"

"Nothin' out of the ordinary," he said, immediately on guard. "But you know how it is."

"I do seem to remember you were a basket case before ours." She crossed her arms over a sweatshirt several sizes too large. Dale's, maybe? "How's Tori doing?"

"Oh, she'll be fine once she gets her exams out of the way. And she's gonna take off some extra time from work, too, so she can concentrate on the wedding." He laughed, but it didn't sound like him. "What little of it her mother's left for her to worry about, anyway."

Joanna unzipped the backpacks the kids'd dumped on the floor when they'd come in, then disappeared into the utility room off the kitchen, returning a few seconds later with an empty laundry basket. "You're really sure Tor wants me at her wedding?'' she said, disemboweling the packs of three days' worth of dirty clothes, which she dumped into the basket.

"It was her idea, I swear. She said it would be good for the kids. Isn't that something? You are coming, right?''

"Hey,'' she tossed over her shoulder on her way back to the laundry room. "You think I'd miss a chance to see you squirm?''

Bobby chuckled, then crossed the kitchen to stand in the utility room doorway, leaning on the door frame and watching Jo stuff clothes into the washer. "We sent Dale an invitation, too.''

Hands full of clothes, Joanna stopped in midstuff. "You did?''

"Yeah. He didn't tell you?''

"We don't talk every day, Bobby,'' she said, pouring detergent onto the clothes and letting the lid clang shut. "And this weekend was crazy.''

Was it his imagination, or was she ticked?

"That was Tori's idea, too,'' he said as she fiddled with the dials. "To invite Dale. Because you'd be already there with the kids and all, so we thought it'd be nice, you know.''

Those big green eyes of hers got even bigger. "Aren't you kind of assuming a lot? About Dale and me?'' Then they narrowed. "Or are you fishing?''

"Maybe,'' he said with a grin. "And I warned Tori he might not come, since for one thing, he really doesn't know either Tori or me all that well. And like you said, maybe you wouldn't feel right goin' together. Not that you couldn't each go on your own, you know.''

She humphed and started the washer.

"Anyway,'' he said. "Tori thought it would be a neat surprise for her mother, too, if Dale came. Since she's got this thing for him, from when he played for the Braves?

We keep tryin' to get 'em together, but for some reason, it never works out. So how'd the show go, by the way?''

For the first time since they'd started talking about the wedding, Jo's smile didn't look like somebody was stepping on her foot. ''Best I've ever done, actually. A bunch of people bought because they'd seen the Santas I sold Dale, too. So I really cleaned up this year.''

''That's great, Jo. It's about time, huh?''

''Yes, it is.'' She yanked open the dryer door to pull out a load of clean towels, fussing at a half-grown red kitten who immediately jumped in.

''So what *is* going on with you and Dale?''

Kitten removed and towels clutched to her chest, Jo pushed past him on her way back to the kitchen, where she dropped the towels onto the table, then took a sudden interest in unloading the dishwasher. From down the hall, music blared and male children, back inside, *vroomed.* His tail wagging, Chester trotted into the kitchen and on over to sit on Bobby's foot.

''It's…complicated,'' she said, glasses clinking against each other as she shoved them into the cupboard.

''More than we were?''

''Light-years more than we were.''

''Ouch.''

''Yeah.'' Silverware rattled into the drawer as she sorted it out, then she twisted around, one hand on the counter, the other parked on her hip. He knew that pose well. And it irked him to realize he still wasn't totally immune to it. ''You wouldn't by any chance be so hot on this working out between me and Dale in order to get me out of your hair, would you?''

The logical thing would be to lie through his teeth. Except he'd finally learned that, sooner or later, lies come back to bite you in the butt. And he had one very, very sore butt by now.

''Okay, so maybe the thought had crossed my mind once

or twice." At her snort of disgust, he added, "So sue me for wanting you to find somebody again. If that happened to also take some of the burden off me…"

"So much the better."

"Well. Yeah." He rubbed a hand across his mouth. "You remember that night when I brought the kids back late and you lit into me?"

A smile twitched around her mouth. "And which night might that be?"

"Right after the boys' birthday party? When I gave 'em their bath and stuff? Anyway, I'm ashamed to admit this…but I was kinda sending out signals like maybe I was regrettin' our splitting up."

"Oh. *That* night. I wondered what that was all about." She grabbed a cookie from the plate and started munching. "One question. Why?"

"Because I thought maybe if that's what you thought, it might prod you into, you know, looking elsewhere. You don't have to look at me like that, I know it was stupid, okay? But Tori was bugging me, and…and I was desperate."

"Oh, Bobby," she said on a sigh, then sucked in a breath. "Please tell me you didn't decide Dale needed some prodding, too."

"I might have…said…something in passing. But, babe," he added when she let out a squeak, "only because I could tell he was already interested, I swear. All I did was give him the all-clear."

"You set me *up?*"

"Jesus, Jo—somebody had to! Otherwise you would've sat here and rotted. So who better than me, huh?"

"Never mind your track record in that department's not exactly stellar."

"Okay, so my previous attempts bombed. But Dale and you…that's different, right? He's a good guy, not like those jerks I tried fixing you up with before—"

"Mom! Dad! Listen to Ry!"

The boys barreled into the kitchen, sliding across the tiled floor in their socks. Ryder clambered up onto the bar stool and thunked an open *Captain Underpants* on the counter in front of him. "I picked it up an' looked at the words, and I just *knew* 'em in my mind, without having to sound 'em out or anything!"

Face glowing and eyes gleaming with power, he read a whole chapter and most of a second one—Matt only had to supply one or two words—before coming up for air, grinning at Bobby like he'd just won a big prize for something. Bobby's heart swelled in his chest as he high-fived the kid, only to go *fsssst* when Matt said, "Wait'll you show Dale!" and Ryder beamed and said, "Yeah!" before both boys took off again, thumping from one side of the hall to the other on the way back to their room.

Bobby started when Joanna touched his arm. "It's okay," she said gently. "Trust me…you're in no danger of being usurped."

"Damn," he said. "How do you read people's minds like that?"

"Not difficult when what you're thinking is written all over your face."

He let out a whoosh of air. "To tell you the truth, I totally forgot that if you got another man in your life? It would mean another man in theirs, too. Then these past two weekends, it was 'Dale said this' and 'Dale said that'…and then that art class, and…"

"And how many times did Dulcy or the boys call you last week?"

Bobby stuffed his hands in his pockets and smirked. "I get your point."

"So there you are. Dale's a novelty to them, Bobby. But he's more like an overgrown camp counselor, not a father figure. Believe me, Dale's no more interested in being a dad than your children are in having two of them."

He heard the edge to her voice. "He doesn't want kids?"

"No," she said after a moment.

"But don't you—?"

"Frankly, I'm not sure what I want anymore. And can we please change the subject?"

It was totally weird, the way you could still worry about somebody you weren't even involved with anymore. "Sure, babe." He averted his gaze, thinking maybe he was making her uncomfortable. But then, maybe it wasn't him making her uncomfortable. Maybe it was Dale. And if it was…if Bobby'd put into motion something that was only gonna hurt Jo…

Shit.

"I'll be fine," she said.

"You know, you've *really* gotta stop doing that because it's freaking me out." She laughed, so he felt a little better. Then he said, "That was really something, Ry, reading like that. I guess he takes after me. A late bloomer," he added when she lifted her brows in question. "Some people, you just can't force to get it together before they're ready. Although in my case, God knows my mother and you sure tried."

Looking a little relieved, like she was glad to have moved on to another topic, she smiled and said, "So what happened with Tori?"

"Timing and luck," Bobby said, and Jo laughed. "But what the people who do have it together don't understand is that they gotta be patient with us slowpokes. Eventually, we do catch on."

"Wow," Joanna said. "This is really you talking?"

"So help me God, Jo…I'm so tired of screwing up, of constantly disappointing or ticking off the people I care about. And I can tell…" He glanced down for a second, then back up at Joanna. "I can tell Tori's worried, that I won't be able to hold up my end of things. That she's gonna have to go to school and work and take care of the baby and the house and everything because I'm gonna somehow let her down.''

''She told you this?''

''Not in so many words, no. But I'm not totally clueless. Living with you all those years taught me how to read a woman's signals, you know?''

Jo got that worried look on her face again. ''One piece of advice, okay? Don't rely on signals. Signals have a nasty habit of getting scrambled. You want to know what she's thinking, ask.''

''Aw…do I hafta?''

''Yes, you hafta. And now you hafta get outta here so I can get these twerps ready for tomorrow.'' Except when he was nearly to the door, she said, ''Bobby? I really do wish you all the best. You know that.''

''Yeah, I do,'' he said, then let himself out, wondering why on earth he'd thought things would get easier as he got older.

After Bobby left, Joanna wandered down the hall to check on the kids. Dulcy, as usual, was deep in an online chat with five million of her closest friends. And from the boys' room emanated periodic whoopee cushion blats interspersed with howls of laughter. And far be it from her to interrupt their bonding. So she wandered back out to the laundry room to transfer the just-washed clothes to the dryer, thinking that here, at least, was something *she didn't have to think about.*

Did everybody else have relationships as weird as hers, or was she exceptionally blessed in that department?

Why hadn't Dale mentioned the invitation? Was he deliberately avoiding the subject? Or had he simply forgotten as he had about her father's already inviting him to Thanksgiving?

And what was such a damn secret about this foundation or whatever it was that he couldn't talk about that, either

Granted, she only had Karleen's iffy conversation with Ben to go by, but still. It certainly fit into the larger picture, didn't it?

Whatever the larger picture was.

She bumped the dryer door shut with her knee and set the timer, thinking about what Bobby had said, about needing to be patient with the people who didn't get it. Unfortunately, patience had never been one of her finer qualities. Just ask Bobby. Of course, *God* would have lost patience with Bobby, she imagined. How Tori had managed to effect the changes Joanna had seen in her ex-husband these past few months was anybody's guess. But more power to her.

But Dale wasn't Bobby, she thought on a sigh, pushing the start button. Big Mama hopped up onto the thumping dryer, then *mrrr-owed* to climb up onto her shoulder for a hug. She hauled up the massive cat—much to Chester's annoyance—and carried her into the kitchen, letting herself sink into the soothing rumble of the cat's purr.

Could she be patient enough with Dale to wait him out?

Could she be patient enough with herself?

"Mom? Are you listening to me?"

Shaking herself from her ruminations, Joanna blinked at Matt.

"Sorry…what?"

"I said, can me 'n' Ry have some of those cookies?"

"*May Ryan and I please* have some of those cookies?"

"What*ever*. Jeez. Can we?"

"Sure, honey. And don't give any to the dog," she said to their backs as they thundered across the kitchen floor.

Would somebody *please* tell her what the hell she was supposed to do?

Chapter 21

The following Friday night Dale woke up with a start in Joanna's bed, feeling like somebody'd clubbed him. The extra hours he'd had to keep the store open to accommodate Christmas shoppers was taking its toll, that was for damn sure. It was nearly ten by the time he'd dragged himself to Joanna's, and although he'd rallied long enough to show the lady a good time, he passed out right after. So he had no idea how long he'd been asleep when he jerked awake, out of one of those too real dreams that leaves your heart thundering in your chest, even though the sleep images shatter into a thousand unrecognizable splinters the instant you come to. On the floor beside him, Chester whined in question, his tail thumping against the rug.

"Go ask your mother," Dale said, only to swat dog hair out of his face a moment later. "Okay, okay..." He threw back the warm, Joanna-scented covers, the chill in the room stinging his skin as he swung his legs out of the bed and willed his vision to adjust to the darkness. Wondering why she hadn't stirred, he glanced over his bare shoulder to discover he was alone in the bed. Which probably accounted for why the dog was after him and not her.

Damn, it was freezing in here. To keep his privates from shrinking to the size of a walnut, Dale pulled on his jeans and T-shirt—where the hell was his hooded sweatshirt, anyway?—the check Joanna had insisted on giving him for the roof crinkling in his back pocket. There'd been no point in arguing with her about it, since clearly this was something she needed to do. He also didn't bother asking how she'd managed to hit the amount right on the head. He did, however, inform her that he'd be making a donation in her name to any local charity she liked, which apparently earned him some major points.

He sure did like the way the lady showed her gratitude.

Even if she had been acting weird the past little while. Since Thanksgiving, he thought maybe.

But then, ever since his conversation with Ben, Dale supposed he had, too. Especially as he'd been so wiped out with the store, maintaining the status quo was about all he'd been able to do. He came over several times a week, he and Joanna slept together when the kids weren't there, watched movies or played board games when they were, but even he had to admit they were all kinda spinning their wheels. Not that he necessarily had a problem with that. But he could see where Joanna might.

He sat back on the edge of the bed to pull on his socks and think about this. What they had here, he supposed, was one of those limbo situations where nobody knew what they were supposed to do next. Or even if there was a "next." Which might not even be worth thinking about except…okay, okay, he was happier when he was with Joanna than when he wasn't. And it wasn't just that she was different from any other woman he'd ever known. She made him feel different, too. Better, somehow. Like he didn't have to watch his back all the time, or try to live up to some kind of expectations. He could simply be who he was, and she seemed to be okay with that.

Except—he stood, his hands on his hips as the dog danced around his feet—Joanna's accepting him as he was for a short-term affair and her being able to for the long haul...well, there was no getting around that, was there? Especially since that sighting a few weeks back.

Granted, as the days passed without any attempt to make contact, Dale breathed a little easier. If the past stayed in the past, then maybe this could work. But if it didn't...

And maybe he should stop worrying about things that might never even happen and go deal with what had.

Dale and the dog tried to get through the bedroom door at the same time, which provoked some mild cussing on his part and a soft yike on Chester's. Damned if she hadn't plugged the Christmas tree lights back in—Joanna was one of those people who started Christmas right after Thanksgiving—but by now he realized the kitchen light was on, as well. He shuffled down the hall, yawning when he hit the kitchen. And there she was, sitting on the cold tile floor in about a hundred layers of clothes, each one uglier and baggier than the next, clunking things right and left into a large black garbage bag gaping open at her hip. At the prospect of food—even food that had evolved into new life forms—Chester forgot all about having to do his business and trotted over to help.

She'd twisted her hair up and stuck a pen or something through it to hold it on top of her head, although lots of little curls still waved around her neck and shoulders like frantic worms. Then she twisted around and saw him and said, "Hey, there" in that quiet way she did, and that provoked a feeling he'd been prone to more and more over the past little while, one that started out small and quiet and warm in the center of his chest, building and building until he felt like sunlight might spill out of his fingertips.

Dale yawned again, then slid his hands into his pockets. "I suppose you know it's after three in the morning."

She glanced up at the kitchen clock, said, "So it is. Huh," then stuck her head back inside the refrigerator.

"You always clean out your refrigerator at three in the morning?"

"No. But I should've done it a month ago and since I couldn't sleep anyway, I figured I might as well do something productive instead of lying there and listening to you snore."

"I do not snore."

"Yes, you do. Well, actually, you make these cute little snuffling noises, but close enough to count."

"Cute? I think I'd rather snore."

"Whatever. And besides, you've usually done your pumpkin act long before this."

He waited a moment, then said quietly, "I guess I kinda passed out, huh?"

"It's okay," she said, her voice muffled from inside the fridge. "You were dead on your feet when you got here. Could you run me a bowl of hot water and give me the cruddy sponge from underneath the sink?"

"I love it when you talk dirty."

"Watch it, bub. I've got some stuff here—" grunting, she wrenched open a plastic container, rearing back and making a face "—that's got serious biohazard potential."

And even though he was half asleep, even though she was sitting there surrounded by some pretty nauseating-looking stuff, he laughed, and crouched beside her, and took her face in his hands, stifling her "Wha—?" with a kiss.

One of those nice, long kisses with a lot of promise behind it.

Only not the kind of promise he was used to getting.

Or giving.

"This isn't gonna get the refrigerator clean," she whispered.

"Do you care?" he whispered back, guiding her to the floor and trying to figure out the route to her breasts through all those clothes.

"Not really—"

"Hey! This is *my* sweatshirt!"

"It was the first thing I laid my hands on—no, not under there, the next layer—in the dark."

"Now it's gonna smell all girly," he said, still trying to sort out all those damn layers.

"Poor you. Wait…could you just…hit the fridge door with your heel to close it? Yeah, that's it. Oh, for God's sake, Chester, go *away!*"

"*Now,* dog. Jesus, your nipples are like ice cubes."

"Hey, I just provide them," she said as the dog sat and rudely stared at them, his head cocked to one side. "Temperature regulation is your department."

"Through all those clothes?"

"Be creative. And what is it with you and floors anyway? Whoa…what *are* you doing?"

"Being creative. And the last floor experience was your idea, if memory serves."

"At least," she hissed, "I chose…a carpeted…*oh!*… surface. Oh, for the love of Mike, what *now?*"

The fool dog had started barking at them—probably because they looked like a couple of idiots, all tangled up in all those clothes and limbs and whatall.

Laughter bubbled from her throat like sparkling water and he said, "You laughing at me?"

She wheezed out, "N…n…no, of *course not!*" on a shriek of even louder laughter when Dale started cussing and flailing at the dog, who'd grabbed hold of his sleeve and was trying to pull him off of Joanna.

"Remember your fling with the Great Dane?" Dale bellowed at the stupid beast, who blinked as if to say, "Oh, yeah," then went off somewhere just in time for Joanna to reach up and grab the front of Dale's sweatshirt and pull his mouth down on hers again. And finally, *finally*, they got everything sorted out and he made her beg a little—not too much, though, or she was liable to slug him—and he thought how he'd never grow tired of hearing her gasp of wonder and welcome when he entered her, not if he heard it a thousand times. A million.

How this was a woman who didn't need flowers and sweet words to get her in the mood, and how he'd never known anyone who deserved them more.

And how he wanted to be the one to give them to her.

For a lot longer than a little while.

She gasped a *"Please!"* and he cushioned her bare bottom with his hands and plunged a final time, a primal act of possession and conquest that, when it came right down to it, was nothing more than a load of crap. Because it was Joanna, with her body and scent and laughter and goodness, who possessed *him*...or as much of himself as he knew how to give. It was Joanna, now crying out a release more taken than given, who'd conquered him...at least enough to be thinking along the lines he was thinking.

So was his own shout one of victory...or of being vanquished?

And did he really give a damn which?

They lay there for a while, waiting for things to settle down and their brains to get going again, sharing heartbeats and their mingled scents and a moment not real likely to get Hallmark's vote. The dog came over to make sure they were still alive, his whiskers tickling Dale's ear.

"Eat your heart out," Dale said to the dog, and Joanna chuckled and kissed him again.

"And you thought I didn't know how to have any fun."

"Never said that." Tugging several of the layers up and down and closed so they wouldn't freeze, he smiled into her eyes, wondering how it was possible to feel relaxed and anxious at the same time. "Just thought you'd forgotten how."

"Amazing how easily it comes back to you." Then she suddenly wriggled out from under him, mumbling something about the floor being hard and cold as she stooped to gather up the now empty containers strewn all over the floor.

Dale got up, as well, wondering what had happened and knowing damn well that any comments about time of the month could seriously impact his life expectancy. Still, that had to be the shortest afterglow in the history of sex.

"What's goin' on, Joanna?"

"Nothing," she said, not looking at him as she carted the containers to the dishwasher.

"Oh, no…don't you dare go acting like a normal woman on me, expecting me to read your mind. I'm no good at it, never was, and doubt I ever will be. So if something's botherin' you, just tell me flat out."

At the word "out," the stupid dog started spinning in excited circles, then made a dash for the patio door. Her mouth pulled tight, Joanna jerked it open to let him outside, then faced Dale, that indecipherable look in her eyes.

"Why didn't you tell me you got an invitation to Bobby's wedding?"

"What? I don't know, it just slipped my mind, I guess. You don't mean to tell me you're mad because I forgot to tell you about a stupid wedding invitation?"

"I'm not *mad*…" Her brow all knotted up, she rammed her hands into her robe pockets. "I don't know what I am. Or what we are. I mean, I just let you seduce me next to green beans dating back to the Neolithic age, but…"

Her gaze tangled with his for several seconds before she stormed out of the kitchen. Dale followed, reaching the living room in time to see her sink crossed-legged onto the old leather sofa, her face in her hands.

''But what?'' he said.

She lifted her head, looking so miserable and balled-up Dale thought his heart would split in two. ''I'm trying to be patient, I really am, but I'm lousy at it and I hate, hate, *hate* being in limbo, which is what I feel right now because even though I know this is only supposed to be temporary, it still ticks me off that you never mentioned the wedding invitation and I'm sorry, but it *really* chaps my hide that you *still* won't spend the night and that's not your problem, it's mine, and *dammit,* why am I crying?''

She lunged for a tissue from the box by the sofa, but only half of one came out and the box thudded onto the floor, which seemed to agitate her even more.

While Joanna honked into her mangled tissue, Dale sat beside her on the sofa, trying to figure out what to say, but his brain was too busy running around in circles and screaming to do that. And anyway, Joanna apparently wasn't finished.

''I feel like the kids, thinking this is *so* not fair, because I like having you in my life, and in my bed, but…but this is making me *crazy! You're* making me crazy!''

Dale now knew what that expression meant about icewater in his veins.

''You sayin'…you want out?''

''No, you idiot!'' she said, slugging him in the arm, but not hard enough to hurt. ''But I keep thinking any second, you're gonna say *you* want out! *That's* what's driving me nuts.''

''Let me get this straight. I'm making you crazy, but you don't want me to leave you?''

''Yes. I mean, no. I don't want you to leave.''

Dale pulled her against him, mainly because he'd bust if he didn't, nestling his cheek in all that soft, sweet-smelling wild hair. And after a long, long time, he said, ''I'm still the same man I was when we started this, Joanna.''

''I know that.''

"And I still don't want a kid of my own."

A beat or two passed before she said, "I've already got kids, don't I? Another baby is..." She lifted one hand, like maybe the words she was looking for would fall into her lap. "A 'maybe.' A dream. You're..." She snaked an arm across his stomach, then twisted around to look into his eyes. "You're *here*. And *now*. Why would I want to give up something *real* for a 'maybe'?"

It seemed like about five hundred years passed while the words formed themselves in his brain, made the long, arduous journey from brain to mouth, and finally escaped into the room.

"You don't really know me."

Another five hundred years passed before she said, "I know everything I need to."

He thought about that, realizing this woman had made him think about relationship issues more than he'd done with all the other women in his life combined. And he sighed. Not a sigh of contentment, though, because fear still lurked around the edges of his mind, that eventually she'd get past whatever it was she felt now and realize there was more. More he wasn't giving her. More he couldn't give her because he simply didn't know how.

Still, whatever this fragile thing was that he'd found with this woman...well, there was no denying it was scary, and he had no way of telling if it would last, but he sure knew it was more than he'd ever had before.

And that had to count for something, didn't it?

"You got any eggs?" he said into her hair. "For breakfast?"

He could feel her breath hitch. "You like 'em scrambled or sunny-side up?"

"Sunny-side up."

"Fine...just as long as I don't have to watch you eat them."

But he could hear the smile in her voice.

* * *

Tori was about to get back in bed after going potty—this having to get up in the middle of the night business was for the birds—when her stomach growled. She grimaced at the glowing clock on her nightstand—4:00 a.m. was way too early for breakfast. Her stomach growled again, as if to say, *Yeah, so?*

On a sigh, she threw on her heavy fleece robe, yanking the tie closed as she tiptoed across the carpeted bedroom so she wouldn't wake Bobby, only to nearly wet herself when she opened her bedroom door to see Dulcy opening *her* door five feet away.

Tori quickly shut her door behind her and whispered, "What on earth are you doing awake?"

The girl's shoulders hitched under a blue terry-cloth robe. "Couldn't sleep. And I'm hungry."

"Me, too." Tori hesitated, then said, "Bagels and hot chocolate sound good?"

"I guess." Twin raccoons grinned up at Tori from Dulcy's feet. "Are there any blueberry ones left?"

"I don't know. Let's go see."

They padded down the short hall in silence, Tori thinking, *I can do this, I can do this.* There were indeed blueberry bagels; Tori popped two into the toaster, then filled a pair of mugs with milk, setting them in the microwave.

"So how come you can't sleep?" she said.

Another shrug. The microwave dinged; she took out the mugs and brought them to the dining table where they both stirred Nesquik into their hot milk, their spoons' clinking against the mugs substituting for conversation.

"You know," Tori said through the teensy-tinsy opening in her throat, "I'm a pretty good listener."

Dulcy lowered her mug to the table with a soft thunk, staring at it for several seconds before saying, "I don't feel like talking."

"That's okay. I'm just saying, if you feel you need to?

I'm here." First one bagel, then the other, bounced up out of the toaster. Tori rose and snatched them out of the slots, dropping them onto a pair of plates. "Wanna get the butter and cream cheese out of the fridge?"

She half expected a "get it yourself," but Dulcy got the stuff and brought it back to the table. With a pair of knives, to boot.

For several seconds Tori watched Bobby's daughter slather cream cheese on her bagel like she was plastering walls, her brow knotted. When she couldn't stand the ringing in her ears anymore, she said, "You get your dress for the wedding yet?"

"Mom and I are supposed to go looking for it tomorrow." Dulcy's knife clattered on the plate. "Even though it's like, so pointless. Me in a dress, I mean."

"Really?" The butter glistened on Tori's bagel like liquid gold; it was everything she could do not to cram the whole thing into her mouth at once. "I would've thought you'd jump at the chance to get all dressed up. I always did."

"Yeah, well, you would."

Tori lowered her bagel. "Why do you say that?"

"Oh, please. You're like so gorgeous. I mean, you look good no matter what. Me?" She blew a disgusted sigh through her nose.

"Stay right there," Tori said, getting up from the table. She went to the living room and pulled a photo album off the shelf, then returned to the kitchen, flipping through the leaves until she found what she was looking for.

"There," she said, plopping the open album in front of Dulcy. "That's me at your age."

"Ohmigod! No way!"

"Yep. Bucky Beaverette, huh? Of course, the five million zits kinda distract from the teeth, doncha think?"

Dulcy squinted at the photo, clearly trying not to laugh. "What's with the hat head?"

"Lovely, isn't it? Unfortunately, no hats were used to achieve that effect. My favorite part, though, are the ears sticking through the straggly hair."

"God." Dulcy looked up at her. "You were dorkier than I am."

"Oh, *way* dorkier."

After a sip of hot chocolate, Dulcy said, "So what happened?"

Tori sat down and turned the album around. "Time, mostly. After I went through puberty, my hair started to behave and my skin cleared up. But I didn't get braces until I was in my senior year of high school, after I got a part-time job so I could pay for them myself. So I spent most of my teenage years feeling pretty down about myself."

"Wow." Then, with a sigh, the girl grabbed her wild hair and held it out from her face. "But nothing's gonna change this. My mother's got it, my grandma's got it…I'm *doomed*."

Tori laughed. "And I would've killed for curls when I was your age. Anything to hide the ears. Besides, your mom's really pretty, don't you think?"

Dulcy made a face, then took another bite of her bagel. "*Dale* sure seems to think so."

Tori closed the album and set it off to one side so it wouldn't get butter on it. "You don't like Dale?" she asked quietly.

"Sure I like Dale. It's just…" She shook her head.

Tori leaned toward her. "I'm not a snitch, Dulce."

"Oh, right. Like you're not gonna tell Dad everything I say."

"Only if you tell me something that leads me to believe you or somebody else is in danger. Anything else…no. I swear."

Behind her glasses, the girl's eyes filled with tears. "Okay, after the divorce? Maybe I didn't like having to go back and forth between Mom and Dad at first, but I got used to it, sorta. And at least I knew when I was with her, I *had* her. Same with Dad. And suddenly there's all these other *people,* and…and things were fine the way they were!'' Tears trickled down her cheeks. ''But now Dad's getting married and you're having this baby, and Mom says she and Dale aren't serious about each other, but if that's true, how come he's there, like, *all* the time? And if she gets married, too…'' She wiped at her tears, shaking her head. ''And I know I sound like a selfish brat, but I can't help it, you know?''

Tori felt like her chest was going to cave in. ''I do know, Dulce. Look, I was ten when Mama decided to get married again. And I remember thinking how I didn't want to share her, either. And how she could be so happy if I wasn't.''

''Yeah?''

''Yeah.''

Dulcy blew her nose in a napkin. ''But your mother's second marriage didn't work out, either, right?''

''No, it didn't. But this one sure has. And if Leo'd been my stepdad when I was a kid, things would've been real different.'' She tapped one nail on the rim of her plate and said, ''You really don't want me to marry your father, do you?''

She sniffed. ''I don't know. Maybe.''

''Because you don't like me?''

''Because you're too young to be my mother.''

''Well, guess what, honey? I don't *want* to be your mother, how about that? Besides,'' she added as the girl's eyes went wide, ''you've got one of those already. A pretty nice one, too, from what I can tell.'' Tori broke off a piece of her now cold bagel and stuck it in her mouth. ''Used to think it'd be fun to have a sister, though. Somebody to go to the mall with and teach how to do makeup and stuff.''

''Yeah?''

''Yeah.''

''Even after the baby comes?''

"Especially after the baby comes." She pushed the last bite of bagel into her mouth and said, "I'm thinking we can leave the kid with the guys and take off every now and then, just the two of us."

Dulcy smiled, but it faltered after a second or two. "It's just that I'm scared, you know? All these changes and stuff…it's all crazy."

Suddenly, Tori had a devil of a time swallowing the bite in her mouth. "Yeah. It is."

Dulcy got up to put her empty mug and plate in the dishwasher, offering Tori another tiny smile before shuffling back down the hall to her bedroom.

With a heavy sigh, Tori leaned back in her chair, frowning at her now cold chocolate as she swirled it around in her mug.

Adulthood was *totally* overrated.

By noon on Bobby's wedding day, Joanna decided things couldn't have been more chaotic in her house had it been *her* wedding day.

"Mo-om! What am I going to do with my *haaaaaaiiiirrrr!*"

Or Dulcy's.

Tossing a "AreyoudressedyetDale'sgonnabehereanyminute" at the boys, Joanna flew out of her bedroom, whacking her hipbone on the door frame in her split to get to her traumatized daughter. And didn't it just figure, that after the hell Joanna'd gone through to get Dulcy into a dress for this wedding, now she'd turned into the she-child-from-hell, begging to wear makeup and insisting she had enough to put into a bra and how could she go with her nails all chewed up like this?

Not that Joanna couldn't relate, but still.

She skidded to a stop behind Dulcy's vanity chair, where her daughter sat glowering at her reflection in the mirror.

Except the glower eased up long enough for the child to say, "Wow...you look great!"

For once, Karleen had brought over an outfit that wouldn't make Joanna look either frumpy or sleazy. The deep teal crepe dress skimmed her body without strangling it, exposing just enough collarbone to be intriguing. And she had to admit the double-tiered hem fluttering at her calves made her feel powerfully feminine. Especially with the high-heeled, strappy, black-satin sandals she'd resurrected from a past life. Her feet were going to freeze, but at least they'd look good.

Palming her daughter's shoulders through the sleeveless purple-velvet sheath they'd finally agreed on after many, many, many heated words in many, many, many stores, Joanna glanced at herself in the mirror over Dulcy's witch woman hair. Joanna had forced as much of her own as she could catch into a French braid, although plenty of stray corkscrew curls still framed her face, blowing raspberries at her.

"Thanks, sweetie. So do you."

"Yeah, right! Look at this!" she wailed, batting at her hair. "I can't get it to do *anything!*"

"Ponytail?"

A horror-stricken expression looked back from the mirror. "Mom! Eewww." Horror turned to pleading. "C'n you do mine like yours? Pleeeease?"

Never mind that Joanna had offered that very thing this morning, only to be met with a touch-my-hair-and-die expression.

"I suppose so. But you have to sit still since we don't have much time before Dale gets here. Did you talk to your father this morning?"

"Yeah. He sounded pretty nervous."

"Getting married is a biggee. I imagine he is."

"Especially as he's already been married once, huh?"

"Maybe," Joanna said noncommittally as she sectioned

off Dulcy's hair and began to braid. "But in case you're wondering, just because a first marriage doesn't work out doesn't mean a second one won't."

"Mom. I know that. Ouch! You're pulling it too tight!"

"Sorry." Joanna partially undid the braiding. "So…how are you feeling about things today?"

"About Tori, you mean?" Her skinny little shoulders bounced, but her expression went cagey. "She's okay, I guess. At first I thought she was like this total airhead, but we've been talking and stuff, and I don't think that anymore. Did you know she got As on three of her exams?"

"No, I didn't—stop wiggling, sweetie. That's great."

"Sorry. Yeah, she's like real smart. And pretty cool about a lot of stuff. Like she said we could go hang out at the mall if I wanted to."

Not just smart, Joanna thought with a smile. Downright brilliant.

"That'll be fun."

"Yeah, maybe. So…you and Dale seem to be getting along better, too, huh?"

Joanna commended herself for staying cool. Yeah, there'd been a definite shift in their relationship after the love-among-the-refrigerator-ruins episode. He'd even owned up to the charitable trust into which he channeled a great deal of his income, confirming Karleen's hunch. And he'd volunteered the information, to boot, even if he was still keeping the reasons for his setting up the trust close to his chest. But she wasn't kidding herself: Dale was clearly feeling his way. There'd been no promises given, no commitments made. And that was fine with Joanna, who frankly had to admit she was doing her share of way-feeling, herself.

"We're just enjoying being with each other for now," she said, finishing up Dulcy's hair. "As for what comes next…" She shrugged. "We'll just have to see."

"Do you think you love him?" her daughter asked quietly.

A question Joanna hadn't allowed herself to ask. Yet. So all she said was, "We've only known each other a couple of months, you know—"

The doorbell rang; the dog barked; two pairs of eight-year-old boyfeet pounded down the hall. Dulcy and Joanna did a final primping in front of Dulcy's closet mirror, then joined the boys—who were dressed, thank God, even if Matt's shirttail was hanging out from underneath his sweater.

Joanna rounded the hall corner and froze.

The man did serious justice to a suit and tie, God help her. The hair could still do with a trim, but who cared? Everything else was just...

"Wow," he said softly, blatantly giving her the once-over. "When you decide to fix yourself up, darlin', you don't mess around." Then—before she could slug him—he said to Dulcy, "And who is this knockout?"

"Da-ale," she said, giggling. "It's *me,* Dulcy!"

"Get outta here!"

"Uh-huh," she said, nodding her head and making all her own little curls bounce around her face. "Mom let me wear makeup and heels!"

One step removed from open-toed army boots, in Joanna's opinion, but yes, they were heels.

Then the usual life-with-children madness ensued while the boys tried to find their shoes and Dulcy suddenly decided the mohair shawl her grandmother had lent her was too itchy so *now* what was she gonna wear and everybody had to go pee and dammit, why was the phone ringing?

"I'll get it!" Dale yelled.

Bless the man. Grinning, Joanna zipped back to her bedroom, digging an ivory swing coat out of her closet Karlee had talked her into buying three years ago, then zipped back to the living room to hand it to Dulcy, her smile fading when she caught Dale's frown.

"Oh, man...I'm so sorry," he said into the phone. "No, no...of course not. And tell her we're thinking of her, okay?... Yeah, you, too, buddy."

Dale hung up and met her gaze, his hand still on the receiver. Instinctively, she pulled Ryder to her.

"That was Bobby," he said quietly. "Tori lost the baby this morning."

Chapter 22

On what should have been her first full day of married life, Tori shifted underneath the afghan on her mother's sofa, watching but not really seeing the figure skating on TV. Over in front of the bay window, about a thousand ornaments glistened softly on the eight-foot-tall, fiber-optic Christmas tree, Bobby's and her present to her mother for taking care of all the wedding arrangements. It had been Mama's idea for Tori to come stay with her and Leo for a while after the hospital said there really was no reason to keep her, since it'd been quick and uncomplicated. As if that was supposed to make her feel better. Tori could tell Bobby'd been hurt when she'd agreed, but at that moment she couldn't deal with Bobby's feelings. Sorting through her own was taking all her energy as it was.

All the wedding decorations were gone by the time they'd gotten back.

She'd felt terrible, ruining everyone's day, knowing people'd probably bought new clothes or rearranged plans. And all of Bobby's relatives who'd come from out of town! A some point, they should probably reimburse people for their travel and lodging, at least. Because there'd certainly be no wedding now. Not for a while, anyway.

"Tori!" She looked up when Mama opened the front door, her hands full of Albertsons' shopping bags. "What are you doing out of bed?"

"They told me there was no reason I couldn't get up if I felt like it," Tori said, trying to keep the edge out of her voice. "As long as I don't overdo it or anything."

Her mother set down her purse and the groceries, then removed her sweater coat, all the while watching Tori as if she might explode; Tori turned away from the worried look in her eyes, dreading the inevitable question. "How're you feeling?"

Empty. Scared.

Lost.

"Fine, Mama," she said. "Just tired."

Her mother sat with her on the sofa, rubbing Tori's feet through the afghan. "You know, it's not all that uncommon with first pregnancies—"

"Mama. Don't."

"Well. I'll just go take the groceries to the kitchen. I thought maybe I'd fix country-fried steak for tonight, if that's okay?"

Tori looked up, forcing a smile. "That sounds great, thanks."

No sooner had her mother left, though, than Bobby came out of the kitchen with a cup of tea, his expression even more heart-wrenching than her mother's. Tori stared at the TV, wishing she wasn't thinking some of the things she was, wishing she didn't feel as if somebody'd tied her brain up in knots. She swallowed back the hot, choking sensation at the back of her throat.

Bobby set the tea on the end table where she could reach it, then sat beside her, leaning forward with his hands clasped between his knees and staring at the screen.

"This pros or amateurs?"

"Pros."

"Who's ahead?"

"I don't know. I came in late."

He nodded, then said, "God. I feel so *stupid.*"

Tori turned her head slowly, as if her neck hurt. "About what?"

"That I don't know what to say. To make you feel better."

"There's nothing you can say," she said after a moment, but gently. "I just need time. And you being so good to me…that helps."

"Does it?"

"Of course it does," she said, her insides cramping. But too high up to have anything to do with the miscarriage.

"Who was on the phone?" he asked, pulling her feet into his lap and massaging her instep. It felt nice. Comforting. "While I was making your tea?"

"Oh. Joanna. She said the kids wanted to come over for a minute, so I said that was okay."

He looked surprised. "You really don't mind?"

"That your kids said they wanted to come see me?" She managed a tiny smile. "What do you think? Dulcy called me last night, did you know that?"

"Oh, yeah, she told me when I talked to her this morning—"

The doorbell chimed. Tori carefully shifted, lowering her feet to the floor so she wouldn't look like an invalid. "Joanna said she was on her cell, that's probably them."

Bobby answered the door; the kids came in first, a little more subdued than usual. Dulcy had brought her a little potted rosebush, dotted with the tiniest, most perfect white roses Tori'd ever seen.

"I hope you aren't too sad," the girl said, her eyes shining and Tori reached up to pull her down for a hug, smelling her sweet shampoo and thinking that one day, she really did want to have one of these.

The boys hung back, close to their father, looking lost. Then Joanna was beside her on the sofa, giving her a hug, too, and telling her she wasn't going to say she knew how she felt, because she didn't—which Tori thought very admirable of her—but that she still felt terrible for her, all the same. And Dale was there, which she hadn't expected, looking like a giant in her mother's living room and wearing that awkward expression men do at times like these, his hands in his pockets.

"I'm real sorry," he said to both Bobby and her, and Tori's insides relaxed a bit, just from knowing she was surrounded by people who cared so much.

Then she decided to stop feeling sorry for herself, especially when it hit her that—finally!—her mother and Dale were in the same place at the same time.

"Mama!" she hollered. "Come see who's here!"

They made small talk for the few seconds it took for Mama to reappear; only when she did, instead of looking delighted, or even embarrassed, every bit of blood drained from her mother's face.

"It's Dale McConnaughy…Mama?"

The room had gone dead silent, as if everyone had stopped breathing. Tori's gaze flickered between her mother and Dale, who looked for all the world as though somebody else had taken over his body. Not only did his smile die, but his eyes went so hard and cold, Tori actually shivered. Joanna got up and went over to him and touched his arm, looking both baffled and scared out of her wits.

"Dale?" she said gently. "What is it—"

"I spotted you a few weeks back, did you know that?" Dale said to Mama, his voice low. "Even got a P.I. to check up on you to make sure I wasn't hallucinating."

Mama's hands knotted in front of her. "I swear, I had no idea you'd moved to Albuquerque until Tori mentioned you were seeing Joanna. And I still c-couldn't believe it, couldn't believe...of all the crazy things, that we'd b-both end up here, that—''

Dale turned to Joanna, cutting Mama off. ''You and the kids take as long as you need. I'll be out in the car. And Tori...'' Her heart twisted at the pain in his eyes. ''Forgive me for acting like a jackass, honey. I know this is the last thing you need, but I just can't stay. I'm sorry.''

''Dale!'' Joanna said. ''What on earth is going on?''

''Ask her,'' he said with a brief, bitter glance at Mama, then let himself out.

Nobody seemed to know what to say. Or do. Ryder crept over to Joanna, silently leaning against her even though Tori could tell her mind had gone right out the door with Dale. Tori looked up at her own mother, staring at the closed front door like a statue.

''You and Dale already know each other?''

It seemed like centuries before Mama finally looked at her. Then, with a small smile that nearly broke Tori's already mangled heart, she said. ''He's your half brother sugar. My firstborn.''

''Excuse me,'' Joanna said. ''I'll be right back.''

Dale hadn't been in the car a full minute when the passenger side door opened and Joanna scrambled inside.

''Talk to me,'' she said.

''Forget it.''

''Excuse me, bub, but that policy you have about no talking about the past? Consider it canceled.'' He didn't have to see her expression to know how mad she was. ''You told me your mother was dead.''

He swallowed down the bile at the back of his throat and said, ''No, what I said was, my parents haven't been in the picture for some time. You drew your own conclusion, Joanna, I really don't want to discuss this right now.''

''Tough.'' Her arms were crossed over her chest so hard

he didn't know how she was breathing. "So you knew. She was here, I mean."

"I didn't know she was here in Albuquerque, not for sure, until a little bit ago. And I sure as hell didn't know she was Tori's mother." He could barely hear his own voice over the vicious pounding in his head. "That I'd walk into that house and run right smack into...*dam*mit!" He banged the palm of his hand on the steering wheel, then clutched it, strongly tempted to rip the thing right off the column. "What kind of sick cosmic joke is this? All the paths our lives could've taken..." He let his thought drift off, still far too poleaxed to make sense of any of it.

"And maybe there's a reason fate brought you two together again?"

He jerked at the sound of Joanna's voice. Jesus. He'd forgotten she was even there.

"I don't believe in that crap."

She made a sound that wasn't quite a laugh. "After what just happened? How could you not?"

Wasn't much he could say to that, was there?

"So," she said, "is your father still alive, too?"

"No. Hasn't been for more than twenty-five years."

"Can I trust you're telling me the truth this time?"

Fury tangling with a million other feelings inside him, Dale speared Joanna with his gaze. "Since I caused his death, yes, ma'am. You can *trust* that I'm tellin' the truth this time. Now would you please go back inside and give me some time to think? Or is that too much to ask?"

Understandably enough, she looked like she'd been shot between the eyes. But he could also see her try to compose herself. He suspected she had a pretty good fight on her hands over that. "Only if you promise we'll talk later."

Yeah, he knew that was coming. And he could've taken the easy way out, placated her with promises he had no intention of keeping. "And I told you already, that part of my life's not open for discussion."

"Oh, right. You drop a bomb like that, and you expect me to just forget about it? To go on as if nothing's happened?"

He blew out a sigh. "No. I don't expect you to do anything. But I am asking you to do what I need you to do, instead of what you've determined I need to do, okay?"

"No, it's not okay," she said, and he heard her voice shaking. "Not anymore. Yeah, it might've been okay before this, before I knew as much as I do now. Or as little, depending on how you look at it. Before I knew just how deep those childhood wounds of yours went." She paused, then said, "Before I fell in love with you."

A sensation like hot ice streaked through his veins; Dale snapped his head around to meet the fiercest expression he'd ever laid eyes on.

"Yeah, you heard right. Deal with it." Then something softened in that expression, something that scared the crap out of him. "And you know what? Despite what you've just said, despite not knowing a single detail, I still trust that man I fell in love with."

She clasped the door handle, then looked back at him. "I swear to Almighty God, I can deal with anything you tell me. Anything. What I can't deal with is you not being able to trust *me*."

The whole car shook with the force of the door's slam after she got out. "Don't bother waiting," she said through the glass. "I'll have Bobby take us home later."

Muttering a string of curses under his breath, he peeled out like some idiot seventeen-year-old.

The silence that slammed into Joanna when she went back inside wasn't that echoey, staticky kind when people suddenly stop talking about you, but heavy and sodden, like a wool blanket left out in the rain. Six sets of eyes now veered to her as if everybody was looking to her to somehow—she squelched a sigh—fix things. Or at least to smooth out the initial lumps and chunks of shock enough to get the story down.

Unfortunately, all Joanna wanted to do was to go somewhere and fall apart. Alone. But nope. Not gonna happen, at least not yet. Her own emotions going at it tooth-and-toenail inside her skull, she suggested Bobby take the kids away for a bit, until…well, she didn't know until *what*, but whatever transpired within the next little while, the kids didn't need to be part of it. And after she'd doled out hugs and kisses and reassurances and they'd gone, it occurred to her that as often as she'd been pissed at Bobby over the past dozen years, that was nothing compared with how she felt toward Dale right now.

Which only proved how screwed she was.

Joanna heard herself say, "Why don't I go make tea?" even as she thought, *What the hell am I doing? I don't even know these people!* a revelation that trailed her into Edith Medina's immaculate kitchen and seemed in no hurry to shove off even after she'd clunked three filled mugs into the microwave, punching the timer buttons hard enough to crack the first joint in her index finger. All she knew was, *somebody* was gonna tell the truth tonight, by gum, if she had to reach down their throats and yank it out of them.

Except her anger went a little wobbly around the edges when she carted a tray with tea and milk and sugar back out to the living room and saw the devastated expressions on both women's faces, their misery effectively drowning Joanna's own. At least for the moment.

She set down the tray, then sat on the chair opposite the sofa, fixing cups of tea for each woman as if they were children. When she handed Edith her tea, the older woman finally said, "You really don't have to do this, you know."

"I know." Joanna stirred sugar into her own tea, then leaned forward. "But your daughter's about to become my children's stepmother. And I'm love with your son. Even though, after tonight, we might never ever speak to each other again. So.'' She leaned back, nestling the tea against the frozen tightness in her chest. ''Since Dale won't tell me what happened, that leaves you—''

The front door swung open, letting in a whoosh of cold air and a grinning, middle-aged man Joanna assumed was Edith's husband. His grin collapsed, however, the minute he caught sight of his wife's and stepdaughter's faces.

''Edie? What's wrong?''

''Leo,'' Edith said with remarkable grace. ''This is Joanna. Bobby's ex-wife?'' Clearly confused, Leo reached over to shake Joanna's hand as his wife said, ''Sit down, honey. I've got something to tell you.''

Once Leo came on the scene, Joanna's role as moderator took a major back seat. Not that she was complaining, even though remaining a more active participant might have kept her from obsessing about the look on Dale's face earlier. She'd seen that expression before, many times, although usually in eyes too young to understand the fear that had put the look there to begin with. In a grown man's eyes, however—especially one as proud as Dale—it was ten times more heartbreaking.

''So I'm your fourth husband? Not your third?''

''I didn't deliberately set out to deceive you. Either of you,'' Edith said to Tori, anguish crushing her words. ''I swear. It was just such a horrible, horrible marriage... I guess I figured if I didn't talk about it, maybe it would fade away, like a bad dream.''

''Even though you had a son?'' Leo said. ''Or did you think you could pretend him away, too?''

''I *never* forgot Dale,'' she whispered, a tear slipping down her cheek. ''Not for a minute. It was Dale who turned his back on me. Not that I blame him—''

''Ohmigod,'' Tori said on a soft gasp. ''All that time you were watching him play baseball...''

Edith took her daughter's hand in both of hers. ''Ca

you imagine what it was like, never being able to say to a single person, 'That's my son up there'? Then when you told me about the party, how you'd actually met him and all…I thought, *Oh, Lord—what's gonna happen if we do meet up someday?* I mean, I never figured in my wildest dreams there was any chance of that, not with him living in Atlanta all that time. That he'd someday move to Albuquerque, let alone that he'd end up knowing you. Not in a million years.''

Tori pulled away, hugging herself. ''You should've told me, Mama.''

''And you have no idea how many times I wanted to. But I kept thinking, what would be the point?'' She looked up at her husband, then at Joanna. ''The last thing I wanted was to make an even bigger mess of things than they already were. But it looks like I did just that, anyway.''

''Edie?'' Joanna asked softly. ''Why don't you start at the beginning?''

The meticulously groomed little woman nodded, took a deep breath and said, ''It's no secret that I'm an alcoholic. But what few people know is that I started drinking when I was thirteen. My whole family had been drunks, see, so when I married Dale's daddy when I was seventeen—and already pregnant—it didn't occur to me to question how much my husband drank. I just thought that was the way of things, y'know?

''What I didn't know, however, was that there's a difference between a quiet drunk and a violent one. My parents might've been three sheets to the wind half the time, but nobody ever got mean.'' A sad smile skittered across her features. ''Wayne got mean. And I felt trapped and helpless and had no idea how to get out of it. Wasn't like there was a whole lotta help in our itty-bitty town for women like me. So the more he hit, the more I drank. Then he started hitting on Dale. And if I tried to stop it, he'd only hit me worse. And I got real scared, if I went too far, *he'd* go too far and kill me, and then what would happen to my boy?''

Joanna reached over and took the woman's trembling hand in hers. ''And you didn't have anybody you could go to?''

Edith shook her head. ''I tried to go back to my folks, once. But Wayne showed up and hauled us back home, threatening to kill me if I ever ran away again.'' Pain streaked across her features. ''I lost two babies after Dale, thanks to Wayne's…method of keeping me 'in line.'''

Leo bolted out of his chair and stomped across the room, his back to his wife. She hardly seemed to notice.

''I was out of it so much in those days, I was only half aware of what Dale was doing. I mean, I knew he went out and played ball a lot—anything to stay out of his father's way—but I didn't think much of it. And I only know what I was told after it was all over, because to this day I don't remember anything of what happened that night.

''It was after supper, I know, because Wayne was home and had already gotten on my case about something or other, I don't rightly remember, and it doesn't really matter now, anyway. In any case, it was still light out, but Dale hadn't come home yet after school. By the time he did, I was in my own world. And Wayne went after him. Dale was ten years old and a skinny kid at that. Wayne was nearly six feet tall and weighed more'n two hundred pounds.''

She paused, clearly fighting for control. ''They tell me Dale said he called out for me to help him. But I never heard it. So when Wayne took a swing at him, Dale swung back. With the baseball bat he still had in his hand.

''The neighbors told me Dale had come screaming to them that he'd hurt his daddy bad, that I was…'too sick' to help him.'' She paused. ''Wayne died two days later without ever waking up. And needless to say, the count took him away from me, even though Dale was never charged with any crime.''

Her own eyes burning, Joanna felt sick for that terrified little boy of nearly thirty years ago, left to deal with his father's drunken rage all by himself. That Dale had turned into the gentle, patient man he had was nothing short of a miracle. But as angry as she wanted to be at Edith for putting a child in such an untenable situation, she couldn't. Especially when she asked, ''And Dale never forgave you?'' and Edith's sad smile twisted her insides even more.

''If I'd've been able to straighten out after that horrible day? I don't know. Maybe he would've. In time. But there's a certain class of folks, in some parts of the country, that everybody else pretty much figures as lost causes, anyway. And being part of that class, I guess nobody thought I was worth the time or trouble or tax dollars to help. Oh, I wanted my baby back, in the world's worst way. But there was nobody to help me figure out how to do that, how to break my dependence on the booze. I actually managed to sober up for a short period of time, when Dale was around thirteen or so. So they let me have him back on a trial basis, to see how it'd go. But with no support system, with my family still drinking themselves under the table every time we all got together…'' She shrugged. ''He was with me maybe a month? And I can still remember the look on his face when the sheriff came to take him away again.

''He went to live with the coach up at the high school, a middle-aged widower who lived with his unmarried sister. I heard Dale was doing okay, and I decided to believe that. I had to believe that or go out of my mind. And slowly, it began to sink in that if I wanted to get, and stay, sober, it was up to me, and me alone. So I moved to the nearest town with an AA group and started going to meetings. When I'd been on the wagon for two years, I went to see my boy one last time. But the damage was done. He had his baseball and his friends and a decent home environment, and he didn't need me. Didn't...trust me. Said I'd betrayed him one too many times, and he wasn't fool enough to believe I'd changed this time. He basically told me he never wanted to see me again.

"I met Tori's daddy not long after, though. A man who didn't drink, with a good, steady job, somebody I thought was offering me a real home. But when I brought up Dale, Walter made it very clear he did not want to start off our marriage with a sixteen-year-old stepson, and as I was already pregnant with Tori, I once again found myself between a rock and a hard place. So I thought, *My child is nearly a man now*. It was too late by then for me to be his mother, anyway."

"So you gave up."

"I prefer to think of it as letting go. I clearly did not deserve Dale. I've come to believe that some mistakes can't be rectified, that the best we can do is take them for the learning experiences they are and move on." She took Tori's hand in hers and smiled at her daughter, then looked at Joanna. "I take it Dale's a good man?"

Joanna smiled, despite the sensation of sharp rocks tumbling in her stomach. "When he's not being stubborn as all get-out, yes, he is."

That got a small smile in return. "Well. That's good to know. That he turned out okay and made something of himself in spite of what I did to him—"

"Oh, for the love of God, Edie!" All three women jerked at the sound of Leo's voice. He'd been so quiet, Joanna had almost forgotten he was there. "Are you even listening to yourself?" He took a step closer, his face red, his hands fisted at his sides. "You know why I fell for you, even though I'd told myself there'd be no one after Barbara? Because you're one of the strongest women I've ever met. Because from the first time we talked, you refused to let me feel sorry for myself. Well, now it's time for me return the favor. So you screwed up! So what? Name me one person who hasn't!''

"But…aren't you mad at me?"

"Hell, yes, I'm mad. In fact, I think it's safe to say I'm next door to furious right now. It's gonna take me some time to get over you not telling me the truth. But if you want to make me *real* mad, you just keep on about how sorry you feel for yourself because you made some mistakes along the way.''

"But—"

"But nothing. And now," he said to Joanna and Tori, "if you two don't mind…" He stomped over to the coat-rack by the front door, removing his coat and a long sweater, presumably Edith's. "I think my wife and I have some serious talking to do about where we all go from here. Which we can do over dinner. Come on, Edie," he said when she didn't move. "You know I can't think on an empty stomach.''

"But my hair looks a sight—"

"Your hair looks fine. Besides, it's not your hair I'm gonna be paying attention to. Now come on, wouldja?''

After they left, Tori got up to sit on a little stool in front of the tree, staring into the slowly undulating lights. Joanna felt a pang of sympathy for the young woman, who must have felt, in the midst of this latest development, as though everyone had forgotten her.

"It's been one helluva last couple of days, huh?" she said.

Tori cracked a tiny smile. "To say the least. God…" She forked one hand through her long hair. "I just can't wrap my head around the fact that Dale's my *brother*." Then she lifted her eyes to Joanna. "Just for the record? I always thought Mama was the best mother in the world. She always made me feel…like there was nobody more important than I was.''

"I don't doubt it.''

"No, no...you don't understand." Frowning, she crossed her arms over her middle. "Now I'm wondering if she was only trying to make up for what she missed with Dale. Like I was her second chance or something."

"You think she loved you out of guilt?"

After a moment, Tori nodded.

Joanna went over and sat on the edge of the sofa, mirroring Tori's pose while she searched for the right thing to say, thinking any time now she'd be perfectly happy to ditch the Dr. Brothers persona. "I don't know your mother, Tori, except from what I've seen tonight. Which was hardly the best way to meet somebody. But I think you're wrong. About her seeing you only as a second chance. Besides, even if that were true, it seems to me most people see second chances as blessings. Not obligations. Like Bobby does with you—"

At that, the young woman burst into tears...huge, shuddering sobs barely muffled when she sank her face in her palms.

Not knowing what else to do, Joanna got to her knees and put her arms around her, rocking her while all the girl's anxieties and doubts and fears came tumbling out like one of the boys upturning his bin of Lego.

After a moment Joanna said, "And you haven't said any of this to Bobby, have you?"

She turned a tear-ravaged face to Joanna. "How could I? How *can* I? I know how much he loves me and—" She sucked in a breath, as if trying to inhale her words.

"And...what?"

"I can't let him think he's failed again."

"Because *you* don't feel you're ready to get married?" When the young woman nodded, Joanna said, "And how is that his failure?"

"It's not. I do know that much. But if I love him, why don't I want to be his wife? And now that the baby's no longer an issue—" She snapped shut her mouth, hugging her knees as if trying to fold into herself, to become invisible. "I don't mean that the way it sounds, I swear."

"I know you don't. But it's okay to admit what you're really feeling, you know. To take whatever time you need to…well, do whatever you need to do. Time you could have taken even if you hadn't lost the baby," she added gently.

"You didn't."

"No. I didn't. And it took Bobby and me nearly nine years to figure out we'd made a mistake."

Tori seemed to think about that for a long time, then let out a huge sigh. "I kept trying to pin our problems on all this…outside stuff, you know? Like the way Bobby seemed to be so spacey all the time, for instance. Or…" She glanced over at Joanna, then away. "Or you still being such a big part of his life. Or that Dulcy didn't seem to want me to be part of hers. Only the more all the outside stuff seemed to work itself out…the harder Bobby tried to get it together…the more scared I got. And I finally realized the big old scary monster wasn't out there somewhere. It was right *here*." She pushed her open hand against her chest, her chin wobbling. "But…I still love him, Joanna," she said on a whisper. "And I don't want to hurt him."

"Tori, look at me." When she did, Joanna said, "You see what happens when people aren't honest with each other? When they decide it's better to let things slide rather than dealing with them? Did you notice the look in Leo's eyes when he realized how much your mother had kept from him? And Dale and I…" She shut her eyes for a second, then opened them again. "Is that what you want to happen? To slip into a marriage you don't really want, at least not yet, because it seems easier than the alternative?"

Tears glittered in her eyes. "But what if I lose him completely?"

"Trust me, honey. Or better yet...trust Bobby." She smiled. "Because I doubt he wants to lose you, either."

Tori eyed her warily. "Are you sure?"

"Hey. I sure as hell could never get him to write things down."

That got a little laugh, which sounded pretty good considering everything else that was going on.

A second later Bobby and the kids returned. Quieter than usual, curiosity lurking in their eyes, her children huddled together in the tiny foyer with their hands stuffed into their parka pockets as Joanna hustled Bobby into the kitchen.

"What's up? Where's Edie and Leo?"

"They went out to get something to eat. And to talk." At his raised brows, she said, "It's a long story, which I'll let Tori tell you."

Bobby glanced out toward the living room, then back at Joanna. "And you and Dale?"

"Who knows? But hey—what fun is a relationship without a monkey wrench or two thrown in, right?"

Her voice caught. And those big old puppy-dog eyes that used to make her nuts got very solemn and un-Bobby-like. "Damn. You're in love with him, aren't you?"

Suddenly too choked up to speak, she simply nodded. Bobby swore, then gave her a one-armed hug. "You want me to take you guys home?"

She cleared her throat and managed, "Actually, I think I'll call Karleen. You need to be here right now. With Tori."

His dark brows crashed together. "She okay?"

"She will be. But right now she needs...to talk. And you need to listen—"

"Mom?" Dulcy appeared at the doorway, looking worried. "Are we going home soon?"

"Yeah, sweetie, in a sec." Then she touched her ex-husband's sleeve and said, "And most of all, she needs you to say what you really mean, not what you think she wants to hear, okay?''

''I'm supposed to understand that?''

''Yes. And after thirty-three years, it's high time you did.''

Twenty minutes later Karleen came to pick them up. The kids all clambered into the back of her SUV; one look at Joanna's face, though, and Karleen's said spill it now. Joanna gave her the *TV Guide* version of the day's events, fighting to keep her emotions out of her voice so she wouldn't spook the kids. But Karleen was no kid.

''Man. That sucks.''

''Yep.''

She glanced over. ''So how're you doing?''

''I haven't had two seconds to figure that out,'' Jo said, thinking what a terrible liar she was because she didn't need *any* seconds to figure out that she felt as though somebody'd ripped her guts out with a grapefruit spoon. That in spite of her best intentions, she'd managed to once again fall in love with the wrong man.

A man who she knew was out there somewhere, a helluva lot more torn up right now than she was.

Dale showed up at her house, later that night, wearing that grouchy I-don't-wanna-do-this face with which Joanna was all too familiar. In the strange glow from the multicolored Christmas lights she'd strung along the portal, he looked like a recent escapee from hell.

''Kids asleep?'' he asked, still standing outside.

''Hours ago, yeah. Why are you here?''

''I'm not entirely sure, to be honest.'' Dale frowned. 'You been crying?''

''Woodsmoke irritation,'' she said, blowing her nose in tissue as Karleen said from inside the house, ''Is it him?''

''Yep.''

Karleen came up behind her. "So you gonna let him in or what?"

"I haven't decided yet." Joanna narrowed her eyes at him. "You gonna let *me* in?"

"That's not fair, Joanna—"

"And once again, we meet our old friend Impasse."

Dale dragged her out onto the porch, pulling the door shut on a sputtering Karleen. Then, in a gesture that was pure Dale, he slipped off his leather jacket and plopped it over her shoulders. "So how much did she tell you?"

"Your mother?" Deciding it was too damn cold to go the no-really-I'm-fine-but-thanks route, Joanna poked her arms through the jacket sleeves, even though two of her could've fit inside. "Enough for me to get mad at you all over again for thinking it made more sense to shove it all under a rock instead of handling it—"

"Yeah, well, before you go getting all high and mighty on me, maybe you oughtta consider that I *was* handling it, in the only way that made sense to me. And maybe to you it looks like I'm some kind of wuss because I never talked about my past—"

"I never said that!"

"—but that's because I'm not a whiner, okay? It's like I said all along, it's my business and nobody else's. I had a choice, after what'd happened. To let it get me—and believe me, there were plenty of times it nearly did—or to rise above it. I chose to rise above it. To enjoy life, rather than let myself think about how crappy mine had been for so long. Because damned if I was gonna give folks a reason to call me a *victim*."

"And what on earth made you think anybody would do that?"

"Talk about living under a rock," he said on a snort.

"Okay, so maybe I don't have any firsthand experience in this—"

"Damn straight you don't. So don't be judging me."

"I'm not judging you, you idiot! I'm trying to help you!"

"I don't need your help. And I sure as hell don't need your sympathy."

Except there he stood, all that bottled-up pain disseminating off him like a cat sheds fur. Maybe it wasn't sympathy, or help, he was after, but he sure as hell was here for *some* reason, wasn't he?

Joanna wrapped herself more tightly in his jacket, crossing her arms to keep it closed as she stepped off the porch and walked out farther into the yard.

"So…you used baseball as sort of a therapy?" she said, looking out toward the road.

She could sense him jerk behind her, as if startled she'd figured that one out. "Not the word I'd use," he said, "but I'll admit there were plenty of days when throwing that ball over and over was the only thing keeping me sane. And the only thing I had any control over."

When she turned, she could only make out his silhouette. Probably just as well. "And you got good at it."

"I got good at it. And I know there's lots of folks think playing sports is a waste of time, but it sure as hell was a better alternative than any number of other things I could've fallen into."

"But don't you see?" she said, thinking as fast as she dared. "That *control* you thought you had was only an illusion. Not that what you've done isn't admirable, if not astounding. Because you're right—too many people in your situation do become whiners. And they certainly don't give most of their money away to charity! But in the end…" She took a deep breath, then let it out. "If it only lets you live half a life, it's still a lie."

He glanced away, then back at her, a muscle ticking in his jaw. "Well, then, that's my decision to make, isn't it?"

"Not when it involves other people."

After a second he said, "I take it you mean you?"

"No. Your mother."

"My mother?" The words were so brittle Joanna half expected to hear them shatter and tinkle onto the flagstone walk. "Well, if you think that, then we are definitely not on the same page." He paused, then said, "What exactly did she tell you, anyway?"

"That both she and your father were alcoholics," she said softly, with as little inflection as possible, even though she felt as though her insides were being shredded. "That he used to beat both of you. That one night you came home late and your father came after you and your mother was too drunk to do anything about it, so you took matters into your own hands and got him before he got you. And that the county took you away from her because she couldn't stay sober long enough to take care of you. And that…" A shiver raced up her spine, although whether from the breeze or the wound she sensed she was about to open, she wasn't sure. "And that she finally decided, after a couple of tries, it was better for you to live with someone else."

He pivoted a quarter turn, enough for her to see his profile lined in the scant light from the porch, to see every muscle in his body go hard as steel.

"It must've killed her to have to give you up—"

"That is such *bullshit!*" He turned on her so fast she nearly lost her footing. "And if that's the way she's seeing it, either her memory's gone soft after all these years or she's working a major con on you!"

"That's not fair, Dale! You weren't there! You didn't hear the regret in her voice—"

"No, Joanna, *you* weren't there!" he roared, closing the gap between them. "You weren't there in that social worker's office when my mother told me she *didn't want me,* that I was nothin' but a burden and it was better for *her* if I lived with somebody else!"

"You were just a kid! Maybe you misinterpreted—"

"Why the *hell* are you taking her side?"

"I'm not taking anybody's side, for God's sake! I'm just trying to get at the truth!"

"The truth? Well, then, try this on for size. Try to imagine what it's like to be a ten-year-old boy facing a skunk-drunk, raging two-hundred-fifty-pound bull coming at you with a broken beer bottle. Try to imagine swinging the bat in your hand as hard as you could, just to stop the bull long enough to save your own hide. Try to imagine the sound of wood cracking a skull, the sound of those two-hundred-fifty pounds crashing onto the wooden floor. Then imagine your own mother, staggering out from her bedroom, and the first words out of her mouth being, 'Oh, God—what've you done? What've you done?' and a look on her face like I hope to God never to see again. Never mind that my father beat the tar out of her on a regular basis, that she let him do the same thing to me. When push came to shove, it was him she mourned. Him she missed. Me? Well, when they came and took me away, I suppose that was her real deliverance, wasn't it?"

Against skin so hot she felt feverish, wind-iced tears stung her cheeks.

"Oh, God, Dale, I'm so sorry—"

"No!" he bellowed, batting her hand away when she reached out to him. "This is exactly why I don't talk about what happened! And it's exactly why…why…" His throat convulsing, over and over, he lifted one hand to brush her hair out of her eyes, the wretchedness in his own nearly making her cry out. "Dammit, Joanna…why couldn't things have stayed the way they were?"

Then he turned and walked away, his burden of hurt and confusion tagging along behind like a pair of maltreated puppies.

Chapter 23

At the sound of the doorbell, Dale peered through the verticals to see Bobby's car parked out in front of his condo. For several seconds he seriously considered pretending he wasn't home. Except Bobby'd parked right nex' to Dale's car, so he was busted.

He swung open his door, wearing the least hospitabl face he could manage. Unfortunately the expression facin, him wasn't a whole lot better.

"Damn," Dale said. "You look worse than I do."

Bobby smirked, then lifted the pizza box in his hand: "Thought you could use dinner. And maybe somebody t talk to."

It'd been a good three days since he'd last talked to an, body other than his employees and customers. And h wasn't in any hurry to break the streak. "You thoug] wrong. On both counts."

"Well, *I* could, then. On both counts. And since there nobody else around that fits the bill, you win. So you bett let me in before this gets any colder."

Dale told himself the only reason he let the guy in was that it seemed a shame to let free pizza go to waste. Not that he was really hungry or anything. Once inside, Bobby dumped the Domino's pizza carton onto Dale's dinette table and peeled off his baseball jacket, eyeing the vintage pinball machine in the corner of the room for a couple seconds before returning his attention to Dale. "This is shapin' up to be one helluva Christmas, huh?"

"Actually, it's about on a par with most of mine." At Bobby's snort he added, "Okay, so maybe this one's suckier than most." He walked over to the table and flipped open the box. "Ah, hell—mushrooms?"

"So pick 'em off if you don't like 'em. Got anything to drink?"

"There's Cokes in the refrigerator. Help yourself."

Dale was still contemplating which slice had the least mushrooms when Bobby came out of the kitchen. He reached past Dale to select his own slice, then walked out to the living room, sinking onto Dale's couch. "Don't know if you care or not, but Tori's taking all of this pretty hard. You might want to get in touch with her, y'know? No matter what, none of this is her fault."

"Yeah. I know. And I do care. Even if it's a little strange, suddenly finding out I've got a sister."

"I can imagine." Bobby took a swig of his Coke, then said softly, "Turns out she doesn't want to get married after all."

Dale's head whipped around. "Because of what happened the other day?"

"No. Apparently she's been thinking about it for some time." He bit off another chunk of his pizza, but not like he was really interested in it. "What she said was, she was only goin' along with it because of the baby coming, but now..." He shrugged. "She doesn't really think she's ready."

"I'm sorry to hear that...are you laughing?"

Bobby stuffed the rest of his crust into his mouth, then got up to get another slice. "You wanna hear something funny?" he said, chewing. "Turns out neither one of us was being honest. She was afraid to tell me she didn't want to get married because she didn't want to hurt my feelings. And I was doing the same damn thing. Don't get me wrong, I do love her. And I really wanted this baby. But I'm not all that sure I was as ready to be married again as I thought I was. Not yet. I mean, I kept seeing that look in her face I used to see in Joanna's…" He shook his head, then sighed. "Only it's taken me this long to figure out *why* she used to get that look. Think maybe it's time I figure out how to fix that before I go screwing up another marriage."

"So you two broke up?"

"Not exactly. She says she loves me, too. In fact, she was scared if she told me the truth, she'd lose me altogether." He grinned. "You know, that's the first time a woman ever said she was afraid of losing me? Kinda made me feel good, if you wanna know the truth. So we're just gonna back up a bit, see how it goes." He took a pull of his Coke, then sat down. "If she needs some time to figure out what she wants to do with her life, I figure that's the least I can do for her, right? Besides…well, she's got a lot on her plate right now. Being there for her mother and all," he said, looking pointedly at Dale. "Not to mention getting to know her big brother."

Dale flopped onto the recliner opposite the sofa, bouncing when it sprang open. "Yeah. That's what makes all of this a bitch."

Bobby polished off his second slice of pizza, then wiped his mouth with a napkin. "Because you feel like Edie abandoned you?"

"That'll do." He looked at Bobby, thinking how it's never occurred to him to connect the Edie Leo'd been talking about at the poker party to his mother, who he'd neve heard called anything but Edith Jane. "I suppose you know the story by now."

"Tori told me, yeah. You wanna tell me your side?"

Dale let out a short, dry laugh. "You think I have a side?"

"There's always two sides to these things. So if you wanna talk—"

"I don't."

"Suit yourself," the other man said with a shrug. "But let me just say this, and you can do whatever you want with it, okay? It has to count for something, how well Edie's done by Tori. Not to mention the fact that your mother's been sober since before Tori was born. Now, maybe that doesn't mean diddly for her relationship with you, but it does mean she finally found the strength to overcome the booze, at least. A lot of alkies never do. I should know. I've got one brother who refuses to admit that he even has a problem, let alone do anything about it." He shrugged again. "Just thought you could use a different perspective, that's all."

"And Joanna put you up to this."

"Comin' over here?" Bobby's eyebrows lifted. "You gotta be kidding. Like I'm gonna go down that road. Although I can tell she's worried about you."

"Well, you tell her she doesn't need to worry about me. I'm fine."

"One, tell her yourself. Two, Jo worries about the people in her life the way other people eat or sleep or breathe. And three, you're so full of it, I can smell you from over here."

Dale kicked down the recliner's footrest and sprang to his feet. "You want any more of this pizza—"

"Don't be an idiot like I was, Dale. Don't walk away from her because it's easier than dealing with all the stuff you don't *want* to deal with."

Dale slammed shut the pizza box, then spun on Bobby. "I *am* dealing with it, dammit! Just not the way everybody else, including Joanna, thinks I should! I don't owe my mother anything, least of all an olive branch. And if Joanna can't deal with *that,* then there's nothing to talk about.''

Bobby folded his arms across his chest, regarding Dale steadily. "You know, I'm beginning to think what women say about us is true.''

"And what is that?''

"That we've got one-track minds. That once we get something in our heads, there's no blasting us out of it.''

Dale took a last swallow of his Coke and crushed the can in his hand. "Joanna doesn't need me in her life.''

"Why do you think that? Because she kicked me out on my ass when she realized what we had wasn't working and wasn't ever going to work? Because she can survive without a man in her life? That doesn't mean she doesn't need you. And you sure as hell need *her.*''

"What I don't need,'' Dale shot back, "is her judging me according to her standards.''

"Yeah, it's a real bitch the way she holds up mirrors in front of our faces, isn't it, making us see exactly what we don't want to see about ourselves?'' Bobby got to his feet, slipped his jacket back on and walked over to the door. "Keep the pizza. I got leftovers comin' out my ears.''

As soon as he heard Bobby's car leave, Dale carted the leftover pizza out to the Dumpster behind his building and tossed it in. Then he kicked the Dumpster for good measure, wondering if he'd ever be able to breathe again without it feeling like somebody was ripping out his insides.

"So you haven't talked to him since that night?'' Glynnie said, dumping some frozen pseudo-Chinese dinner kit into her Sam's cart.

Joanna did the same with a giant box of corn dogs, thinking, *And why is it again I thought I wanted my mother to "be here" for me?* "What would be the point?''

"To keep the lines of communication open?''

"He's already cut them, Mom."

"You think he wants to stuff the whole thing back in the closet?"

"My guess is, it's already stuffed and the door's locked for another thirty years." She sighed. "What is it with men, thinking they have to be so damned invincible all the time? The minute the shell cracked open, he was off like a shot."

"Well, for heaven's sake, Joanna—think about it. Whatever his mother's motivations may have been, in his eyes she gave him away like an old coat. More than once. If you had issues with me and my work, imagine how he must have felt. So what does he do? He erects the toughest, thickest wall he can around himself, so he can never be hurt again. And a lot of what made up that wall involved not talking about his past—"

"And when the past caught up with him, it left him feeling vulnerable." Joanna plunked a six-pack of orange juice into her cart. "I did figure that out already, Mom."

"And did you also figure out," her mother continued, in full courtroom cross-examination mode now, "how frightening it is for a man who's buried his emotions for all those years to suddenly have those emotions stripped bare? Criminy, Joanna—under the best of circumstances, most men don't know what to do with their feelings...." Glynnie eyed the family-size lasagna in Joanna's hands. "Is that any good?"

"The kids love it. So I do, too."

Her mother got one of the lasagnas for herself and said, "Anyway, I see it every day in my work, men who wear their stability like a medal coming unglued in situations most women would take in their stride." She slowed down in front of the mini eclairs, but kept on going. "It must be a real pain in the butt for them, thinking they have to be strong all the time."

"Not a problem Bobby's ever had to deal with," Joanna said with a grunt.

"Oh, even Bobby, in his own clueless way, is afraid of being weak. They all are."

Joanna thought about that as she pushed her cart into the next aisle, stopping to load up on milk.

"Which is when, ironically enough, we have to get pushy," Glynnie said.

"Mom." Joanna let the glass door swing shut and moved on to the butter. "It took me about a thousand years to figure this out, but you can't...will a person to be some-body they're not. To be who you want them to be because it would make *your* life easier."

"So you're just going to give up?"

The four-pack of butter tumbled into the cart. Across the aisle, the Muppets were murdering "The Twelve Days of Christmas." Joanna looked at all the other shoppers, going about their mundane business, none of whom had a clue how treacherously close the woman a few feet away from them was to losing her already tenuous grip on sanity.

"What choice do I have?" she said at last.

"Do you have a choice about loving him?"

Now Bing was crooning "White Christmas." "No," she said on a sigh.

"I'm not talking about trying to change him, honey," her mother said gently. "But I'm guessing Dale doesn't know how to trust, because nobody's ever given a reason to. You may be his only chance. Because if you let him go, you'll only be reinforcing what he already *thinks* he knows about women. Right?"

Joanna pushed the cart into the Christmas goodies aisle picking up a bag of bright, glittery bows that she didn' need since she already had enough recycled bows to las until she was ninety. Except they were so pretty and cheer ful and she really, really needed *cheerful* right now.

"Oh, God," she said on a rush of air, crinkling th pretty, cheerful bows to her chest. "I can't do this."

"Sure you can," Glynnie said, dumping her own bag of bows into her cart. "You're my daughter, aren't you?"

"Oh, God," Joanna said again.

Needless to say, she could think of nothing else the rest of the day. Half of her thought her mother was off her nut—as far as Joanna could tell, the fastest way to make a man run for the hills was to get in his face the way Glynnie had suggested. Unfortunately it was the other half, the half that agreed with her mother, that was going to get her into trouble.

Oh, well. Wasn't as if she hadn't been *there* before.

Since it was Friday night, the kids were with Bobby. Who'd been at sixes and sevens himself since Tori had moved out, but—sorry—he'd just have to muddle through this one on his own. Joanna had her hands full. And her stomach, since she'd fortified herself with at least a half dozen pieces of her homemade fudge. Even so, she punched in, then cut off, Dale's number a good twenty times before she finally let the call go through.

His machine picked up. Joanna panicked. Hang up? Leave a message? Did he have Caller ID? Was this the dumbest thing she'd ever done? Was there a special place in heaven for stubborn women who loved the wrong men—

"Hey! It's me," she said when she suddenly realized the machine had beeped at her to leave a message and it was too late to turn back now. "Uh, hi," she said again, shutting her eyes and willing herself intelligent. And calm. Calm would be good. She opened her eyes again and sat on the sofa, only to bounce right back up and start pacing. "First off, this isn't a drunken phone call. Although God knows it would be easier if it was, because then I wouldn't feel obligated for any of this to make sense. Which doesn't mean this will, but…oh, hell."

Chester sat to watch her pace, offering whatever encouragement he could. So she dragged in a breath and said,

"Look, I've been thinking all of this over, and okay, so maybe I can't imagine what it must've been like for you, having to do what you did. Or how it must've felt, being forced to defend yourself because your mother couldn't. And if you thought for a moment I'd...I don't know, what *did* you think? That I'd condemn you for defending yourself? That I'd be afraid of you because of it?"

She paced some more, and Chester encouraged her some more, and she said, "As far as your mother goes, God knows I'm in no position to know whether she should've, or could've, fought any harder for you. I really do believe she loves you and that she's sorry for what happened. No, a lot more than sorry. Wrecked, is more like it. And she's not conning me, okay?"

Pushing at the knot between her brows, she said, "And that's probably just ticking you off more, isn't it? Damn." A rush of air left her lungs. "I'm really not taking sides, Dale. How could I, since I have no idea what it was really like for either of you back then? Except...okay, I've got to say this, because if I didn't, I wouldn't be honest...but it makes me sick to think if I ever screwed up with my own kids, they'd never give me a chance to make it up to them. It's weird, though, huh, the way we can latch hold of something from when we were kids and drag it through our lives, like...like a raggedy, filthy baby blanket. Doesn't do us a damn bit of good anymore, but somehow, we just feel safer with it.

"And I have no idea where that came from. But then, I'm totally winging it here, so bear with me. I guess what I'm saying is...what?" She let out another sigh. "That I guess we all try to avoid things that might hurt us, don't we? I sure did, convincing myself I had everything I needed with my kids and my business, because the alternative meant opening myself up again. Risking making another mistake. Getting screwed. Figuratively. And literally, I guess," she added on a little laugh. "Then you came along and shook me awake. And here I am, in love again…'' The last words caught in her throat; she waited until she could speak without her voice shaking. ''…and scared to death…and probably making a total fool of myself over the phone. And if I get cut off before I'm finished, I'm going to be seriously pissed.

''Anyway,'' she said, the rest of her words tumbling over each other, ''the whole reason I called was to let you know…that I'm not going anywhere. I'm not your mother, I'm not your ex-wife, and I don't abandon people who are important to me. For God's sake, look at me and Bobby, right? So what I'm saying is, if you need me, I'm here. If you want me, I'm here. But the rules of the game have changed. This time, I'm playing for keeps, you got that? And if you decide I'm worth trusting…''

Her pulse pounding, she took another deep breath and said, ''If you agree to play by the new rules, then come over on Christmas morning. But you have to bring a present. And it's not something you can buy, or wrap up, and I'm not going to tell you what it is. That one, you're going to have to figure out on your own.'' Clutching the phone so tightly her fingers cramped, she whispered, ''My heart is yours, if you want it. But if you take it, you can't give it back.''

She punched the off button, then sank onto the sofa with her hands covering her face, thinking she might throw up.

Chester crawled up beside her and laid his head in her lap.

The cats, however, with their superior wisdom, kept their distance.

Dale stared at the phone after Joanna hung up, feeling like he'd swallowed broken glass. He stabbed at the erase button, accidentally hitting Play instead. So he listened, again. And once more after that. Because, in spite of how stupid it was, he wanted to hear her voice again.

To hear her say again she'd never leave him.

But he couldn't take the challenge he knew she was issuing him. He wasn't like her, wasn't the kind of person who could rip himself wide open and scrutinize all the jumbled, exposed parts, then rearrange things so they made sense again.

He just wasn't.

The condo suddenly felt like a coffin, airless and cramped. Dale grabbed his jacket, punching his arms through the sleeves as he strode out to his car. The crisp, cold night air, tinged as usual with the scent of mesquite and hickory, seared his lungs; Christmas lights mocked him with their frenzied cheerfulness as he drove through his neighborhood and out onto Coors Boulevard, heading north.

He had no idea where he was going.

He had no idea about anything.

He drove most of that night, clear to Taos and back, arguing with himself, mostly. Thinking about Joanna and what she was offering, about what he knew he had to do to accept what she was offering and how little he wanted to do it.

And how much he couldn't stand the thought of what it would mean if he didn't.

He got back to Albuquerque somewhere around six in the morning, well before dawn. The waitress in the Denny's where he stopped for breakfast was friendly enough, but mercifully unchatty. Except, long about the time he let her pour him his third cup of coffee, the middle-aged woman— Carmen, according to her name tag—said, "Looks like somebody had a rough night."

"Yeah." Then he heard himself say, "You ever been faced with a decision you just did not want to make?"

"Sure," she said in a voice that sounded like she had rocks for tonsils. "More'n once."

"What'd you do?"

She laughed softly. "Made it and got on with my life."

"You ever regret any of those decisions?"

The brunette seemed to think about that for a moment. "Only once. And that was because I didn't listen to that little voice tellin' me I was going in the wrong direction, y'know?"

Dale smirked. "Little voice?"

"Hey, don't knock it," she said, handing him his check. "We all got 'em. Just gotta be quiet enough to hear 'em. You all done, honey?"

He nodded and she cleared his place, leaving him to his coffee and his thoughts and more little voices than a body wanted to hear this early in the morning.

Loud, obnoxious little suckers they were, too.

And the loudest, most obnoxious one of the lot sounded an awful lot like Bobby.

Don't walk away from her because it's easier than dealing with all the stuff you don't want to deal with.

Dale gazed out the window by his booth, watching the sun rise over the Sandias. Although the city streets were clear, it had snowed in the mountains overnight, the Crest glittering against a crystal-blue sky. Another voice skipped through his brain. Joanna's this time. Except the words weren't any he could actually remember hearing her say out loud.

Don't do this for me. Or your mother. Or for anybody else. Do this for you.

Then he heard, like she was standing right behind him, *I love you. No matter what.*

He got up, making sure to leave Carmen a hefty tip.

Twenty minutes later he pulled up in front of a nondescript little ranch house with a pair of white, light-decorated reindeer in the middle of the rocked-in front yard. What, if anything, might come of this, he had no idea. But it was time he stopped letting his past suffocate his present.

Because all those years of denial hadn't made him any less of a victim, had they?

As he walked up to the front door, he felt Joanna right there with him, nagging her little heart out.

And that was okay.

"So. How're you doing?"

Joanna looked up at Bobby from putting the Christmas breakfast dishes in the dishwasher. Sunlight streamed through the windows, gilding her pancake-and-sausage-scented kitchen; her father and Chester were outside, supervising the boys on their new bikes; Dulcy had vanished to try on the roughly two dozen new outfits she'd gotten; and her mother was in the living room, ticking off cats by clearing away the mountain of ripped wrapping paper and ribbons covering every square inch of the room. If it weren't for the boulder lodged in the center of her chest, Joanna might even have been enjoying herself.

"About Dale? Oh, the usual—it was nice while it lasted, it was just one of those things, easy come, easy go..." She let the dishwasher door slam shut. "Take your pick."

"Aw, Jo—"

"I'm fine, Bobby. Let's move on, shall we? So how are *you* doing?"

Bobby shrugged as he poured himself the last cup of coffee. "Actually, I'm doing pretty good. Tori and I decided to take things one day at a time, see how it goes." He poured milk into his mug, his spoon clinking against it as he stirred. "She really wants to finish up college, maybe work for a couple years before she gets married. And it's not like I've got any pressing plans," he finished with a grin.

"She's worth waiting for?"

There was a conviction in his expression she'd never seen before. "Yeah. She is. We both just have some growing up to do before we settle down." Joanna snickered attacking the splattered stovetop with a sponge as he added, "I'm having dinner with her folks tonight, in fact."

At the mention of Dale's mother, the sadness and frustration Joanna had been so desperately trying to fend off for the kids' sake smacked her right between the eyes. Swallowing back stupid tears, she started scrubbing harder.

"Aw, hell, babe," Bobby said softly. "I wish there was something I could do."

Joanna wiped her sweat-shirted shoulder across her eyes, then dumped the leftover sausages into a Ziploc bag and tossed them in the fridge. "Hey. Put your butt out on a limb, sometimes the limb breaks." She closed the refrigerator, then turned around, leaning against the door with her arms crossed. "You know what your idiot ex-wife did? Left this long, rambling, totally insane message on Dale's machine the other night. Nutso Female of the Year Award—" she pointed at herself "—right here. At the moment he's probably thinking he's well rid of me."

"Somehow, I doubt it."

"Yeah? You know something I don't?"

Bobby screwed up his mouth, then blew out a sigh. "I went to his place a few days ago, and we got into it about you, and believe me, babe—the face you're wearing now's *nothing* compared to his that night. He's got it for you bad, honey. Real bad—"

"Whoa, whoa, whoa, back up, buddy—you went over to Dale's and *got into it about me?*"

"Yeah. I did. Wanna make something of it? And look at this," he said, walking over to the patio door and peering outside. "Looks like Santa hadn't quite finished makin' all his deliveries."

Shoving her righteous indignation to one side, Joanna tromped over to the patio door, muttering, "What are you talking about?" Her eyes grew wide at the sight of the horse trailer attached to an unfamiliar pickup, both coming to a stop right next to the paddock.

They got a lot wider, though, when Dale got out of the truck.

Behind her, Bobby chuckled. Joanna turned to him, her eyes narrowed. "Why am I getting a bad feeling about this?"

Grinning like a fool, her ex plucked her Peruvian sweater off the hook by the door and plopped it over her shoulders. "You can chew me out later. Right now—" he yanked open the patio doors, spun her around and shoved her outside "—you got bigger fish to fry."

Then he closed the patio door behind her.

And locked it.

Except for a crow cawing at the top of one of her cottonwoods and the sound of hooves stirring restlessly against the floor of the trailer, it was ominously silent. No kids, no father, no dog, no nobody. Except her and Dale. Who was leaning his long, lean self up against the truck's front fender, wearing worn jeans, cowboy boots, his leather jacket and the kind of grin a woman dreads down to her toes.

"Merry Christmas, honey," he said, those blue eyes twinkling, and her heart went bonkers.

Against her better judgment, Joanna took a step closer. "Is that…a horse butt I'm looking at?"

"Yep. The rest of the horse is in there, too. In case you're interested."

She was now close enough to see it was a palomino. At least, from what she could tell from the back end. "You bought me a horse?"

"No, ma'am. I bought *me* a horse. But seeings as how he won't exactly fit in the condo, and since you have this empty stable and all…" He shrugged.

"I didn't know you rode."

"I don't. But I figured you could teach me."

She'd closed the gap between them by now, close enough that over the pungent, heady scent of hay and horse she smelled him. Him and her own hope and desire and fear, that any minute she'd wake up.

"You mean to tell me you just took it upon yourself to park a horse in my stable, expecting me to take care of it?"

"Now, who said anything about you taking care of it?"

"Well, since I live here and you don't…what are you doing?"

"I think it's called holding my woman close."

"Oh." She smiled, nestling against him, her hands on his chest. "Your woman, huh?"

"Yeah. I kinda like the sound of that. How about you?" And he lowered his mouth to hers and pressed her close enough to feel their heartbeats mingle, and she wrapped her arms around his neck and kissed him back, thinking she was about to pop from being so happy.

After enough kissing to hold them for a bit, he tilted her face up to his. "Like I said, the horse is mine. And I intend to take care of it, so you can just unknot your panties right now. But you said something about bringing you a present?"

"Oh, God." She dropped her forehead onto his chest. "I don't suppose you could forget about that phone call?"

"So…you telling me you didn't mean what you said about not going anywhere?" Her head jerked up as he added, "And all that stuff about if I took your heart, I couldn't give it back? That was just talking through your hat?"

"No! That part, I meant—"

"Then that's all I want to know." He wrapped his arms round her again, resting his chin on her head. "But, damn, honey…I'm such a mess."

"Takes one to know one."

He chuckled, then kissed her again, and once more after that, then she said, "Let's get this critter out of this tin can so she can see her new digs."

Dredging up memories from long ago, and praying the

mare knew what "back" meant, Joanna slipped into the
trailer from the side door, unhitched the lead and gently
backed the horse down the opened gate and through the
gate into the paddock. The mare turned right back around
and stuck her head over the fence, clearly looking for some
affection. Grinning, Joanna took hold of her bridle to stroke
her golden nose, blowing into her nostrils the way she used
to do with her grandmother's horses. The mare nodded,
whuffling in her face, then reached up to lip-nibble
Joanna's hair.

"She's so beautiful," she said, laughing. "What's her
name?"

"Butterscotch."

Joanna laughed again, sliding her hand farther up on the
bridle—

"What…? Oh, my God," she breathed. Tied with a thin
satin ribbon to the bridle ring, the diamond flashed in the
morning sun. Her gaze zipped to Dale. "Are you serious?"

If she hadn't already been out-of-her-head in love with
him, the half-hopeful, half-tickled-with-himself look on his
face would have done it for sure.

"Only way I could figure out how to let you know I was
done playing around…" He reached up and untied the ring,
then held her hand and slipped it on her finger. "…and
was ready to play for keeps. Fair's fair—if I can't give you
heart back, then you can't give mine back, either."

"Are you really sure about this?"

"Well, see, I could walk away from you, which would
probably make my life a helluva lot easier—"

"This is true."

"—except then you'd probably plague me in my dreams
every night. So I figure, if you're gonna keep me up every
night anyway…it might as well be in the flesh."

"This is crazy," she said, gawking at the ring. Which
was big enough for her to decide, right then and there, t

next time he wanted to pay for a household repair? She was *not* paying him back.

"You having doubts?"

She looked deep, deep into his eyes. "Not a single one."

And his smile was the only gift she'd ever need, ever again.

It had not escaped Dale's notice that Joanna had accepted his off-the-wall proposal without asking a single question about anything that had caused the rift between them to begin with. He could see them in her eyes, though, although not so much about whether he'd done what she'd thought he should do, as simply a curiosity about what he'd done, period. However, serious discussion had to wait until after the kids had made over the horse and Bobby and Roger had shaken his hand and even Glynnie—with what looked like definite tears in her eyes—had given him a big hug and told him in no uncertain terms she expected him at her house for Christmas dinner. But eventually things calmed down and everybody went away—Bobby to Tori's, the kids with their grandparents—leaving him and Joanna alone to hash things out.

Dale suggested a walk, since it was highly unlikely he'd be tempted to mess around with her out in public, which he definitely would if they stayed in the house. So off they went, traipsing down to the *bosque* with Chester in tow, holding hands like a pair of teenagers. It felt real good. It felt *real*, period.

"I went to see my mother," he said at last, after they'd been walking for a while and talking about this and that. The important stuff, he'd discovered, they agreed on. And the little things didn't really matter, when it came right down to it.

"I figured you probably would," Joanna said.

"But not because you thought I should."

She laughed. "I'm very relieved to hear that. So what happened?"

He thought about their conversation, the remorse in his mother's eyes, how he could tell she wanted to hug him but he wasn't ready for that yet.

"We talked some. Agreed to meet again after the New Year and talk some more." He squeezed Joanna's hand. "Gonna take a lot more than a conversation or two to resolve things between us."

"I know that," she said softly, letting go of his hand to slip her arm around his waist. It wasn't easy, them walking together, since her legs were so short. But they eventually got a rhythm going.

Dale watched Chester dash off after something or other.

"When I was still really little," he said, voicing memories he'd refused to even acknowledge before a few days ago, "there was lots of laughing and hugging. Mama used to sing to me, all the time. And read to me, too, like you read to the boys." He laughed. "Lord, I could ask her to read the same book three times a night, and she'd do it. Then along about the time I started school, things got real bad, I don't know why. The nights…the nights were the worst. I'd lie in bed and listen to him hittin' her, wanting to get up and stop him, scared to death he'd come into my room and start in on me for no reason. My father had never wanted me, I knew that. But I sure as hell thought Mama did. That she loved me. And I would've done anything in my power to help her, to get back the mama who used to sing to me. Except what power does a little kid have?

"I was sick to my stomach that night, after I'd hit my father. But you know what? I felt proud, too. Proud that I'd finally gotten brave enough and big enough to save her. To save us both. And I remember thinking, *She doesn't have to be afraid of him anymore. Now things can go back to the way they were.* Instead, I only discovered my be wasn't good enough. Not to make her love me the way she used to, not to get her to stop drinking.''

"So you decided never to let anybody get close enough to hurt you that much again."

"I was ten years old, Joanna," he said. "I have no idea what I was thinking. Not then, anyway. Later though, after she pushed me away for the last time, I guess I did decide from then on, life was gonna be played by my rules. That the things I was good at, I'd be very good at or die trying. And to never let anybody see what I wasn't good at."

"And now?"

"Now I have you to remind me when I'm acting like a fool."

She stopped dead, throwing him off balance. "You were never acting like a fool, Dale! And if it sounded like that's what I was saying, I apologize. You were acting like some-body who'd felt betrayed by the one person he should have been able to count on. And your mother was too confused and too much a victim of her illness to even begin to un-derstand how you might interpret her actions…''

"Hey, hey, sweetheart…" He took her face in his hands, thumbing her cheeks. "It's okay. I understand. Or at least, I'm trying to. And you're cold. Let's go back."

She called the dog and they turned around. On the way back to her house, he told her more about what happened in the aftermath of his father's death, how no charges had been filed since he was only ten, for one thing, not to men-tion riddled with bruises and cuts and burns from his fa-ther's abuse, as his mother had been; about how he'd lucked out when it came to his foster care, how Jasper Wyman had been instrumental in jump-starting Dale's ca-reer; how that both Jasper and his sister Bea had been gone for many years.

And he talked about Meredith and how that had been a mistake, about how she'd dumped him when she found out he'd have to retire and she'd no longer be in the limelight as a pro player's wife; about how he'd never wanted his name associated with the foundation before this because he didn't want folks coming around and asking why.

About how he loved kids but had never wanted any of his own because he couldn't bear the thought of somehow not being whatever it was his child might need him to be.

About how being with Joanna had uprooted every single thing he'd thought about what he wanted and needed. Or, more accurately, what he thought he didn't need or want.

"I'm even thinking…well, maybe I wouldn't mind having a kid of our own someday," he said, and again she stopped dead in her tracks to look up at him. They'd taken the long way around, coming back to her house by way of the road fronting it.

She pushed her hair out of her face. "Don't say that because you think that's what I want to hear."

"I'm not. Believe me. I'm just saying…I'm willing to look at some maybes I wasn't before this."

A soft smile spread across her lips. "I have everything I could possibly want, right now. If we do have a baby, great. If we don't…" She shrugged. "That's okay, too."

"Then why in tarnation are you crying?"

"Because it feels good, dammit," she said, wiping her eyes. "You should try it."

"I've got a better idea," he said, and kissed her. For good, long time.

"Hey, over there!"

Startled out of their embrace, they both looked across the road to where an older man with a belly that probably preceded him into a room by a good five minutes was leaning on the top of his post-and-rail fence.

"Oh, God," Joanna muttered under her breath. "That's the guy who owns the dog Chester knocked up." Then she smiled and waved. "Hey there, Mr. Shaw! I just got myself engaged!"

"Oh. Well. Congratulations, I guess. Thought you might like to know…Gladys had her pups."

"Oh?" Joanna said, then muttered something that sounded like, *There is no way I am letting this man ruin my day.* "How many?"

"Sixteen, all told."

Dale felt her nails dig into his arms, right through three layers of clothes. "Wow. Didn't know Chester had it in him."

"Well, see, ma'am. That's just it." Dale saw a blush steal across the spider-veined cheeks. "I'm thinkin' now maybe Chester's not the father after all."

"Oh?"

"No, ma'am. Actually, from what I can tell, it appears the pups look an awful lot like that bloodhound that lives down the road a ways. So I won't be bothering you any further." He turned to go, then pivoted back. "Y'all wouldn't be wanting a puppy now, would you? I mean, one might be nice to mark the occasion of your engagement, don't you think?"

Eyes laughing, Joanna turned to Dale. "Great Dane mixed with bloodhound?"

Dale blew out a breath. "Gonna be some big dogs."

"Yeah. I know." She turned back to the older man and said, "Why don't you put us down for two? They'll be good company for the horse we just got."

The older man gawked at them for several seconds, then walked back to his house, shaking his head.

"God help me," Dale said, "I've fallen in love with a crazy woman."

"Yeah, well—" The sunlight teased all those alien curls as she looped her arms around his waist, grinning. "You've only got yourself to blame for that." Then she whispered, "Welcome to my life, Mr. McConnaughy."

He touched her face, soaking in the smile that was for him alone, that he knew would be his for the rest of his life, and reveled in a happiness he'd never believed could be his. "Glad to be here, Ms. Swann. Now what d'you say we go inside and have ourselves a proper celebration?"

Laughing, she said, "Race you back!" and took off toward the house, Chester barking his fool head off the whole damn way.

*   *   *   *   *